FORGOTTEN CITY

BOOK TWO

K.A KNIGHT

Monstrous Truths (Forgotten City Book Two).

Written by K.A. Knight

Edited By Jess from Elemental Editing and Proofreading.

Proofreading by Bookish Dreams Proofreading.

Formatted by The Nutty Formatter.

Cover by TrifBookDesign.

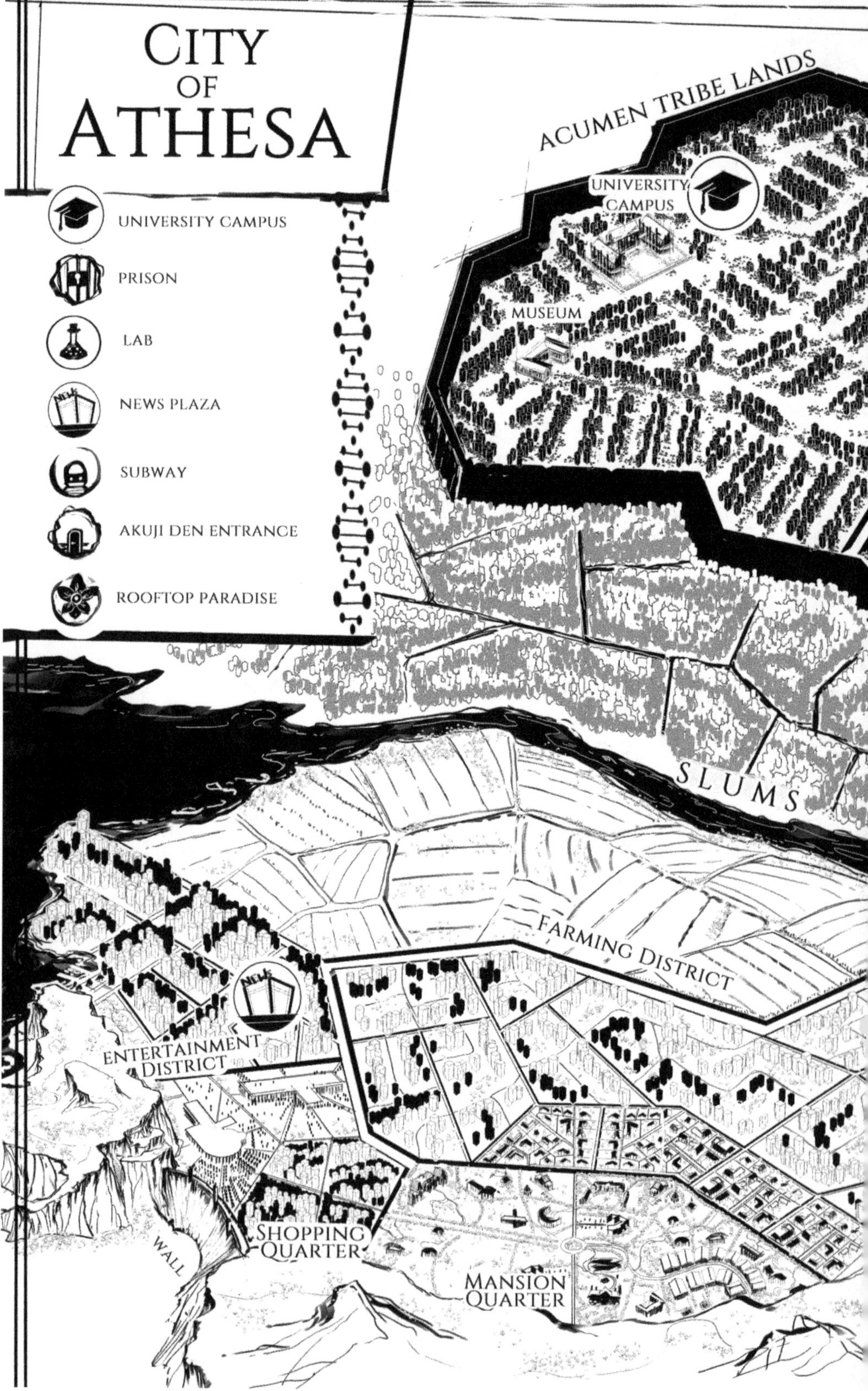
CITY OF ATHESA
UNIVERSITY CAMPUS
PRISON
LAB
NEWS PLAZA
SUBWAY
AKUJI DEN ENTRANCE
ROOFTOP PARADISE
ACUMEN TRIBE LANDS
UNIVERSITY CAMPUS
MUSEUM
SLUMS
FARMING DISTRICT
ENTERTAINMENT DISTRICT
SHOPPING QUARTER
WALL
MANSION QUARTER

DARKLINGS_TRIBE_LANDS
BUNKER
PRISON
POLICE HQ
GRAVE
ROOFTOP
DUMP
ZOO
SOUTH DOOR
NIGHT FANG TRIBE LANDS
ARIA'S ENTRANCE
PARK
RESIDENTIAL DISTRICT
SOUTHERN CLIFFS
SPECIMENT RI2

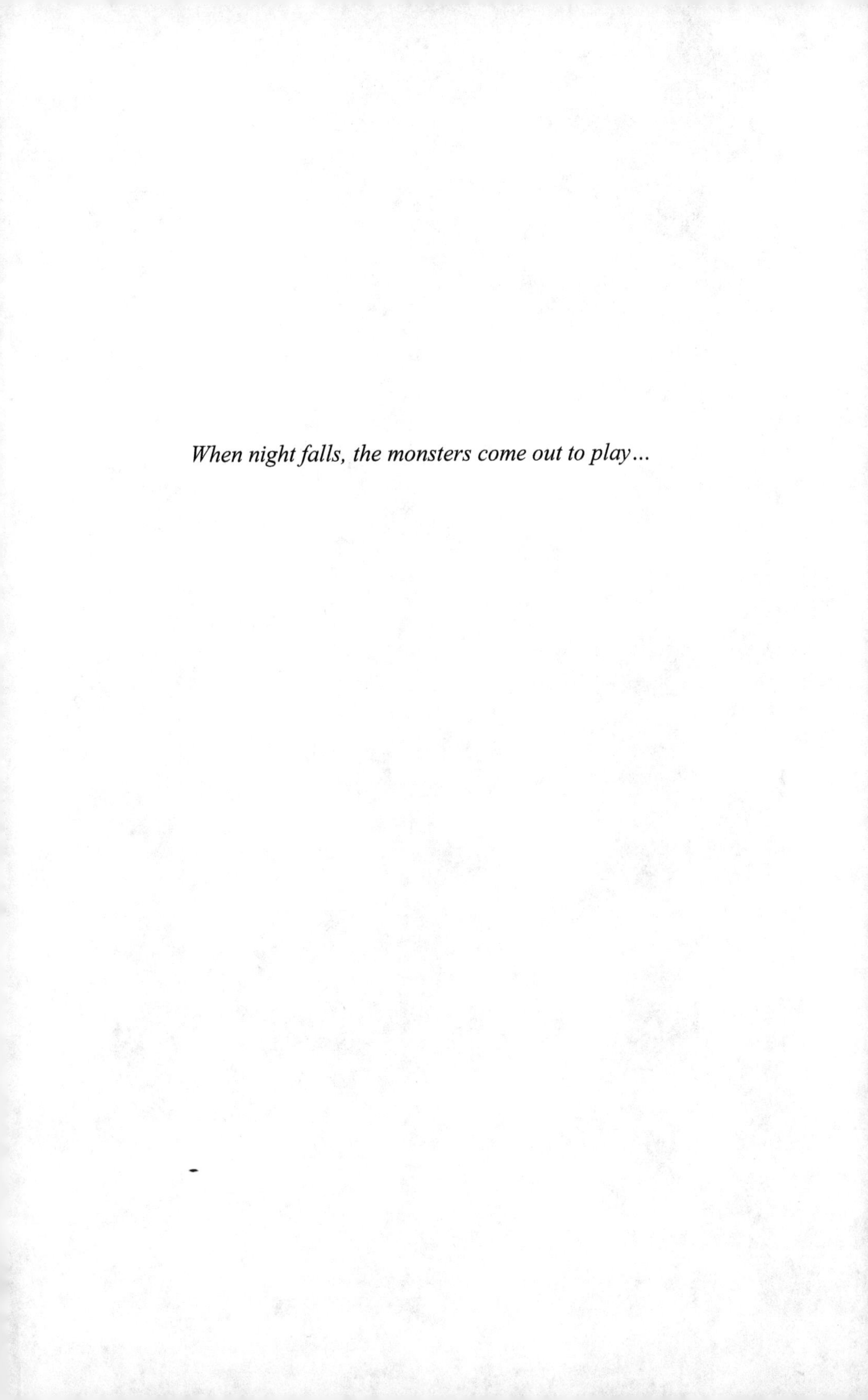

When night falls, the monsters come out to play...

PROLOGUE

TALIA

Blowing out a nervous breath, I crane my neck back to once more look at the place I will be working. Nano Industries, which is a lab here in Athesa's residential district, is spectacular.

The tallest building there is, it's a shining beacon throughout the city, and I get to work there. More than that, I get to make a difference and change the way we live. Nano hired me for my specialty training in genetics, but my true passion is something I can't tell them yet, not until I earn their trust. I know I will have to work my way up from the bottom, but hopefully, after I complete the research they want and give them the results, I can look into what I want—no, *need* to.

I want to research the effects the cultivated food we are making is having on the poorer section of our world, especially regarding the children. My eyes flick to the slums I can just glimpse behind the taller buildings. I've been there a few times, trying to help as much as I could, handing out food and clothes, but after the last time, when I gave a little girl a coat and I found her with her throat slit for it the next day, I stopped going. I knew I couldn't help that way. No, I needed to do something bigger and more important to change our way of life.

While we live across the bridge with more food and riches than can be counted, they suffer with diseases that were eradicated years ago, ailing health, and even birth defects that could easily be avoided. A lot of it stems from the food rations that are handed out every now and again, but it's more than that. It's affecting the kids on this side now too. It is rare, and the cases are few and far between, but my friend at the hospital let me look at their readings and I was right.

Our bodies and chemistry are changing.

I need to figure out why and how to stop it before it's too late.

Nano is the place to do that. Squaring my shoulders, I slick back my blonde hair, tug my black-framed glasses back into place, and storm inside like I'm going to war.

Most of the morning is a rush. I'm sent to security to have my fingerprints scanned, as well as my eyes, body, and hands. My blood is taken, as is my height and weight. I'm subjected to screenings and more tests before I'm given security clearance. The in-depth tests make me raise my eyebrows, but I guess it makes sense. The research they do here is very important, and it wouldn't do for someone who didn't belong to get their hands on it.

Once escorted back from security, I am shown around the lobby and scanned through the turnstiles. I'm just waiting for the elevator when a disturbance has me and the man escorting me turning around to watch.

There's a woman fighting security as she flings questions at them. She wears a camera around her neck, hanging from a thick strap. Her black hair seems to catch and absorb all the light. She is bold and reckless and nothing like me. Her curves are enough to even have me looking down at my boring body, especially in the unflattering jumper and slacks I'm in. She's wearing a tight white top tucked into black jeans with a big belt and a leather jacket slung over her shoulders. Her eyes sparkle as she carries on fighting them as they yank her from the lobby, shouting.

“Journalists,” he snaps, annoyance lacing his tone before he forces a smile as he looks down at me. I ignore that. I’m used to men using their height against me, their stature. I’ve been looked down on my entire life. It didn’t matter that I was born into money or that my parents were scholars before they died. All that matters is that I am trying to get into a male dominated field and they hate it. It makes them feel nervous and weak. I became good at using my words and keeping my eyes down, simply letting my work talk for me.

I worked harder than every single person to get my PhD, and I refuse to be cowed now. I have given up my entire life in the pursuit of research and the hope of bettering our world.

I tilt my head back and nod with a smile that’s well practiced—mocking yet not enough to be called on. My momma would have been proud. I take after her, after all.

She was just another woman trying to change the world created by men.

“Please.” He gestures for me to step inside the elevator, and I do, turning to face the doors as they slide shut and we shoot up into the air towards my future.

ONE

THREE YEARS LATER...

TALIA

Kicking off my trainers, I collapse onto my sofa with a groan, not bothering to turn the lights on after dragging my exhausted self inside my penthouse apartment and locking the doors. The moonlight from the floor-to-ceiling windows lights the spacious, modern apartment enough for me to feel a twinge of loneliness. I have no one to come home to, no one to care if I'm late, and no one to worry that it's been two days since I was here.

There was once, but not anymore.

He betrayed me. I thought he loved me—hell, I thought I loved him, but I guess I was more in love with the idea of him. I liked not being alone and having someone who shares the same values and ideals, but it was all a lie. I'm starting to realise there is strength in loneliness, but during nights like this, I miss my parents.

I turn to stare at their painting above the fireplace. It used to hang in their mansion, but I never wanted their life. I wanted to pave my own way, so the mansion remains untouched, and the only thing I took was this painting. My mum's familiar brown eyes and blonde hair, and my dad's grey eyes, which swirled like a storm, just as mine apparently do when I'm angry, just makes me miss them even more.

I miss them something fierce tonight. I wish I could just call them and hear their voices one more time as they remind me that what I'm doing is worthy. Yet wouldn't they be disappointed? Three years ago, I set out to work my way to the top so I could change things and help people, but here I am. I am no higher up, just a lacky scientist double-checking research and working on things they seem to trust me with.

Nothing important nor world changing.

I'm stuck in limbo, working every day. I nod submissively to men who look down at me, men dumber than me, and silence my voice and ideas for fear of what might happen again.

"Mum, what shall I do?" I sigh, talking out loud like I often do to reason out my problems. She used to say there was always a logical solution to everything, but right now, one evades me. "Do I stay and hope I can one day get to do what I want? Or do I leave and try myself? I have enough money. I could buy a building, start my own small lab, and make a name for myself. It would be hard, nearly impossible if Nano blocks me, which I think they would. They don't like to be rivalled… I think I made a mistake working for them. I know they do good and help people, but I'm starting to think it's only at their expense and on their terms. Am I wrong?"

There's no answer, so I drag myself up and to the kitchen. I make a quick, healthy meal of chicken, rice, and veg, but after the first few bites, I push it away. It's a reminder that people are starving right now, and it's unsettling my stomach. Shaking my head, I force myself to shower off the day, the leers, and comments, and collapse naked into my emperor-sized bed.

My wet hair is spread messily across my silk cushions, and my glasses sit closed on a pile of notebooks and research textbooks I keep next to my bed. My old boyfriend used to call me a triple threat—beautiful, smart, and submissive. He actually called me that once, saying I knew when to bite my tongue, and I hate that he was right. I back down so easily. The only time I don't is when it's something I'm truly passionate about, otherwise I try to find a logical way around it, which often misleads people to believe I'm cold and emotionless.

Robot bitch is the term I hear most often.

The second is cock tease, all because I decided to embrace my femininity and changed from loose clothes to form-fitting dresses that make me feel like I can take on the world.

Flipping over so I'm facing the plain white ceiling of my boring apartment, I find myself wishing for something to change. Anything really. This cold, sterile life I am living is wearing on me, and the research that once excited me doesn't anymore. I feel like I'm wasting my potential.

I fall asleep with hope on my mind.

TWO

CATO

The stars shine brightly through the glass dome above me as my tail lazily wraps around the wooden leg of the bench I lie on. The recent book I borrowed from the library rests on my rising and falling chest. My left arm dangles off the side, touching the once beautiful mosaic floor of my favourite place.

Sitting up with a sigh, I hold the book tightly, like a precious treasure, and climb to my feet. I stretch out my muscles, which are tight from sitting here so long as I read. My eyes sweep greedily around the space. I'm in the art section of the museum, the paintings keeping me company as I wander through the halls. The ropes that once protected the valuable art are long gone, most of the walls are stained, and some of the paintings are missing, though I tried to save as many as I could. Leaves blow in from the open front doors, travelling deeper into the museum.

The monument is forgotten, like us.

The huge, domed ceiling in the next section makes my breath

catch, as always. The intricate marble structures and paintings must have taken years to create, and now they have been left behind to rot with no one to appreciate their beauty but me.

Don't get me wrong, my tribe appreciates beauty, art, science, and knowledge, but most prefer to spend their time scouring the human libraries or researching our people. It's a noble cause, and one I should be focusing on, but something called to me this night. It was a whisper, and I couldn't resist. It led me here, and now some foreign feeling pounds through my heart.

Change—that's what it felt like, but I couldn't logically explain why.

Unlike the Nightfangs, which is the tribe my friend Akuji rules, who trust their instincts to keep them alive, I prefer to focus on what I know and can prove. However, I cannot deny my instincts, which are screaming at me that everything is going to change soon. Frowning, I force myself to speed up. I burst out of the once double front doors and onto the cracked steps of the building. Before me is the square that my people have claimed as ours.

It has an intact water fountain proudly standing in the middle, with a huge, bronze statue set in the heart, lions around the bottom, and a man with a scroll standing proudly between them—Professor Athesa, the man who established the concept of science and society as we know it.

Passing the statue, I spot candles burning in the library and smile softly, knowing my friends, my people, will be there, but I head to our home instead.

The university campus stretches before me. There were once buildings between it and the museum, but they were destroyed in the war, and we built tracks to easily access our base, or den, as the warrior tribe calls it. There's a roar, and I lift my head, my eyes narrowing as I stare into the distance. It was far away, in the Darklings' land. It's none of my business, yet I stand here for a moment longer, wondering which poor monster has been killed now.

No, it's none of my business.

Rolling my shoulders back to ease the tension there, I move through the double doors of the old, red brick building. The main university building, which somehow survived the war, has stunning architecture and spans the whole block. It once held classrooms, theatres, lecture rooms, and more, but it's all changed now, thanks to us. We've made it our own. We built skywalks between it and the buildings on either side, which were also part of the university, expanding the area for our tribe. We don't take in rogues often, but we do sometimes take in wanderers from the warrior tribe.

After all, I was one before.

We have had a few children born in the last few months alone, so we need to expand the nursery. It's situated in the middle of the complex so they are the most protected. Unlike Akuji's tribe, we don't live underground all the time. We have converted basements for those who prefer it, but after a few years, our people created barriers for windows and doors that descend at sunrise to protect our people. It means we can work through the day if need be and also use more rooms in the building. The tunnels under the university were also extended to reach farther out in the city, so as not to limit ourselves like the daylight does.

One of my main research goals is to lessen the effects of the sun. Although we are nocturnal creatures, some of our people, including me, think we could boost our natural aversion to sunlight so the next generation of our people can have all the best opportunities.

The horn sounds—a warning that dawn is a few hours away. The alert reminds those who are spread out across the city and those who guard the perimeter of our lands. During the day, our cameras turn on, allowing us to watch for any humans. Not that they wander in here, but you can never be too careful. At night, they recharge using the moonlight. It's genius, really, even if I do say so myself, considering I created them.

Once inside, I greet my people, answer some questions, and

converse before escaping upstairs to my lab. It's built on the top floor, and since it's constructed of old science classrooms, it's not as state of the art as I would like, but it will do, and it's all mine. Even the bravest of our people don't like being that close to the sun during daylight, worrying it will somehow get to us. Me? I trust in our creations, and I lead by example. It also gives me the space I need to focus on my research in solitude after a hard night of leading our people.

It's a job I also love, but under it all, I am a scientist more than I am a leader. They still continue to elect me year after year, saying I am the best they have ever had. Logically, I know I have advanced our tribe and expanded our territory, as well as brought peace between the Nightfang tribe and our own, the Acumens, but sometimes, splitting my time makes me testy.

Hence the need for silence.

Here, I can evaluate my complicated feelings and roaring instincts. I have fought long and hard to maintain control over my beast and to be a logical being rather than an emotional one, but sometimes it's hard. We are hardwired to fight, mate, and follow our beast's instincts, but that doesn't mean I have to be nothing but a monster.

I can be so much more, and I will.

Sighing, I set my book down at the door, wash my hands, and slide into my lab coat. It's a little snug again—the fourth time this year. I will need to make a new one out of scraps I find in the city, but wearing it brings me back to my logical human side, rather than a bumbling monster playing scientist.

I know the other tribes respect the knowledge we can provide, but they think we are strange. That's okay, though, since not all of us need to be obsessed with fighting and killing. There is enough room in our city for all of us, hence the split of our tribes.

Sitting down at my notes, I chew on my pen as I read over them again. It's on another formula to test for resistance to sunlight. I never test them on anyone but me, but I feel like I'm getting close.

Closer, anyway.

But there's something missing, something I cannot synthesise in our DNA nor understand.

What the humans did to make us is mostly a mystery, despite the research I was able to find. If only I had more, I could change everything…

I could save our people from our own nature.

If only…

THREE

TALIA

Groaning, I pull my eye from the microscope and take off my glasses, rubbing the bridge of my nose as I slump back into my chair for a moment. I'm rechecking someone's research, and yet again, it's wrong, which means I'll have to spend the next week fixing it without getting any credit.

I jump when there's a noise behind me. Whirling around, I sweep my gaze over the lab but find nothing. Everyone else has left for dinner, leaving me alone in the lab that takes up the entire side of this floor. I narrow my blurry eyes and notice a man walking across the walkway connecting this glass-enclosed lab with the lab opposite. That must have been where the noise originated.

Shaking my head at my foolish, jumpy nature, I put on my glasses and straighten. I grab my tablet to start correcting the formula when I hear the whoosh of the lab door opening. I don't think anything of it at first, but when there is no chatter or the sound of coats being put on, I turn slightly and leap to my feet. Stumbling into my work bench, I gawk at the man standing before me with an arched eyebrow.

"Dr Hayes." I scramble up and check myself over to make sure I'm presentable. I peer at him, my cheeks heating at his cold expression as he watches me. "How can I help you?"

After all, it's not every day the lead doctor of the research facility comes down to see you. In fact, I've only met him once, during my interview, and he terrified me. I'd read his research during my master's program. It's ground-breaking. He has a top rate mind, and he was brutal in my interview, and the way he watched me…well, it freaked me out.

Now he's watching me with the same gleam in his eyes, like I'm an experiment, but then he blinks and it disappears. "Ms Ledger, is it not?"

"Erm, yes." I duck my head to hide my flash of irritation. Of course he forgot me. I'm nothing, but it doesn't stop my annoyance since he hired me himself and I've been here doing all the hard work.

"I need to speak to you," he states bluntly.

Excitement courses through me. Has he heard about my research project on the side I plan on presenting this year? "Of course, sir. If this is about the upcoming research presentation, I am ready—"

"No, not about that." He makes it clear he doesn't even know what I'm talking about, and I sag before nodding. "Come to my office in ten minutes." With that, he leaves without even checking to see if I agree.

Bastard.

Groaning, I look back at the research I need to get done. I know I'll be working late to complete it if I have to stop for this meeting.

Let's hope it's important.

I knock on the doctor's door nervously. It's on the very top floor of the skyscraper. I was forced to wait in the lobby of his office for twenty minutes, despite him calling me here. The more I waited, the more angry and agitated I grew, until I was almost bouncing in my seat, much to the annoyance of the prim, middle-aged woman behind the receptionist's desk.

"Come in," someone calls, and I hurry inside. When I get a look at his office, I gape.

It spans the entire top floor, with floor-to-ceiling windows showcasing the city of Athesa and the wall beyond. For a moment, I linger on that before peering around. There's a stone balcony outside, with seating areas and warmers. Inside, the office is decorated to immaculate, if not cold, taste. There is modern artwork and pictures of him doing research everywhere. The floor is hardwood, not carpet, and unwelcoming, just like the man sitting behind the huge desk. Opposite him, on four chairs, are other men I don't recognise—all middle-aged and forgettable—and there are two empty chairs there. I clear my throat and step farther in.

"You wanted to see me, Dr Hayes?" I say dumbly.

He gestures to the chair, and I nod, hurrying across to perch on the edge.

I nod at the men in the other seats, but they just watch me. Something in their eyes makes me look away. Uncomfortable, I wait for Dr Hayes to speak, knowing he hates being interrupted and questioned.

"Ms Ledger, we have an important field research task we think you will be perfect for." He poises his hands on his desk before him. The sunlight frames him, and it wouldn't surprise me if he moved his desk to make that impact in every meeting.

Then what he said hits me…

Field research? I've never been in the field. My area of expertise keeps me in a lab, just the way I like it. Things can get complicated in the field, and research is muddled since there are too many factors to take into account, but it's the first assignment I have been asked to join, so I can't turn it down.

"Will I be the lead?" I question.

He looks at the men, almost smiling. "Of course."

A lead in a field assignment for Dr Hayes? That would open doors that would allow me to research what I want. I could make a name for myself.

"Can you tell me about the research?" I ask, and he nods.

"Yes, but you will sign an NDA. This does not leave this room. It is top secret." That makes me raise my eyebrows, but I nod, and he carries on as if he was waiting for my confirmation before telling me what exactly he wants me to do. "We are researching the *monsters*" —he spits the word— "and trying to understand what happened, how we can help them, and how we can find peace."

I blank at that. I didn't know they were researching the monsters, but it makes sense. They are a phenomenon. Nature is amazing, and even though what happened between our species was terrible, I can't deny they are incredible specimens.

"But when the war broke out, some important research was left in our lab in the Forgotten City."

"I see." I don't really. "And you want me to…"

"Retrieve it, of course." He smiles like it's easy.

I laugh as I look around, thinking they are joking, but they aren't, so I sober quickly. "And how would I do that?"

"By going through the wall, of course."

I jolt at the new voice—a deep, dark, confident one I would recognise anywhere. I twist in my chair, gawking at the man I didn't see until now. He's leaning against the wall, looking out at the city he runs. After all, he's the president.

What is the President of Athesa doing here?

This is a lot bigger than I first thought. I sit up straighter, the pride I feel at being chosen almost making me beam at them. I am finally being recognised for what I can offer, and I cannot help feeling prideful of that, but then I slump. How can I do this? Despite the fact that it's an amazing opportunity, I would surely not survive it.

"Through the wall… I wouldn't survive," I say in confusion.

"We have a contact, a…woman from the slums who can apparently get through the wall and back. She's been doing it for years, according to our contact."

“Whatever for?” I ask in shock.

“Money, of course. What else? Either way, it works for us,” he answers dismissively, brushing it aside. “She has agreed to take you in during the day. That way, you will be safe. She can get you there and back before nightfall. Nothing will happen to you, and we will have the research we need.” He sees me hesitate and leans forward, imploring, “It would mean advancement for our species and understanding where there is uncertainty. And for you, Ms Ledger, it would mean an open contract and endless funding to research whatever your little heart desires.”

I stare at him, shocked. Is he telling me that if I do this, I can research anything?

Yes. I read it in his eyes. It’s a good incentive, excellent actually, and I know deep down, it’s the only way I will get there. I will never get noticed otherwise, left to wither and die in a lab doing others’ works.

Am I actually thinking about this?

I can’t be, that’s crazy. I don’t even like going outside!

“Why me?” I ask instead of outright denying their request.

“We see your potential, Ms Ledger, and this is your chance to show us, me, why I should trust in your dedication to the field. Plus, you’ll be the first scientist over the wall, the first scientist to explore monster nature. Think of it now…”

He’s right.

I can’t do this, though, I really can’t. Not only do I not even like being around other people, but I also wouldn’t have a clue what to do in a monster infested city. Whoever the woman they hired is, she’s obviously insane for going back there all the time.

But the funding…the research. I could save so many.

“Yes. I will go.”

The words are out of my mouth before I even have time to think through the implications.

I’m going through the wall.

I’ve lost my mind.

FOUR

TALIA

The next few days are a whirlwind of preparations. It's so funny watching my colleagues' faces when they realise I've been chosen for fieldwork. They don't know what, of course, but it doesn't matter. I hold my chin higher as I sign contracts and listen to the explanation of what I need and where it is. I'm given a map, and I force myself to go out, get a bag, and fill it with things I think I will need, including new shoes and casual clothes.

When everything is spread across my bed, ready to be packed, I panic. What am I doing? I can't do this, but I have no choice. I signed a contract. I can't go back, not now.

Early the next morning, I'm picked up at my building in an armoured army vehicle and escorted to the bridge that leads from Athesa to the slums. Carrying my heavy bag, I swallow nervously as I trot across the bridge. Once I cross it, the world completely changes.

The streets turn to dirt. There's no clear path anywhere, with rubbish piled all over. There are no streets and signs, just shacks and shanties built on top of each other with walkways strung between them. I hurry past a brothel, where a woman hangs from the window, smoking something.

I jerk back with a little scream as a rat runs across my boots. Blinking and lowering my head in embarrassment, I tug my hood up, remembering what they said about being nothing but a shadow. I follow their directions. I get lost once or twice, my nose crinkling at the stench and the people sleeping rough. The kids are too skinny, dirty, and scared, while the older people are tired, weary, and defeated.

I end up giving over some rations before I force myself to keep moving, needing to keep some for myself as I finally turn the corner and reach the place where I am to meet my guide. When I see her, I stop in shock. She blended in for a moment, but when I finally make her out, I don't know how she ever could have.

She's like no one I have ever seen before.

Her hair is what draws me first. It's a bright, shocking red, like the colour of spilled blood, intersected with lighter ginger strands.

Her eyes make me gulp. They are a brilliant emerald green, like jewels my mother once owned, and so stunning, they actually shock me for a moment before I take in the rest of her face. Her features are all hard edges, with a small scar above her pouting pink lips. There is nothing soft about this woman. She's a survivor. She's also strong. Defined muscles are obvious on her arms and legs, where mine are all soft. Her tucked in waist shows she's from here and probably used to fighting to eat. Where I am sparkling clean and perfectly put together, she's smudged in dirt and dust like she can never quite get rid of it. Her clothes are torn and worn, but she is more beautiful than any woman in Athesa. She's a natural beauty, something people pay and strive to be, and here is she, huddled in a dirty alley.

The determined tilt of her chin tells me this woman is not someone to mess with, as does the hard gleam in her eyes as she watches me move closer.

She turns her head without removing her gaze from me and then spits something on the ground, making me jump. She notices, of course. "You're late," she snaps.

I blink in shock and fear. I really don't want to annoy this woman. She scares me a little. "I was told—" I begin, but she interrupts me, her voice low and throaty.

"The sun is up, and we are already behind schedule. If you want through the wall, then we move now. You don't leave my side, you stay silent unless I talk to you, and you never wander off, understood? If you do, I'll leave you."

I know she means that. She would leave me. I like that I know where I stand with her, even if it's brutal and not at all cultured. "I understand," I answer, wanting her to know I won't let her down. I feel the need to win her approval for some reason.

Sighing like I'm a nuisance, she looks me over, and it's clear she finds me lacking. "Take off the hood."

I hesitate, and annoyance flashes in her eyes. "I… Um, I was told—"

"Take it off." She rolls her eyes. "I'm not going to hurt you or try to get your secrets—I have my own—but I need to know what I'm working with."

Uncertain, I reach up and pull it down. I keep my eyes on the ground for a moment before I flick them up to meet hers. I nervously fold the cloak and put it in my brand-new bag, and then I stand here as she surveys me. The sneer that tilts her lips has my heart sinking, even as she tosses me something, a scrap of fabric she had been holding.

"Here."

I catch it.

"Tie this around your eyes," she orders.

I wrinkle my nose at the stench, checking it over. She snorts, and I meet her eyes. "Why?" I demand.

"So you don't know the way in, duh," she snaps, getting annoyed. "Stop with the questions and do as you're told. It might just save your life."

Great, Tal, annoy your guide. She's definitely going to leave my ass. Still, despite the circumstances, intrigue fills me, and I wonder how she gets through the wall.

"How will I see?" I finally ask.

"That's the point—you won't. You'll hold the back of my jacket until we are through. Once we're over the wall, you can remove it. Also, you're too clean. You know you're going to get dirty, right?"

I blink, not sure what she means. "They are just clothes."

I can tell I've annoyed her again. The flash of hatred and envy that crosses her face is enough to have me shrinking back and tying the thing around my eyes.

"Fine, let's go." I can't see anything at all, and disappointment fills me at not being able to see the wall up close. She moves nearer, and I feel her tug at the fabric before grunting in approval.

I stumble from the force, and she grabs me, making me jump. Her hand is warm in mine and scarred where mine is soft. Night and day. She's a fighter, I'm a scientist, and for a moment, I feel ashamed of that—ashamed that I grew up comfortable when she clearly didn't. "Don't let go at any point. If you get lost, I'll leave you."

Fear fills me at what I am about to do. I was so stupid. I need to talk, to babble like I do when I'm nervous, even though I know she doesn't want to talk to me. "What's your name?"

There's a heavy pause, and I wonder if I have pushed her too far when she finally answers. "Aria."

I roll the name around in my head and nod. It's strong and to the point. Beautiful. It fits her.

"What's yours?"

"Talia," I respond instantly.

"Well, Talia, I hope you know what you're doing," she mutters, and I wince, knowing I really don't. I was so stupid to agree to this, but there's no going back now as she leads me away. I try to keep track of our direction, but it's impossible. The sound and smells are foreign as I stumble behind her sure, silent steps. It's embarrassing when I realise how heavily I'm breathing in fear and how loud I am compared to her.

She directs me with blunt, clipped words, and I follow her without hesitation, having no other choice.

We stop suddenly, and I pant, knowing we are close now. I can almost feel the huge wall's presence. "You'll need to get to your knees and crawl now. Hold onto my foot. I'll go slow and it's going to be cramped, so do not freak out and scream."

I want to argue, to jerk back, but she lets go of my hand. "Okay," I squeak out. There's nothing for a moment, and then her hand is there again, lower, and it tugs me to my knees. I drop into the mud with a wince as she places my hand on her boot. When I nod, she starts to move slowly so I can keep up.

I sigh, wanting to see where we are, but a moment later, something fresh and amazing smelling brushes over my nose, and I know we are through the wall. I can almost feel the wide-open spaces around me, my eyes darting around behind the blindfold, desperate to see.

I'm dragged to my feet and pushed back. I hit something hard, and my hands spread on either side as I trace it. Concrete. Scarred. Uneven.

The wall.

I'm touching the wall, which means I'm through.

I'm in the Forgotten City.

"Do not move, do not look, and do not make a sound."

I couldn't even if I wanted to, but I silently beg her to hurry up and take off this blindfold because above the fear, I feel excitement.

Then she does just that, tugging down the blindfold and stepping back. I wince at the sudden onslaught of sunlight before my mouth drops as I take in our surroundings.

Compared to Athesa, it looks desolate and destroyed, but under that destruction is so much beauty, it steals my breath. The miracle of nature and manmade structures leaves me silent. I spot birds in nests on lampposts, dogs asleep in cars, and flowers and plants growing everywhere, even through the holes in the concrete below us. It stretches out like a forgotten metropolis, and there is something so achingly beautiful and real about it.

"In the hurry to escape, everything was left behind." Aria's voice suddenly cuts through my examination, explaining, "Some tried to buy their way out of the wall, but it didn't happen." She nods to her left, then down to the dirty wall in the distance. "Down there is a mass grave of people. None of them were buried, just bodies piled on bodies. They are all decaying skeletons now, with claw marks and blood decorating the wall."

I blanch but nod. This might be nature's city now, but it's also filled with monsters. Yet I can't help but think they didn't seem to destroy everything, more left it to decay.

There's something else as well.

The silence.

In Athesa, it's always so busy. There are cars, people, cameras, and sounds of the city, while here, there is nothing. It has my shoulders relaxing in a way I didn't know I needed, even as it makes me slightly unsure. "It's so…quiet."

"It comes alive at night." She smiles, and I share a quick smile with her for her joke.

But the reminder of what lives here has me wrapping my arms around myself and eyeing the city differently. Where are they hiding? Are they watching now?

Aria looks back at me. "Where to?"

Her question prompts me to focus on the mission, even as I look around nervously. She stops in front of me, her unafraid gaze settling me a bit as I eye her. She doesn't look scared at all. Instead, she looks happy and peaceful, as if being here is akin to me being in the lab.

How strange.

"Where to?" she repeats.

Oh, right. "I, erm, I have a map." I hurry to pull it from my bag and show her what they gave me.

She takes it from me and scans it with a roll of her eyes before peering closer at it. "Fucking hell."

"What?" I ask nervously. She glares at the map as if it offended her, and then her gaze rises, and the anger I see there almost makes me stumble back.

"That's in the middle of the city."

"That's a problem?" I ask, concerned about the slight edge of nerves in her eyes. She ignores me for a moment, folding the map and shoving it in a pocket, which is fine by me. I don't even know how to read it anyway.

"Only if you like being alive." She groans. "I stay on the outskirts if I can. That deep in the city, there are too many big buildings and underground entrances, and too much darkness, which is where they like to lurk."

"Oh." It's all I can muster. Fear pounds through me so hard, I'm debating on running back through the wall with my tail tucked between my legs.

Rolling her shoulders with a shrug, she pulls some shades down to cover her eyes and turns her head. "We better get moving."

"We are still going?" I almost scream.

"I need the money, and you need…well, whatever you need, so yeah, we are going, but we are going to need to move fast. No breaks and no stopping if you want to get there and back before night-time."

"What happens then?" I inquire, even though it's a dumb question.

"When the sun goes down, the monsters come out to play." She laughs and starts walking towards the monster infested city. Her steps are silent and purposeful, and she avoids everything as if she knows it's there without looking.

I rush after her, not wanting to be left behind, but I have to keep looking between my feet and her, and it means I stumble and make a noise. I can tell it annoys her. "Wait, please," I beg, needing her to slow down.

"Shh," she hisses, turning and pointing at my feet. "Watch your steps and lower your voice."

"Sorry," I whisper, following her lead. "How—What do we do if we meet a monster?"

"Run like hell and hope for the best?" She laughs.

I shoot her looks, trying to understand and settle my mind, because curiosity is taking over, making me nosey. After all, a scientist's job is to understand. I've always been curious, if not scared of what happened over the wall, and here's a woman who knows something. If I didn't take the time to ask, I would kick myself later, scared or not.

Plus, talking will help me calm down as we venture farther into the city.

"You've never encountered one?"

"No one has and lived to tell the tale," she reminds me. "We all know the lore, though, and how dangerous they are. They can kill a human before we can even scream. I don't particularly want to be lunch, do you?"

I shake my head, watching her move around a lamppost with ease. I can't move the way she does. Her movements are all slick and smooth, made for ground like this. I'm made for labs. "Good, then let's hope we don't meet one."

I almost laugh again, even though I'm scared. "Let's."

FIVE

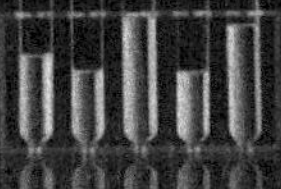

TALIA

Aria doesn't talk much after that. I take the hint and follow her through the city, trying to keep up. Where she's silent and sure, I'm clumsy and loud. It's embarrassing, but I can't help it, especially since my boots are killing me, yet I don't complain. She already thinks the worst of me, and I really don't want her to leave me here.

Instead, I focus on the city as we move deeper. The shops are either raided or destroyed. The buildings are partially demolished, and the roads are ruined. Debris and remnants of the city were left discarded here like carcasses. It's almost sad, and I wonder who occupied the houses and shops. Where are they now?

Did they get out?

There's also evidence of monsters. Footprints, claw marks, blood… That is enough to have me shivering in fear.

After what feels like hours, I'm exhausted, sweating, and wondering why the hell I took this job. With each heavy, painful step, I remind myself I was a fool for thinking I could do this.

Without a word, she swerves towards a building and hurries up the stairs. I hesitate but hurry after her. The steps creak with our weight, and spiders scurry out of our way, nearly making me scream. She bounds out of a metal door, and I follow after her. Without a word, she hops onto a crumbling edge of the rooftop, swinging her legs like she's having fun. "Sit and drink," she orders as she looks out at the city.

She hasn't even broken a sweat, and for a moment, I envy her. "You are fast," I mutter, panting embarrassingly. I sit next to her and guzzle some water, my lungs screaming at me.

"Don't drink so fast. You'll make yourself sick, and you need to ration it. They cut off the water and power a long time ago," she snaps, and I freeze before my cheeks flare with heat and I look away.

I can sense her disgust, and it makes me slump. She's right—I shouldn't be here. "I know that, shit, I'm sorry. I'm so bad at this."

"You wouldn't be my first choice," she teases. "So why are you here?"

The fact that she asked makes me sit up a little. She doesn't know why, that's for sure, but it's the interest in her voice that has me peering back at her. She's framed by the sun, her hair glowing like a flame, while I simply blend into the background with my limp, sweaty blonde hair and boring eyes.

I want to tell her, but I'm not sure I'm allowed to, so I tell her as much. I expect her to be offended, but she shocks me yet again. "Talia, do I look like the type of person who blabs? Or, for that matter, do I look like a person who has anyone to blabber to?" She smirks. "You don't have to tell me everything."

She's right—it can't hurt. Plus, I need to talk to someone. "I work for a lab, part of the government. They left some research here, and that's all I know. I'm to retrieve it."

"And they didn't send a team, an army, through the front gate?" She frowns. I know what she's thinking, I thought the same thing.

"They wouldn't make it," I offer, still unsure if she's not right. "They wanted it done quietly and fast."

"It's a coverup." She nods, understanding now. "Still, why you? Not to be mean, but why not a super soldier or spy?"

I don't even hesitate to tell her. She can judge me all she wants. She already hates me, and for some reason, I want to convince her I'm not all that bad. "I honestly don't know. I didn't ask. I've been waiting for years to conduct hands-on research and to be able to do what I am trained for. This is the only chance they have given me, so I can't mess this up, Aria. I'll get the research, and they will finally let me research what I want to."

"Which is?" she asks, seemingly interested and not just pitying me.

"I want to do an analysis of the effects our cultured food sources are having on children and the underprivileged," I answer truthfully. "I want to help make this world a better place."

"You're about the only one who wants to then, kid."

Kid? I'm clearly older than her, but then I think about it. I'm only older in age. She knows this world better than me, so in her eyes, I'm probably a child, bumbling and unknowing.

Her words register, and I frown. "What do you mean?"

"The government will never change. They like the slums. They keep the poor, poor and the rich, rich. There is a clear pecking order. They won't ever do anything to change that because it benefits them. The rich earn more and live longer and better, while the poor kill each other for scraps. It's the way they like it and the way it will always be. Nothing will change that. Sorry to burst your bubble, Talia."

I frown, looking away. I've believed in the good of my people and what we are capable of and can do my whole life. I know we aren't perfect—I hate the slums and want equality—but nothing is perfect, and there are good people who can change it…right?

There was clear truth behind her words, however, so she obviously believed it wholly, and for a moment, my entire world seems to spin as I think back on my life and my society.

Is she right?

No, she's not. There is good in this world and the capability for change. She's jaded. She's seen the worst of humanity without any good, and that would make anyone feel this way, but I've seen the beauty, strength, and kindness humanity is capable of.

She's wrong about us.

"You're wrong—some want to make this world better, and I'm one of them. I'll make it happen. We can do better than we have before."

She watches me with something akin to respect. "I hope you're right," she murmurs as I stare at her. "Now drink up, we need to keep moving."

The next few hours are hard. We talk more though. She seems freer with me than before, almost respectful, until I offend her about her work. I explain why and where we are going, and she even finds me new shoes once she realises mine are hurting me, but she's always on guard. It's clear she doesn't like my pace, especially after we have a run-in with a wild animal she thinks was near us.

I'm almost relieved when we spot the skyscraper that leads to the lab. I hurry across the square, my scientific brain locking on the building. It's only when I have my hand on the door when I realise it's quiet. Looking around, I spot Aria staring down at a hole worriedly.

"Aria?"

Turning away, she hurries to my side and follows me inside. It's dark, the sunlight unable to pierce the shadows, and I peer into it nervously. She suddenly splashes light across the reception area, which is so similar to the one I work at, it has me freezing for a moment. "You're up, Doc. Lead the way."

Shivering in the dark, I worry my lip but move around the furniture, her light showing the way. I search for what they explained… Ah, there is the entrance to the lab. It's hidden, though I don't know why. Maybe to protect their research?

It's not uncommon.

I turn from the elevator to the wall. It looks like every other panel, but I'm hoping this is what they described, since this is the only logical choice here. "I hope this is it." I raise my hand hesitantly and press it to the wall. I can almost feel the warmth of the mechanics waking up, and then there's a beep so loud, it makes me jump.

A green light makes me pull my hand away, and then a section of the panel swings inward. A door. I peer inside to see metal steps leading down. To the lab? Rolling my shoulders back when I smell the antiseptic, I step inside. Each step makes me braver as I feel more at home, more comfortable.

Electricity buzzes to live, lighting up the area as I cling to the metal railing. "Here we go," I call to her, and I hear her torch click off. I spare her a look. She looks unsure, but I'm not.

This is the right place!

We made it!

I hurry down the metal stairs, navigating them with familiar, sure steps, unlike outside. The familiar, comforting feel of a lab makes me confident and strong. The lab is displayed before us, ready to be explored, and excitement fills me. Air-con blows over me, and I grin, almost laughing. I feel Aria watching me, but I leave her to it as I hurry to find the research, her warning about needing to be out of here by nightfall echoing in my head. Despite the fact that I itch to explore the sprawling lab and the secrets it holds, I focus on our mission.

I boot up the computer. It's an older version, but it comes to life quickly enough. It should have every file I need to start with.

"How long?" Aria demands, her voice uncertain, and I blink, trying to pull myself from the computer as I flick through files and notes.

"Hmm? Oh I'm not sure."

I focus back on my work, feeling her annoyance, but it fades in the face of excitement at what the files could hold. I follow my directions and take the vials I need, crosschecking their labels carefully with the data on the computer to make sure they correlate and are the correct ones. I pull the bag from under the desk and carefully pack them into the insulated interior, knowing they need to be kept cold. Hopefully, this will last until we get back. It's all I have to work with.

I work as quickly as I can, mentally checking things off as I work through the cultures and fridges. I double- and triple-check everything, but the next thing on the list isn't there, neither is the next and the next. I frown. Maybe it's somewhere else?

But no, it should be here. So where is it?

"What is it?" Aria demands. I didn't know she had been watching me so closely, but she must have been able to sense my confusion. Her eyes are uneasy where she stands on the stairs, as if she does not want to enter the lab, which makes me frown harder.

"Some of the samples are missing," I admit.

"Did you double-check? Maybe they were put into a different fridge."

I nod, hurrying to check anyway, meticulously opening everything to make sure. "No, they are definitely gone…but they should be here." I crouch on the floor before turning to meet her eyes. There's only one logical solution. They were taken. But why? By whom? "Who would sneak into the city and steal samples?"

"No one good," she mutters, but then there's a massive crash from upstairs. I jump to my feet, backing away in fear, but she only seems determined. "And that is our cue to go. Grab your shit. Now."

I hesitate. There is so much more I need to grab. If I go back without it, I will lose all their support. "I still need collect data—"

She hurries to me. "No time." She throws my bag at me and yanks me to my feet. "That could be anything or anyone, and I'm not sticking around to find out. This will be enough. We go now, or we die."

That gets me moving, because she's right, and it's more important we survive this than locate the missing samples. We can always come back. I follow her up the stairs, where she stops at the top. I swallow my fear at her stiff back. It's not a monster, is it?

If it is, what do we do?

I want to ask, but I stay quiet, following her lead.

There's another crash, and she turns to me with a finger pressed to her lips, telling me to stay silent. I nod, and she turns forward, stepping out. I follow as close as I can, not wanting to be left alone. I don't see anything, but I spot something outside.

The sun is starting to set.

Oh my god.

We are going to die here!

My eyes drop to something moving outside, and I almost scream. Aria is focused on the sun with fear in her eyes—fear I've never seen in her before. "Aria," I hiss.

"I know," she mutters, but she's not seeing what I am.

"No, look." I point it out, my hand shaking. There, beyond the glass, is a fucking tiger, an animal I've only ever seen a clone of in the zoo, since most died out here in the city…or so we thought. It's watching us, smashing into the glass as it keeps its eyes on us, searching for a way in. My heart pounds, and I'm sure it can hear it and taste my fear as it licks its fangs.

"We move fast and silently now!" Aria orders, grabbing me and yanking me after her. She pulls me outside and into a sprint across the square. My eyes go back to the tiger, and I almost scream when I see it bounding after us.

Then it roars.

"Run!" Aria yells.

I push myself to race at her side, but we are too slow. We are going to die. Oh my god, we are going to—

I scream as Aria goes down next to me with the tiger on her back, biting her shoulder. It's huge, double her size, and so strong, I freeze for a moment, but the fear and determination on Aria's face gets me moving.

I won't leave her to die, not when I can help. It's foolish, but I rush to the tiger to help. It turns to me and roars. Its eyes are now locked on me—a new moving target. "Go!" Aria yells. I glance at her to see her reaching for something, but my eyes cut back to the tiger as it prowls towards me.

It shadows my every step, Aria's blood dripping from its mouth. I flick my gaze to her to see her determination. She holds a rock in her hand, and she's swaying slightly on her feet, but she's standing strong. "Run now!" she screams and lets loose. The rock sails through the air and hits the beast. It turns sharply, its tail snapping across me, knocking me back as he roars at Aria.

My eyes go to her, imploring her to run, to come with me.

But it's between us…

"Go!" she demands and then runs, despite her wound. The tiger starts to chase her, and I have no choice. I can't be left here alone. She told me to run. I was told to listen to her, so despite my fear, guilt, and worry, I turn and run.

I hear it roaring and her running feet. I falter, debating going back, but I can't. She told me to run, plus I might not find her again. No, I'll run. I'll listen to her. She's smart and capable. If I bumble around, I'll put her in danger. She'll find me again, I know she will, so I run, blinded by my own fear and tears.

The city remains silent around me as I plunge into the darkness of the Forgotten City.

As the monsters awaken.

SIX

CATO

Frowning, I stare out at the city beyond, the invisible line between my tribe and Akuji's standing before me. There is nothing to signify it, yet I know it's there. I heard things—things that shouldn't be possible if no one was on alert.

Screaming.

Human screaming.

Human female screaming.

I hesitate again, needing to find out what it is, but I do not want to cross into Akuji's territory. We might be okay, friends even, but he couldn't allow that to stand. Then again, if there are human females screaming in his territory, he's probably there already.

Just then, I hear something closer—small, running feet.

It sounds almost like a child. It is not one of ours, though, because they are too loud and unsure, and then I hear her muttering. Her fear hits me full force, the stench of it making acid rise in my throat. It's pure terror, and for some reason, it sends my heart into overdrive. A growl rips from my lips as I pace the line, and then I see her.

She stumbles at the end of the road, stepping over my territory and into Akuji's. Her head whips around, looking over her shoulder. There are tears in her eyes, which are the colour of a storm, lighting up like thunder cracking through the night. Her hair is a blonde halo, flowing around her as she rushes back around and falls again. She hits the ground hard with a sob before pushing to her feet and backing away.

She's lost, confused, and scared.

I've never seen a human female, only the male warriors they send in here. How did she get through the wall, and why is she running? And from whom? Was she the one that screamed? It seems likely. Maybe one of Akuji's warriors found her and is trying to kill her for crossing the wall.

For some reason, that thought fills me with fury, and before I know it, I've stepped over the tribal lines, drawn by her fear. A sick feeling tears at my stomach, my heart thunders, my claws slash at the air, and my tail lashes behind me. My entire body roars at me to save her.

To protect her.

To cherish her.

Where did that come from?

I have no time to stand here, shocked and confused, however, as the scent of fresh human blood hits me. She's hurt! Her head whips around, and I realise I let out a growl. I don't know much about humans, but I know their eyesight is poor in the dark, so she probably only sees my shadow, but it sends her scrambling backwards. Another scream rips from her throat as she tries to get away from me.

Something deep inside me tells me she will never be able to get away from me, though, no matter how hard she tries.

It gets me moving, knowing we are in danger. She's in danger. If Akuji's warrior catches her here, which he will from the scent of her blood and the sounds of her screams, then she is as good as dead, and even the thought of that makes me wild. Red bleeds onto my vision.

I could be killed for this, for treachery and for crossing tribal lines, but none of it matters when the little whimper she lets out rocks me to my very core. I want to tear this city apart and kill anyone who dared to hurt or scare her.

She's mine! Not theirs!

When I reach her, she curls in on herself, holding her hands up as if to ward off a blow. Her face is pale and terrified, and I find myself aching to see those stormy eyes again. My heart pounds at being so close to her, because below the scent of her fear and blood is something so sweet and enticing, it wakes up every cell in my body. It reforms me until I'm a beast, and I reach for her without conscious thought.

I need to touch her, taste her, and protect her. It's not an instinct I can fight, and no logic can change what I'm doing, not when she whimpers again. Holding her softly, I cradle her against my chest. She's so tiny, she weighs nothing.

Another whimper slips from her lips, and the sound rips out my heart. I have to make it stop. "Shh, everything will be okay," I tell her, but my voice is growly, and she shrinks farther into herself, her lips quivering. I don't have time to comfort her or prove I won't hurt her, not when whoever made her scream could be chasing her.

Keeping her close, I quickly stride back into my land. Only then does the worry in my shoulders unravel, but I still have an injured, scared, human female in my arms. My people might be loyal, but they won't take kindly to her presence, so I cover her as much as I can. Luckily, most of my people are out at this time of night, but I take the back stairs one leap at a time until I'm locked away in my lab and living areas. Once there, I block the door so they can't just walk in, which they wouldn't necessarily do, but one can never be too sure.

Looking around, I find a place to put her. There isn't much here, I don't need a lot, and for a moment, I hate that I don't have a comfortable nest for her in the big room. Instead, I settle on a section of the floor with a counter on one side and a wall on the other, trying to make her feel safe.

I'm reluctant to put her down, but I force myself to, frowning as she groans. Her eyes remain closed as she curls around something, a bag of sorts, and her face is turned away from me as if waiting for a blow.

It hurts a lot.

"You're safe now," I tell her, trying to soften my voice as much as I can. I even move away so she doesn't feel cornered, but she stays like that. I fetch her water and some food, and she doesn't move, but she shivers, so I grab a fur, wrap it around her, and then sit at my desk.

This research is important, but I can't think about it now, although I pretend to. My eyes go between her and it. I hope she will relax, talk… look at me.

I hope she will flash those mesmerising eyes in my direction again.

I can be patient. I can wait forever if I need to.

My body tells me this human is mine, though I'm not sure why, but I plan to find out.

"Who are you?" she croaks out. Her voice flows through me, lighting every inch of me up, making me hers.

SEVEN

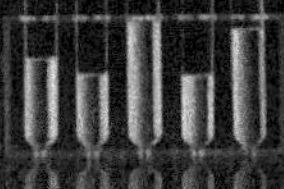

TALIA

He's huge. It's my first thought. He's also not at all what I was imagining the monsters to look like. I've studied some of the old news reports, but they never looked like this. This man is almost…gentle-looking. Perched on a chair too small for his seven foot plus frame, he's hunched over as if he's uncomfortable with his size or trying to make himself smaller for me.

When I first saw him, I was terrified. He was just a massive shape coming towards me, and I was sure I would die after racing through the city for what felt like hours, but then he picked me up. I couldn't even stop him, the strength I felt in his arms astounding me. He lifted me like I was nothing more than a feather. I didn't even look where he was taking me, sure he was going to kill me when we got there.

Aria would have fought, but not me. I froze. I curled up and prepared to die, and then he put me down and walked away. I felt him watching me, but out of the corner of his eye.

He gave me water and warmth. Why?

The monsters hate our kind. So why did he help me?

Who is he?

"Who are you?" I ask again, sitting up slightly and wrapping the fur tighter around me. A delicious scent wafts off it, but I resist burying my nose in the pelt and inhaling it. He still might kill me, but I can't be scared forever. Even now, my fear is ebbing away, being replaced with exhaustion.

My voice is stronger this time, and I know he hears me. Turning his head slightly, he watches me carefully as if he's worried I will scream again.

He probably doesn't want anyone else stealing his kill.

The thought makes me laugh maniacally, and he frowns as he observes me, probably thinking I'm crazy. I'm not so sure I'm not. After all, I'm trying to converse with a seven-foot red monster who's sitting on a rolling office chair in what looks like a high school science lab.

"My name is Cato," he finally responds. Despite his gruff exterior, his voice is almost soft, providing a balm to my terror, and I relax before I realise it.

"Okay, Cato, why am I not dead yet?" I ask, and he flinches back as if he's offended by the idea. I shrink under his anger, hoping I've not pushed him too far.

Turning away with a growl, he slowly breathes in and out, giving me time to stare at him. His skin is bright red, like a flame, highlighting muscles stacked upon muscles. His arms are almost double the size of my body, and his broad chest is bare. He wears tattered shorts, his only clothing, which hang low on his waist. He has two black eyes, a long, regal nose, and thick, lighter red lips. Black horns jut from his head, curling up into the sky, and for some reason, I want to touch them. His hands are massive, and his fingers are long and tipped with black claws, which could easily rip me apart. A red tail lashes behind him in agitation.

"Don't say that," he says.

"Sorry," I squeak out, pressing back into the wall.

"I am not going to hurt you," he sneers like he hates that I think that, but why wouldn't I?

"Okay," I murmur, not wanting to annoy him. If I want to survive this, I need to keep this monster happy before he decides to eat me like a fucking snack.

"What is your name?" he queries, looking back at me. He watches me like he truly sees me, noticing every flaw and defect, while also hanging onto my every word. Nobody looks at me like that. I'm invisible, even to my lovers, but this monster observes my every move like it intrigues him, and that unnerves me. I wonder what he can see.

"Talia," I answer.

"Talia." He drags out my name, ending with a slight growl that sends a shiver through me.

"Yep, and you're Cato," I reply dumbly, and then let out a little scream when he suddenly appears before me. I didn't even see him move, but his face is almost pressed to mine. That delicious scent wafts to me again, almost making me lean into him as I pant.

"Say it again," he murmurs.

"What?" I ask in confusion, distracted by the expanse of red skin before I realise I'm checking out his muscles and jerk my eyes back to him. Most human males would smirk, but he doesn't seem to notice the effect he has on me.

It's clearly been far too long since I've had sex if I'm checking out a red monster.

"My name," he implores.

"Cato?" I repeat, and he groans, his eyes sliding shut.

"Again."

"Cato." I search his face, noting the tiny scars across his skin. His lashes are tipped red, and fangs hang over his lips. I ache to trace his face. It's all angles, and his features are beautiful in a deadly way. His eyes open, the black swirling with red, locking me in place. "Your eyes are turning red," I whisper.

Snarling, he sits in the chair with his back to me. His hands fist on the table, and his chest heaves with his ragged breathing. I remain silent, not wanting to push him when he's so clearly fighting something. Maybe he's trying to resist killing and eating me?

I want to tell him I wouldn't make a good meal, that I'm too fatty, but I can't. I continue to watch him, worried any little noise will cause him to snap.

"I will not hurt you," he states, his voice strong and determined. He glances over at me, and his eyes are black once more. I want to ask him what that means, but I don't. "Not ever."

"Why?" I question.

"Because it would be like ripping myself apart," he whispers before he turns to face me. "Why were you screaming? Were you chased? I smelled blood."

"Not mine," I whisper. "My friend, she was hurt."

"By one of us?" he asks, freezing.

I shake my head. "A tiger." He slumps slightly. "I have to go back and find her—"

"Someone from Akuji's tribe will have found her by now, as you were very loud. I cannot walk back into their territory, they will kill me, and if you go back, they will have you as well, and I will not let that happen."

I blink at all the information, filing it away to ask about later. "Have her? Will they kill her?" I go cold all over.

"I do not know," he admits. "But I will not take that risk with you."

I slump like all of my strings have been cut. "Aria," I whisper. "Please, you have to let me go. I have to find her!"

"No!" he roars, and I shrink in on myself. "You will stay here where it is safe, until I figure out what to do."

"Please, Cato," I beg, despite my fear. "She needs my help."

He stands. "I will go and see if I can find her. If I can't, I'll come back. Is that acceptable?" I nod, and he points at me. "Do not leave this room. Outside of this room is my tribe. The building is filled with them. They won't hesitate to kill you, do you understand?"

A building filled with monsters? "Yes," I croak out, and he watches me for a moment before snarling again.

"Stay here. I will not be long." He strides to the door and rips it open, and then I hear it click shut. I sit where I am, shocked. What is happening?

I haven't had a moment to breathe since the tiger attack, and now I'm locked up with a monster who just left me in a building full of them. I almost laugh before I slap my hand over my mouth. Despite what he said, I need to get out of here, find Aria, and get back over the wall. But how will I do that?

I start by standing up, ignoring the ache in my body from running, the burning of my eyes from crying, and the drying blood on my skin as I hurry around the room, searching for anything to help. I blink in shock when I open a fridge to find some of the missing research.

Motherfucker… The monsters took the research.

Why?

I hesitate, but I don't have time to ask questions, so I shut the fridge. My search only turns up more and more research and notes that intrigue me. Whoever it is, they are a very capable scientist. Could it be a monster?

But why?

Blowing out a breath, I focus on the only door in the space. I have to go out through there. Rolling my shoulders back, I storm over and unlock it. When nothing happens, I peek my head out, and when I still hear and see nothing, I slide one foot out, but then there's a roar of laughter before there's one of anger.

It's so loud, it slams through my heart, sending instant terror coursing through me so hard, I stumble back through the door. I desperately grab the closest thing—which happens to be a chair—and I push it in front of the door, but my panic consumed brain knows it's not enough, so with all my strength, I push a desk in front of it and scamper back to the corner of the room, grabbing a blade I found on the side.

My lungs scream as I hyperventilate, and my body shakes from adrenaline.

When nothing happens, I slump slightly, suddenly exhausted as the adrenaline leaves me cold and shivering. That was dumb—really dumb. Who did I think I was, trying to waltz out of a monster den?

Okay, so I can't just walk out there. For some reason, the monster, Cato, didn't want to hurt me. In fact, he seemed appalled at the idea, but that doesn't mean it won't change. However, I can work with that for now, because the monsters out there want to hurt me just like he said. Better the enemy you know and all that jazz.

I'll stay here until he gets back, and then I'll wait for him to sleep, wait for them all to sleep, before I make my grand escape into daylight. That's the only reason I tell myself I'm trusting this man, even though it's a lie and my heart aches at the idea of leaving.

How absurd.

EIGHT

CATO

I know the other human isn't in my territory, but I couldn't deny Talia. She looked so scared, but she was still determined to race into the city of monsters to find her friend. That loyalty? Yeah, it did strange things to my heart, until I found myself agreeing to go look for her. I shouldn't have left Talia alone, but I didn't have much choice. My dread that something could happen to her has me searching as quickly as I can for her friend, but when I reach the border of Akuji's land, I know I have no choice. I cross it, sticking to the shadows and moving quickly. I was taught by his people, so I know their locations, what to look for, and how to stay silent.

It works, and I don't run into anyone, but when I reach the square that haunts me to my dying day, the place I both hate and love, I smell it.

Blood.

There is a lot of it, and it is not Talia's. Her friend? It has to be. Aware I'm putting myself in danger, I step out into the open and follow the blood trail. I form lies in my head. Akuji might let me get away with it, but some of his people ache to fight, ache to enforce their laws and impress their reigner. They wouldn't hesitate to try and kill me, and then I'd have to kill them all, which would start a war we don't want or need.

Just for her, my Talia.

She is mine. The feeling is undeniable. I'm not sure why, but I won't look at it too closely. I'm running on instinct, my heart clenching at having to tell Talia her friend is badly hurt. Suddenly, the blood trail veers to a dead-end alley, and I freeze, smelling Akuji. It's strong. He's either still here or was here not long ago, so despite the fact that Talia needs to find her friend, I get the hell out of there. I will not risk a war between our people, not even for her.

I guess some of my intellect still remains, although the rest of it fled when I laid eyes on her. The closer I get to my land, the more my nerves increase and my steps hasten. I don't think my people will enter my rooms without being called, but if they heard her, or worse, she tried to leave?

A flash of red fills my head before I push it away. Once back at my den, I take the stairs in one leap. I rip open the door, blinking in shock when I watch a desk, a chair, a whiteboard, a box, and some cloth bits fly across the room from where they were behind the door.

There's a squeak, and my eyes land on Talia. She's in the back corner of the room, her eyes wide as she watches me with a scalpel in her hand. The terror in her gaze instantly has guilt filling me, so I close my eyes and breathe through my panic and anger, relieved to find her okay, even if she is scared. I shut the door and hold my hand out to show her I mean no harm, then I slowly move across the room.

The closer I get to her, the faster her heart races, the stench of both fear and relief filling the air. I ignore it as I stop before her and crouch. "It's okay, it's just me." I reach for the blade, not liking the fact her hand is shaking and she might cut herself, but she mistakes my intention. I must move too fast, even though I try to slow down and hunch to make myself smaller. Her instincts kick in, and she lashes out. I don't even feel the tiny butterfly cut, but she freezes and her eyes widen as fear explodes through her. Slowly, I extract the blade so she doesn't hurt herself and pocket it. When I stand, she jerks back with a squeak that makes my heart hurt.

"Talia, it is okay, it's nothing. I will not hurt you," I repeat, and then I retreat to give her room to think. My eyes stay on her as I sit. I feel a small cut on my cheek, but I ignore it. I watch her, worried about how pale she is.

Her head drops, and she wraps her arms around herself for a minute before she shakes it off and then looks at me. Her gaze travels over my face, which I like too much, but then guilt pops into those stormy eyes. "I'm so sorry about your face," she whispers. "I panicked."

"It's fine, I've had a lot worse." I grin, but she shakes her head and forces herself to stand. Her eyes dart to me nervously as she moves around the room. I watch her, wondering what she is doing, but when she turns back to me, she takes a deep breath, and with more courage than I thought humans possessed, she stops before me and lifts the cotton swab she is holding to my cheek. "Let me clean it."

I freeze, not even breathing or blinking. I do not want to scare her away, not when her delicious scent is wrapping around me, hardening my length again and making me think of things I have no right to ponder with such a small little human—a human who fears me. Licking her lips, she leans closer, and I watch the glistening pink flesh and wonder what they would taste like.

"This might sting," she murmurs, but I don't move as she touches the cut. It does sting a little, but I let her clean it. She mumbles to herself as she does, an adorable muttering of words that has my lips quirking and an ache blooming in my chest. I yearn to reach out, snatch her to me, and crush my lips to hers and see if she would mumble then.

When she steps back, she seems more confident, but worry still lingers in her eyes. "I don't think it needs stitches, but I don't know how fast you heal."

"It will be gone in an hour," I admit with a slight shrug. Her eyes widen in wonder, and I see the questions flickering through her eyes. Interesting. "You can ask," I offer, but she shakes her head.

"Sorry. So, Aria, did you find her?" she asks, voicing the one question she's been wanting to ask since I walked in. I think she's scared of the answer, however, since her friend isn't with me. She discards the swab and leans near me, watching me carefully.

"I'm sorry, Talia," I begin. "I found a blood trail." I don't mention how much, not wanting to upset her further. "It led deep into Akuji's territory. She wasn't there, but..."

"But?" she prompts, focusing on me. Her eyes are alight with a fire that shouldn't have me nearly panting with need.

"But I also smelled Akuji, the reigner, the leader of the Nightfang tribe whose land you were in," I explain.

She sags before turning and screaming, muffling it with her arm. I fly to my feet, reaching for her, but she recoils like she feels me, and with a flick of her hair, starts to pace. "Fuck, fuck, fuck. He has her, right? Shit, what if he killed her?" she whispers to me. "Would he kill her?"

"Akuji? Maybe, if he felt it was necessary. He's no friend to the humans, but he could have easily killed her then and there, and he didn't, which leads me to believe he wanted her alive for something."

"Logic, I can work with that. You're right—if he wanted her dead, it would make sense to do it then. If he has taken her, there is a chance she's alive, albeit slim if she was bleeding. But I can work with a slim chance." Her brain is magnificent to watch as she works through every scenario and outcome.

A scientist's brain, I realise with a start.

"Talia, are you a scientist?" I question.

She freezes, eyeing me carefully. All that confidence, all that fire is gone, and her face is pale. She scurries across the room, and I instantly hate the distance between us. Wrapping the bag in her arms, she leans into the wall.

"What's in the bag?" I ask, trying to engage her in conversation. She flinches, obviously hearing me, but she doesn't speak. "Okay, how about why were you in the city?"

Nothing.

"Talia?" When she doesn't respond again, I stiffen. "Are you cold? Hungry? Tired? You can sleep," I urge, but she continues to ignore me, and I hate the silence. I miss her warm, soft voice that settles this chaotic feeling she has incited in me.

Frowning, I move closer, trying to catch her gaze, but she turns away. I still catch the tears in her eyes though. "Your friend will be okay." I find myself lying without knowing why. It's not logical, but I can't help myself. Her tears and almost silent sniffles cause agony to tear through me until my voice is rough and desperate. "Talia, please, nobody will hurt you, okay? Please, little one, stop crying. Your tears are killing me."

She continues to ignore me, and I find myself talking to her anyway. Slowly, her tears abate, but she still doesn't talk or look at me. After an hour of watching her, I want to scream or rage, anything to get her attention. I am desperate for her voice, for those stormy eyes to lock on me and make me feel both weak and strong again.

It's better than this…cold shoulder.

Fuck, it's driving me crazy.

All forms of logic are gone.

I should be working. I should check on my people. I should send a message to Akuji, but I do none of those things. Instead, I watch her, begging her to talk to me.

"Talia, why did you come over the wall? Why did your people risk a female?" I demand, and she flinches, her eyes flaring for a moment before she turns away. Sighing, I retreat to my desk, forcing myself to focus on my work, but even still, I steal looks at her, hoping each time those lightning eyes will be on me.

But they never are.

NINE

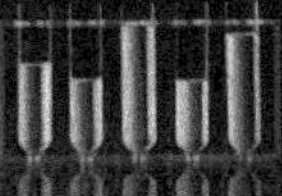

TALIA

Akuji has her.

The words repeat in my head. This monster, a leader of a tribe, as Cato called it, has my friend. I know Aria can look after herself, she's the strongest person I know and is more comfortable over this wall than anyone else, but it doesn't mean she's indestructible or immortal. She was bleeding and hurt, and then a monster kidnapped her.

Please be okay.

I know I get attached too easily, something my exes always told me, but when I see the good in someone and get to know them, I don't hold back. Life is too short not to love and bond with other people, and Aria is loyal, strong, and funny. It was very hard not to like her, and despite the fact that we came from very different walks of life, I find myself missing her and her quick wit.

She would know what to do, but it seems that it's up to me to save her this time. Right now, though, fear and exhaustion are taking its toll on me. My brain is shutting down, and I can't fight it, even as much as I need to.

I fall asleep hunched over my research, a protest on my lips.

I wake suddenly, my head jerking up before I let out a groan at the crick in my neck. My entire body is aching and still exhausted, and my brain is slow to process as I rub my neck, wondering where the hell I am.

Did I fall asleep at the lab again?

Everything comes rushing back, and my eyes slam open as I turn my head to find the monster who kidnapped me…or saved me, depending on how you look at it. When I see him, I relax slightly. He didn't touch me or hurt me. In fact, there is a blanket draped over me, and I'm clearly on his bed, whereas he is hunched uncomfortably over his table. His horns dig into the workbench, which is slightly scarred as if he does that a lot. His arms pillow his head, and his face is turned towards me as if to watch me, even in sleep.

Yesterday, he just watched me for hours. It was unnerving. One look into those black eyes, and I knew he could see down to my very soul, so I looked away, not wanting him to find me lacking like everyone else does.

I find myself drifting to my feet and moving closer to inspect him. While he's asleep, he seems almost peaceful, softer, and less scary. His lips are curled in a small smile I ache to trace. His nose is strong, his eyes are like almonds, and his lashes look like crescents on his red cheeks. His features are all sharp angles—sharp enough to cut me. Even with horns, he's truly beautiful. If he were a human, he would have been a model. My eyes drift to his wide shoulders, which are so muscular, my mouth dries for a moment, and then to his flexing back that I study for an embarrassing amount of time before my eyes roam down his arms.

His huge biceps and veiny forearms flex as he sleeps, making me swallow as my perusal finally ends on his huge hands, tipped with black claws. Everything about this monster, Cato, screams danger, yet he looked at me with kindness. He covered me to keep me warm, looked for my friend, and hasn't hurt me.

Yet I know he will. After all, I'm a human and he's a monster, and we are enemies, but why does that thought fill me with nausea? Shaking my head at my foolishness, I look around. It must be dawn. I know enough about monsters from Aria to know they sleep during the day.

Now is my shot.

I find myself hesitating before I force myself to ignore that madness. I hurry to my bag and strap it on and then hesitate again. Snarling at my idiocy, I drag the blanket with me and softly drape it over his back. I freeze when he stops snoring, but then he sighs softly.

"Talia," he murmurs, the sleepy sound of my name on his lips doing something to my insides I don't want to ponder. When he starts to snore again, I relax and quickly hurry back a few steps. Sucking in soft breaths and ignoring my screaming heart, I move to the door.

It's now or never.

As I open the door, my eyes go back to the monster. He looks so lonely, the room empty, bar research and notes. I ache for some reason before I turn and hurry downstairs. It doesn't matter that he intrigues me, that I have so many questions my head aches, nor does it matter that he helped me or that he was kind.

He will turn on me. They are monsters, after all.

I need to save myself and my friend.

I freeze when I'm through the door. We are at the end of some stone steps, and when I peer over the rail, I groan. My thighs cramp at the idea of descending them, but I have no choice. I hurry down them, keeping my footsteps as light as I can, trying to remember how Aria moved. By the time I'm down two flights, though, I'm panting loudly and sweat drips down my body, but I still push on. Four more flights down and my thighs cramp, but after one more flight, I reach a set of double doors.

Looking left and right, I move quickly to them, but when I open them, wincing at the creak, there is some kind of metal shutter covering my exit, and despite how much I try, it won't move. I know it's useless, so I shut the door and look around.

There has to be another way out.

Fear fills me at the idea of exploring a building filled with sleeping monsters, but I have no other choice, so I randomly pick right and move through the corridors. I start to relax when I don't run into anyone, getting cocky. It's why I don't see them until it's too late.

The corridor breaks into a room, and in that room are hundreds of sleeping monsters curled around each other. Furs and pillows lie everywhere like a giant nest. I just gawk, my foot held mid-air above the tail of one sleeping in the doorway.

The chorus of snores and growls makes me pale as I stumble back. I'm about to turn and run when I see stairs leading down to another door.

It has to be a way out.

Fuck.

I'm so fucked.

Logically, I know there has to be another way out, but I don't have time to find it. One of them could wake up at any minute, even Cato, so I infuse steel into my spine. Channelling Aria, I step over the sleeping giant. I slowly make a path across the room, spotting the best route, but unfortunately, it also takes me through a dense section where I have no choice but to practically crawl across them. After slow going and sweating through my clothes, I finally reach the other side and do a happy dance before turning and sprinting down the stairs. The door is metal and unlocked, and I yank it open, hurry in, and shut it before letting out a loud puff of air as I lean against it.

I hear a noise and stand upright. I'm not outside. I'm in a fucking tunnel.

Okay, a nice tunnel, but it's still a tunnel, which means I'm underground, in the dark, with monsters.

I really suck at this.

The light is dimmed to create a softer ambience, but it still allows me to see the marble floor and pale white walls covered in paintings and maps. It's almost spotless and looks like something from before the war. It's obvious it's part of the building above, which has me intrigued, but I spot some open doors and hear snores coming from them, so I slowly slide across the floor, wincing at the squeak of my shoes. I move slower here, and when I reach a door, I hurry past it, not even peering inside.

I don't want to be caught.

The tunnel seems to go on forever and winds through the earth until I'm lost, but then it turns, and at the end are double doors—double doors that are closed with a monster sitting on the floor beside them, snoring away.

A bin with flames is next to him.

If he's on watch, he sucks, but it works for me, so I thank a deity I don't believe in and slowly move past him. At the door, I keep my eyes on him as I open it and slide through.

Biting my lip, I look around and almost groan. I'm in another building. Grumbling to myself, I start to walk, noticing it's lighter here. Daylight pierces the fog of darkness, and when I step out into another room, I see why. There are skylights above, letting in rays of light. I almost bask in it, knowing that means I'm safe for now.

Until I hear the door opening behind me.

TEN

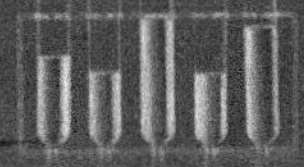

TALIA

I whirl, my mouth dropping open when I see the monster lingering in the darkness beyond the doorway. His usually soft face is hard, his eyes are flashing red, and his hand grips the handle with a strength that dents it as he watches me. The sunlight separates us. He is in the dark, and I am in the light. For a moment, a tangible thread connects us, almost drawing me back to him. It's that silly thought that has me stumbling back a step, which in turn seems to kick him into action. Slamming the door behind him, he steps into the shadows. His eyes flick to the light coming in, and that's when I remember what Aria said.

Light hurts them, so they never come out during the day.

I soon realise why when, with gritted teeth and determined, flashing eyes, he steps into a ray of sunshine. He instantly winces, his hands fisting as he takes another deliberate step towards me. At first, nothing happens, and then his skin begins to heat, the evidence obvious as he begins to stagger. Uncertainty gleams in his eyes as his skin begins to blister, but he still pushes forward, a hiss escaping his lips.

More and more blisters appear on his skin as he stumbles towards me through the light.

"Cato, no!" I yell, rushing forward in an attempt to stop him before stilling myself. Why am I trying to protect this monster? It doesn't matter that he was kind to me, that he didn't hurt me, nor that he looked for my friend. He's still a monster.

"Talia," he hisses, his knees almost giving out as a pained moan escapes his lips. "Talia left."

His voice is garbled, and I slap my hands over my mouth as I watch blood bubble on his lips. "Go back!" I demand, my eyes going to the door that would lead me to freedom. "Cato, go back!"

"Not without—" He coughs and falls to his knees in a ray of sun. "My Talia."

"Shit, shit, shit," I mutter, looking from the door to the monster watching me with dark, agony filled eyes. "I hate you right now!" I scream as I rush to him and throw my shoulder under his, trying to heave him up. All I succeed in doing is grunting like a wild animal at the size and weight of him. "Come on then. You need to stand, or I'll leave."

That gets him moving. He stumbles to his feet but leans into me, swaying as I drag him towards the door. It's slow going, and by the time I'm back there, his skin is completely blistered. Throwing open the door, I try to push him inside, but he grabs me tightly, despite the pain he's in, and pulls me with him as if knowing I plan to run away again.

The monster inside of the door is gone, and Cato leans heavily into the wall, panting as he glares at me. "Could have been hurt," he rumbles.

"Yeah, yeah, but I wasn't, and did you honestly just expect me to sit around and wonder when you or you people were going to murder me?" I throw up my hands but rush to him when he starts to slide down the wall. Rolling my eyes, I get us moving again. "Come on, let's get you back before you melt into a puddle or something."

"That…doesn't…happen." It's slow going, and he leads me

through a side entrance I didn't see, which takes us straight to his floor. That would have been handy to know before I played hopscotch with monsters downstairs. Once we are back in his lab, I'm sweating like hell and exhausted from helping the big bastard upstairs. He collapses onto the floor, and I hurry to the med kit I found and drop to my knees beside him.

Eyeing the expanse of blisters across his body, I start with somewhere safe—his hands and arms. As I clean them, he doesn't move or open his eyes.

"You could have been hurt," he slurs, and my eyes dart to him before focusing on what I'm doing as I search through the box for the cream. His voice comes out stronger with every word though, which is a good sign. "It was stupid, Talia, and you are not stupid. Don't do that again. Ever."

I ignore his order and locate the cream. Popping the top and squeezing some onto my finger, I turn and start to slowly massage it into his skin. "Sorry," I murmur when he jerks away. He slowly settles back, and I begin the arduous task of applying it to his whole body.

As I apply the burn cream, I meet his eyes, which are watching me warmly. The expression is too intense, so I look away.

"Look, I won't apologise for leaving. I was trying to save myself and my friend, but since it didn't work and I'm back here again, I can't keep being scared of you. So why did you save me?" For a moment, I don't think he will answer, then his hand turns and he cups my own. When I meet his eyes, they are as confused as my own feelings.

"I don't know," he admits. "I always act on logic. Every action, thought, or word is carefully thought out, and I know the outcome, but I couldn't help myself. There was no logic when I first saw you, only this intense need to protect you. When I saw you, something scrambled inside of me, and I had to save you. I don't believe in fate or destiny, Talia. I am a scientist, but I couldn't stop myself."

I don't know what to say to that, so I remain silent, and after a moment, he lets me get back to my work, but something shifts inside of me. The fear I was carrying for the big monster disappears, despite the fact I try to hold onto it. Maybe it's because I realise we are so similar, or maybe it's because I don't know why I feel drawn to him either.

"Why did you save me?" he asks softly.

I meet his eyes. "I don't know either."

He nods like that makes sense and looks at my hands on his skin. "You are good at that, but I should have told you it's not necessary."

"What do you mean?" I hesitate.

"I heal very fast naturally." I blink as a million questions come to mind, and he chuckles. "You can ask. I can almost see them in your eyes."

"How fast? Does it depend on the state of injury? Can you heal anything? What about—"

"Whoa, whoa." He chuckles. "Yes, we can heal almost anything. No, we aren't immortal, but most wounds heal quickly. As for how fast, it depends on the severity of the wound and the age of the monster. I heal the quickest of my people."

"Show off," I mutter, and we share a shy smile. Despite his words, I apply more cream. "Then why did you let me carry on?" I finally ask, scared of his answer.

"Because I like the feel of your hands on my body," he replies instantly, no shame in his response as he relaxes.

Sitting back in shock, I watch as his skin starts to heal, the burns almost melting into his skin like they were never there. Ten minutes later, all that is left is pink skin, and after the next ten, nothing.

It's as if it never happened.

"Incredible," I whisper.

"Yeah, that level of healing leaves us exhausted though," he mumbles, still answering my questions, but his eyes are closed, so I don't comment again. Instead, I sit back on my heels. Suddenly, I yelp as I fall. I didn't even see him move, but I'm dragged into his arms and flipped. His back is to the door, and his huge, red body is wrapped around mine.

"Can't run," he explains tiredly.

Huffing, I smack his arm. "I won't, now move, I can't sleep like this."

"So warm," he purrs, nuzzling my neck, and I freeze as that purr spreads through his whole body, vibrating it.

"Cato, this is inappropriate," I whine.

"Sleep, Tally." He pushes his leg between mine. My eyes fly wide at the feeling of his huge knee pressed against my pussy.

Oh yeah, because I can sleep with a massive, red monster pressed up against me.

I must say it out loud, because he chuckles softly. "I don't know, I don't think I will sleep as hard as I will wrapped around the tiny soft human."

"You're delirious," I argue.

He kisses my neck, and my pulse jumps. "Relax and sleep," he orders.

Huffing, I try to wiggle to get comfortable when it's obvious he has no intention of letting me go, only to still when something massive prods my back.

"Little Tally, I wouldn't do that."

Eyes widening, I stay frozen as he laughs again.

"Sleep, human."

For some strange reason, I do.

Moaning, I burrow deeper into the heat, curling around it and sighing when it seems to tighten around me… Tighten? I slam my eyes open and stop breathing as I blink in confusion at the red skin before me.

Red skin.

Warm.

Cato!

I try to jerk back, but the arms holding me don't even budge. I'm wrapped around him like a monkey clinging to a tree, plastered to his body. He doesn't seem to mind, though, holding me with one hand on the back of my head and the other on my ass.

"Erm, Cato?" I squeak out. He rumbles out a purr, only pulling me tighter until my face is squished against impossibly hard muscles and a slow, steady heartbeat. Wiggling, I manage to lift my hands and push at him, but he doesn't budge an inch. Blowing out a steady breath, I crane my head back to see him already awake and looking down at me with a grin.

"Dude, you are heavy," I mutter "Now move."

"Do you feel better after a sleep, Tally?" he murmurs instead, reaching up to move my hair out of my face for me.

"Tally?" I narrow my eyes. "Don't call me that."

"Of course not, Tally, now let's get you some food. Humans need that, right?" he questions.

I watch Cato as he works at his desk, unsure what to do. After he got up to order food, he sat down at the desk.

"What's your research?" I ask, trying to fill the silence, still feeling uncertain after waking up in his arms.

"Why were you in the city?" he asks casually.

I stay silent, and he turns back around.

"That's fine, you'll tell me when you're ready. As for my research, I was trying to find a way to extend our immunity to sunlight to help strengthen us during the day, since it's our only weakness."

"Only weakness? How very cocky," I mutter.

"Not cocky, Tally, just truthful." He winks, and then he comes back a moment later with a plate of food and hands it to me. When I take it, our fingers brush, and the electricity that sparks between us leaves me gasping. His smile turns smouldering, but then he sits before me, watching me as I pick at the food. The truth is, I'm too confused to eat, but when I stop, he nudges the plate, so I carry on eating.

"How far have you gotten on your research?" I find myself asking.

He seems to blush then, scrubbing at his neck nervously. "Not far. I've managed to successfully avert any birth defects and research our genealogy to help with reproduction and illness in our people, but this? It eludes me for now."

The determination in his voice is familiar. "You will," I state. When I'm finished eating, I sit back and watch him. "So what now? I'm guessing your people will wake soon, and they will find and kill me, right?"

"No," he snaps, seemingly angry at the idea. Not angry…

Furious. His eyes flash a red colour I've seen before but don't understand, nor do I plan to ask about in the face of such power and rage.

"So what now?" I ask softly.

"You will stay here. I will send a message to Akuji about your friend. When we know how she is, we will come up with a plan."

"And until then?" I demand. "How long could it take for him to reply?"

He shrugs. "I don't know." Standing, he holds out his hand. "Come."

For some reason, I almost giggle before sobering. I place my hand in his, and he lifts me softly. Keeping hold of my warm palm, he leads me across the room to a door that was locked yesterday. He pulls out a key and unlocks it. I eye it, and he chuckles.

"I don't like people being nosey. I give my people every inch of my life, but here? It's my haven." I look around at the lab then and back to him, nodding in understanding. It's his safe place away from people and expectations, where he can just think and be alone. He softens when he sees my expression and pushes in the door. "It's a habit to keep this locked. I'm sorry."

I step inside as he flicks something, and I can't contain my gasp. Compared to the cool, almost barren lab next door, this room is completely different. I'm not sure if it used to be an office at some point, but it's beautiful. The carpet is soft and luxurious. There are steel blinds drawn across floor-to-ceiling windows, but curtains have been drawn to make it more homey. String lights illuminate the space, strung across the ceiling in a zigzag pattern. There's a cactus near the door and plants all around, even covering an old desk pushed into the corner. The place is an L-shape, and to the left, hidden from the door, is a comfort zone.

There is not a bed, but there are mounds and mounds of furs and blankets. It looks so comfy, my body actually aches. There are posters and books lying around everywhere in purposeful stacks. I wander in, dragging my finger over their bindings. From biology to romance novels, he seems to have it all, and they are clearly well looked over and read. There's a partially open door, and I move over, my eyebrows rising at the bathroom I find there. It's stocked with a shower, a bath, a toilet, and mirror. It's modern and spacious. Just then, my bladder screams at me, and I turn with an embarrassed wince.

"It's amazing. Ah, can I use the facilities?" I ask.

"Of course. I'm sorry, Talia, I should have thought about that last night." He frowns, but I just nod, shut the door, and hurry to the toilet, but when I sit, nothing comes. I'm too nervous. "Um, can you hear me with your monster super hearing?"

There's a pause and then a huff, almost like a laugh he tried to cover. "Yes, but I am not listening, Tally."

Grumbling, I try to pee, but I can't. "I can't go when you're listening," I whine.

There is another laugh, and then suddenly, soft music wafts through the air, and I relax, finally peeing. After I'm done, I wash my hands and face with water from the sink, cupping it to drink some before drying my hands and opening the door. I ache to wash away the blood and sweat, but I don't want to keep him waiting.

I find him with his back to me, crouched down under the desk. He's flipping through some old records. Perched on an old filing cabinet I didn't notice before is a record player playing the soothing tones of soft jazz. "I'm not sure what music you like."

"Any actually. I can appreciate the beauty in rock, hip-hop, jazz, and orchestra. They each have such different sounds, but the way they are made? Magnificent." I smile as I move closer.

He grins up at me. "I feel the same."

"I actually used to play the piano," I offer as I sway with the music. He puts in another record, and a soft, romantic song plays.

"You did?" he asks as I twirl to the music, unable to help it. He smiles, watching me before standing and moving towards me. He takes my hand and tugs me closer. I gasp as he starts to sway.

"Cato," I start, but he hushes me, lifts me, and twirls me, making a laugh burst free as he pulls me back and sways again.

"The piano?" he prompts.

"My mother taught me when I was younger. It was the only time we spent together. She was always very busy. She was a good woman, an inspiration, but I always missed her, so piano was our time. She made me understand the logic behind each key, each piece, and I fell in love with the order and the ability to create. It settled me. It was peaceful and grounding," I murmur as I sway with him.

"You stopped playing?" he surmises.

"When she died," I murmur. "It made me sad."

Frowning, he pulls me closer. "I am sorry, Tally."

I nod and just sway with him, and then he suddenly spins me out again, making me grin, and the bad mood is broken just like that. We dance around his room for this song and the next before he pulls me closer, resting his chin on his chest to look down at me with sparkling eyes and a soft smile.

I stare up at the monster in the warm white lights, the music wrapping around us, and I can't remember why I ever feared him.

"Cato, why don't you hate me like the rest of your people?" I ask, needing to know.

He stills. "Why would I hate you? I understand the hatred of the people who…hurt us, but you? You did nothing to me. How could I hate someone who's so innocent? So beautiful and strong? We are both smarter than blind hatred. Maybe, Talia, you are making me realise that not all humans are bad."

"And that not all monsters are feral, killing beats." I grin.

Smirking, he leans down and presses his lips to my ear. "Oh, I am feral. Don't mistake that, Tally. I am feral for you. I spent all night wondering what your human skin would look like flushed with me inside you." He pulls back and spins me as I stumble in shock.

What on earth?

He laughs harder at my blushing cheeks and shy look as he pulls me closer again and lifts me, grinning as he holds me in the air. "You are so cute when you blush, Tally. Your skin looks like mine. I wonder if I could make you blush all over. But don't worry, you're safe for now." He lets me slide down his body and dips me just as the music ends.

We are both panting and staring at each other. Slowly, his smile fades and his eyes flash with hunger as he holds me tightly. Pulling me back up slowly, he releases me, but his hands flex like it was a struggle. I instantly miss the heat of his touch. The way he watched me made me feel beautiful and desired.

I realise that for a moment, we weren't enemies. We weren't monster and human. We were just us.

What is happening to me?

ELEVEN

CATO

Licking my lips, I force my gaze away from Talia. She glows in here, shining with an inner light I can't describe. Her lips are curled in a shy smile, and those addictive eyes sweep me away with their stormy depths. She's beautiful.

I've never been drawn to anyone before, monster or not. I've never felt the lick of flames until now. I know all about our physical needs and have seen and heard about the mating hazes my people go through, but I never understood their lack of control and possessive nature.

Until her.

She makes the madness make sense.

It terrifies me how quickly she is wrapping me around her tiny, little human finger. "Wait here, okay? Feel free to explore or shower. They can't get through. I will lock the door for your safety. I need to check in with my people and send the message to Akuji."

She nods, sobering at the reminder, and wraps her arms around herself. I ache to grab her and make it better, to feel her melt against me again. When I woke up with her wrapped around me, I couldn't breathe or move a muscle. I just lay there for hours, watching her sleep. I adored the way her nose would crinkle, her eyes moving under her closed lids, and the soft breaths that would blow across my skin and leave me hard and wanting by the time she woke up.

Sleep was a necessity for my body. Never before had I actually wanted to crawl back into my nest. I used to hate the weakness of needing to rest, but now I'm counting down the hours until I can sleep with her and hold her tightly. I want to feel her against me, where she fits perfectly and belongs forever.

Turning away before I say something stupid, like begging her to love me, I hurry to the door, but when I look back to shut it, she's standing in the room looking so alone and lost, it hurts.

"It will be okay, Tally. You're safe here. I would never let anyone hurt you." With that, I shut the door before I storm back in there and wipe that worried look away.

Once downstairs with my people, I handle any issues that have arisen, from a fire in a food barn to problems at the perimeter and quarrels within our ranks. It's a long process that I used to find joy and purpose in, but all I can think about is getting back to Talia. I want to see her smile again, smell her scent, feel her against me, and explore that brilliant mind of hers.

I almost ache with the need to race back to her side.

It's illogical and I hate it, yet the image of her storming towards me with determination in her eyes as she gave up on her chance to escape is seared into my brain. As is the image of her with her head tilted back and her eyes alight with laughter and joy as I pulled her close, the warm lights of my nest making her glow like an angel.

This human is completely and utterly taking over my every thought. Where before there was logic and reason, now there is only need and possessiveness.

It's distracting, and more than once, I am having to ask people to repeat their issues. My comek, my second-in-command, watches me worriedly, and hours later, he finally pulls me aside as I scrub at my face.

"Okay, spill. What's wrong, brother?"

"What? Nothing," I mutter guiltily.

"Uh-uh, I know you. That's not your *I'm distracted trying to save our entire race* or *caught in a scientific problem* expression. This is something else, so tell me," he urges, growling. He wants to protect me, to help. Unlike most of the people here, he isn't obsessed with knowledge and peace. He is like Akuji and the old me—a warrior. He left with me because he's my best friend.

We have been together since we were kids, since our parents died in the war. We had many looking after us, but it wasn't the same, so we stuck together, just two orphaned boys. When I decided to leave the tribe and come here, he followed me without protest, telling me he would follow wherever I wandered. It didn't matter to him where he settled, as long as it was with me.

His brother.

His family.

Guilt eats at me for lying to him, but I know his thoughts on humans. He hates them with a fierceness that scares me, especially knowing how close Talia is to him. Once, I didn't care, understanding his anger at them, even as I felt nothing towards them. He let his anger at the loss of his family and friends fuel his hatred, whereas I let it change me. Logically, I thought it through, and I recognised blind hatred wasn't smart. I was always curious why.

Why they made us.

Why they hate us.

Why they want to kill us.

Not him, he just wanted to kill them all. For a moment, I hesitate. I should tell him. He could help me with this problem, but the idea of him and Talia in a room together makes terror race through me. My brother would kill the human I cannot seem to stop thinking about—the human who restarted my old heart.

I let my shoulders sag and focus on his searching eyes. "It is nothing. I am just tired, I was up all night working on that new formula, and it didn't work."

He sighs, accepting my answer. "I'm sorry, brother, but you know you will find the answer. You always do. There is no one smarter than you," he teases, nudging my shoulder. "How about we go to the aqua?"

I hesitate. Usually, I would take him up on it. The aqua is a place for relaxation, and after being stuck in my lab, I would always drink away the problems plaguing me and listen to the chatter of my people. That familiar atmosphere and the burn of the ale would usually allow my brain to look at the problem with new light, but not tonight. The idea of leaving Talia unprotected and being away from her makes me sick to my stomach.

"Not tonight, brother." I clap his shoulder. "I need to figure this out before I can relax, but have fun and find yourself a mate for the night."

"You know I will." He chuckles. "Are you sure though? You look wound tight. We could spar?"

"Stop babying me." I snort. "Go find a female to make wild."

Laughing, he nods, and with one last look, he hurries away to do just that, and my smile drops. I feel guilty for lying to him. Would he hate her? Wouldn't he help me if I asked? I frown, truly wondering if his loyalty to me would override his blind hatred, and for once, I don't know.

I hate that I'm questioning my brother after everything we have been through, but I won't take it back.

I won't risk her.

Not even for my family.

After making my final rounds to check on everyone, I finally grab some food and water and head back upstairs after ordering my people not to disturb me. They don't question it, so used to me locking myself away for days. It usually means I'm close to cracking a problem.

Not this time. This time, I am the problem.

I know my duty, which is either to kill the human or have her sent for questioning. But there has never been a human female over the wall, only soldiers. Surely that changes things? Besides, I couldn't do that to Talia, not now. Not after she cared for me. I couldn't betray her that way. Not even for my duty or my people.

I have no idea what I'm going to do about it however, but that's a problem for a later date.

Excitement and anticipation thrums through me the closer I get to Tally, but when I unlock the door and search for her, my heart melts. Some foreign, warm feeling flows through my body as I watch her. She's curled in my nest, her hand fisting the fur, and her hair is spread around her. Her plump lips are parted, and her eyes are closed.

She's beautiful.

Desire courses through me. It's so strong, something I've never felt before her. A human. Maybe something is wrong with me, like my brother thinks, but I can't seem to care with her in my nest.

I want her, crave her. Why else would I put myself and my people at risk?

But the question is what is she to me? Why do I hurt when I'm away from her? Why does happiness fill me at the sight of her in my space, rested and clean? Why does her scent wrap around me and warm me like nothing else ever has?

I crouch before her, softly moving some hair from her face with a claw and frown at the sharp weapon against her perfect, paper-thin skin. She is so small and fragile compared to me. How could this ever work, and more importantly, why does the thought of her going back to her people cause agony to pierce my chest?

Rubbing at it, I stand, leaving the food and water next to her, and head back to my lab, intent on working. I need to distract myself from the turbulent emotions I don't know how to contain or understand.

All because of one human.

If only my people knew.

TWELVE

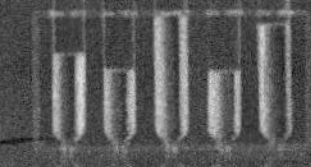

TALIA

I'm warm, warmer than I've been in a long time, and content. A feeling of safety wraps around me, pulling me back to sleep, but a noise has me frowning and blinking my eyes open. A yawn splits my lips as I sit up, frowning deeper as I look around. For a moment, I can't figure out where I am. My apartment doesn't have fur…

Then it all comes back, and I bolt upright, but I don't see Cato, only a plate of food and drink next to the bed. Sliding to my feet, I stretch and look around. Did he come back yet? After he left, I had a nice, warm shower. It took three times to clean my body and hair from the last few days, but once I was clean, I felt so much better. My clothes were filthy, however, and I really didn't want to put them back on, so I washed them and left them to dry, then found an old sheet which I tied into a makeshift night shirt. It hangs from my willowy frame as I look around. I can't tell if it's night or day or how long I have been asleep, but my stomach is still full and I feel more rested.

That's when I hear it again.

Slipping out of the open door, I spy Cato, and my breath shudders in my chest. For a moment, I forgot how imposing my monster is. *My?* No way, delete that thought. Not mine. Just a monster. But there's something so achingly beautiful about him as well. Since he's focused on the samples before him, I allow myself to lean into the door and greedily watch him without concern about earning his anger or worse —his interest.

I recall the feel of those massive hands on my body last night, and I shiver, hating to admit it almost felt…good.

He's bent over his desk, his massive shoulders rounded, flexing the muscles on his back, and my mouth turns dry. His enormous, muscular arms flex as he moves with slow and purposeful actions. His black horns catch the light as I trace their curled length with my gaze before looking at his face. It's all square jaw and sharp edges, with a human-like nose and big, pouty lips, even with the huge fangs hanging over them. His eyes are tilted up and almost lined black, and his tail flicks behind him. When he sits back with a frown, I find my eyes dropping to the wide expanse of his chest.

He's a scientist, but I've never quite seen a scientist like him. He's built like a wall, all solid muscle and sharp, firm lines of abs and pecs.

If you look past the red skin, flicking tail, and horns, he's almost human.

My traitorous body gives a pulse, desire coursing through me, but I ignore it, hoping it will go away. Instead, I focus on his deft fingers as he works with quick, sure strokes, his eyes alight with purpose as he studies what is before him.

As I watch him, I realise he carries the same air as me, the same loneliness and determination. My heart aches for a moment, and he must hear me, because his head jerks up, then his black eyes land on me and lock me in place. I lose myself in his gaze, as if he's stealing my very soul, unable to look away as he watches me right back. Something flashes in those dark depths, something I cannot begin to explain.

When he finally looks away, I sag, released from his gaze and almost panting.

Fucking hell, Talia, get it together.

"Did you eat?" he murmurs, and when I shake my head, he frowns. "I didn't wake you, did I?"

"No," I answer. "What are you working on?" I tread closer, my arms wrapped around my waist as I stop behind him and peer over his shoulder. He seems to freeze, and I realise my breath is blowing across his neck. A slight growl emits from him, and I quickly step back.

Maybe he's territorial of his work, like I am, or he doesn't like someone peering over his shoulder. Either way, I stop, not wanting this massive monster pissed at me. He could kill me so easily, yet he turns slowly, allowing me time to see his movements, as if sensing my fear and unease with him.

"Sorry," I whisper.

He frowns as I avoid his gaze and crooks his finger at me. I freeze, glancing between him and the table, and slowly move closer. When I reach him, he pulls me in front of him. I stiffen at his hands on my hips, but he either doesn't notice or doesn't care as he turns again so I'm practically between his thighs. I am so small compared to him, his chin is at my shoulder as he leans over me to show me his work.

"I'm trying to pinpoint what, exactly, in our DNA is affected by sunlight," he murmurs, showing me the samples.

"If you can locate that specific point, you could isolate it," I reply, impressed with his work. He jerks against me, sucking in a breath.

"Exactly." His voice is darker, growly, and I quickly step away, putting my back to the table to face him. His eyes are usually black, but now there is some red flooding them.

"Why do your eyes do that?" I find myself asking.

"Do what?" he queries, tilting his head.

"That." I gesture. "Change colour."

He jerks and turns away, breathing slowly, and when he turns back, they are black again. "Sorry," he mutters. "It is something that happens to us sometimes."

"When?" I question, too curious for my own good. He watches me before coming to some sort of conclusion.

"Extreme emotion—anger, sadness, happiness, lust…" He trails off, and I gulp. He grins slightly. "It's different than the haze, but similar bodily reactions."

"The haze?" I ask, happy to keep asking since he's answering. It will help settle my curiosity and stop me from analysing why he was turned on by me being so close. It certainly wasn't anger or sadness.

He nods. "A biological reaction, a predatory trait. It takes control of us when our emotions become too strong or we are threatened. Usually, if we are in danger, it makes us more monster than man, leaving us stronger, faster, and feral, but in that state, we recognise no one or nothing. We could hurt anyone if they get in our way. We try very hard to come back from that state. The first monster who escaped from the lab lived and died in it, and through the generations, we have gotten better at controlling it, though it helps that we aren't at war anymore and free to find happiness."

"But before?" I prompt.

"Before? Most of us existed in the haze during the war. We fought to stay alive, filled with bloodlust. We killed many, the death of our own only heightening it. Some still exist in the haze, rejected from tribes for not learning control. They are dangerous, very dangerous, and they would kill their own if they had the chance."

"Why?"

"The longer you remain in the haze, the more your mind unravels, until you eventually go mad or can't come back." He shrugs. "I've seen it happen, and it was not pretty."

"Oh, you saw it happen?"

He nods, glancing away before meeting my gaze. "With my father. When my mother died escaping the labs, he went into the haze. I was just a youngling, protected by our people who went underground while our warriors fought the war above. But I saw him enough to see him slide into the haze. Even when the humans were driven back and the wall started to be built, he couldn't come back from it. He was lost, mad with grief."

"Cato," I whisper, taking his hand and squeezing it, hoping to ease the pain in his voice. "What happened to him?"

"They said he was killed during the final days of the war, but my brother and I found out the truth a few years ago." When I simply wait, his shoulders fold in. "One of our own had to kill him. With no humans left to slaughter, he turned on his own people, so lost in his pain and grief, and they had no choice but to end his life so he could return to his mate."

"But you and your brother…" I shake my head. "You lost them both?"

"He isn't my biological brother. He lost his family in the uprising as well, and we bonded over it and protected each other, but yes, I lost both of my parents. It was a very long time ago, and my people looked after us, loved us, fed us, and raised us as their own."

"Wow." I squeeze his hand, trying to offer comfort, knowing how hard losing your family is. "I'm glad you had them and weren't alone."

Something in my tone must alert him, a bitterness I suppose, because he glances up at me with knowing eyes. "Like you?"

He told me his story, so for once, I find myself opening up about mine. I nod and look away, staring at my small, pale hand in his much bigger red one. "My parents died when I was young, fifteen. It was my birthday the day after I found out. I had no one. No one cared what happened to me, no one made sure I was fed, happy, or healthy. It was very lonely, and I missed them. I had the money they left, and since I was nearly an adult, I was left to my own devices in their house."

"Tally." He pulls me closer, and I find myself pressing my head to his chest, his steady, beating heart giving me the strength to carry on as he strokes my back.

"No one cared at all, Cato. I was completely alone. I survived, I had to, and I made them proud by being the best I could and focusing on my studies, but it never felt like enough. I still miss them so much." Tears fill my eyes, and I try to hold them back, but they fall anyway—tears I didn't shed, even when I found out about their deaths.

I've never been able to cry, as if I'm too numb, since I was a teenager forced to grow up way too fast, just like him.

"I have no doubts they would be proud of you, Talia, my human. You are so strong and intelligent. You adapted to survive and strive to make the world a better place. I see it in your kindness and unparalleled strength. It's normal to miss them," he murmurs, stroking my back as tears wet my cheeks and his chest, but he says nothing about it. "I'm so sorry you were alone, and I hate that you had to go through that by yourself."

Sniffling, I pull back slightly, and he cups my cheeks and looks into my eyes before wiping away my tears. "What happened to them?" he finally asks.

"They were killed in an accident," I whisper. "A stupid freak accident. One minute, they were there, talking about cake for my birthday, and the next, they were gone, and the world was a little less bright and a lot more cold."

He nods like he understands, and I guess he does.

We are both orphans.

"You are not alone anymore, Tally," he promises as he leans in. My eyes close without permission as he softly kisses each eyelid. "And I bet they are so very proud of the woman you've become."

I don't know why, but that makes me cry harder, and he just holds me as I do. This monster, this…this man, who should hate me for simply being human, holds me as I grieve over my parents. He soothes and protects me, holding me so tight, I start to feel safe for the first time in a long time.

Slowly, I begin to settle down, and my cheeks heat, feeling embarrassed by my outburst, so when I pull back, I avoid his eyes and clear my throat. Taking pity on me, he squeezes my hand and lets me go, putting space between us. He probably knows I need it with how raw I am feeling. "How about we eat, and then you can help me with my research?" he offers, and my head jerks up. How did he know that I needed to focus my brain again? To turn back to logic to feel grounded and safe in what I know after that?

He does it too—I see it in his knowing eyes.

"I'd like that," I murmur.

After eating in companionable silence, he brings me back to the lab and shows me his current hopes for his research, and I help him with the samples. I'm just checking one over for him when I catch him watching me. He's not staring at me worriedly, like I might ruin his experiment, but with warmth.

"Thanks for letting me help," I murmur.

He nods and glances at his own sample.

"At least you don't think I'm a dumb blonde." I grin, and he frowns in confusion.

"What does the colour of your fur have to do with your intelligence? Is there a correlation in humans?" he wonders out loud. I can't help but giggle, and he brightens at the sound.

"No, it's just a saying." I roll my eyes. "Human men will use anything to put women down to make themselves feel better."

He's quiet for a moment, but a tug on my hair has me turning back to see him combing his fingers through my locks, stroking the strands. "They are idiots. For what it is worth, your hair is beautiful. It makes me think of the sun, as if I can finally see that bright, brilliant beauty trapped in these strands." He drops my hair and focuses back on his work like he didn't just melt my panties and heart as I gawk at him.

I never gave much thought about my hair, but now I can't help but smile, my cheeks warm as I look at it. I wonder what else he likes about me, but I'm too scared to ask.

When he sits back as he checks something over, my eyes catch on my bag, and something inside me drops as I remember why I am here and what I should be doing.

It's definitely not flirting with Cato.

That's when I realise I no longer fear him. How strange.

"We will have to wait a few hours for the results," he tells me, carefully putting away the experiment. He's totally unaware of my inner debate, but when he looks at me, he frowns. "Tally, what's wrong?"

I can't get over that nickname, but I swallow and look from my bag to him. He follows my gaze, and his eyebrow arches. "Did you hear anything about Aria?" I ask, diverting his attention.

He shakes his head, and his eyes go back to the bag. He once asked why I was here, and I owe him that much, despite the fact I shouldn't tell him. "I was sent here to collect samples from the lab," I admit. "They left research here. That's where we were when we were attacked. That's what's in the bag."

"Not all of it," he murmurs, watching me. "I took some a long time ago."

My mouth drops open in shock. He unlocks a cupboard and gestures for me to look inside. There are notebooks and frozen vials. I hesitate before grabbing a notebook and flipping through it. "I never knew what any of it meant. I know enough to decipher some of the code in regard to our genetic makeup, but no more. It obviously has to do with how we were created."

"I don't understand." I bring my gaze to him. "Created? These are genetic blueprints." My eyes widen, and I stare at him as the pieces click into place. He watches me warily. "They… You were created in that lab?"

He nods slowly. "My people were, and then they bred more of us."

"You… The humans…" I shake my head, working through it, and he sighs.

"The lab was all we knew. Many died there. The experiments were rough on us. The first few of us were more monster than human, but it was slowly diluted into what we are now. Eventually, my people fought back, tired of being oppressed, abused, and hurt."

"The war," I mutter, and he nods again. My whole world shifts, and I grab the table for stability as my world crumbles around me. Everything I thought I knew was wrong, a lie.

"We escaped. We just wanted to be left alone, and we tried to flee, but they would never let us go, not after what they did to us. They trapped us, but they never expected us to fight back. All those genetic predator instincts they bred into our DNA turned on them, and they couldn't win, but they also couldn't tell the truth."

"They lied to us all. I always wondered how you came to be. Some said aliens, some said a natural disaster, but I could never figure it out." I shake my head. "And no one was ever allowed to ask."

Dumb. I'm so dumb.

"They created you, and they tried to kill you when you escaped." I peer at him. So many thoughts run through my head, but one is prominent. "You must hate me."

"Not you, Tally. You are innocent in this war, just like me. We are just collateral damage, but that is why I took the research, to help me with my own and to stop them from ever getting their hands on it."

"And then I came to take it." I sag. "Fuck!" I tug at my hair. "I didn't know, I swear. I should have, but no one ever questioned it. I grew up with the wall in place and knowledge that monsters were real, but I never even thought to—" His hand covers mine, stopping my rambling.

"It's okay, Tally," he whispers.

"No it's not." I leap to my feet and pace. "They perverted nature. They tried to play god, and the world could have been destroyed by it! But why now? Why are they coming for the research now…" I turn to him. "They need it, but why? They need the experiments they did on your kind."

"I don't know," he replies. "I didn't even know that was why you were here. How about we find out together?"

"What do you mean?" I ask, my whole world crumbling. Are the people I work for truly the enemy? The true monsters?

They created them, a whole new race, and then they tried to eradicate them so the truth couldn't get out. All of those lives were lost for their lies…and I work for them. I was sent here to give them exactly what they want, and I don't know how Cato doesn't hate me, because at this moment, I do. I was so blind, so stupid, thinking I could make a difference.

Not anymore.

Straightening my spine, I meet his eyes. "I won't give them the research, and I won't allow them to hurt anyone else again, but I need to know why they sent me here and what they need so I can figure out their plans. If they are willing to not only create a new sentient species and experiment on it, but to start a war to cover it up, then they are capable of anything and I worry what that means, not just for humans, but you as well."

He watches me with something akin to hope in his eyes as he nods slowly. "Then we will find out. We will figure out what the humans want." He stands, towering over me, but unlike the humans who do it to overpower me, he simply does it because of his height. "But know this, Talia. I will never let them hurt my people again."

I nod, knowing it's not a threat, but a promise. If I ally with the humans, if I get what they want and give it back, then he will kill me, and I don't blame him. They have been tortured, used, and abused for so long, not to mention killed for simply being alive, for being created, so he has no reason to trust humans.

I want to give him one though.

I want him to trust me, I realise, and something in me warms.

I thought I was supposed to help the people of Athesa, but maybe it was always this. Maybe I was always meant to help these monsters, these people, who have known nothing but pain and betrayal since birth.

Maybe I was always meant to find myself here, with him, to stop it from ever happening again.

THIRTEEN

TALIA

"There are some missing, aren't there?" I'm cataloguing the research, trying to make sense of it. If I can, hopefully, I can help them.

For once, I feel like I'm actually helping, like I'm doing something I should be doing.

It's as if fate brought me here, a construct I never believed in before now, but I can admit there must be a guiding hand to land me here in this lab with the capability to read this research and help Cato and his people. He lifts his head from where he's crouched next to me, reading off labels.

"I think I left some behind," he murmurs.

"And I didn't get them all. Tiger attack." I shrug. "That means we need to go back if we want to understand it all and protect it. It would be best to keep it here. The lab will be the first place they search, and when we don't come back with it, who knows what they will send."

"You're right," he agrees, and I blink before slowly smiling.

"That's the first time I've heard a man say that." I chuckle.

Standing, he grips my chin and tilts it up with a frown. "Not a man, Tally, a monster." He moves away, grabbing something and putting it into bags. "If we are to get the research, we need to sneak in. It's in Akuji's land, so he might let me get away with it, but if his people find me and a human in the one place they hate?" He shakes his head, and the warmth that had been invading my body from his touch and words flees, only to be replaced by cold stark fear. It was so easy to forget I should fear the monsters, since Cato would never hurt me. He's kind, gentle, and smart, so yeah, easy to forget, but he's very serious, so I nod stiffly.

"I'll do whatever you say."

"You? Obedient?" He chuckles again as he comes over, slinging a bag over his shoulder. "Even I don't believe that, Tally." He winks. "We'll sneak out. I'll have to carry you through their land, since it's less likely we'll leave your tracks and scent, plus I'm faster and quieter. We get in and get out. You stay at my side at all times, understood?"

Part of me chafes at the stern command, but I see the worry in his eyes and I know he's only doing this to protect me. "Understood."

Towering over me, he searches my gaze. "I mean it, Talia. I will protect you, but I need you to listen to me on this. We are knowingly walking into another tribe's land without invitation and invading the desecrated sanctuary where many of our own died. We have to be careful and smart."

Standing, I take his hand in mine and squeeze it. "I promise, Cato." I need him to believe me for some reason, and when he sighs in relief, it's obvious he does. "Let me cause a distraction to clear the way," he mutters, and then he's gone. I wait behind the door, almost bouncing on my toes.

Fear and excitement war within me—fear from being in danger, but everything is dangerous over the wall, and excitement for finally being out of the lab and getting my hands on the missing research. Maybe we'll even find Aria, since that's where it all started.

As much as I like being in a lab, I miss fresh air and seeing the sun and sky.

I miss being free.

My whole world has shifted since I've been over the wall. My mind still scrambles to make sense of everything, but there are some things I'm certain of.

One, humans created the monsters.

Two, they experimented on them and hurt them until it started a war.

Three, they built the wall to contain their mistakes.

Four, they want the research back.

Logically, I am assuming it's so they can continue their experiments, something I cannot allow to happen. Look what happened last time they did. We lost thousands of people, as did the monsters, and our lives were irrevocably changed.

Five, I trust Cato with my life, and certainly more than I ever trusted a human.

Six, I can do good here. I can help.

Seven, Aria may be hurt or in danger, and I need to help her.

Eight, monsters are scary but also not the villains they are made out to be.

Nine, I don't miss my life over the wall, only the safety and certainty it came with.

Isn't that strange?

I'm still getting used to everything and Cato has been nothing but kind and answering every little question I might have, one that popped up earlier was about the power and he proudly declared he had managed to fix the grid for them all.

Smart monster.

Cato comes back and takes my hand, hurrying me down the stairs. I almost stumble as I try to keep up with him, so he lifts me into his arms, carrying me bridal style, and just leaps down the staircase. We are moving too fast to see, and it starts to make me dizzy, so I bury my head in his throat, keeping my eyes tightly shut, even as I feel the jostle of us moving, and then the scent of fresh air blows across us. Even then, he doesn't slow, so I keep myself as still as possible, sucking in a deep breath and stiffening at the scent of him.

A scent that burrows into my body and seems to awaken every inch of it.

It's musky, male, dark, and almost foreign, but it's so sensuous, it wraps me in a protective, sensual bubble, making every inch of me throb even as I relax. I feel both safe and aroused. God, I hope he doesn't notice, but he seems intent on keeping us safe, moving faster and faster. I feel us leaping and turning corners, but I don't lift my head.

If I did, I would be sick.

"Are you okay, Tally?" he murmurs. His voice is in my ear, and he's not short of breath, despite the fact he's carrying me and sprinting like he's in a race.

"Fine," I squeak out, and his chest rumbles with a mix of a purr and a laugh, making me smile, even as I burrow closer. His hands tighten on my thighs, pulling me securely into the circle of his arms.

"Not far, just keep quiet, okay?" he says.

I nod, not trusting my voice, and just hold on for the ride. I focus on him instead of the way my stomach rolls, moving past his delicious smell to the feel of his skin under my fingers. I loosen my death grip and lightly stroke his red skin. It's so soft, like velvet, and it feels like pure silk over metal. His muscles and body are so strong, it almost hurts, but I find myself stroking his shoulder, exploring until a growl vibrates his body, and then I still.

"Stop distracting me, Tally." He huffs, but there's an edge of amusement in his tone, so I blush hard, realising I had basically been petting him.

Jesus, Talia.

First I'm sniffing him, and now stroking? Thank god we finally stop. I open my eyes to see us storming into the lab's building. After stopping, sniffing hard, and looking around, he softly sets me on my feet. I wobble for a moment, and he keeps his hands on me until I nod and step forward. He steps back and follows me to the lab's door, watching my back.

I glance back, blinking for a moment as a memory of Aria in that exact place blends with the current image of him. Shaking my head, I hurry down the steps, almost slumping when I don't see Aria there. I know it was a long shot, but I had hoped…

"Talia?" Cato calls.

"Sorry," I mutter and finish heading to the first lab, booting up the computer and logging in with my details. As it loads, I glance up to see Cato looking around, and I realise it probably brings back a lot of bad memories here. Fuck, I'm insensitive.

"You can wait outside if you want," I offer softly.

He blinks and looks at me. "Logically, places cannot hold memories or ghosts…" He trails off and remains silent for a moment before continuing, "But this place always feels wrong to me, haunted, and their screams still echo in my head."

"I couldn't live in my parents' mansion anymore. It felt like it was haunted by them. I hated it. It used to be so warm and filled with life, and then it was just a shell," I tell him and hold out my hand. "So I know what you mean, but it's better when you're not alone."

He takes my hand and lets me pull him into the lab.

"I can't erase what was done to you and your people here, but I can try to make it better. I can try to make sure it never happens again with your help."

"You have it," he replies automatically, making me smile up at him.

"Then let's get to work." I squeeze his hand and then let go, turning back to the computer.

"Let's." He nods.

Hours later, I lean back from the computer. I've copied everything across and password protected it on this computer so if anyone accesses it, I'll know. Cato has been busy checking the entire lab and transferring the contents of the research into the bags we found here. We plan to move it back to his lab for storage so it will be safe from their hands.

When they find out I betrayed them, I will lose my job or worse, but I have to. I can't let them get away with this.

"That's everything, I think." He nods as he stands, stretching his arms above his head. His horns catch the light as if he's sucking it up into his shadows, so I quickly look away, not wanting to be caught staring again.

"Talia?" he asks, and I make a mumbling noise. "I know this has to be hard for you." Shit, he thinks I'm worried about the humans, which I guess I am, but my main concern is how attracted I am to a monster. I can't say that though.

"Yeah." I just shrug, unsure what else to say.

"Humans did this. They pushed us to our breaking point, and they are the reason the war started. Now they clearly want another one. I know this is hard, but you are doing the right thing," he reasons softly.

"Am I?" I ask as I look back at him. "What they did?" I shake my head, feeling sick. "But what if your people use these—"

He moves closer and takes my hand. "We won't, you know me better than that. Yes, there are some who want to start another war with humans, mainly the Darklings, who are crazy, but then there are us, Acumen and Nightfang, who just want to be left alone and live our lives." He searches my gaze before sighing. "Let me show you why you should trust us."

Standing, I let him lead me through the labs to a corner, where he looks down at me. "Remember, we don't blame you, Talia. I don't." That scares me enough to make me focus, and when he leads me down the corridor, horror and disgust eat away at me.

He's showing me the cells where they were kept and hurt. They go on forever. Steps lead farther down into the lab, heading to more cells, and the more we pass, the more the sickness claws at my throat. There is still dried blood in some, and some even have bones of dead monsters…even small ones.

Like kids.

"Stop," I beg, sliding to a stop and hanging my head, tears blurring my eyes. "Please stop."

"Talia." He sighs, rubbing my back. "It's okay, it's our history—"

"It's not okay!" I scream. "None of this is okay!" I gesture around us. "We take an oath to do no harm, to research things that could help people, not this—not trying to play god to hurt and harm innocents."

I stumble back from him, wrapping my arms around myself as my tears fall.

"You should hate me, you should kill me. I wouldn't blame you. Look at this place! I can almost feel the pure agony and hopelessness in these walls. And to think this was under everyone's feet, and they either didn't care or didn't want to know." I shake my head again, my eyes darting to him. "I get why your people hate us, so why don't you hate me?"

"Because you are not them," he answers sternly, stopping before me. "You are not the monsters they are, Talia. You are good. I see it in your gaze. Just like all monsters are not evil, neither are all humans, I know that. Yes, what happened to us is horrific and still scars our people even today, but we are free, and you are going to help us stay that way, aren't you? Isn't that why you wanted to come here?"

I nod, and he softens, his gaze warming. "That's why I don't hate you, Talia. How could I when you were lied to as well? Being born human doesn't make you like them, just like being born a monster doesn't make me a killer. Yes, we are supposed to hate each other, but I don't hate you. Do you hate me, Tally?" His voice is soft at the end as he tilts his head down to steal all of my vision. The cells disappear, and all I see are those black eyes and familiar smiling lips.

"No, I don't hate you," I murmur, and his gaze roves over my face as I trap the words inside.

I don't hate him at all. In fact, I like him too much, and it scares me.

FOURTEEN

CATO

After helping her collect herself, I shoulder the bags and place the one I can't carry on her lap as I lift her into my arms again. She cuddles into me, so soft and warm, and for a moment, I just look down at her, admiring her blonde hair, the sight of her pale skin against my red complexion, and the softness of her curves against my hard muscles. It just feels right, like she belongs here in my arms.

Swallowing back that thought, I head back into the city, wanting to get out of Akuji's territory before someone finds me, because if they so much as even look at Talia… Fuck the agreement, I would kill them.

She's mine.

I hurry through the city, slightly slower than my fastest pace, because I saw how pale she was on the way here and I don't want that. Although every second out here puts us at risk, it's better than her feeling sick for a little bit. When we cross the line into my lands, I slow even further, and she lifts her head to look around as I stride through the streets, purposely avoiding the areas covered by cameras and where my people patrol. They will hear me if I get too close, but I normally wander around, so they won't even second-guess it. Plus, the wind steals her voice when she speaks softly, and they would need to be close to hear her heartbeat.

She's as safe as she's going to get in a city full of monsters.

"It's beautiful," she whispers as she looks around. "Even the destroyed, forgotten bits. There's so much life here. I always thought everything would be dead." She shakes her head, watching the owls hooting as they fly around, the bugs seeking shelter for the night, and the nocturnal animals scurrying through the buildings. "But it's not. It's full of life, so innocent and pure."

I look around, seeing it from her perspective. "It is. I love my lands. It's a shelter for all, a place of knowledge and learning and preserving beauty."

She nods as she looks at the work we have done to fix buildings and clean up as best as we can.

Unlike Darklings who destroy and Akuji who lets it crumble, we are rebuilding.

"I can se—"

I cover her mouth, my eyes narrowing and nostrils flaring. That's when I hear it—his feet. I would know his footsteps anywhere.

Snarling, I look around before seeing the shopfront. Glancing down, I put my finger to my lips. "One of my people is coming, stay silent and low," I demand in a whisper as I hurry over and place her in the storefront before shutting the curtain one of my people hung. Moving as far away as I can, I curl my hands into fists on the bags as an excuse of where I have been as he draws closer before emerging through the shells of buildings. When he sees me, he's not surprised, only stopping when he reaches me.

"Brother," he greets.

"Brother." I take his arm in greeting, and when he looks me over, he snarls, "Damn it, I told you to stop going back there. Akuji will kill you."

"He'd have to catch me first," I joke, stopping my eyes from darting to Talia's hiding spot, even though I want to ensure she's okay. It's almost a physical need, and I find myself angling my back to her to protect her from him before I realise what I'm doing. "What are you doing out here anyway?" I ask, switching to leader mode. I know tonight is his one night off from protecting our people. He usually spends it escorting women to warm his furs or getting drunk.

"Looking for you." He rolls his eyes, knocking horns with me. "Since I haven't seen you much recently, I thought we could go exploring or something."

"I have—"

"Research to do," he finishes, mocking me before grinning. "Figured. You truly are a shitty monster."

"Want me to roar at the moon and rip into some animal?" I laugh, making him chuckle.

"No, but I'll take some sparring or even bedding some females at least, or males if you're into that."

I look away for a moment, and he tilts his head. "What's wrong? You're acting shifty, more so than normal."

"No, I'm not," I snap.

"Brother, I've known you since we were kids. You can't lie to me, you never could. You make a good leader and a great friend, but you are a shitty bad guy." He grins, but it fades when I just stare. "What is it?"

I sense his worry, and guilt eats away at me for lying to my brother. "Nothing, I'm just tired."

"Lie," he retorts, and I snarl, hating he has that ability over me, although the same goes for him. Something is clearly bothering my friend, but I haven't even asked, too worried about Tally. I'm a bad friend and a bad leader, but they have others to protect them while she only has me, so I'll be selfish for a little bit.

"Cato," he demands, "what's going on?"

I don't know how to answer, I don't want to lie to my friend, but he has enough reasons to hate humans and I know he would hate Talia. He would kill her to protect my people, and just the thought almost makes me see red.

"Cato?" he questions, stepping closer. He eyes me warily, looking for signs of what's going on. The reason why he is so good at protecting our people is because he's very observant, but not even the dumbest monster could miss what happens next.

Talia sneezes. It's a small, cute sound, but it may as well be a declaration of guilt for how loudly it shatters the silence.

His eyes go to the curtain, turning red as he races over and rips it away to expose Talia. He snarls, grabbing her by the hair and hauling her out. "A human, brother. Look what I found." He obviously thinks I didn't know she was there or I don't know her, because he throws her to the ground, getting ready to kill or attack her. Watching her curl into a ball, her face scrunched in terror, has me doing something I never would have contemplated before—I attack him, tackling him to the ground.

His expression changes into one of shock as he stares up at me, the pain racing through his eyes chased by anger. He roars as he throws me away, turning to me with betrayed, accusing eyes. "Brother."

"Leave her," I demand. "That's an order."

"She's a human!" he spits before charging me. I deflect and knock him back, and we quickly descend into a full-on fight, our horns clashing as we slash our claws at each other. We are on even footing since we trained together, but then I manage to pin him, my worry for her making me stronger.

The haze has almost taken over, but I manage to push it back slightly so I can snarl out, "She is mine!"

He freezes below me, his eyes wide. "Cato—"

"She is mine!" I roar, the haze lacing my voice. "You will not touch her!" I pound my fists into the ground on either side of his head, cracking the concrete as he watches me warily.

"You would kill your brother over a human?" he asks softly, sounding so hurt and small, like when we were kids.

It pushes the haze further back, and I sit up, throwing him a glare.

"No, but if you try to harm her again…" I trail off before turning to her. She's on her knees with her hand in front of her mouth. "Tally, are you okay?"

She hiccups out, "Yes," before rising to her feet and coming to me. Collecting her in my arms, I swing her up and bury my head into her neck, settling my fear with her scent.

I nearly lost her.

I nearly lost her.

The haze surrounds me again, and I tighten my grip on her, needing her close. I slide my hands over every inch of her body to check for injuries.

"I'm sorry, I'm so sorry. I couldn't help it. I'm sorry, Cato," she mumbles over and over.

"Shush, Tally, it's okay," I murmur, kissing her hair. With her head cradled in my palm and her legs wrapped around my waist, I turn to my brother, who watches me with dawning horror and disgust.

"You have made a big fucking mistake, Cato," he snarls, and I know he's right—not only did I harbour a human, but I attacked a brother, a member of my tribe, to protect her.

Stepping back, he eyes me like a stranger, and that drives the knife right into my heart. "Brother, I—"

"You will answer to the tribe for your crimes," he snarls, his nostrils flaring as he looks at Talia in my arms. "And the human will as well."

FIFTEEN

TALIA

"Cato?" I ask, scared.

He looks down at me and smiles, but I can tell he's worried. "It's okay. Just stick close to me, all right?"

I nod, and he slides me down his body. He grabs the bags, and with one last lingering look at the other monster, Cato pulls me after him. My eyes go back to the man who attacked me. He didn't hurt me, but he wanted to, and if Cato hadn't been there, I have no doubt I would be dead.

He was so fast and strong, I didn't stand a chance. It gives me a new appreciation for their species, not to mention Cato. He was stronger and faster than the other monster. I find myself drawing closer to him, even as I note the sadness in the other monster's eyes before his gaze lands on me and narrows in hatred.

Is it for my kind or for what it's done to Cato? I don't know, but I know I'm about to be paraded in front of a group of monsters and that my fate hangs in the balance. I just have to trust Cato and hope I won't end up dead before I'm able to save Aria.

Cato keeps his eyes on me, clearly worried, and when we approach the building they sleep in, fear blooms within me. I'm walking straight into their nest, and this time, there will be no running or hiding. I'll have to answer to them, and if they choose, they could kill me.

I've reached out before I know it, slipping my hand in Cato's much bigger one. He looks down at me and stumbles over a step before curling his claw-tipped fingers around mine and squeezing. He's showing me I'm not alone and letting me know he'll protect me with just a look and a touch. It gives me the confidence I need to walk into that building, hand in hand with a monster.

He keeps hold of my hand the entire time, despite the whispers, glares, and roars for answers as we are led before his people. I thought we would just be marched before them, but I was wrong. A meeting was called, and they filled into a lecture hall in the building, where we were left upon the stage. Cato's brother prowls before his people, shooting me disgusted looks the entire time, but I refuse to shrink away, especially when Cato stands strong and tall at my side, taking it all with a steady calmness that seems to affect even me. Eventually, his people quiet down and he clears his throat.

It's clear they respect and care for him—it's evident in their hurt.

"My tribe, I am before you today because I broke our laws. I harboured a human." Roars go up, but it's hard to tell what they are saying. It's clear, however, that they are angry. Not necessarily at him, but at me. "She was hurt, scared, and running through our lands." I was, was I? Did Cato just lie to protect me? "She is a female, and not a soldier, but a scientist."

Eyes swing to me, and I realise their fear makes them dangerous. He groans, scrubbing at his face. "Please, let me explain."

I step forward then. "Can I speak, please?"

Cato looks to me before nodding, and I wait until they quiet down enough for me to speak. I don't know what I will say, but it's important. If Cato is to be held accountable for this, then they deserve the truth. I mean them no harm, even if they never believe me.

"Yes, I'm a scientist. I understand why that must be frightening, but I swear upon my life I am not here to hurt you, nor am I like those who did. I believe in science, in the ability to find the truth within the universe to explain the unexplainable, never to cause harm. Not ever. I did not know the truth of what my people did, but I was sent here to collect their experiments. As soon as I learned of the truth, I felt sick to my stomach, and I refused to. I was helping Cato collect their research and hide it from the humans who would use it against you again. I know you probably don't believe me, and that's okay, but please, don't be angry with Cato. He didn't kill me because he felt sorry for me. I was weak and stupid, running around your world without understanding the consequences. He hated keeping this from you, but once he found out why I was here, he wanted to protect you from my people and what they did to you and still clearly want to do to you." I glance back at him. "He's a good man, torn between duty and doing what's right." I look out over the lecture hall filled to the brim with monsters of all ages and sizes, a sea of red as I beg for their understanding.

Beg for a monster's life, how strange.

"I didn't know what my people did. I know that's not an excuse, but it's the truth. He kept me alive because he thought I could help, that I knew something, and I did. I wasn't just any scientist, I was working in their lab. Not on this, but on other research. I was surrounded by them at all times and looked down on for being a woman, so they talked freely around me. I know more than they ever could have thought. I know how they think and what they want. I won't give it to them, even if it costs me my life. I want to help you. I don't deserve your mercy after what my people have done, but I'm asking for it anyway. I'm asking for you to let me help you, and if you cannot, I understand, but please, please don't take this out on Cato. All he is guilty of is loving his people so much, he was willing to break your laws to keep you safe from those who would hurt you." I look at his brother. "Even if he hated it. Thank you."

I step back to find Cato watching me, his jaw dropped and eyes warm, before he clears his throat. "We were just coming back from the lab when we were found. I should not have lied. I should have presented the tribe with this when I found out, but I…I wanted to protect you. We had just found a way of life, of safety and freedom, and I was hoping to preserve that. I know it's wrong, I should have shared my concerns, but I did it out of love, that I promise you. I will not ask for mercy, I will abide by whatever you wish, but if your wishes are for me to step down or for me to be exiled, please know this—I am lucky to have been your leader and see our people grow from such pain, and I hope one day, you can understand why I did what I did."

There's murmuring as he steps back, and I take his hand again, suddenly nervous now that my bravery has gone. "Now what?" I whisper, worried for our future.

Despite what may happen, I know I would do it all over again, even if I ended up back here, facing a sea of angry monsters, standing next to the one creature in this world I should hate but don't. It's worth it to protect them, to stop what my people were doing and protect this city and these monsters.

Even if they hate me, it was still worth it.

"We live in a democracy, Talia. Everyone gets a say in our tribe," he murmurs. "A vote will be cast, a vote for our future, for my leadership and exile…and for your death."

I shiver, and he holds me tighter.

"I will not let them kill you. Despite everything I fight for to keep our freedom, I would say the hell with it all if that's what it came to, to keep you safe."

"We vote!" Cato's brother yells, but he looks back at me with a considering look before his gaze moves to his friend. He's worried for him. Despite his hatred for me, he's worried for his brother and what this means. He was just doing his duty as well, and I understand his abhorrence of my kind.

The voices all blend into one, and I close my eyes, waiting on their answer. A species who has been nothing but hurt by humans is deciding my fate. Fitting, I suppose, but I can't blame them if they call for my death. I knew the risks when I came over the wall.

I open my eyes, watching as sheets of paper are passed down to the front and given to an older monster, who starts to read them and count. Cato squeezes my hand and looks down at me, his voice lowered just for me. "Whatever happens, trust in me, okay?"

I nod. "Aways," I murmur, squeezing back. "Thank you for saving me that day."

"You saved me, Talia," he whispers as a yell goes up.

We both turn back as the man stands. "The votes are in. For Cato, our leader, the vote is clear. You will be forgiven for this transgression, but do not let it happen again. Despite everything you have done for us, your duty must still come first."

Cato nods, his relief clear. Despite what he says about wanting space and sometimes feeling worried about his duty, it's clear he loves it and loves helping people.

"For the human." The man's eyes swing to me, neither angry nor hopeful. "She will be allowed to live, but I think I speak for us all when I say it is under the provision that she helps us, and if she in any way betrays us, she will be put to death immediately."

"Understood," I respond, almost slumping. I am to live. They believed us. I grin up at Cato, and he grins at me.

I know we dodged a bullet. They are more worried about what the humans want and gaining my help than killing me. One death versus their entire race, they truly are the smart ones. No wonder they have lasted this long.

"Then I suggest we get back to our desires, no?" Cato calls. "They won't do themselves." That causes some chuckles, and although I know some will still be angry and probably resentful, they clearly trust in him. They start to scatter, some watching me with interest and others with outright hatred.

Cato's brother stops before us, glaring at me. "I will never trust you, and when you mess up, which you will, human, I will destroy you." He glares at Cato and storms away.

Cato snarls, watching his retreating form before looking down at me. "Stay here, I need to talk to him." He hesitates and leans down, pressing his forehead to mine. "They won't harm you now, okay? Trust me and this. Just don't run away." He chuckles, and I nod, wrapping my arms around myself as I watch him go after his brother.

I'm now alone with the lingering monsters. I meet their gazes and smile shyly, my cheeks blushing under their regard. "So, erm, do I get a tour?"

SIXTEEN

CATO

"That's all you have to say? Threaten the woman?" I roar at my brother, chasing him outside.

"The human!" he roars, turning on me, the space between us bigger than it has ever been. We have been inseparable since we were kids. When I left Akuji's tribe, he followed me, always trusting in me.

"You have never doubted me before, so do not start now, brother," I beg, hating the hurt in his voice. He's surrounded himself with anger, letting it rot his soul. I don't know when I stopped hating humans or started to think of Talia as different, but knowing that my best friend, my brother, hates her and wants to kill her destroys me.

"I never doubted my brother, but you? I don't know you. The brother I knew would have killed the woman the first time he saw her for everything they did to our people, to us, and our parents!" he yells, his eyes flashing red as he faces off with me. "He would not have kept her like a fucking pet and protected her, especially from me!"

"I did what I had to for our people—"

"They might have bought that, but I saw it in your eyes—you want her. It's simple and plain. You want the human." His lips curl in a sneer. "You chose her over your own people, your duty…and me." He pants as he stares at me. "I don't know you, so I certainly don't trust you, but congratulations, you get to keep the human. Do not expect me to stand around and watch as you destroy yourself and our people." He turns, but I won't let him leave until we finish this.

"Brother, do not do this. Our people need you, I need you."

"You never did," he says, facing away. "You never needed me, but I needed you. You were the only family I had. I looked up to you so much and trusted you with everything. I would have given anything for you. Now, you're just a stranger. You will make us weak and destroy us, but hey, at least you aren't the only monster keeping secrets and humans." He tosses a crumpled note at me and then fades into the darkness, walking away from me and our brotherhood like it was nothing. The ache makes me rub my chest, even as I grab the note, curious what he's talking about.

I might have just lost my best friend, my brother, for Talia, and yet I can't regret it, especially when I read the note.

Cato, my friend.

Can we meet? I have a human here searching for her friend, and I think you have her. Talia?

-Akuji

Akuji has Aria. I almost slump in relief, glad to hear Talia's friend is alive and well. She was so worried, so at least it's one less concern for her, but they want to meet. That could mean anything. They could take Talia. I hesitate, but I know what I have to do.

I won't lie to her, and I won't hurt or risk my tribe anymore, so when I find the first runner, I send a message back. I tell him it can wait until tomorrow night, since it's nearly morning, but in reality, I want to keep Talia to myself a little longer.

At least for now.

SEVENTEEN

TALIA

"No, I won't ever grow horns." I giggle. The kid at my side nods seriously, looking back at the bunch of little ones following me. They are a mix of ages, with eyes ranging from all black to a bright orange, short to fully grown tails, and horns of all sizes, since those are still growing. They are cute as hell. After Cato disappeared, they cornered me on the stage and started peppering me with questions. A female who introduced herself as Noya told them to at least let me sit down if they were going to quiz me, so now I'm following a herd of children and a few adult monsters back into the sleeping area.

"What about a tail?" one whispers.

"Nope." I grin. "I like your eyes. How come they are orange?" I inquire, seeing as fair is fair.

"My mummy says we are born with orange eyes, a mix of the red and black, and when we get older, they turn completely black." He shrugs, making me nod in understanding.

It's a bit like a few feline animals.

Back in the sleeping chamber, I answer a few more questions from the little one at my side, who seems to do most of the talking. The others appear shy or scared, which makes me sad.

Letting the kid lead me over to a pile of furs, I sit cross-legged as he crawls over with a book in his hand. "Will you read to us?" he asks, his big orange eyes peering up at me. Tiny little fangs hang over his lip, and adorable little black horns sprout from his head. Swallowing, I feel a pang deep in my chest as I watch him. "Please, human Talia?"

"Please?" comes the echo of other kids as they look at me.

I glance up at Noya, who just grins and nods, and then I see a few other adults drifting in, some still wary but drawn by the children as I turn back. "Sure. What's your name?" I ask as I take the book and peer down at the fairy tale he's chosen. It's something my mother read to me when I was little.

"Groff." He grins as he settles closer, the other kids relaxing on the blankets also.

"A very strong name." I grin. "You can just call me Talia if you want," I whisper like it's a secret, and he giggles.

"Humans are funny. Mummy said they were scary."

"Some are," I tell him softly. "Some are very bad. Your mummy is smart," I say brokenly before gripping the book and looking down. "Okay, let's read."

As I start to read the story, doing the dramatic voices like my mother used to—deepening it for the bad guys and making it tinkling and high for the fairy—I notice more and more monsters drifting in until the whole room is packed. Every eye is on me as I read. I blush like crazy but forge ahead as the kids laugh and call encouragements. I even act out a few bits, making them scream and giggle.

The sound goes straight to my heart, cracking it further.

After all, I'll never hear that sound of my own.

My voice cracks as I carry on reading, but my despair soon disappears as I lose myself in the story, almost giddy with excitement as they all draw closer, forgetting their mistrust of me. It's almost like we are bonding, and I would read a hundred books if that were the case.

There's a small noise, and I lift my head to see Cato in the doorway, his mouth open in shock as he looks around the room. I smile softly just for him before ducking my head and reading as Groff nudges me with his tail.

"'And they lived happily ever after. The end,'" I finish a while later. I shut the book softly and put it down, looking around to see a few kids fell asleep, but not Groff. He's watching me curiously, and before I can react, he clambers into my lap. His little hands grab my shirt as he peers up at me, his tail lying across my leg. I hear someone growl, but I don't move as I look down at this little boy, who's trusting me and bridging a gap he didn't even know was there. It just proves if we aren't brought up with hatred, it isn't there, no matter our differences.

"My mummy said humans were scary, but you aren't. You are kind. You won't hurt my family like the other bad humans, will you?" he asks innocently, with that naïve knowing only kids seem to have.

"Never," I promise vehemently. "I would never hurt them or you. I would die before I did." In that moment, I realise that's the truth.

Groff nods solemnly before smiling brightly at me. "I thought as much. Do you have kids?" he asks around a yawn.

My heart slams, and my stomach rolls. "No." My voice cracks.

"Okay." He sighs and snuggles closer. I freeze before wrapping my arms around him, and within a minute, he's snoring softly. Closing my eyes for a moment, I just let myself believe this is real, that he's mine, before it's dashed away. Turning to Noya, I whisper, "Where do I lay him down?"

"Just there." She nods at a fur.

I hold him tightly as I stand, and as softly as possible, I carry him over to the fur Noya indicated. Crouching, I lay him down as tenderly as possible and arrange his little tail before tucking him in and stroking away the tuft of brown hair sweeping into his face. "Goodnight, little one."

I move to Noya, who's watching him softly. "Thank you for allowing me to do that," I tell her.

She glances at Groff and smiles. "Always. You don't have kids?"

Licking my lips, I hesitate, and she looks at me as something akin to understanding passes across her face. "I can't have them, or it would be very unlikely. That's what they have told me anyway. I had two miscarriages before. I, erm, lost the baby," I admit when she looks confused. She is the first person I've told since I found out from the doctor. "I've always loved kids and wanted a big family, since I had no one else, but I guess some things aren't meant to be. I babysat all neighbourhood children growing up for money, but I can't have my own. Thank you for letting me hold him for a minute to know how it felt."

She takes my hand and squeezes it. "A tribe is a family. We share everything, even our children. You can look after them anytime," she jokes, making me grin softly. "I am sorry, Talia." Then, unexpectedly, she pulls me into her arms. Those who had been listening around us wrap their arms around me, holding me tightly, and for the first time in years, I cry as the monsters hold me, letting me mourn what could have been if my body didn't betray me.

They hold me until I stop, and when they step back, Noya wipes my face for me, holding my cheeks and searching my gaze before nodding as if coming to some conclusion. "*Refresol*," she whispers before stepping back, and the others repeat it. Before I can ask what it means, Cato appears.

"Okay, I'm stealing her back," he teases, taking my hand and waving goodbye to them as he starts to lead me to the lab. Exhaustion sets in halfway, and he swings me into his arms without asking. The day's events are catching up with me, but I wrap my arms around him and look up into his eyes. I want to ask what happened with his friend, but something else takes precedence.

"What does *refresol* mean?" I ask softly.

He blinks and looks down at me before smiling. "One of us, why?"

I can't help the smile that covers my face. "No reason." I lean my head against his chest, and before I know it, I'm succumbing to sleep as I'm carried in my monster's arms.

EIGHTEEN

CATO

Looking down at Talia in my arms, I can't help but think it's all worth it. Despite the agony in my chest over the fight with my brother, I don't regret saving her or bringing her here. Leaning down, I kiss her head softly, grinning when she makes an adorable little noise and scrunches her nose.

Kicking open the door to the lab, I step through, then lock it behind me before hurrying to my room, where I lay her on the furs like she did the child. After taking off her shoes, I tuck her in, staring down at her. When I found her in the middle of my people, I was worried, but she had been laughing. The way she brought the story to life for them won them over. They were assuaged by her kindness and pure soul, which was easy to see.

No wonder they called her one of them.

Unable to help it, I kick off my own coverings and slip into the furs, lying next to her. I want to pull her into my arms, but I won't take advantage of her when she is asleep. Instead, I settle for smelling her in my furs and feeling her warmth close by. I close my eyes and settle in, but something heavy lands on me. My eyes open to see her arm across my chest as she slowly inches closer. I barely breathe as she curls into my side. She throws her leg over me, nuzzles her head into my side, and then climbs over me and sprawls onto my chest, her legs and arms wrapped around me.

My heart races as I wrap my arms around her and hold her tight, unable to stop the heavy feeling she creates in my chest. She was so scared of me when she first woke up, and now she's curled around me like a kitten, so trusting and beautiful.

When her foot brushes my hard-on, I groan, nudging her so she's not lying directly on it. All it takes is a sniff of her to arouse me, but like this, with her warmth and curves pressed against every inch of me? Yeah, I throb painfully, but it's more than just for her body. It's for her mind, her soul. Watching her with my people made me think of things I shouldn't want, especially with a human, but I can't seem to stop my feelings for her from growing.

She can't stay, can she? She's human, and she belongs with her people like I belong with mine.

The idea of her leaving actually causes a physical pain, but she can't ever be mine.

The lie burns in my chest, as does the fact that I did not tell her that her friend is alive and okay just to keep her with me.

NINETEEN

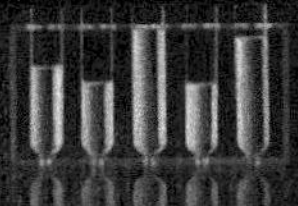

TALIA

When I wake up, I'm curled around Cato, and he's asleep. I just blink, confused how I got here and why I'm wrapped around him like a koala, but he doesn't seem to care. One of his hands grips my ass, and the other is in my hair, holding me to him.

Shit.

I try to slide off him, and his eyes fly open, searching for a threat. When he realises I'm awake and moving, he relaxes and lets me go. "Morning," he mumbles around a yawn. He's so sleepy and cute, I have to look away, ignoring the burning in my cheeks. I must have climbed all over him in my sleep.

My ex did always say I was a hugger.

"Morning," I reply, and I rack my brain for something, anything, to say. As the silence stretches on, he arches his eyebrow, and I panic until I finally blurt, "Did you hear anything about Aria?"

His face shuts down as he rolls from the bed and gets to his feet. "Not yet," he answers, but his voice is strange.

Sitting up, I pull my knees to my chest as I watch him. "Okay," I whisper softly, but he's stiff. Was it the cuddling? No, if it had been, he would have woken up feeling awkward.

Is he lying to me?

No, Cato wouldn't. I let it go and head to the bathroom. After showering and using the toilet, I find him hard at work, and I join in. Usually, he's chatty and fluttering around me, but today he barely looks at me, and I find myself missing his gaze and touch. I easily got used to working side by side with him and much prefer it over working alone again.

Following his lead, I stay quiet as I collect the research. They wanted this research for a reason, we just need to find out why.

After a while, there is a knock at the door, and once Cato gets it, he comes back with trays of food. We eat in silence again until I finally can't take it anymore. "Okay, what's wrong?"

"Nothing," he mutters, but he won't meet my eyes.

"Cato, you won't even look at me. Is this about…about me sleeping on you? I can sleep in a different room if it makes you uncomfortable."

His head shoots up. "No," he snarls, making me blink before he softens with a sigh. "Sorry, I was just worried about my people. I shouldn't have taken it out on you. No, you'll sleep in my nest with me, where you are safe." He smiles tenderly then. "Finish eating, and we will have some fun. We both need it."

"Fun?" I repeat.

"Fun." He grins. "You do know what that is, don't you, Tally?" he teases, prodding me with his tail.

Laughing, I smack it away, more relieved than I care to admit that we are back to normal, but there is still a shadow in his eyes. I don't ask, though, because if he wanted to tell me, he would. I bet it's about his friend. He was clearly upset about it yesterday. When he's ready, he will tell me. I just hope he doesn't let it eat him up. Maybe fun would be good.

Once we've eaten, I slip on my shoes, and he leads me downstairs.

I wave at some people I know before Cato tugs me outside, stealing me away for himself before the kids can reach me.

"You're mine tonight." He grins down at me. "So hurry before the brats find you," he teases and pulls me after him as I laugh.

"Where are we going?" I ask as he guides me across a square. There's a statue in the middle I want to get a better look at, but I don't have time with him pulling me after him.

"To see my favourite places of course." He grins back at me, his eyes twinkling as he pulls me to a giant building across the square, with once white stone steps and pillars outside. It has a peaked roof with Old World Museum written on it, and excitement pools inside me.

"Museum? Really?" I almost clap as I hurry to his side.

The building stretches as far as the eye can see, and it's obvious it used to be beautiful and busy with life. Some windows are shattered or gone entirely, and some have small lights peeking through them like there are monsters inside, but when I step into the leaf-covered marble foyer, none of the destruction matters.

It's stunning. "Wow," I whisper as I spin, taking in the high ceilings with paintings covering every inch, clearly hand done, a domed top, and what used to be a reception area.

When I drop my head back down, I see Cato staring at me, his lips parted and an unreadable look in his eyes, but my body knows it and heats. We just stare at each other, the hunger written starkly across his features making heat crawl through my body until he suddenly looks away, freeing me from his gaze.

"It's beautiful," I tell him, and he glances back at me, purposely flicking his eyes down my body and back up to meet mine.

"It certainly is."

I can't help the blush that stains my cheeks so I turn away again, wandering around to explore and see as much as I can. He follows after me, always on my heels, but in companionable silence to let me see everything. The fact I know he's there, watching and protecting me, has my heart beating double time, which he can undoubtedly hear. When we move into a huge, open space filled with paintings and a skylight above showing the stars, I find myself sitting on a bench and looking around.

Cato makes a noise, and I look at him. "What?" I ask, a smile playing on my lips.

"This is my favourite spot," he murmurs before sitting next to me, his thigh pressed against the full length of mine. His tail, which I don't think he even notices, wraps around my ankle and pulls me closer. "Last time I was here, I had this feeling… Not very scientific of me, I know, but we are instinctual creatures, and as much as I try not to be, I still am."

"A feeling?" I prompt, looking over at him and realising he belongs here. He is equally as mysterious and beautiful as the art surrounding us.

"That everything was about to change," he whispers, his eyes dropping to my lips before he stands and holds out his hand to me. "Come on, let me show you something else."

I lift my hand and place it in his, his huge palm dwarfing and warming mine as he softly tugs me to my feet and leads me from the museum. He shortens his long strides to match mine and makes sure his body is to the outside to shield me from all prying eyes and potential threats. His eyes scan the horizon, but when I squeeze his hand, he glances down, and his face softens as a smile curls his lips.

"You suit the night," he says randomly, making me tilt my head in question. As if he understands the gesture, he carries on. "The moon shimmers in your blonde hair, making it look like spun gold, your eyes light up with the stars, and your pale skin shines so bright, you might as well live up there with the celestial gods."

I stumble to a stop and gawk at him, but he's oblivious, just tugging me along like he didn't just say the most beautiful things anyone—human or monster—has ever said to me. "Cato," I call, tugging him to a stop until he turns to me. "You can't just say stuff like that and continue walking!"

"Why not?" he asks, his brow furrowed in confusion.

"Because… Because…" I huff, making him grin as I point at his face. "Stop being so cute and nice!" I storm past him, hearing his laughter chasing after me. A moment later, he takes my hand again and steers me in a different direction, towards the library. We head inside, and he happily waves at his people there. They wave back. Some eye me curiously, while some outright ignore me.

Rome wasn't built in a day, and it's better than eating me.

Though I wouldn't mind if Cato did…

No, bad brain!

He leads me through the stacks. The scarred, wooden structures have clearly been cleaned and righted, and when we break out into the middle, I gape. It's beautiful, it truly is. Tables are scattered in the middle, filled with monsters reading by candlelight. I can't help but feel at home here. The bookcases spread around us in a circle and stretch as far as the eye can see, with a huge, iron staircase towards the back leading to an upper level, where there are more bookcases. Some of them have spaces on them, some books are bent or crinkled or even destroyed, but it's clear they have spent a lot of time cleaning and fixing this place. The walls are cracked but clean, some of the windows are busted but taped over, and candles hang in lanterns, covering the space in a warm, welcoming glow.

The flooring has been scrubbed, and even though some of it is scarred with what looks like claw marks, it is definitely still beautiful. "This place is so cosy," I murmur as he lets me look around, and then, without a word, he gives me a tour of the building. He shows me books still locked behind cases, and the ones they couldn't fix, which are piled carefully in the back. There's a monster there working through as many as he can, trying to save them, which both surprises and endears me.

Then Cato leads me upstairs, his claws clicking on the metal rail, and once there, he releases my hand. "Wander to your heart's content," he instructs.

I do, moving through the stacks and running my fingers across the spines. I slide some out to flip through, grinning at the fact that they have been looked after. They even have labels for borrowing them. My heart settles and peace fills me the longer I wander. Being here is like being at home, and for a moment, I can almost imagine the library I used to spend my childhood in, curled up reading in a corner to pass the day. Eventually, I decide to find Cato and have to search the aisles to do so.

When I find him again, he's leaning back, his legs folded against the opposite bookcase. His head is tilted to the side, and he holds a romance novel in his hand, the tome looking tiny in his huge grip. For a moment, I just watch the way his eyes flick eagerly across the page, the way his claws softly flip to the next one, and how his mouth moves with the words as if he needs to speak them out loud.

I lean my shoulder into the case next to me and accidentally knock into a book. The sound is quiet, but his head snaps up. He settles back when he spots me, and a welcoming smile crosses his lips as I blush furiously at being caught watching him. "What are you reading?" I ask to cover for me perving on him.

There is just something about a huge, scarred monster reading a book that is so incredibly attractive.

He holds out his hand, and I take it, expecting him to sit me down next to him, but instead, he lifts and drops me between his parted legs so my back is to his front. He notches his head on my shoulder and wraps one arm around my middle to grip the book, the other playing with my hair as his tail encircles my ankles. The move was so natural and quick, I just sit here blinking.

We cuddled last night, but I was asleep. With me awake, it feels very intimate. His breath wafts over my ear, and I can feel his heart's soft if not slightly racing rhythm, the hardness of his muscles, and the movement of his lips as he continues to read. I settle back and read with him, focusing on the words and not on the feel of this very large, muscular man pressed up against every inch of me. Slowly, the nerves fade as I become absorbed in the story.

I gasp when the heroine runs away from the love of her life over a miscommunication, and Cato holds me tighter. Turning my head, I bury it in his arm, hiding. "I hate these parts," I mutter. "I know they usually end happily, but that part between letting it all go and fighting for happiness? It terrifies me that they won't be strong enough to fight for it."

"Me too," he murmurs. "But that part is also my favourite." I look up at him, and he smiles. "It's the moment they realise how much they love each other and just what they are willing to risk to keep that person. Yes, it's scary, change always is, and the pain? Of course it hurts, but it's the best type, don't you think? When they finally get their happy ending, they will deserve it that much more."

"I guess I never thought of it that way," I whisper as he delicately pushes a stray hair behind my ear. "Still, I usually have to close the book and walk away for a little bit."

"Then let me read it to you," he murmurs, and I close my eyes as his voice washes over me, reading me chapter after chapter until the couple end up back together again. All the while, his low, purring voice transports me into the story. The soft stroke of his hand across my side, thigh, and arm grounds me, and when he starts to read the makeup sex scene, I turn bright red and shift my body, both nervous and aroused. I hear him inhale, and a slight growl escapes his throat as he tugs me closer, letting me feel the very hard, long evidence he isn't unaffected either. He doesn't stop, though, and I don't ask him to.

We remain locked in a bubble as he reads me smut, our desire growing between us until I'm almost panting and his voice is crooning.

"'Sliding down her silken thighs, I drag my tongue along the arch of her foot before slowly kissing up the legs I have been imagining entwined with mine for months now. I stop and taste every inch of her freckled skin, memorising the star constellation on her flesh so I will never forget. Groaning beneath me, she arches up, seeking my mouth, and when her hand tangles in my hair and pulls me up, I go willingly. I sink into the kiss as she wraps herself around me and holds me tight. Her wet heat welcomes me as I settle between her legs—'"

"Fucking hell," I whisper, trying in vain to ignore the throb between my legs and the tightening of my nipples.

"You okay there, Tally?" he murmurs in my ear. The bastard. He did it on purpose, and if he didn't, he's the most sexually unaware man I've ever met. I hate the fact that I sigh and lean into him, rolling my hips slightly. Grunting, he grips my left hip and holds me still, his claws pricking my skin. "Don't do that," he rumbles.

"Do what?" I ask innocently.

"Rub against me like that. I had to sleep with you wrapped around me, Talia. Every inch of your sweet, soft human skin was against mine, and now here you are again, rubbing me like a cat in heat. Your body is begging for me to give in and taste you like I want to."

"I… We…" I stumble over my words, and he chuckles softly, licking the shell of my ear.

"I can smell your arousal, Talia, so behave, little human. It's very hard" —he drags out the word, making me swallow— "to read as it is."

"I know, I can feel it," I quip, unable to help myself.

"Don't talk about it, just ignore it," he mutters, rearranging himself before diving back into the book. When he finally finishes reading, we are both sexually frustrated but also grinning from the happy ending.

"You were right—it was worth it," I murmur as I turn in the circle of his arms to see his face, but his expression has me freezing. "What?" I ask. His face is so serious. "Cato?"

"Walk away right now, Talia," he rumbles. My eyes widen and my heart hammers in desire when I recognise the pure intent blazing in his eyes. "Right this second, unless you want me to kiss you."

"What?" I whisper.

"I have wanted to since the moment I met you. I've been fighting it, not wanting to scare you, but I can't… I can't not kiss you with you looking at me like that. So walk away now, Talia."

"Tally," I respond, licking my lips. His eyes track the movement, and he fists his clawed hands on the floor as if to stop himself from pouncing on me. "You call me Tally. Don't stop now." I don't know why that seems important, but it is.

"Tally." He drags the word out, his forked tongue flicking across his lips as he watches me. "Walk away."

"And if I don't want to?" I question, being brave for once in the face of such need. No one has ever wanted me that way, as if they are in physical pain because they need me that much. Only him, only Cato, and he's right—I need him to kiss me. I need him to make that move, because I never will, but I want it.

This monster slowly wormed his way into my heart and soul, with his protective arms and soft-spoken words. He danced with me under the lights, read to me in the library, and protected me from his people, while also working with me side by side. It's not hard to admit that I care for him, and I'm curious about what he's offering.

"Last warning, Tally," he snarls, his eyes flashing red and only glowing brighter the longer I linger before him.

"I'm not going anywhere." I tilt my chin up defiantly. "So what are you going to do about it?"

He moves so fast, I don't even have time to brace myself. One moment, I'm on my knees before him, and the next, I'm on my back on the floor with him crouched above me, forcing himself between my legs. I gasp as he rolls his hips and lets me feel his hard length. "You should have run, little human."

"Do your worst." I smirk, knowing I should be afraid, but I'm not.

Not with him.

"Don't say I didn't warn you, little human," he snarls, his voice feral. This isn't my soft-spoken Cato. No, this is the monster, and he's ready to claim what he wants, which just so happens to be me.

He moves just as quickly as before, his lips descending on mine. I expected sweet, soft, and unsure, but no. He slams his lips onto me, his fangs catching on my bottom lip, and he sweeps his forked tongue inside my mouth, tangling it with mine. The kiss is so hard and fast, I have to fight to keep up. Those sharp fangs dig into my lip, and when he pulls back, I find myself arching up and licking at them as he watches me.

"You taste so sweet, Tally," he rumbles, keeping himself effortlessly poised above me with one hand as he tangles his claws in my hair and tilts my head back before slamming his lips back onto mine.

He loses himself in me as much as I lose myself in him. Moaning, I wrap my legs around him, becoming consumed by the kiss.

He sweeps away any reservations I had, and my body lights up just as much as his eyes. Desire surges through me, and I grind against him, moaning into his mouth.

He's going to drown me in the flames, and I can't seem to care.

My nails drag along his chest and shoulders, making him jerk closer and nip my lip until we both taste blood. Suddenly, he stops and jerks back, slamming himself into the bookcase. Panting heavily, his lips red from our kiss and stained with my blood, he reaches up and touches them as I sit up to see him.

"You're bleeding," he snarls, shaking his head as his eyes start to fade to normal. "Fuck, Tally!" He lunges at me, opening my mouth and checking my lips, so I pat his hands.

"Cato," I say, repeating his name, but he ignores me. I see anger and self-hatred arching across his features, so I cup his cheeks hard so he will look at me. "I loved it." I lean in and kiss him again, tasting my blood on his mouth. "You didn't hurt me, I did it to myself. Stop panicking and trust me to know my limits."

He licks the blood on his lips, and his eyes flare for a moment, but he searches my gaze. "You sure you are okay?"

"I'm better than okay," I promise, kissing him softly. "How about we go back?"

Nodding, he gets to his feet and takes my hand, but the whole time we are leaving the library, he shoots me considering, almost fearful looks, and there's a distance between us that wasn't there before.

I hate it.

TWENTY

CATO

Once out of the library, I'm in a foul mood. I shouldn't have done that, I shouldn't have kissed her, but I couldn't resist, not with her big, hungry eyes looking at me like that while her body rolled against mine. The musk of her arousal wrapped around me so tightly, it was hard to breathe. I couldn't not kiss her, it was impossible.

I hurt her, however, and in doing so only reminded myself of how fragile she is. She's human and not as strong as us, so I should be protecting her, not ravaging her mouth so hard, I can still taste the sweet tang of her blood.

The fact that it nearly has me spilling annoys me further, and hatred courses through me. She glances at me as we walk, but I can't meet her eyes, afraid of what I will see there.

I can take a lot, but one thing I cannot take is Talia being scared of me. Not ever. Not once I realised what she is to me—my mate.

It was so obvious all along, but I was fighting it and ignoring the signs, because it's doomed to end. Unlike the book we read, we won't get a happy ending, not a human and a monster. Our differences are worlds apart. We belong in totally different places, and Talia could never survive here. The fact that her blood still stains my tongue is proof of that, but it doesn't stop me from wishing for a moment that she was mine.

I had known it deep down, but when I looked up to find her watching me, it was like something clicked deep inside of me, and with roaring clarity, I knew it. She is my mate, my forever, my one person. No wonder I knew change was coming. I was sensing her, the person meant to be my partner, yet how can she be when we are not equal? She is a smart, beautiful human, and I am a feral beast, making her bleed from my need for her.

My mood only sours further, and once we're back at our rooms, I leave her there, needing to walk away before I drop to my knees and beg for her forgiveness. I hurt her, the worst sin of all. Even before I knew she was my mate, it would have wrecked me, but knowing the incredible, smart, fun, and capable Talia is meant to be mine and I destroyed it makes me nothing but the beast they call us.

I find myself wandering through the streets, growing angrier and angrier at myself. Not only did I lie to my mate, but I hurt her all within the span of two days. I'm a terrible male and an even worse mate. If we could be together, she wouldn't want me, and for good measure.

I don't deserve her.

Eventually sick of my self-pity and dark mood, I head back, dreading seeing her again, since she can read me so easily, but when I hear laughter, I follow it, and my whole world slides to a stop. She's reading another book, and my people and younglings are gathered around, listening raptly as she descends into a fake roar, making them laugh harder. My mood instantly lightens as I watch her.

She's okay.

She's fine.

I find myself sitting with everyone else, and hours later, she yawns and bids everyone goodnight. I move through their masses, extracting her from a pile of sleeping younglings, and lift her into my arms. She curls up into them so trustingly, my heart skips a beat. Her fists clench against my skin as she sighs and peers up at me, half asleep.

"I missed you," she whispers.

"I missed you too," I reply, leaning down to kiss her head. "Sleep, I have you."

"I know you do." She yawns as I carry her upstairs and gently settle her in the bed before stripping off her shoes and tucking her in, but tonight, I don't get in next to her. I need to keep my distance, because it is going to hurt like hell when she goes back.

It will destroy me in a way nothing ever has, because even now, after a few days, I cannot imagine my life without her.

Hours later, as I'm struggling and failing to work, I hear a noise. I rush to her side to see her kicking in her sleep—a nightmare. I stroke her hair away from her face and lean down. "Shh, Tally, you're safe, everything is fine. You're safe," I promise, and she slowly wakes up, blinking.

"Cato?" she asks sleepily.

"It was just a bad dream," I tell her. "Go back to sleep." I stand, but her hand darts out and grabs mine.

"Sleep with me, please?" she begs, her big eyes imploring me, and I can't deny her anything she wants, even if it will make it so much harder to let her go.

Slipping into the bed next to her, I keep some distance between us, but she slides over and buries herself in my arms.

"Tally." I try to pull away, but she just lies in my arms with her legs between mine. She's oblivious to the reaction it creates in my body and my internal struggle, but I refuse to move away.

"What was your dream about?" I ask, and she stiffens in my arms, so I pull back to see her face, spotting the tears in her eyes. "Tally, talk to me!" I demand, running my hands over every inch of her to check for injuries. She laughs and wipes at her eyes before patting my chest.

"I'm not hurt."

I relax, but only marginally. Her tears are like a physical blow to my already aching heart.

"It's just…tonight and then last night with the kids." She shakes her head.

"You don't like kids?" I inquire, confused.

"No, no, I love them!" she replies before sighing and meeting my eyes. "I can't have them. I always wanted kids, but they told me I might never have them."

"Oh, Tally." I pull her closer, wrapping my arms around her as I kiss her head. She cries into my chest, sounding so pained that it rips my heart to shreds. When she calms a little, I pull back and wipe her face before meeting her eyes. "I'm sorry, I truly am, but just because you cannot have them biologically doesn't mean you can't have them if you don't want to. There are other ways—"

"I know that," she whispers.

"The kids here are all of ours, despite who bears them. We are all a family with responsibilities," I explain, "but you would be an incredible part of that." I could see that now, her looking after the kids…but what if it hurts? "Would you like me to ask them to stop making you read to them?"

"No! Please don't."

I sense the pain there, so I pull her closer. "I could never deny you anything, I just don't like seeing you hurt. But, Tally, you think this makes you less than. It doesn't. You are still Talia. You are still a woman. An incredibly brave, smart, funny, kind, and sometimes stubborn woman."

"Cato." She tries to stop me, but I force her to look at me.

"This changes nothing," I promise, and it doesn't. Yes, I want kids, and the idea of Talia carrying my kids is bliss, but I'm also a possessive, jealous man and would hate sharing her attention. I just hate this is a hurt I can't take away. With or without kids, she is still Talia.

She is my mate, my intended, and I wish I could give her everything she wants.

Even if she won't be mine.

"The right man will not only understand but love you for it," I tell her, even as the words feel like razors.

"You think? I've never told a partner. I was too scared to because despite the fact they all say it's fine at the beginning, they eventually want a family, a perfect family and wife, and I can't be that."

"Then they are fools," I snarl. "There would be nothing more fulfilling than having you and your love. Kids or no kids, they would be the luckiest man in the world. Children are incredible, the hope for the future, but there are many other ways to become a mother or not at all if that's what you want. Some things are not meant to be, and that's okay, it doesn't affect who you are. You're a scientist, Talia, and an incredible woman. I have no doubt that if you put your mind to it, you will find a life that will make you unbelievably happy, and you deserve that."

"And what about you?" she queries, searching my gaze.

"What about me?" I ask, perplexed.

"Don't you deserve to be happy? I see you here, surrounded but still alone. Are you happy, Cato?"

I swallow as my heart thrums with the truth—the truth this one little human sees right into the core of.

"Right now, with you in my arms, I am," I admit truthfully, and the bright smile she gives me makes it all worth it as I lean in. "Now sleep, and I will protect you from any more nightmares. Nothing will ever hurt you while I am around, Tally."

"And when you are gone?" she whispers, closing her eyes as she leans into me.

"It doesn't bear thinking about," I admit softly as I kiss her head and close my eyes, trying to imagine my life before her. She's right—it was lonely and unfulfilled. She brought purpose and colour back to it. She brought the sun, so how will I ever go back to living in the dark alone, longing for a mate I can never keep?

TWENTY-ONE

TALIA

The next morning, I watch Cato. He's different today, more reserved and acting cold towards me. He still brings me food, makes sure I drink, and answers my questions, but there is a distance between us that makes my heart ache. Rubbing my chest, I find my eyes drifting to him again, wondering if I freaked him out last night with my tears and confessions. He doesn't seem like the type to shy away from the hard stuff, though, so why is he pulling away from me?

I miss feeling his eyes and hands on me.

I miss him, and he's right here.

"Have you heard anything from Aria?" I find myself asking, and he stiffens before shaking his head at me. I frown at his reaction and focus back on the research before me. Biting my lip, I remember the way he kissed me yesterday, as if he couldn't get enough of me, and the way he held me last night so sweetly, protecting me from my dreams. He also comforted me about my biggest insecurity and didn't seem to care about my body's own self-sabotage.

I should be able to have kids. I'm a woman—it's biological.

Or that's what is drilled into us from a young age.

Our worth is only measured by our wombs.

It took me a long time to realise that I'm still a woman—stupid, I know—but that's what I felt like. Not being capable of bearing children made me feel like I wasn't wanted nor desirable, like I wasn't complete, yet he knew and got to the heart of the issue. Cato reassured me about the things that were worrying me.

How can he go from holding me so tightly and promising me I'm whole to not looking me in the eye? It hurts, if I'm honest, and I find myself slumping into my work, worrying I said or did something without realising it. Maybe he's starting to hate having me around like everyone else eventually does.

"Nothing at all?" I find myself asking, trying to start a conversation.

"No," he rumbles, but I narrow my eyes. Something is nagging at me. He won't look at me, and he's clearly feeling awkward…

Is he lying to me?

I had a feeling he was, and now I'm sure of it.

"My ex used to lie to me," I start without looking at him. I feel his head snap to me as I carry on. It's not something I've told anyone before, but I have to make him understand. He's silent as I speak while looking at the research. "I loved him, or I thought I did. I think I was more in love with the idea of him and of us, of not being alone anymore. I shared everything with him, my hopes, my dreams, my fears…and my research." I pause briefly, letting that sink in.

"I was working on it in my spare time, so no one else knew. It was my passion, my hope. I was going to present it at the next open call to try and give myself a name so I could research what I wanted, but I was an idiot. I didn't see his greed until it was too late. He was an okay scientist, but he didn't have the drive to create his own research or notice the problems around us. He couldn't see past orders. Instead, to make a name for himself, he stole my research and passed it off as his own. To this day, he's working on it, being funded and praised."

Shaking my head, I curl my lip in disgust. "When I confronted him, he lied to my face and then continued to lie. He gaslit me to make me seem crazy, and it worked because I'm a woman and he's a man. He got away with it, and now I find it really hard to trust anyone." I purposely meet his eyes, letting him see my anger and disappointment over the fact he would lie to me.

"So when someone lies to me, I never forgive them," I tell him as I lock eyes with him and see the guilt eat up his pupils. "You are lying to me! Where is she?"

"Tally," he starts, holding his palms up. "Let me explain."

"No, I want the truth! I trusted you!" I scream, tears filling my eyes when I realise it's true. I trusted him, the only person I have since my asshole ex. I trusted him, and just like everyone else, he's been lying to me. All those soft, sweet moments are now tainted when faced with his guilt.

"Tal—" The door slams open, and we both turn to see his brother there.

He ignores me completely, his eyes on his friend and leader. "There's an emergency!"

Cato is on his feet in seconds, striding out of the door. I hurry after him, panting as I race down the stairs, but I'm unable to keep up. He stills at the bottom, watching in horror as one of his people screams as he is carried through the door. Blood covers nearly all of his body, and his horns are broken, but there are no obvious wounds since he's writhing too much to see anything.

"What happened?" Cato barks, a transformation coming over him. He's fierce, protective, and in control. Everyone snaps to attention.

"Human attack at the border," one of the males yells. "They were trying to find their way in. We stopped them, but Freck was shot."

"In there, now. We need healing supplies," he commands. "You, get water and send out word to patrols." He barks out orders, and I watch, dry-mouthed, as they rush to do his bidding, and when those blazing eyes turn to me, I almost shiver with desire. "Back upstairs, Talia, now."

He turns away, expecting me to follow his command, but fuck that. Someone is hurt, and I can help. Pushing all my anger and worry away for the moment, I hurry after him. The monster has been placed on a table, and the room is filled with supplies. Tying my hair back, I barge through their masses to see Cato looking him over, but he's unsure. "Where's the healer?" he demands.

"No one can find him," someone else replies worriedly.

"Let me help," I demand, and Cato looks at me, his brow furrowed in question.

"Our bodies are similar enough, and for fun, I got a medical degree." I reach across and take his hand. "I can help."

He stares into my eyes for a moment before inclining his head. Ignoring the whispers around us, I whip off my lab coat and turn to wash my hands. "We are going to need to clean him to find the wound first. I need towels, water, and antiseptic," I demand. "Cato, you're going to help me."

After thoroughly washing my hands, I move back to the monster. The supplies are there, and together, we quickly clean him up, searching for the bullet wounds. I spot it in his lower abdomen and feel around the wound. "Help me turn him slightly to the left." He does, and I peek over. "Through and through. No bullet inside of him, that's good. It's a bleeder, but I don't think it nicked anything important." I talk as I work, my hands sure and steady as I work to help this man. I feel eyes on me, but for once, I'm not nervous.

I'm confident, and when we clean, sew, and dress the wounds, I talk them through it. All the while, they stay and watch. When I'm done, I clean the rest of him before checking his horns. He passed out a little while ago, but when I prod them, he wakes up. His hands snap up to grab mine, and I freeze and look down at him. His eyes are red. Knowing Cato is ready to intervene, I hold up my hand to stop him.

All he sees is an enemy, so I keep my voice soft. "It's okay. It's Talia. I'm just helping you. You are safe, you are okay." I repeat it until he drops my hand and his eyes fade back to black.

"Sorry," he croaks out.

"Don't be," I tell him as I inspect the wounds. "You are going to be okay," I promise. "You are doing so well. You'll need to rest, no monster activities for a while, but otherwise, you'll be okay." I pat his arm in reassurance.

"Yes?" he asks, afraid.

"Yes." I nod as I clean some minor cuts, and when I'm happy he's okay, I look back to his face and smile. "You are going to be okay," I assure him once more, knowing he probably needs to hear it. I squeeze his hand and meet his pained yet relieved eyes. "I promise. Do you want any pain relief?" He hesitates, embarrassment in his eyes, and I lean in so only he can hear me. "There is no shame in it, but if you don't want the others to see, I can sneak it."

He softens and nods, and I quickly hide the syringe before plunging it into his arm. Soon enough, he's asleep. Good. He needs rest. Stepping back, I sigh, my shoulders sagging with exhaustion now that the adrenaline has worn off. My bloodied hands and arms hang limply at my sides, and when I glance up, I meet Cato's eyes. They are burning bright red and locked on me.

Swallowing, I look away and meet the confused gaze of Cato's brother. Without a word, he slips away, but not before I see him nod in respect.

"Come on, you need to clean up," Cato murmurs, taking my hand, his own covered in blood as well.

"But—" I start, looking back at my patient.

"Someone will stay with him and call if you are needed. I promise." When I agree, he leads me away, telling his people to take watch. We head upstairs hand in hand, all my anger at him lying to me gone with what I just saw and did.

The truth of the humans.

We hurt and kill these innocent people who are just trying to survive. I'm glad I could help, but it doesn't lessen my anger over it happening in the first place. I stay silent, lost in my head, and so does Cato. He's probably worried about his people.

When we are back upstairs, he leads me to the bathroom, kissing my hand softly. "Get undressed and showered. I'll be back in a minute. I'm just going to check the border reports and ask for some food."

I watch him go before stripping off my clothes. There is blood on them, so I carefully fold them and leave them on the bathroom floor. Pulling my hair tie out, I drop it into the pile and crank on the shower, watching the spray hit the porcelain base until steam curls around the room. I step inside and tug the curtain closed. Leaning my head back, I let the water sluice over me before turning and pressing my hands to the wall. I watch the blood-red tinted water swirl around my feet before being washed away.

I hear him enter the bathroom, and I can't bring myself to care, even when the shower curtain is pulled back. Usually, I would hide and gasp in horror, but I'm just so…drained. I stand here, not even looking at him, even as I feel his eyes roving over every inch of my body, heating my skin better than the shower.

"We need to talk," I tell him.

"We do, but first, let me help you clean off and thank you."

"Thank me?" I ask, lifting my head to see him watching me carefully.

"For saving one of my own when you didn't have to. You showed us all today just what humans are capable of. Yes, Talia, I plan to thank you for being so fucking amazing and not taking it out on my people. For saving him."

He holds my gaze as he steps into the shower with me. I turn, my eyes widening as I crane my neck to stare up at him. Grinning, he leans in and kisses me softly. My eyes slide closed as I lose myself in the soft, sweet kiss, but as quickly as it started, it ends, and I'm left blinking my eyes in shock when he drops to his knees before me.

"Cato," I whisper.

"Shh, Tally, just shh. Let me thank you, my little human," he murmurs, his voice rough as he stares at my body, licking his fangs. "You are so beautiful, it hurts. If only you knew what you did to me, how wild you make me, and how out of control you make me feel when I strive for constant order. You make me feel alive, Tally, just as much as you make me feel this voracious hunger."

What can a woman say to that? Not much, since Cato parts my thighs softly and gazes at my pussy so long that I start to get self-conscious. I try to close my thighs, but he keeps me spread wide for him, licking his lips as his bright red eyes clash with mine again.

"I wonder if you taste as delicious as you smell," he purrs.

Fucking hell.

Without waiting, his tongue darts out and drags across my wet folds, and he hums, digging his claws into my thighs to keep me still for him. "Fucking delicious," he rumbles before diving in, attacking my cunt with his mouth.

There is no rhyme or reason or any finesse, and I almost wince. Gods, why did I think sex with a monster would be any different than with a human man? All they care about is their own pleasure, not if I enjoy—

Fuck!

His teeth catch my clit, and I nearly scream from the sudden pleasure. His eyes dart up to mine as he growls, "I see," wickedly, and then attacks my clit.

He licks, sucks, and explores the rest of me, seeing what makes me moan, what does nothing, and what has me gripping his hair and grinding into his face. He uses it like a plan of attack. That analytical mind stores the information away and uses it to make my knees weak and my cries louder.

Once he seals his lips around my clit, I come apart with an embarrassingly loud scream, clutching his head to my pussy as I jerk and moan. When I come down from the high, I blush, releasing my tight grip on his hair, but he keeps licking me softly.

"Cato," I whine.

"Again. I need to taste every drop of your cum. I want to hear you scream and feel you claw at my head again," he snarls, dragging me closer and practically making me straddle his mouth.

Embarrassment flares through me for a moment before it fades into simmering pleasure as he lashes my clit. It's almost too much.

He doesn't relent, growling for me to come. He pushes his tongue inside me, filling me with it and making me fuck it. My feet almost slip, but he holds me in place as he feasts. My head falls back on a cry as I reach down and tweak my nipples, feeling him watch me before one clawed hand bats mine away and he takes over. He twists them harder, the edge of pain making me cry out as I grind into his mouth.

"I'm so close. Oh fuck, don't stop!" I yell, smashing my pussy onto his face as I reach for another release.

His claw pricks my nipple as his tongue thrusts into me, and I tumble over that edge once more, coming on his tongue as he purrs and pets me. He licks up every last drop just like he promised before he sits back. His smug, satisfied face grins up at me, and just then, my legs give out. His hands dart out, catch me, and pull me to him as he kisses me softly, letting me taste my own release.

"You are so perfect," he purrs, holding me to him. "And you taste even better than I imagined. I could live on just your cunt, Tally."

Fucking hell. Maybe sex with monsters is different after all. Grinning at my no doubt dumbfounded expression, he lifts me and sets me on my feet. My eyes drop to his huge, throbbing, leaking cock, which is bobbing desperately for my attention.

Standing, he captures my hands when I would have grabbed his hard length and then kisses them. "This was about you, Tally, not me. Trust me, I got enough pleasure out of watching you come for me." I shiver at the hunger in his voice before nodding, and he gently turns me.

I hesitate, but his hands grab the soap before he slowly starts to lather every inch of my body. He washes away all traces of today, each soft stroke of his hands making me relax further until I'm boneless. When he washes my hair for me, I almost cry with the careful, treasured way he does it.

He dries me off after our shower, carries me to the bed, and tucks me in next to him, making it awfully hard to stay mad at him. If he were human, I would accuse him of doing this just to lessen my anger, but I know he didn't. He did it because he wanted to, because he cares for me, and the scary thing is, I care for him too.

"I never wanted to lie to you, Talia, but I was scared of losing you." He doesn't look at me as I sit up. "It sounds crazy, I know, but if I told you, that would be it. You would go with your friend and leave me, and I would be left wondering if the rest of my life would have been different if you had just stayed, because I'm crazy about you. I never believed in destiny or fate, Tally, until you. Nothing made sense with you, yet I couldn't stop myself. Logically, I knew we were enemies, but I couldn't stop myself from falling anyway. You make me crazy in the best possible way. You make me believe in something beyond only what we can prove and see. You make me believe in love, in happiness, and in the future. You make this doubter a believer."

I just stare, having no idea what to say, but he doesn't mind.

He kisses me softly. "Just let me hold you one more time, and then I'll tell you everything. I'll let you go, Talia, just like you want."

But is it really what I want?

TWENTY-TWO

CATO

She's quiet, which is terrifying, but she doesn't move away. She lets me hold her, feeling so soft and perfect against my large body. It makes my heart ache, because I know my arms will feel empty without her inside them.

My heart will be empty without her love in it.

My smiles will be cold without her to see it.

In such a short amount of time, Talia has become my everything, and it terrifies me. What will be left when she is gone once more? Before, I was a leader, a scientist, but now I'm a mate, a leader, and a scientist in that order. A mate puts their love's happiness first, and I will do the same with her, even if it breaks my own heart.

I should have never lied to her. It was stupid, and I'm thankful she seems to be forgiving me, but I need to tell her the truth, the whole truth, and let her make her own decision. I don't want to be anything like the humans or the man before me. I don't want to hurt her, only to help her and love her fully by embracing her independence, her mind, and her intelligence.

Holding her tighter, I let myself believe for a moment this could last forever, but I know it can't. I slip from her arms and slowly gather some clothes I found for her. When she sits up, I take the opportunity to dress her, stealing touches and glances, unable to speak as I stare into her knowing, sad eyes.

Both of us feel the end of this racing towards us.

When she's dressed, I braid her hair in a warrior braid, wanting to leave something of myself with her when I'm gone so she might think of me once or twice, since my whole life will be consumed with her until the day I die.

She takes my hand and kisses it as I stand and lead her back to the lab. Once there, I sit heavily and watch her. She steps between my legs, and before she can make empty promises or try to make me feel better, I tell her the truth, which I should have done as soon as it came. "Your friend, Aria, is fine. She is with a friend of mine. Akuji, the leader of the Nightfang tribe, is a good and honourable man." She sags and tears build in her eyes, so I pull her into a hug.

"Thank God, I was so worried."

I feel even worse, so I just hold her tighter, offering comfort. "They want to meet. I let them know you are okay as well and set a neutral location. We are just waiting to hear back, and then I will take you to her. I promise." What I don't tell her is that walking away from her will rip me to shreds and leave me an empty shell.

Pulling away, she stares up at my face. "And what then?"

"Then you go home," I mutter bitterly.

For a moment, something akin to pain flashes in her stormy eyes, giving me hope.

"It will be okay," I reassure her, kissing her. "Until then, why don't we have something to eat, and then you can check on your patient? I'm betting you are wanting to."

She grins. "You're right."

"I usually am." I wink as I retrieve the tray of food left outside the door, my eyebrow rising at the piles of human food. It seems my people have fallen under Talia's spell as well and are thanking her the only way they know how—by looking after her like they would if she were one of our own.

She laughs when I put it between us, and we fall into a comfortable silence as we eat, both stealing looks at one another. All I can taste is her, even as I swallow the food, wishing I was eating her and wondering if she would let me pin her down and feast on her again. When she's done, I take her hand, and then we go to check on my warrior. He's asleep, so she gently checks his wounds before turning to me in shock, making me laugh.

"We heal quickly." I shrug, leaning into the door.

"This is sealed up and already scarring," she whispers before redressing the wound and coming towards me. "How quickly?"

She's asked questions before about healing, but seeing it in action is something else.

"It depends on the wound, but with that? The scar will be gone tomorrow. Good treatment" —I wink at her, making her blush— "combined with rest and food speed up our healing. I once had my arm almost torn off and it healed within four cycles," I explain, and she nods. I see her eyes lighting up with interest and questions.

Gathering her close, I kiss her head because she's just too damn adorable.

"You can ask away," I encourage her, and she almost jumps up and down as questions flow from her mouth. I answer as many as I can, watching her take the information and catalogue it away.

Just like I do.

As she talks, I just stare. She's magnificent.

Her stormy eyes are alight with an excitement that makes me hard, and her brilliant brain turns me on like nothing else.

Sighing, she leans into me some time later, empty of questions. "I get why you lied, but don't ever do it again. Never." She narrows her eyes on me, and I can't help but grin.

"Who thought I would ever be scared of a tiny human?" I tease.

Huffing, she slaps my chest. "And don't forget it."

I'm chuckling with her when a noise behind me has me turning to see a messenger, and I instantly sober. "They agreed to meet," he informs me. "Neutral ground, here." He hands over the note.

"It took a long time," I remark with a frown.

"Sorry, there were Darklings in the neutral territory, so I waited them out, not wanting the message to be intercepted."

"Darklings… They never come out of their holes. What are they up to?" I mutter.

"I don't know, but nothing good." He hesitates, looking to Talia, then back to me. "They… They looked like they were gathering for something—something big."

Rubbing my head, I dismiss the messenger to rest. Another worry. Darklings showing their ugly heads is never anything good, but I can't deal with it now. Instead, I look at the message and sigh, knowing we need to get ready and leave if we are to arrive on time.

"Come on, Tally, it's time to see your friend."

And it's time for me to say goodbye and walk away from the best thing to ever happen to me.

TWENTY-THREE

TALIA

The meeting is in what used to be a small park not far from Cato's territory. Still, we have to gather some warriors, which takes time, and then make our way through the city. He insists on carrying me, and when they start to run, I realise why. They are at least double my max speed, and something that would have taken me an hour only takes about thirty minutes.

The moon is high in the sky when we stop just beyond the meeting. I turn to ask Cato why, and he presses his finger to my lips and leans down. With his mouth to my ear, he whispers, "I just sent a warrior to check the area and make sure there are no traps or anything. You never know. When it's clear, he will alert us, and we will go in, but I need you to promise to stay behind me until I say okay, no matter what you see, okay?" He pulls away and gives me a very serious look. "Please, Tally."

That's what has me promising. My heart is beating so fast, I feel sick, knowing Aria is close. Part of me is relieved, knowing that she's okay, but the other half is sad this will probably be goodbye between

Cato and me. He has come to mean a lot to me, even if I can't really understand how or why.

When his warrior comes back, we move through the building we were hiding behind. They take the stairs in massive leaps that has me closing my eyes, and once on the roof, I look down to the park. There is a big red alien sprawled on some grass, his eyes closed and mouth moving as he talks to…Aria!

I want to shout, but then we start to jump over the edge of the building. I almost scream but manage to swallow it just as we land. Well, Cato does, cushioning the blow as his warriors spread out, meeting the other red aliens. They are big and clearly warriors, judging by their scars and weapons, but they are not all that different from Cato's people.

I don't spend time analysing them, though, because my eyes go to Aria. I slip from Cato's arms, and his hand wraps around the nape of my neck, comforting me and reminding me of my promise. Her eyes drink me in the same way I am her, noticing she is uninjured.

She looks great, like she's thriving here. Her skin is glowing, her eyes are bright, her hair is braided back ornately, and her clothes… She looks like one of the warriors, almost like the one who scoops her into his arms. I stiffen, but she just grins up at him.

He's a big bastard, bigger than even Cato, and covered in scars with more weapons strapped to him than I can count. "Akuji," Cato whispers to me, and I nod, watching Aria worriedly. Akuji straightens, and I move back, suddenly scared at the imposing sight he makes. Of course Cato catches me and shelters me in his arms, and I soften like the wimp I am. Aria grins at me suddenly, and I grin back, unable to stop myself.

The relief inside of me is so profound, I almost cry, my hands itching to pull her into a hug she would probably hate. I barely hear the words exchanged by Cato and Akuji, keeping my eyes on her. Aria is obviously following along, because she smacks her monster, then more words are exchanged before Akuji suddenly looks ready to attack Cato, and I almost scream. Cato seems unbothered, stroking every inch of skin he can to settle me, and I force myself back into the conversation.

"I meant no offence," Cato rumbles, and my whole body lights up, remembering the way he rumbled between my legs.

Aria slides before Akuji, scolding him like a child before looking at me. Something gleams in her eyes before her chin goes up with a defiant expression. "Fuck this," she mutters, and using her impressive speed and muscles, she slips away from Akuji. I do the same to Cato, who snarls after me as I meet her halfway. We embrace, our limbs tangling as she holds me tightly and tears form in my eyes.

I thought I had lost her. I thought I was all alone.

I want to tell her everything, but I'm choking my words back, not wanting to cry on her. She would hate that. When she pulls back, she notices the tears in my eyes but doesn't comment.

"I thought you were dead," I murmur, her eyes searching my face as I search hers.

"Nah. I did adopt a monster and a tiger though." She laughs, and we both glance over when there's a purr. I spot a tiger moving through the other monsters and swallow hard, not willing to look at it further after what happened with the last tiger.

"Of course you did."

"And you?" she questions, her voice stern and scary. "Do I need to kill them?"

I hear Cato, but I ignore him for now. "No, no, they have been… nice," I hedge, wanting to tell her everything but unsure where to start. I smile, unable to help it, knowing she'll get a kick out of it as much as I will. "I promise I'm okay. I'm working, actually."

"Of course you are," she repeats, making us both grin at each other.

We're just two women from completely different walks of life brought together by chance and bonded by pain and trauma. I never knew how important it was for me to see that she was okay, but now I'm almost crying in relief, so happy to see a friendly face.

"You have a brave human there, Akuji. I truly meant no offence. I know names are important to warriors and their mates. I did not know," Cato calls from behind me, interrupting my and Aria's moment.

The big monster, Akuji, comes up behind Aria, and I gulp. "Well, now you do," Akuji replies, winding his arms around Aria and pulling her away from me, leaving me unsure, so I step back to Cato, needing his strength. "You are my human's friend. I am glad you are not dead. She's quite crazy, so I feared she might have killed them."

When Aria softens, I look at the big monster to see the same love I see in hers reflected back in his eyes. That has me smiling at him, and all fear I felt for him leaves me. No one could be bad if they love her and her him.

"Yeah, I've noticed that about her. The same goes for her though. I might not be as strong or as capable as her—"

There's a growl coming from Cato, which I roll my eyes at.

"But I care for her. If you hurt her, then I will try my hardest to do some damage."

Akuji smirks at my threat, as does Aria, but he nods in respect. "Understood, human."

Aria pulls away from his arms and slings her own around me. "You need to tell us everything that happened. Seriously, I was so worried, and I don't like that feeling," she tells me softly, and I can tell it cost her to admit that.

I struggle for words, as so much has happened, but I settle on simple ones instead. "This is about more than you and me, Aria."

"What do you mean?" she asks, frowning at me, obviously feeling the heaviness behind my words. I lower my voice, feeling Cato drawing closer but needing to get this out.

He doesn't stop me, he never would, but I lean into him, needing that support now more than ever. "The research they sent me to get was gone for a reason. Cato had taken it. He feared what it contained and the ramifications of the humans getting their hands on it again." That makes her raise her eyebrows, but I hurry on, needing to tell her everything. "The information contained, Aria… It shocked me to my core. The humans did this, Aria. They made them."

"I know," is all she says, and I gawk for a moment before shaking my head, needing her to understand.

"But it's more than that, no wonder they want this information back. They would go to any lengths to protect it."

"Talia, tell me," she demands, clearly wanting to get these answers from me.

"It's so much more, Aria." I shake my head, knowing I probably look scared of the truth, of what I will find when I dig deeper. "What they did to them, what they are continuing to do—"

"Incoming!" someone yells, interrupting my words.

Aria is yanked behind Akuji, and Cato pulls me behind him, so I can barely see what's happening. I peer through gaps as a man rides up on a horse—well, a monster. The horse is a huge, black beast, and the monster on top of it is no less scary, with a wicked smirk showing cracked fangs. One of his eyes sports a massive scar, and it's white compared to his other black eye. His body is huge, bigger than any monster here, and more scarred. He's a darker red also, standing out against the sea of brighter red monsters. Behind him is an array of similarly coloured scarred monsters.

Cato and Akuji work together to protect me and Aria, who refuses to cower like I do.

"Samael," Akuji calls, and Cato lets him speak, happy to watch. No doubt Cato is looking for weakness, for threats, and forming a strategy to protect his people and me.

"Akuji," he greets with a sneer. "Thank you for our latest fighter, he fits in well."

"Why are you here?" Akuji demands as I shrink further into myself when the monster's gaze focuses on me. That one look is filled with such disgust, I actually shiver.

"There was a meeting called, was there not? We were invited." Samael grins, leaping from his horse.

"Yes, but you never come to them," Cato replies in confusion. Laying my hand on his back, I move closer, seeking his comfort and protective arms. He needs to focus, but I am unable to stop myself.

"Well, now we do," Samael snarls. His voice is dark and edgy and filled with such anger and hatred, it hits me like a whip.

This one hates humans a lot, but he also seems to hate everyone. I never want to be around him alone, that's for sure.

"And why's that?" Akuji demands.

"Because it interests us. The fact that you both have humans standing next to you and not chained up shows me how weak you are and how much you might not care," he sneers, pacing before us like a caged animal as I shrink into Cato.

He reaches back, wrapping one arm around me.

"Care?" Akuji repeats.

"That human warriors are currently surrounding the wall with weapons." Samael smirks as he drops that bomb.

My eyes widen as we all stare, and then chaos ensues.

TWENTY-FOUR

CATO

"What?" Akuji snarls.

I try to remain calm, even as I pull Talia closer, needing to protect her. I'm worried they are here for her.

Akuji must be having the same internal debate, because Aria comforts him. "They didn't come when I was over the wall with Talia, so it's not for us. It's strange, though, that they would do it now."

"Why?" I demand, needing to understand so I can better protect Talia.

"They only came now, after the other woman came through the wall, so what do they want? You? They would have come before now if they wanted another war with the monsters, and if they wanted us, they would have come days ago. So logically, they want the woman." Aria's eyes go to Samael. "The woman you took."

"You took a woman?" I roar, red covering my vision. The idea of this…this bastard kidnapping an innocent human woman triggers my protective instincts to be more beast than man. I feel her hand, her soft little hand, at my back, anchoring me, and then her lips ghost over my skin there, back and forth, until I'm no longer debating ripping Samael's head clean off.

If only Talia knew his reputation, what he is capable of, and what he is. She would be terrified even to be near him. He's more monster than any of us and has proven it time and time again with his actions—actions that landed him in the Darkling territory all alone years ago before he started his own tribe of misfits.

In fact, I shuffle us farther back away from him, not trusting him or his erratic behaviour, not near my mate. I don't want to start a war, but if he so much as looks at her again, he's dead.

"She came into our territory through the wall. The laws are clear," Samael snaps.

My fear for the innocent woman only ratchets higher. She has no idea what she walked into. She was probably running from the humans, and instead, she stumbled into something much worse.

My logical side rears its head then, because if she was running and willing to enter the forgotten city filled with us to get away from whomever was chasing her, then she must know something big, something we could use to protect our people and mates. Akuji must be thinking the exact same thing, because his words echo my thoughts.

"She must know something," he murmurs. "We need to find out what."

"She is our prisoner, so we will discover what she knows." Samael smirks viciously.

Blood roars in my ears. I know he will torture her and do unspeakable things to her. Akuji wasn't around when Samael went off the deep end, becoming nothing more than the monster even our people called him.

He was always different, and we all understood why, but he gave into that.

He became the darkling, a monster even our people fear, and now he has a human as a prisoner—one of the very creatures he hates most in the world.

"If you hurt one hair on her head, I will rip you to pieces," Akuji warns, once again proving we are in sync.

"He won't," Aria says slowly, meeting Samael's eyes. "Because if the humans want her and they find out he killed or hurt her, then they will come for him and his people. He would be responsible for starting a war again, and if I'm not wrong, breaking your laws. Isn't that right?" She looks at her mate then, and I see the pride shining in his eyes. The fool. I shake my head, pulling Talia closer, glad she's not painting herself with a target against that beast.

"That's right, little human," Akuji praises, and I look away, feeling like I'm interrupting something. The way they look at each other… I wish Talia looked at me like that, as if I hung the moon and stars for her, but that's selfish, and I'm happy with where we are. She's my mate, my love, even if she never wants to be. I will never push her or hurt her like everyone else has. I will simply be here to steady her and protect her from a cruel world that doesn't see her greatness, her kindness, and her beauty.

Samael growls a warning, making me unleash my claws as Akuji steps in front of his mate. "Fine, she is your prisoner, but you will ask her, and you will not hurt or touch her in any way. If I find out you did, the tribes will come together and we will destroy you."

It would take all of us. In the time that he has spent licking his wounds in his dark lands to the north, Samael has become stronger and more feral. He's an opponent we don't want to tangle with if we don't have to, but I know, one day, we will, as he slowly sinks into madness.

Not today, though, not with Talia here. She could get hurt, and I would never forgive myself. With my mate's safety in mind, I step in to diffuse the situation before it leads to bloodshed. "Enough. We cannot afford infighting if the humans are coming for us. We have to work together. While we are waiting to find out what the human knows, we must come up with a plan to deter and watch the humans at our borders."

"What do you suggest?" Akuji questions, knowing when to listen to me, since I was the one who first helped split the lands and come up with the tribal territories as well as our safety protocols. Even so, his eyes flick to Samael in warning.

I need to keep his attention before he makes a move. I need him to understand, for them all to understand. My first instinct is to protect our people, but in this moment, I don't really know how, and the uncertainty in my words reflects that. "Like I said, we work together. They haven't attacked yet, which means they are either watching us or waiting for something. We must do the same—watch them and be prepared in case they attack again."

"Cato is right. I say we work in teams to patrol our borders and post sentries on the wall to observe them. That way, we can be prepared if they attack. We should also set traps at every entry point, an early warning system," Akuji responds, thinking through my logic and nodding.

"Logically, they would attack during the day," Aria murmurs. "It's when they would feel safest, in the brightness of daylight. You can't watch them during the day, but I can." She looks at Akuji, sure and strong. "Put me in the rotation."

"Aria, are you sure? These are your people," he questions.

"My people who are threatening to attack and kill innocents, monster or not, and threatening to start another war over their own secrets. They sent us in here knowing that. You are my people. Your people are the only ones who care about me and whom I care about. So yes, I might be human and they might be human, but don't lump us together. I want to avoid a war as much as you, Akuji. Beyond that wall is the slums, where innocent, starving people are just trying to survive. They would be the first casualties, and I won't let that happen."

Samael's eyebrow rises before he shutters his expression. Tilting up Aria's chin, Akuji forces her to meet his eyes, and I look away once more. "You have a warrior's heart, my little human, and I am honoured you chose me as your mate."

Aria chuckles. "So you'll let me do it?"

"I do not control you," Akuji snaps. "I know you are capable, and I will watch from the darkness of the shelters nearby in case you need help."

"Of course you will." She laughs.

Feeling uncomfortable as they just lovingly stare at each other, I try to get us back on track and get Talia away from Samael as quickly as possible. "Samael, do you agree to these terms? Are you willing to post sentries on your wall and report if any attacks are imminent?"

"And if the humans breach our lands, am I allowed to kill them then?" he mocks.

"Of course. They know the rules," Akuji replies. "They cross into our lands, and they die."

"Yet you have two humans with you," he points out.

"Two innocent humans who came here for sanctuary," Akuji almost hisses, his eyes narrowed. "If you want to get to them, you will have to go through me." He pushes Aria to one of his warriors and spreads his arms wide, his head tilted back in challenge. "Come on, Samael, I'm right here. Take me if you can."

Brilliant, we are nothing better than quarrelling animals.

But it works, and Samael submits…for now. We all know it won't last.

It's not in his nature.

"Just what I thought," Akuji sneers. "Stop fighting with us and focus on our enemies. They want something from our land, maybe to start another war. We need to be united as one—one people, one fighting unit. It's the only way we will survive. We will not be the bloodthirsty monsters they created and unleashed. We will be warriors protecting our city, our people, and our home. We will not start this, but if they come for us, they will find a fight they cannot win."

"That's hot," Aria remarks. We all look at her, and she grins. "Oops, forgot about your amazing hearing."

"Fine," Samael concedes.

"We lie low and play the long game, keep communications open between our people." Akuji looks to me then for answers.

"We will continue trying to understand the research they wanted to see and what it means. We don't have nearly enough answers yet," I reply vaguely, not giving much away.

Akuji nods, happy enough with that. "Good, keep me updated. Samael, let us know when the female talks, and if you cannot handle her, send her to my tribe. Aria will get the truth from her."

"Girls club." She holds up her hand and looks around as we frown at her. "Monsters don't high five? Okay then." She drops it.

There's a giggle from behind me, which makes me smile—Talia. The sound is so innocent, so carefree, it has my heart pounding. My fingers itch to pull her close and never let her go.

"Then we all know what must be done. We had better get back to our people and spread the word. I will send weapons to you both," Akuji declares, unaware that I'm debating stealing my mate and running far away where she will be safe from everyone and everything, but I can't. I have a duty to my people, all my people, and Talia wouldn't let me do that anyway.

"We don't need any," Samael spits.

"Fine. Cato?"

"We could do with some. I have been training my people. Even though they don't enjoy killing, they are sufficient, but we do not have enough to go around," I admit.

"Good, I will send some. If the humans want a war, a war they will get."

TWENTY-FIVE

TALIA

I don't want to let Aria go, not because I'm afraid, but because I will genuinely miss her. I don't know when we will see each other again, or even if we will. I have hope, but in this world, nothing is certain.

Anything could happen.

I feel it on the horizon, a change…war.

The humans want to start another war.

I hold Aria, the tiger making her pull away with a laugh. After promising to communicate through the messengers, I watch her go with teary eyes. As soon as she's out of sight, I turn to Cato. He scoops me in his arms and holds me tight, the warmth and safety he offers instantly making me relax.

"Shh, Tally, everything is okay. She will be fine. Akuji loves her, that much is evident. He will do everything he can to protect her, and that's a lot. I wouldn't mess with him."

I laugh, lifting my head to meet his eyes. "How do you always know what to say?" I murmur, searching the black depths of his gaze.

Grinning, he flashes his fangs as he leans down and presses his forehead to mine. "Because we have the same thought process, my little human." Without looking away from me, he calls orders to the others. "Send the word—extra patrols and wall duty. I want everyone on high alert. I will meet you back at the nest. There is something I need to do first." Without waiting for his warriors to reply, he takes off with me in his arms at full speed.

Burying my head in his chest, I close my eyes and listen to his thumping heart, letting it settle my anxiety. The motion of his body is smooth, and he holds me tight as he runs. I don't know where we are going. He has someplace in mind, and I can't protest, not when it means I get time with him.

I'm still mad about the Aria thing, but I can't carry on for too long since he only did it because he wanted to protect me and keep me close. It's kind of sweet actually. I also can't stay mad at him when he protected me at that meeting, keeping that weird Samael away from me. I can almost feel Cato's relief, though, that he gets to take me away and not leave me with Aria.

And to be honest, I feel the same.

I feel happy with him, protected and supported.

Safe.

Who knew that all it would take for me to lean on someone and trust them again would be a seven-foot red monster with a forked tongue and tail? Not me, that's for sure, but I can't help but think I don't see our differences anymore. I only see the things that make him unique, that make him Cato, the man who makes me laugh and talks science with me.

It's scary how dependent I have become, and how much I value his input and his warm smile. The last time my heart broke, I told myself I would protect it in the future and never hand it over so easily again.

But Cato? He's stealing a piece at a time. It was so slow and careful, I didn't even notice until the thought of being parted from him actually made my heart ache and my stomach twist. Leaning in, I kiss his chest and nuzzle closer. He nearly stumbles, and I can't help but giggle. When I look up, he's grinning down at me.

I close my eyes again and just hold on, letting him take me where he wants. Wherever it is, I know it will be beautiful, just like everything he shows me in his world.

Okay, so beautiful might not have been the best word to use. I stare at the crumbling, dirty, cracked cement steps leading to a twisted iron gate with a huge, grimy sign above it declaring it's a subway. The location half is broken off, and the light above it flickers as if it's not quite sure it wants to work.

Honestly, it looks sketchy as hell.

"A subway?" I ask slowly, confused.

Placing me on my feet, he grins down at me. "You should know by now, Tally, not everything you see is the truth here." With that mysterious parting sentiment, he captures my hand and tugs me after him towards the dubious-looking subway.

"Uh-huh, yeah. See, if you brought me here to kill me, could we not? Like, if I'm going to die, I would rather it wasn't in a dodgy-looking subway. Maybe like a meadow? Yeah, a cute little meadow with flowers, and you would kiss me softly and say you have no choice." I squeak as he turns and glares down at me.

"Talia, what on earth are you talking about?" he asks.

"Erm, nothing," I mutter.

He leans down into my face. "I would never kill or hurt you in any way. Doing that would be the equivalent of ripping my own heart out, little human. When will you understand that?" I gulp, and he sighs. "But you need to decide if you trust me or not." With that, he turns and walks away, leaving me there. "If you trust me, you'll follow me, even though you're not sure, but if you don't, I'll take you back to Aria and Akuji now, because I will never stop trying to give you the world, and you will never stop being unsure of it."

I hesitate for a moment before hurrying after him and taking his hand. He doesn't turn, but I squeeze it and slip in front of him. "I do trust you, Cato, more than anyone I ever have before, and that scares me."

"It scares me too," he admits as he leans down and cups my chin. "But I'm not running away just because it's scary. I never will, not from you. I'll always run towards you."

Unsure what to say to that, I just nod, and he grins.

"One day, you'll believe that, and I'll be there waiting with open arms, but for now, let me show you what I wanted to before you thought I was going to murder you."

"Hey!" I protest. "It was a valid thought since you brought me here," I grumble, making him chuckle. The rich, deep sound sends a shiver through me.

I let him pull me down the steps to a metal gate, which he pushes inwards. It opens to a double door, which he easily opens and slips inside, pulling me with him. At first, it's all black. I strain to see, but it's no good, so I reach out and grip his arm. "I can't see." I hate how weak my voice is.

"Oh!" He groans. "I forgot your eyes aren't as adaptive as ours. One second." He lets go of my hand, and I wait. My breathing is loud in the otherwise quiet space, but then I hear a click.

A moment later, light flares, forcing me to close my eyes, and when I open them, they water from the sudden light, but I can see, thank god. He lit two lanterns, which hang from the ceiling in the archway we are standing under. The white tile floor is spotlessly clean, as are the walls, despite some old graffiti. Signs, posters, road signs, and lights have been hung along the walls—everything scavenged from the city.

"Come on." He holds out his hand, and I take it as I look around. He leads me farther to some broken escalators, where a glow comes from the bottom. I follow him down, our steps loud, and as we descend, neon lights start to appear. I see arrows pointing down and bar signs, all lighting the area in a cool glow.

"What is this place?" I ask, my voice soft.

"You'll see," is all he says.

Feeling less like he might murder me, I keep my eyes open wide and scan everything, and when we reach the bottom, I just stop and gawk. "Welcome to the Hideout." Cato grins back at me, sweeping his hand out to encompass the entire area. "It's the one place where my people and those from Akuji's tribe can go and meet in neutral territory. They can drink, eat, and enjoy their time together. It's a place for us monsters to be free." He smirks.

I gulp and just stare, drinking everything in. To the left, they turned an old ramp into a stage, where a red monster lady currently sings in a deep, rough sexy voice. Before her are tables made of old barrels, boxes, and a few wooden tables with chairs spread around and monsters crowded everywhere. To the right is a bar, where three monsters make drinks and food. There's also a dance floor with a few dancing monsters.

There are stairs towards the back leading up to a glass walkway, which seems to have been turned into a viewing area, crowded with talking and laughing monsters.

At the old tracks, there's a subway train that's been transformed as well.

The subway carts are now eating areas, with booths and lounges. Another subway train is a bar, and a third seems to be a shop of some kind. The whole place is lit by neon lights and strung with fairy lights. I can't see beyond the train, but there seems to be walkways there too.

"Beyond are the fighting rings, betting areas, and, well…areas." He winks at me, making me blush as I nod.

"It's amazing," I whisper, and the wide grin he shoots me is worth it as he takes my hand.

"No human has ever set foot here before. You're the first, Talia, and you will be the last." I swallow and meet his eyes, knowing he's giving me much more than his trust, but the trust of all of the monsters. This is their haven, their safe place, and I know the location. He's trusting me and showing everyone he trusts me.

They stare. Some of his people are used to me and either wave or ignore me, while some of Akuji's monsters don't seem surprised, just curious. There are one or two hostile looks, but I ignore them, understanding why they would hate a human and not trust me. They have nothing to worry about, however, because I would never hurt or betray them, especially Cato.

I let Cato lead me through their masses to a booth I didn't notice. It's to my right and almost behind an alcove. One can see everything from that table, and there is a red rope around it. He strides past the rope and leads me into the ripped red leather booth with the table before it marred by claw marks. Pulling me into his side, he lounges back and watches his people. "Your own booth, huh?"

"For the leaders." He grins without looking down at me. "It's so we don't have to fight for a table. It's a perk, one I don't use often."

"You come here a lot?" I ask, leaning into his side with my head turned up to peer at him.

He shrugs. "When I'm not working, so not really, I guess." He frowns as if not realising that.

"You work too much." I nod. "I do the same."

"I guess we are very much alike then," he purrs, leaning down to kiss my head softly.

"I guess we are." I grin and then jump when some drinks are banged down before me. A female glares at me before smiling suggestively at Cato and walking away, her hips and tail swaying. I blink, turning to Cato, who seems totally oblivious as he takes his drink and sips it.

"Erm…" I hedge. "Who was that?"

"Who was who?" he asks, looking down at me in confusion, and that's when I realise he truly didn't notice her or the obvious jealousy pouring from her, which in turn triggered my own. Cato isn't mine, and I guess I never thought about him being with anyone else or them wanting him, but it makes sense. He's strong, capable, sexy, smart, and a leader.

"The female clearly wanted you or has had you and was jealous of me," I admit, grabbing my drink to fiddle with the straw.

"Really?" He frowns, looking around. "Why?"

"Why was she jealous?" I ask bitterly. "Oh I don't know, because you are strong as hell, so sexy it hurts, smart—" I bite it off and sigh. "She was jealous, she wants you. Don't let me stop you. Go ahead." I wave my hand.

Suddenly, his claw-tipped hand grips my chin and softly turns me to face him. "You're jealous," he murmurs as if he's in shock.

"No need to shout it," I mutter, ripping my chin away before sighing. "I just… I get it, okay? You need to be with one of your kind." He lets me ramble, and when I glance at him, he's grinning widely, so I narrow my eyes. "What?"

"You're adorable," he murmurs and leans in, running his lips across my cheek. I try to jerk away, but he holds me tight, gripping my neck to keep me there. "I have not been with anyone here, and the only one I want is you, so don't be jealous. As cute and as proud as it makes me, I don't want you upset."

"Yeah, but you have all these women at your beck and call. I never even thought about it. Oh god, did I make friends with one of your exes?"

He's laughing again, and I cross my arms, fuming as he laughs at me.

"Tally," he begins, but I ignore him. "Talia, look at me now," he orders, so I do, softening when he reaches out and cups my cheek. "You have not befriended an ex—"

"You don't know—"

"I do because I have never been with anyone," he admits without shame, and my mouth drops open as I stare.

"What? You are a virgin?" I whisper. "A monster virgin." I giggle, and he grins. "Oh god, you are!"

"Yes, and proud." He shrugs. "So no jealousy, please."

"But why? Trust me, any woman would beg to be with you. Human or monster," I say, and he eyes me with a grin before shrugging.

"I hoped that one day, I would find my mate, and when I did, I didn't want her to be upset or jealous of my past. That wasn't fair. A lot of monsters are happy to lie with whomever before their mate. We are a very free people, and sex is an instinct, a need, but I was happy to wait for her. To me, sex is more than just satisfying an instinct. It's for love. It is forever."

Wow. I just stare in shock and something else—pain. He's waiting for his mate. His perfect match is out there. I'm guessing it's like marriage but an instinctual thing for him, like animals. He's waiting to give himself to her, and I've been kissing and touching him. It hurts, a lot actually, and I'm suddenly jealous of a woman who might not even exist or he doesn't even know.

"I see." I turn away, sipping my drink. I feel him frowning at me, so I comfort him. "It's an amazing thought process. She's very lucky."

"No, that's me," he murmurs, pulling me closer, but his embrace no longer feels like a sanctuary, because I feel guilty for stealing his touch, his time, away from his mate—a woman I hate already, because she'll have him and I want him.

I want him to be mine, and he never will be.

TWENTY-SIX

CATO

Something is wrong with Talia, but I don't know what. I keep asking, and she just says she's tired. Is that it? I try to take her back to rest, but she wants to stay. She talks to my people, drinks, and even dances with me and a few of my people, but something is bugging her, and I hate that she's keeping it from me.

I'll bide my time, knowing she will eventually share when she's worked through it, just like I do. Until then, I hold her tighter and sway to the soothing croon of our best singer, Rainer.

After dancing, I let her lead me through the subway carts so she can see everything. At the stalls for clothes, she searches through the racks, her hand hesitating over some tight leather pants with lacing up the back and a few other items. Discreetly, I nod at the seller, and when Talia looks away, I pay for them and ask for them to be delivered.

I can see she is starting to tire, so I take her hand, bid everyone goodbye, and lead her back out into the city. Once there, she takes a deep breath. "Can we walk back and not run?" The words are the only ones she's said for a while, so I nod, willing to give her everything if it will make her smile again.

Tomorrow, I have to deal with a potential war, so tonight, I just want to spend my time with her. Unwilling to let her pout, I grab her hand and walk with her, pointing out my favourite architecture or places. I tell her stories as well, and she eventually starts to soften, smiling and even laughing, and I feel like I've achieved a great victory.

I stop to show her the old preschool and the high school, knowing she'll like that. We end up racing each other at the track under the moonlight, and of course I let her win, which she slaps me for. After that, I show her the artist warehouse, which is still forgotten, the kiln left half full and unoccupied tables. She wanders around with the same awe I did, and I can't help but watch her with a pounding heart.

I get to keep her for a little while longer, but how much longer? Won't it make it that much worse when she leaves?

I should be worried for my people, for what the humans are up to, but instead, I'm worried about Talia. What will she do back over the wall if she gets lonely again? Will she miss me the way I will miss her, as if she's taken my entire soul and heart with her? Even now, I can't bear having a few steps between us, as if needing to be close to feel her heat and have the floral scent that's all her wrapping around me and settling my chaotic thoughts.

When she turns to me, I grip her chin, unable to help it, and lower my head to hers. I kiss her and silence whatever she was going to say, and when I pull back, I smile at her. "Couldn't resist," I say. "We should get back, it will be sunrise soon."

"Right, and we should work."

"We should," I whisper just inches away from her lips. "Tell me to stop, Tally."

"What?" she asks, searching my eyes.

"Tell me to stop," I beg as I lean in and kiss her again, dropping my hands to her ass and pulling her close. I groan at the feeling of her body plastered against me. "Tell me to."

She doesn't. She kisses me back, biting my lips and tangling her tongue with mine. She strokes my fangs until I lift her and set her onto the closest table before forcing myself between her thighs. I taste the heady flavour of her on her tongue, feel her warmth against me, and inhale the scent of her arousal.

Laying her back, I kiss down her throat and neck before returning to her lips. I need them on mine as my hands explore every inch of her, tracing her delicious body as she moans for me. Slowly, she starts to pull away before pushing me back. I go willingly, both of us panting heavily. "We should stop," she whispers raggedly, but her voice is confused, like my own would be.

"Of course, Tally," I whisper and kiss her once more before helping her down and taking her hand, wanting to show her that there will never be any hard feelings between us. I will never push her or be upset with her. I will protect her and heed her wishes. She's in charge when it comes to us. My tiny human mate holds my heart and future in her hands, and she doesn't even know it.

We reach home just as everyone is bedding down for the night. She goes to check on her patient as I check on the border patrol. They report the same as before— humans at the border and walls but no movement—which is good for now.

When Talia comes back, she's shaking her head. "He's fully healed and on patrol. Incredible. I'll talk to him tomorrow, but for now, I need a shower and some sleep before we start work."

"Me too, Tally." I take her hand, and when she yawns halfway up the stairs, I pick her up and carry her to our nest. She snuggles into my arms in that way I love that makes me feel complete, and she's asleep before I even reach our rooms. Laying her down, I kiss her head softly as I stare at her beautiful face.

"How did I ever live without you?" I murmur, cupping her cheek. "How will I ever live after you?"

TWENTY-SEVEN

TALIA

I sleep hard, and when I wake up, I know it's been a long time since I fell asleep. Cato isn't next to me, and for a moment, sadness engulfs me before I realise it's probably for the best. I shouldn't have even let him kiss me last night, not when he's saving himself for another, but I was weak, so very weak, and part of me wanted to be his first kiss, even when I know he will never go further.

It's selfish and stupid, so instead of thinking on it or the fact that his scent covers my skin in that addictive way I've come to love, I stumble to the shower. After taking care of business, I find some clothes neatly folded on our nest and blink. My own were getting ragged, but these are the ones I saw last night. I hold them close, tears welling in my eyes as I realise he either went back and got them for me or sent someone. I didn't even say anything, he just noticed I liked them and bought them.

Just like that.

Cato isn't in the other room after I get dressed, so I head downstairs, more comfortable here now. Don't get me wrong, some people are still afraid of me or hate me, but when I wave and greet those I know, I don't feel as scared. I'm bombarded by kids almost immediately, and I laugh and play with them before excusing myself to find my patient and check in. If he was on patrol, he has to be okay, but I need to see for myself. I can barely believe how quickly they can heal. It's incredible, and it also makes me wonder what the humans did to create such quick healing in their genes. Was it a random side effect or something they mixed into their DNA when creating them? As usual, the questions fill my head as I wander the corridors. I ask a few people about my patient's location, and they eventually direct me to the third floor. I take the stairs they indicated and find myself on a floor I haven't been on before.

This has to be one of the living floors. Some of the doors are missing to what looks like old offices and lecture rooms, with beds and cute little houses made within. I spot drawings on some of the walls from the kids, clothes hung up to dry, and weapons piled neatly on the side next to plates and pots. It's domestic, and I find myself smiling as I wander down the tiled corridor. There are notice boards that are still standing, and I stop before one to peer at the home-made posters. There is one for a nest get-together, another for a hunt, and a third for a book group. Looking at that, I can hardly believe these are the monsters we are raised to hate and fear.

They are just like us.

Just then, a loud cranking noise reaches my ears. Turning, I look to the closest room and notice what I thought were boarded up windows at the back are actually shades. The metal shutters are rising, which must mean the sun has set. I guess I'm getting used to this nocturnal lifestyle, which isn't a surprise since I spent most of my time at the lab at night to avoid as many people as possible.

I watch the shades rise and wonder how they did it. Is it based on the time or lack of sunlight?

That's something to ask Cato, because I spot the monster I need leaning into his door farther down. Hurrying closer, I smile at him when he sees me. He smiles back, flashing fang, and the monster he's talking to narrows his gaze on me. That makes me miss a step, but I continue forward.

"Hey, I just wanted to see how you're feeling," I call when I stop nearby, but not too close since the other monster is throwing me dirty looks. It takes all my excitement away, and I find my shoulders rounding like I'm back at school being bullied.

"Great, thanks to you," my patient replies happily, and then he glances at his friend, stepping before me with a growl. "Don't look at her like that, she saved my life."

"She did nothing," he hisses. "She's a human, or have you forgotten?"

"No, I haven't, but maybe you've forgotten the fact that she never hurt us. In fact, she went out of her way to help me. She reads to your kids so you can spend time with your mate, and she's even trying to help us figure out what the humans want at our walls. Stop being an ass and living in the past, times are changing. Not all humans are our enemies."

"We'll see," is all the male mutters before turning on his heel and storming off.

"I'm sorry!" we say at the same time, making us laugh.

"I really did come to see if you're okay."

"Come in." He jerks his head behind him, and I step in to see a huge lecture hall filled with beds. "Sorry it's busy, it's where most of the single patrols and warriors sleep."

"Don't worry about it. I shared a dorm at school with three other girls, it was crazy," I tease. "Come and sit." I point at an abandoned desk in the corner with two chairs. He takes one, and I take the other. He has no shirt on, none of them ever do, so it's easy to see the completely healed wound.

I just stare.

"If I didn't know better, I would think you were checking me out," he teases, making my head jerk up, and a laugh bubbles out of me, even as I turn red.

"Sorry, it's just I've never seen such excellent healing before," I tell him.

"I'll pretend you were talking about my muscles for my vanity's sake," he flirts, flexing his muscles to make me grin. He's funny, harmless too, and I find myself relaxing. I don't have to worry about what he's thinking, if he hates me, or if he wants to kill me. It's nice.

He also stood up to his friend, which means a lot.

"You know, humans aren't bad-looking. They could even be attractive if you can get past the lack of natural defences."

"Don't be so sure. I can knee you in the balls faster than you can claw me," I tease, making him laugh.

"Are all humans as funny and smart as you?" he muses out loud, watching me. Grinning, I lean in like I'm going to tell him a secret.

"No, sorry, I'm one of a kind." I wink, teasing again, and he grins.

"I see why Cato is so eager to keep you." He lifts his head. "Isn't that right, Reigner?"

I turn in surprise. I hadn't even heard Cato sneak up on us, but there he is, leaning against the door with an amused expression. "Stop flirting with her," he admonishes, but it's soft and caring. "How are you feeling? I came to check, but I see Tally has already beat me to it."

"She did. Sorry, Doc." He winks at me. "So, Tally, do you—"

"Nobody calls her Tally but me," Cato hisses. Moving so fast, I don't even see him, Cato drags the monster from his chair and points his finger in his face, and the monster holds up his hands, grinning.

"Sorry, Cato." He smiles wider, definitely not sorry as he winks at me. "See you around, human." He slips past an angry Cato and whistles as he walks off. I'm pretty sure he did it just to test Cato, but I roll my lips in and place my hand on a vibrating Cato. He whirls, but when he sees it's me, he softens as all the fight leaves him.

"Come on, Tally. We need to get you food, and then it's time to work. We need to figure out what these humans are up to." I take his hand and let him pull me to my feet. He keeps it as he leads me downstairs to the others, and I find myself grinning at that, despite the fact that he doesn't belong to me.

I can't be his Tally. Not forever.

After eating downstairs with everyone, we excuse ourselves back to the lab, ignoring the knowing looks. They think we are sneaking away to do something else.

Cato dons his lab coat and even brings me one, and then side by side, we start to work and catalogue the research. We won't have time to go through all of it in a hundred years, but we need to pinpoint what is important and what can help us.

It's a slow, arduous task, but it sets my mind at ease. There's no time for worries or questions, and no time to even analyse the strange feelings I have for my lab mate. We just work seamlessly, barely needing to talk, which to some might seem awkward and strange, but I enjoy it. I hate having to repeat myself or dumb down my intellect to work with others, and with him, I don't have to. He knows what I need or mean, and I do the same for him, understanding his thought process, since it's very similar to my own.

It's relaxing, despite the deadline we are under, and I find myself smiling as I work, thoroughly enjoying myself in the lab in a way I haven't for a long time. I haven't truly enjoyed myself since my mother and father first took me to theirs and gave me my own desk to conduct experiments. Ever since then, I was always racing—racing to graduate, racing to make a name for myself, racing to be better than the men around me.

The truth is, I already was, and if I were born as a man, I would have been promoted many times over and given my own lab before now. It annoys me, because my gender holds me back, and it's something I couldn't understand for a long time. Why does being female affect how I should succeed? Why should it put this invisible barrier on anything I can do? It shouldn't. There was always so much fight and talk for equality among the sexes, yet even now, it still exists. Women still have to fight twice as hard to be at the same, if not lesser, position of a man in the same field.

Our world is broken, meant to keep women down, created and run by men. It always benefits them.

But not here.

Here, there is true equality. Women can be warriors who are just as good, if not better, than men. They can be mothers and work. They can do whatever they want to without judgment or penalisation for being born with a vagina, and maybe that's the reason I'm starting to fall in love with this forgotten city. Despite the fact everyone thinks these monsters are feral beasts, and they are in some ways, they are more advanced than humans.

Hours later, I sit back, scrubbing at my face in annoyance. "I can't make sense of half of these notes. It's so hard to work backwards from the end results."

"Think it through logically then." Cato turns to me, patiently ignoring my rapidly deteriorating mood. "What do they want?"

"I don't know. To create more monsters?" I throw my hands in the air and think that through. "Which, if they do, means they need the original research. Do they want to make more or hide something?" I lean forward, and something seems to click. I look at him, open-mouthed, to see him grinning at me. I narrow my gaze. "What?"

"I just know you can figure this out, Tally. If anyone can, it's you and your brain." He shakes his head. "It's incredible. You were born to do this, to be a scientist and help people."

I blush and duck my head, not used to praise, but he doesn't allow me to, pulling my chin up.

"Never be embarrassed about your success or intellect with me. Own it. You are incredible."

"And you aren't? Look at you." He grins shyly, and I glance back at the research, making him laugh.

"Go ahead, talk it out loud. I know you need to because I have to as well." Cato has been more than happy for me to take the lead on this, bowing to my knowledge on humans and the way they would work. He trusts me to understand it and help his people.

I roll my shoulders back, straightening with purpose. I don't want to let him down. "I'm making logical assumptions here. It's almost like they are trying to replicate something, like an original experiment or bond. I've never seen genealogy quite like this," I mutter. "I can understand some, but I need samples to compare them to. It would make sense that some are human and some are monster, so I'm going to draw blood and give myself a baseline to work on, and then we can categorise everything and try to work through the samples. You can take notes, since you were there. How does that sound?"

When I lift my head, he's watching me, his eyes red with hunger, and then his lips crash onto mine in a blistering kiss before he pulls back. "Sorry, couldn't resist." He grins cheekily. "Draw my blood. Everything I have is yours anyways, Tally."

Something about that feels too serious, too much like a promise of forever, when we know we only have now, so I ignore it, gathering what I need and taking his blood. He watches me intently the entire time. He doesn't flinch or complain, and when I'm done, he softly takes my hand, leans down, and kisses my jumping pulse, making me gasp.

He draws my blood so softly, it's almost erotic, and when he's done, he leans in and licks the little hole. My eyes shoot wide, while his own are still red, and he grins at me wickedly, flashing fangs.

"I love the way you taste, like how I imagine the sun does," he whispers. "All bright, airy, and perfect."

I duck my head, pulling away and putting the samples into the testing machines I need, and when I sit back down, I'm flustered, my vagina almost panting for this monster.

"You know I can smell your desire, right, Tally?" he rumbles, and I turn to see his claws ripping into the table as if to keep himself in check. "It's enough to drive me wild and make me forget everything we should be doing right now. I want to taste that sweet desire that is wrapping around me."

Shit. I try to calm down, but his words don't help. They go straight to my throbbing clit, which practically puts up a sign saying *yes please*.

Not mine, not mine, I remind myself, but when he leans in, closes his eyes, and inhales, letting out a moan, my traitorous body doesn't care he's not supposed to be mine. All it cares is that this monster, this man, excites me in a way no other ever has—not just physically, but intellectually—and I'm done fighting this. I should, but part of me wants to own this, to have him, even for a moment.

His mate can have his forever, but I'll always have this.

"Cato," I whisper, and it's as if he senses my surrender, my thighs so slick, I rub them together, because he finally snaps.

Snarling, he grabs me and pulls me across his lap, bringing his lips down on mine. Reaching up, I grip onto his horns, hauling myself higher until I'm climbing him, grinding myself against that incredibly large bulge beneath me as I kiss him back. I tangle my tongue with his, not even caring when his fangs cut into my lip and the taste of my blood fills our mouths. In fact, it has me moaning, and he swallows the sound. His claws slide down and rip off my coat, and then he grabs my trousers, his brain working as little as mine.

Knowing I am able to bring such a smart man to his knees is addictive.

I giggle, pulling my mouth away, and he snarls before turning my head and licking and sucking on my neck. I moan, and the threat of his fangs piercing my flesh causes me to shiver as he drags them up to my ear. "Do you find how much I want you funny, Tally?" he snarls.

"No," I whimper as he grabs my ass and drags me back and forth on his hard cock. It hits my clit through my trousers, and I'm almost coming.

"Cato," I beg, needing this, needing more.

He hears my plea and answers. Lifting me, he places me on the lab bench, grips my knees, and rips them apart. Careful of my new pants, he strips them off me, stopping to stroke my skin along the way. I leaning back, and the only thing separating us are my tiny knickers.

Snarling, he leans down, presses his mouth against them, and sucks, making me buck my hips.

"Oh fuck," I cry out, reaching for him to anchor myself. He lets me grip his hands as he grasps my knickers and slices them away. Nudging my thighs wider, he stares at my pussy for so long, I start to get self-conscious, but then he blinks and meets my eyes.

"You are so fucking beautiful, so fucking pretty and soft. I can't…" I swallow, thinking he's about to stop this, but then he looks at his hands. "I can't touch you with these. I don't ever want to hurt you."

"What?" I sit up, confused and hurt, and close my legs, but he shoves them open with a snarl.

"Don't you ever hide yourself from me," he snarls and then lifts his hand to his mouth. "I promised I'd never hurt you, Tally, and I won't."

"I don't—" I stop, my mouth dropping open as he puts his thumb into his mouth and bites off his claw, spitting it away. "Cato!" I yell, but he grins at me, biting off every other claw on his hand, and then, with a wicked look, reaches between my thighs and strokes my pussy.

"Much better. Now I won't ever hurt you." He groans, sliding his hands down my wet folds. "Fuck, Tally, you are so wet."

"But, but…" I protest. "Your claws!" I know they are weapons, and every warrior, every monster, has them.

"They will regrow, and even if they don't, I don't care. I don't need them, not as much as I need to be able to stroke this pretty pink pussy."

Holy fuck, that's the hottest thing anyone has ever done for me. This monster, this man before me, might have maimed himself just to touch me. I fall back when he circles my clit, watching my every expression as he explores my pussy. Within minutes, he's mastered what has me whimpering, what has me jerking, and what has my eyes crossing, and he uses it against me.

This monster masters my body within seconds and has me arching off the table, gripping my own breasts, as he strokes me casually.

"Look how pretty you blush for me," he murmurs, circling his expert fingers around my entrance before he meets my eyes and thrusts them into me. I cry out as I explode around them, coming so hard, I almost black out. When I come to, he's still stroking me with soft little thrusts, and when I blink and meet his eyes, he leans down and licks a line across my pussy before he snarls, "Mine."

"Yours," I pant, and it's the truth—I'll always be his, even when he won't be mine. "Please, Cato." I reach down, grip his head, and pull him closer, throwing my legs over his shoulders. His other hand grips my ass and yanks me to his mouth as he starts to feast, lashing my clit with his tongue before dipping it inside me alongside his fingers.

My head falls back with a bang, and my thighs shake as I grind into his face. He growls as he attacks me, eating me like he might die if he doesn't.

"So pretty, you taste so good, Tally. I could forsake food entirely just to eat you, live off you. That's it, my pretty little human, ride my tongue and show me just how badly you want me. Come all across my face so other males see just how much you are mine," he snarls, nipping my clit and making me scream again as I fuck myself on his face and fingers. I shamelessly take the pleasure I need, and he helps, sliding a third finger inside of me. He thrusts them like he would his cock and lashes my clit relentlessly with his tongue until I come again.

I yell as my legs lock around his head and I grind into his mouth, struggling through the intense pleasure until it finally subsides and I slump, his mouth dotting kisses along my pussy.

"Good girl, Tally, such a good girl." His red eyes meet mine as I blink them open. Leaning back slightly, he licks his glistening lips as he stares at me spread out across his desk. "Fuck, you are magnificent. Look at you, Tally. Look at how beautiful you are, how fucking strong. You drive me wild, do you know that? I walk around with a constant hard-on. Even catching your scent on the breeze makes me hard, and now I'll taste you every day for the rest of my life, and no other taste will compare."

Fucking hell. I can't take it. I can't not touch him.

It's wrong, I know he's not mine, but I want him too badly. I want to give back to this sweet, incredible man and show him what true pleasure is.

For a moment, I'll forget everything but him.

No past, no future. Only us and this desire between us.

Slipping to my knees before him, I meet his confused eyes as I grab his thighs and tug him closer. "Let me return the favour. Let me taste you."

"Tally, you don't have to."

"But I want to," I insist, leaning in to lick his hard cock like he did my pussy. His hips jerk, and I grin, loving the power I have over him. "Let me show you just what you've been missing."

"All I was missing was you, Tally, only you," he promises, and unsure what else to say without crying, I yank down his cloth, freeing his huge erection. It's so big, I don't think I'll be able to swallow him whole, but I'll sure as hell try.

Pre-cum glitters on his tip as he groans, so I put him out of his misery and lick the tip of his cock. He gasps, his eyes wide with wonder. Keeping my eyes on him, I wrap my hand around the base, unable to touch my fingers, but that's fine, and with my other hand, I grip his peachy ass, tug him closer, and suck the head into my mouth.

His hips jerk as a snarl rips from his mouth, his chest heaving and hands clenching. I pop my mouth from him and smile. "You can touch me, Cato."

He hesitates, so I grab his hand and put it in my hair. His fingers tunnel into my locks, gripping me as I focus on his cock. I lave it with my tongue, dragging it up and down until his hips are thrusting gently, and then I suck the head back into my mouth, sucking hard until he snarls. His hand tightens on my head, but still, he doesn't do anything but watch me.

He's letting me do whatever I want and not pushing for more, just grateful for whatever I choose to do. I know that even if stopped, he wouldn't hold it against me.

"Tally." My name is like a prayer caught between a plea and a promise. Rolling my eyes up to his, I slide my mouth lower, taking him as deeply as I can, and his eyes fly wide. Humming, I keep my mouth there until his head falls back.

I pull back and swallow him again, mimicking him fucking my mouth, and his hips help me, thrusting gently. Sliding my hand from his ass to his balls, I cup them gently as I suck and lick him, worshipping him the way he deserves.

"Oh, Tally, please, you need to stop."

I refuse. I know he's close and he's wild with it, his hips jerking as he slams himself deeper into my mouth. I hold on as he takes over, fucking my mouth desperately, but then he tries to pull back and I grip him, sucking hard. His cock swells in my mouth, and with a roar, he explodes.

His scorching cum fills my mouth. I swallow reflexively before pulling back and letting some spill down my lips and chin as he watches me, his eyes wide with pleasure and wonder.

Licking my lips, I lean in and kiss his cock before I'm yanked to my feet. His lips crash onto mine, tasting his own cum before he pulls back and presses his forehead to mine as he pants raggedly.

"Tally, my perfect fucking human, how did I ever get so lucky?"

I'm the one who feels lucky.

TWENTY-EIGHT

TALIA

After a long day of working, I head downstairs to see Cato dealing with his patrols and reports. The humans haven't moved from the wall, and he and Akuji have been sending messages back and forth. I sent a few to Aria, but I know she's busy helping on the wall, so I don't worry about getting a response. If she weren't okay, Akuji would have told me by now. Plus, nothing could touch her with him at her side.

"Miss Tally?" one of the kids calls when I wander into the living area.

"Yes, Feur?" I murmur, crouching before him.

He kicks his feet, stealing glances at me. "Mummy says you're very busy and not to bother you…but could you read to us? Just for an hour?" he begs, his big black eyes locked on me. "Pwease?"

How the hell do I say no to that?

"Of course," I murmur and take his hand, letting him lead me over to the others. I don't know when I became the Pied Piper of story reading to monsters, but here we are. I sit heavily and watch them. "Which one tonight?"

"Could you tell us one?" another kid, Tres, asks.

"Me?" I blink. "Erm, I don't really know any."

"About over the wall?" another kid adds. "What's it like where you are from?"

I don't know if I'm supposed to talk about it, but it might lessen some of the confusion between our races, so I settle down. "Well, it's very much like the city you live in, only our divisions aren't between tribes but social ranking—how powerful you are," I explain. "At the very edge of the wall is a place we call the slums. Those who don't have much power live there. It isn't a very nice place, and they struggle a lot." I refuse to lessen the truth. "They starve, they are hurt, and they are often forgotten."

"Why don't your people help them?" one kid asks.

"Because humans are selfish creatures," I answer. "Some of us try to, but there aren't enough of us. Beyond the slums are more homes, shops, and workplaces. Then we have our food produce, like fields and water treatment plants. All of it works like a cog in a machine—"

"I don't get it."

I look around and find a toy, holding it up. "You see how these pieces only fit in their certain holes?" When they nod, I carry on. "That's what it's like where I live. We all have our own places where we fit."

"And where did you fit?" Feur asks.

"In a lab, much like the one Cato has. I was… Well, I helped the humans come up with vaccines, to keep kids like you safe, and food substitutes for those who couldn't get food."

"Did you always want to do that?" another queries.

"Yes and no. I always wanted to be a scientist to help people." I shrug.

"What about your parents?" another calls, making me grin.

"They aren't with us anymore. They died when I was very young," I admit. "They were incredible people, you would have liked them. My father told the best stories every night, and no matter how tired he was, he would act them out for me." I grin. "And my mum? She made the best pancakes ever."

"How did they die?" a kid inquires.

"In an accident," I reply slowly, "but it was a very long time ago."

"Do you miss them?" another asks.

"Very much so. I was heartbroken after I lost them. It hurt very, very much."

"What about your friends?" another calls, and so goes question after question, from my love life, to work, to the city. I answer as many as truthfully as I can without scaring or upsetting them.

"So humans just pick a person and mate them?" one older teenager asks. "It's not based on the mating feeling like we are taught?"

"For humans? No." I shrug. "We fall in love, a chemical reaction. We find the best person for us—no instincts involved most of the time—and if you're very lucky, that person loves you back."

"Have you been in…love before, Miss Tally?" someone calls.

"I have once," I admit.

"What happened? Wasn't he your forever mate?" another girl queries, making some boys gag.

It seems kids, even monster kids, are all the same.

"He wasn't, but I learned a lot from that love. I learned how to be stronger, to stick up for myself, and to trust in myself. I learned how to be alone."

"Alone?" another asks. "Are you alone a lot?"

"Over the wall? Yes," I reply softly.

"Isn't that lonely?" Feur asks. "We are never alone. I don't think I would like it."

"I'm starting to realise it was very lonely. I don't know how I'll ever go back to nights without listening to you all play or reading you stories. You all have spoiled me that way." I wink, and it's the sad truth.

"Don't be sad, Talia," Feur says and climbs closer, taking my hands. "You can stay here with us—that way, you will never be alone again. You can be one of us."

Tears fill my eyes as I stare into his stubborn little face. "I don't think I can stay," I murmur. "I am…different. I am a human, and some don't like that."

"I don't care that you're human." He nods seriously. "You are kind. You read us stories, you play with us, and you make grumpy Cato smile." I grin at that. "Why does it matter if you are not red like us?"

"I-I don't know, buddy, it just does to some people," I tell him. "And that's okay, they have their reasons."

"That's dumb." He huffs, and in that moment, I see the incredible man he will grow to be. "You are no different to us, not inside, and my mummy always says it's what's inside that counts."

"Your mother is very smart," I say, squeezing his hand, "and I wish I could stay, I truly do."

"You do?" another asks.

"Yes. I like it here. I like everyone, and I love the city, but sometimes, we don't always get what we want. Let's not be sad," I tell them when they slump. "I am here now, so how about more stories? I can tell you about the time when I snuck out to meet friends at the lake, only to get stuck on a rock because I was sure there was a monster in the water waiting to eat me!" I pounce, making them laugh.

As I tell them stories, my heart breaks, wishing I could stay like they want me to, and when I'm done, I realise there's a crowd again. I blush hard when I realise they have all been listening to some of the most embarrassing details of my life, but in their eyes, I see nothing but respect.

Cato reaches for me and pulls me into his arms, his mouth going to my ear. "I promise you will never be alone again, Tally."

I just wish I knew that was a promise he could keep.

His destiny is to lead his people and to fall in love with his mate, and when that happens, he will forget all about me.

He will forget about his Tally and the promises he made to her.

But I never will.

That night—or day, I guess—I struggle to sleep, and it seems Cato does too, but we don't speak. He just holds me, and I want to beg for him to never let me go. I want to be selfish for once in my life and beg him to keep me.

I won't, though, because Cato deserves his mate. He deserves to be happy, and I won't keep him from that, because if I asked, he would say yes. He would forsake his future and happiness for me. That's the type of man he is, and I won't do that to him. Instead, I bury myself deeper into his side and feel the countdown on our time together trickling by.

I wonder if he feels the same.

I wonder if it hurts him as much as it hurts me, or if he feels nothing but relief.

I'm too scared to ask.

The next morning, we are both quiet as we work side by side, and I find myself getting frustrated because I find nothing but dead ends. My bad mood only declines as time passes and I don't come up with the answers I know we need. Cato senses it, and after a while, he stops letting me mope.

"Come on, get ready, we are going out."

"I need to work," I mutter.

"And banging your head against the desk won't help," he retorts before cradling my face. "Tally, you aren't doing this alone, but maybe to understand this…" His eyes drag over the research. "You need to see the beginning to see the end."

I frown at that, wondering what he's talking about, but I trust him, so I nod, pad to our room, and get dressed. I don't bother packing water or food, because I know he will. He has an obsession with looking after me and providing anything I might need like it's the best job in the world.

Strange man. I couldn't get my ex to carry my phone for me or hold my bag.

Once I'm dressed, he leads me from the university building and through the city towards the lab. I've been there before, but maybe he needs to be there to show me whatever he has in mind, so I keep quiet, and once we're inside the building, I follow him down the metal stairs.

He doesn't stop, though, he keeps walking, and after hesitating, I do the same.

We head past the labs and around the corner we didn't explore before, not wanting to venture too far. Back here are rows and rows of cells. I swallow down my bile and wander past them. They seem to stretch on forever, but then he suddenly turns right, into a locked room. He breaks the lock and opens the door for me.

Stepping through, I peer at the normal-looking lab, but he doesn't stop. He takes my hand and pulls me across the room. "Cato?" I whisper, afraid to talk too loudly, as if it would disturb the horrors and the ghosts that linger here. "Where are we going?"

"You'll see," is all he says in an equally soft voice.

At the end of the lab is a staircase leading down to a door. The door is locked and coded, and I'm about to try the codes they gave me when he simply rips it open and looks back at me. "The labs were not their only experiments," he states vaguely before stepping through.

I want to ask, but we step into a tunnel. Lights built into the rounded walls give off a very dim glow. It's dark and slightly scary, so I move closer to his back, but he doesn't seem afraid or worried as he wanders through the maze that seems to twist and turn.

"Cato, seriously, where are we going?" I hiss, nerves filling me.

"Trust me."

I do, so I keep quiet after that. An hour or so later, the tunnel simply ends in two metal doors, and he presses his hand to them, breathing heavily.

"Welcome to the bunker," he mutters as he rips them open and steps back.

TWENTY-NINE

CATO

I follow Talia inside, seeing it through her eyes. Though the lingering hatred and pain from this place flashes through me, I need to tell her, to show her, how awful this place truly is.

Yes, the equipment is top of the line, and yes, it looks amazing from here, but it's not.

It's hell.

It's a place even monsters fear.

"I can still hear the screams, though I got lucky. I was only brought here twice for misbehaving. They hurt a friend of mine, and I reacted…badly. I didn't have much control back then, and that lack of control over the haze landed me here, but others…others who were angry, who couldn't control their hatred and fear and got lost in the haze, well…they never came back."

She looks over at me, and I smile sadly.

"Like Samael. I don't know what he did, but one day, he was gone, and during my second punishment here, I saw him. He was just a youngling, Tally, just a kid, and the things they did to him… It's no wonder his mind is fractured. It's no wonder he is the way he is. Even if I cannot stand idly by as he hurts others, I understand why. It's why we call him and his people Darklings. It's why they are the farthest away from humanity…" I shake my head. She doesn't need to know the true depths of their depravity and madness. I look around once more and then back at her. "This place should be a dream for a scientist like me, but instead, it's a nightmare."

"Cato," she croaks out, coming closer. When she reaches up and cups my face, I close my eyes as I soak in her warmth. I let her presence push back those memories that haunt me. "I'm so sorry. I'm so very sorry."

"I know," I murmur, covering her hands as I press my head to hers. "You didn't do this, Talia, but you needed to see. There might be answers here, and if not, you needed to see this to understand."

I feel her nod, her scent wrapping around me and offering comfort. "Maybe it truly is our species who are the monsters," she whispers. "I don't understand how they could have done this or why they did this."

I open my eyes to see my pain reflected in her eyes, the same kind that lives in me. "Because they could." It is as simple as that. They did this to us because they could.

No one cared enough to stop them, and they didn't care what it took or who it hurt as long as they got what they wanted. Our bodies, our rights, were nothing to them. They thought they were better. They thought they were untouchable and therefore could dictate what happened to us and get away with it.

And they did.

They made us the monsters for fighting back, for trying to save our people and keep them safe.

"I hate them," I tell her, and her eyes fill with tears as she watches me.

"I know," she whispers.

"It's not logical, hate doesn't help—"

"Shh." She presses her face to mine, holding my gaze. "Whether it's logical or not, you feel it, and you are allowed to feel it, Cato. If we were solely based on logic, we would be robots. We need emotions to keep us real, to keep us alive, even if those emotions are sometimes unexplainable. Hating the people who not only created you and your kind but then tortured, abused, and used them is not unexplainable. It is obvious and understandable. I hate them for you. I want to burn this fucking place to the ground and then go over the wall and do the same there. I want to scream it from the rooftops so my people finally know the truth. I want there to be riots and chaos, just so I can protect you and the incredible people I've met here."

The determination reflected back in her eyes steals my breath.

"I want to save you all, and I will." Her voice hardens. "I will save you all from them. They will never get this research, and they will never hurt you again. I promise you, Cato, that no matter what happens, no matter what comes, I will protect you."

"My beautiful, beautiful Tally," I murmur, leaning close and kissing her softly. I don't know what else to say. Whatever words that would come from my mouth would be lacking in regard to the strength of my feelings for my mate. Every mate thinks they got lucky, but me? I have been given the most incredible, smart, kind, beautiful, and perfect mate in the world, and I will always treasure that, always treasure her. I might not be able to fully put into words how much this little human means to me, but I will always show her.

I vow it with my lips pressed to hers.

When I pull back, she smiles at me as I pull away, twining my hand with hers. "Come on, let me show you why I brought you here. This won't be easy to see, but I think it might help you understand, or at least I hope it will."

The front of the lab is state of the art, even more so than the lab in the main building. Here, they don't hide anything or spare any expense, but as we plunge into the waiting hell below, using the once working moving stairs, the truth is spread out below the entire city. Tanks hold new-born monsters, suspended in all states and forms. Some are mutilated or wrong. Behind them are tables where blood still remains, as well as skeletons, since the war started so suddenly.

Cages, or cells as they called them, fill each wall, small enough that we could barely lie down. They are stacked on top of each other, offering no privacy or solitude, just bars and glass. There are hundreds of them. Some stand open, while some remain closed with the dead inside. This place was one of the most guarded, and so it was the last to fall. When they evacuated, many of the guards killed the subjects, and all the monsters were dead…bar Samael, who managed to break out in the chaos. When we arrived, he was ripping his way through humans.

"Oh my god." Talia covers her mouth, her eyes wide in horror as she gapes at the hell beyond.

"This is where the experiments began. I'm not sure what they were doing down here after they created us, but it was nothing good. The bits and pieces I heard when I was here made it seem like they were splicing our DNA to try to create different species like us. As you can see, it didn't work, and the things they created were framed like trophies. Other times, they would just cut up our people and test their organs, but they enjoyed it, enjoyed hurting us. Here, Talia, is where it all began. It's where the first monster was created."

Standing hand in hand with her, I look out at the birthplace and torture sanctuary of my people. A human and a monster, both free, both supposed to be enemies, coming back to the beginning as lovers.

Looking up at me, she squeezes my hand, lifts it, and kisses the back. "Let's stop this from ever happening again." With a determined tilt of her chin, she descends the steps into hell, ready to find the missing piece.

TALIA

In this bunker, there are reminders everywhere of the true depravity of humans. It infuriates me. I take my time exploring, making sure I remember every single inch, so whenever I doubt why I am doing this or if humans truly are that bad, I will remember.

Along with it comes respect for every single monster, especially those who survived here, like Samael.

It is clear that he was born with nothing but rage and pain, torn apart by the hands of human scientists over and over. When all you have ever known is death and agony, how could you be anything but a hate-filled monster? Knowing Cato survived this place, that he was here, fills me with pain and fear like I've never felt.

I want to erase this place and the past, but that's not right. This happened. It cannot be erased, and it shouldn't. It should be remembered. It should hurt and make you waver. If not, then their suffering was for nothing.

With Cato's help, we start to organise and pack some of the research in hopes it will fill in some gaps, especially the samples and notes we find. It's clear that whatever they were doing here was much worse than just creating a higher, intelligent species and keeping them captive. And why now? Why do they want it now?

Why risk it all? Unless they have no choice but to…

Maybe something here is the key to the monsters and my bosses need it. If so, I have to find it and keep it safe first, because if the humans surrounding the city are any indication, they are willing to do whatever it takes to get it back.

Even start another war—a war neither side could survive, not again.

We hang on the balance of peace and chaos, and we are all that stands between it.

Once I can't pack any more, leaving the heavy stuff to Cato, I wander back through the bunker, swallowing down the pain I can almost feel drenching the walls like their blood. I let it fuel me, let it fill me, and the more I see, the angrier I become.

I end up behind some cells near a door we didn't look in. I have a bad feeling, but I refuse to cower. I need to see everything to know the truth, so I open it, and tears instantly spring into my eyes. My mouth drops open, and bile crawls up my throat.

My entire soul seems to shudder at the scene before me.

There, in the middle of the room, is a crucified monster—or what is left of them. The skeletal bones are chained outward. The skull hangs down, the horns half bent and broken. The floor in here is stained with blood, leading to a drain under the corpse.

I gag, but I am unable to look away, wondering how anyone could do this.

How could anyone be capable of such inhumanity?

"Shh, Tally, it is all okay," Cato soothes, appearing behind me and turning me to his chest before shutting the door softly. "Shh, let it out, I know, let it all out." He holds me as I break down, even though it should be the other way around. When I lift my head and say just that, his face softens as he wipes my tears away.

"I have had many years to see these horrors. There isn't much that will shock me anymore. Yes, it hurts my heart for my people and that person in there, but it fuels my determination to keep you and my people safe."

"I'm not one of you," I remind him, and after being here, I don't know how he doesn't hate me too.

"You are. You might not have been born with horns or red skin." He winks. "But your heart is all monster, baby, and I plan to keep it that way. So let's get you back. You need to eat, sleep, and relax."

"No, I won't, not until you are all safe," I mutter. I glance back at the door, a furious determination lacing my tone. "I can't."

THIRTY

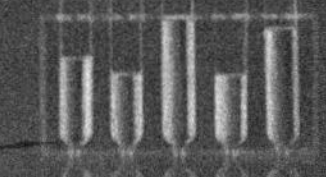

TALIA

Back at the university, I dive into our research, not wanting to stay at that bunker. It felt haunted. I'm trying to categorise as much research as I can to find the important bits, but there is so much. It could take a lifetime to go through it. Cato works tirelessly by my side, only stopping to check on his people and work through any issues that arise. I know he's worried I'm not sleeping, but he forces me to eat, and three days later, I'm no closer to finding what they are looking for than when I started.

Exhausted, dejected, and angry, I let him drag me to bed and curl around me where he orders me to sleep. He's right—if I rest, the answers might come to me. My brain needs sleep to work on the problems. Everything was starting to get slightly hysterical at this point, despite the fact I'm used to sleep deprivation.

I expect to worry on the problems all night like I usually would, but I find myself sleeping hard, and when I wake up, my mind and body are rested. I'm raring to go, but first, I flip over to see Cato still sleeping, which is rare. His eyes are closed, his face is relaxed, and fangs adorably hang over his lip. His tail is wrapped around my ankle to keep me close to him, and when I try to pull away, he growls softly before tugging me closer. I smile as I melt into the circle of his arms.

I shouldn't, since he's not mine, but in the dark, all alone, I can admit I wish he were.

Despite everything, I found the one person, the one man—monster, who gets me, cherishes me, and supports me. He's kind, smart, and charming. He's loyal and dedicated. He's beautiful and protective. He's everything I didn't know I needed, and yet he's not mine.

I'm a selfish bitch, it seems, because I don't pull away. In fact, I lean in and kiss his chest, giggling when a purr starts deep inside of him. I do it again, and the vibration echoes through me, making my breath catch.

"What are you doing, my love?" he murmurs, and when I glance up, he has one eye open.

"Shh, sleep," I order, and a grin crinkles his lips before he flips onto his back, pulling me with him. His eyes slide shut again as he holds me against him and makes a half-asleep affirmative noise.

Grinning, I lay my head back down, but I'm restless. I need to work. Well, not really, that's not what I need, but I won't tell him that. I forgot about his enhanced senses, though, because a minute later, I hear him inhaling deeply before a growl vibrates his chest.

"If you are needy, Tally, you should have said so. Just wake me up."

I look up to see him wide away now, his eyes burning red, but I slide off him. He doesn't let me get far.

"Talia," he warns. Gulping, I stare up at him and blurt out, "Okay, I'm turned on. Happy now?"

"Very," he purrs, grinning at me wickedly, and before I can even protest, he flips us and pins me beneath him, forcing his leg between my thighs.

"Cato!" I groan, knowing we shouldn't.

"If you don't stop overthinking this and talking, I'll fill that pretty mouth," he threatens, and my jaw drops at the dirty warning. He grins as he presses his nose to my pussy and inhales. "Fuck, I love how you smell."

I shiver as his hands tug me closer. "Cato—" I yelp as I'm flipped, my face pressed to the nest. He grabs some of the fur and shoves it into my mouth, making my eyes widen.

"Better." He grins as he tugs off my clothes, leaving me naked, and runs his nose down my spine. He grips my hips and tugs me up so I'm on all fours.

I could spit out the fur, but something about it gives me the right to be brave, as if I don't have a choice when I know that's not true, but I still wiggle my hips and his hand comes down on my ass. "Still, Tally. I'll eat that pretty, needy pussy when I'm good and ready. Now behave."

I whine around the fur, fisting it as I try to keep still. I feel his eyes burning a path over me, leaving me weak and needy, so I part my thighs, and it works.

"You don't play fair, human," he snarls, his voice more beast than man. His hand comes down in a punishing slap on my ass, making me jerk and moan. He does it again, no doubt watching my reaction, and my pussy clenches at the sting of pain.

My clit throbs in time with my heart now as I widen my legs farther, and he finally touches me. His fingers stroke my pussy before dipping inside me, making my eyes slide closed in bliss. "I think you liked that, Tally, but let me check," he teases, and his hand comes down on my ass again, making me clench around him. "Oh yes you do," he purrs, and he does it again. "I love it too. I love watching your skin pinken with my hand marking you as mine, Tally." He grips my hip to hold me still as he leisurely thrusts his fingers in and out of me before his thumb rubs my clit.

The pace is soft and not enough to get me off, but I still push back, desperately reaching for a release he holds back from me. When I finally get close, he stills, leaving me whining, wet, shaking from the force of my need to come. He only starts to touch me again when I slump, winding me back up again.

"Shh, Tally, I'll make you feel good, but I want to play first." He licks my spine before leaving nipping kisses down my body, and then he closes his mouth over my clit. I jerk at the sensation, but just as suddenly as his mouth touched me, it's gone again.

I feel so frustrated, tears build in my eyes, and when he pulls his fingers free, I almost scream.

His wet finger trails up, and I stiffen when it circles my asshole. "Is it pleasurable to fuck you here?" he asks, his brain working again.

I start to shake my head before I shrug. I've never tried it, after all. I never trusted anyone enough to.

"Hmm, well we can explore that together then," he purrs, leaning down and licking around the forbidden hole. I jerk, even as I tighten around his other hand still inside me, making him groan against my skin.

"Please," I beg after spitting out the fur.

He stills, grips my hair, and yanks me up, twisting until I see those blazing eyes. "Put it back in your mouth, or I'll tease you more. Be a good girl, and I'll eat your pussy until you can't even scream anymore."

I scramble to put it back in my mouth, and he chuckles but doesn't tease me again. He lifts my hips into the air and drapes my legs over his shoulders as he seals his lips to my pussy, tasting all of me before thrusting his tongue into me as I writhe.

When his lips finally seal around my clit, I moan my release around the fur, my body going limp in his grip. He doesn't let up, sliding his fingers inside of me and lashing my clit with his tongue until one release rolls into the next. I pull away, too sensitive, and he lets me drop to the furs before turning me. The fur slips from my mouth, but when I look down, he hovers over my pussy with a wicked grin.

"Cato," I start hoarsely, but he sucks my clit hard.

His fangs scrape along the sensitive bundle, and my body jolts as his hands slide up my body to grip my breasts. He tweaks and plays with my nipples before he pops my clit free and climbs up my body, watching his hands on them before leaning down to follow his fingers' path. He sucks and licks my nipples until I'm arching into his mouth.

"So pretty, so soft," he purrs against my breasts, nipping my nipple, and the slight sting of pain makes me come. He watches me and then smirks as he continues his assault. Leaving my nipples hard, engorged, and wet, he sits back and slides his tail up my thighs, flicking my clit before dancing over my wet cunt.

As he does, he wraps his hand around his length, watching me spread out on the furs as his tail slides into me. My eyes fly wide, and I moan. With a knowing grin, he strokes his rock-hard cock as he fucks me with his tail, slowly at first before speeding up with his own stroke of his hand. I writhe, my eyes locked on his movements as I clench around the invasion, around his tail that strokes me inside.

"Look at you being such a good girl. Does my tail feel good inside you?" he asks. I whine, and he groans. "You look so sexy with it fucking you, stretching you. I can barely breathe through my need, Tally," he rumbles, speeding up his strokes on himself as his tail thrusts harder and sends me over the edge once more.

With a roar, he follows, splattering his release across his hand, my thighs, and pussy, his tail fucking it into me as he strokes and drains his cock of every drop, and then he slumps forward. His tail is still inside of me, but it's still now as we both just pant and breathe heavily.

I'm shocked but satisfied, and Cato eventually slides it out of me, getting to his knees and bringing his tail to his mouth to lick it clean.

"Cato," I whisper.

"Time to clean up, Tally." He picks me up and leads me to the bathroom, where he washes me once more, leaving me defenceless and feeling off-kilter. I'm barely able to breathe until he leaves to grab my clothes, and once he brings them back, I dress silently, unsure what to say about what we just did.

It was amazing—okay, incredible—but we are crossing lines we can't undo, and he seems to relish it, even though I'm scared.

"Time for work, Tally." He grins widely, smacking my ass as he passes. "I'll go get us some food while you get started."

I watch him go, shaking my head with a smile before it fades when I remember the truth—he's not mine and never will be. I need to stop getting attached.

Who am I kidding? I am already attached, and it's going to hurt like a son of a bitch when I have to give him up.

THIRTY-ONE

TALIA

"Could it—no, it can't be that simple." I spin my chair, almost falling from it as I hurry to the notes sprawled across the floor. Dropping to my knees, I frantically look them over before swearing when I realise we are missing one of the numbered notebooks. Muttering to myself, I start to crawl across the lab, searching for it, knowing I'm close to a breakthrough.

That moment of realisation reaches for me, and I'm desperate as I scramble across the lab, searching for the missing journal. The note—

"Tally?" Cato calls worriedly, and my head jerks up when I realise he's been watching me from his own chair, concern sparking in his dark eyes.

"Number ten! Where is number ten?" I shout, and his eyes widen as he looks around.

"The notebook?" he asks, confused.

I nod my head rapidly. "Ten, we need to find ten!" I know I'm not making sense, but I feel like I'll lose my train of thought if I speak too many words. Cato, however, does not ask any more questions or try to lock me up in a loony bin. Instead, he jumps to his feet and searches with me, but an hour later, it's obvious it's not here.

Grumbling, I write down my thoughts haphazardly before I forget them and blow out a breath. "We need to find ten."

"Well, nine and eleven are here and marked as being from the lab, so ten must be there. I can go back—"

"I'll go with you." I jump to my feet. "The quicker I have it, the quicker I'll know."

"Know what? What's going on, Tally?" he demands, gripping my face to stop my erratic movements. "Talk to me."

Blowing out a calming breath, I meet his eyes. "If they did what I think they did."

"Which is?" he prompts.

"Spliced more than one animal into your DNA."

"We know they did." He frowns, not understanding.

"Yes, a potent mix, but then when they found the right one, they stopped experimenting, right? Wrong. I think, if I'm right, they carried on experimenting and that some of you are spliced with different animals. But it's more than that. There is something I'm missing, I just can't see it yet."

"Then let's get you to that journal," he murmurs.

I nod, and we hurriedly pack a bag before waving goodbye to his people. He accepts a wrapped parcel of food, and then we are off. Akuji gave us permission to be at the lab, so we go straight there, with Cato carrying me. When we reach it, I drop everything and start to search, as does Cato. When I find it hiding under a table where it must have fallen, I dust it off and leap up excitedly. For a while, he watches me flip through it before frowning and looking at the courtyard.

"I forgot to tell Akuji's men we are here. Give me one minute, Tally. Don't go anywhere." He kisses my head, but I barely hear him, waving him off as I skim the chicken scratch, trying to decipher what I need.

To be certain of what I am reading, I need to double-check the vials and maybe combine them the way they did, otherwise how can I be sure that's what this says?

I'm debating the best way to conduct an experiment when I hear it.

Breathing.

I jerk my head up as I stumble from my stool, realising a monster snuck down here without me even hearing.

Cato's brother.

Fear fills me as I stare at him. "Cato just went to talk to Akuji's people," I whisper.

"I know," he tells me, watching me carefully as he prowls closer. I stumble back a step, and he stills, cocking his head to the side as he watches me. "You are scared of me."

"Wouldn't you be? You want to kill me." I laugh hysterically, wondering if I could get past him or scream for Cato before he killed me.

Probably not.

He observes me for a moment. "I did want to kill you," he admits.

"Yay me," I whisper, swallowing hard. "Wait, did… What changed?"

"I saw the way you were with him, with our people. You're not like the other humans. It doesn't mean I trust you, but…but I don't want to lose my brother." His lips curl inwards, and he lowers his head. "It has always been my job to protect him, to protect my family, and you threatened that, but I reacted badly."

I'm so confused. "I-I don't want to threaten anything," I tell him softly. "I'm trying to help, I really am."

"Humans surround our walls, searching for the research you are holding. You could have given it to them, could have left, but you didn't."

He's right—I had every opportunity.

"And I don't plan to," I state. "What they have been doing is wrong. It's sick. No one should play god."

"I don't know if I can trust that," he says and moves closer. Fear blooms inside of me as I see the conflicting emotions in his eyes.

"You are going to have to," I tell him bravely, "because I'm not going anywhere."

"Do not hurt him," he begs, and I see the desperation in his eyes. "He's all I have left, please don't take him away from me."

"I would never hurt him. It's the last thing I would ever want to do," I assure him, sighing at the vulnerability in his eyes. It's easy to be afraid of him, to hate him, but it's harder to do that when I can see the truth.

He's just worried for his brother and his people.

"I'm not like them. I know you don't believe that, but I want to help. I truly do. What humans did to you…" I shake my head as he flinches. "I cannot begin to make up for that, but I will keep trying. Every day, I will try to make this right, because you all deserve a future. You deserve safety and happiness, Cato above all. I could no more hurt him than I could hurt myself."

His eyes watch me carefully. "You love him."

I jerk at his words. Is he right? I don't have a chance to respond, because Cato comes bounding in, smiling when he sees me before it fades when his gaze lands on his brother. The snarl he lets out breaks my heart as Cato leaps between us, and the pain I see reflected in his brother's eyes is too much.

Placing my hand on Cato's back, I step to his side. "Shh, he doesn't mean any harm. He came to speak to me, not threaten or hurt me. He just wants to understand." I look up at Cato. "He's your brother, Cato. He made a mistake, one I won't hold against him. I don't blame him for hating me or being worried about my presence, and neither should you."

"He threatened you," Cato snarls, his fists clenched.

"Yes, he did, and I respect that. He did it because he loves you, so kiss and make up, boys." I huff. "We have much bigger things to deal with than your dick measuring contest."

Cato peers down at me, confused. "Why would we measure our dicks? Mine is clearly bigger."

"Men." I groan. "It seems even monsters are the same."

His brother sniffs indignantly. “And mine is spectacular.”

“I’m sure you both have very nice cocks,” I patiently offer, “but now we need to get to work. Is Akuji okay with us being here?”

Cato nods and looks down at me. “I also told him you had something to show them, since you are close to a breakthrough, so one of his men is outside to help watch our backs.”

“You are?” his brother asks, and I see hope in his eyes.

“Yes, if you let me work,” I grumble, making Cato chuckle. His brother smiles at the sound and meets Cato’s eyes.

“She sounds like you when we were younglings,” he remarks before lowering his head. “I am sorry for threatening the human. I was just worried for you and our people, but I never should have let my own prejudices and anger take control. If the human Talia can look past them and help us, so can I.”

“See? Teamwork!” I clap.

His brother sighs and gets to his knees. “To make amends, I offer rights of respect.”

“Brother.” Cato sighs, but he looks determined, his teeth gritted.

“It’s the least I can do. I ask that you take this, not just as my brother, but as our leader.” He tips his head back, leaving his chest and neck vulnerable.

“Rights of respect?” I whisper.

“It is a way to show your respect for another and to atone for a wrong by making yourself weak,” Cato murmurs, watching his brother. “It is our way.”

Okay…

I watch as Cato straightens his shoulders, seeming to grow even bigger, his tail lashing anxiously behind him as he approaches his brother.

“Are you sure?” Cato queries.

“I give my life to you. It is in your hands. I ask for forgiveness,” his brother says, the words practiced. “I offer you my loyalty and my life, brother,” he adds, and Cato jerks then hardens before my eyes. He glances back at me, his face unreadable, and I don't know what he sees in my gaze, but he looks back at his brother…and strikes.

He slams his fangs into his brother's neck, who grunts but doesn't falter.

I watch in horror before I realise what this means. Cato could choose to kill him, could maim or hurt him badly, and he has to trust in his friend, his brother. I have no doubts Cato won't do that, but the viciousness of his attack shocks me. Sometimes, I forget just what Cato is capable of.

Right now, he is reminding me, and he knows it.

He releases his brother's throat, not killing him. It's a warning, I realise. A punishment.

When he glances at me with blood on his mouth and fangs, I swallow, but I refuse to look away or be afraid. This is still the man who dances with me, who holds me tight, and who promises to keep me safe. He is the monster who kisses me like he can't breathe without me. This is still Cato. I hold out my hand to him, and the relief that crosses his face makes my heart shudder. He hurries to my side, wiping his mouth before holding me tight, like he was worried I would turn him away.

I reassure him by leaning into his side, my eyes going to his brother, who seems to deflate on his knees. Blood trickles from the wounds on his throat, but his eyes are clear, happy.

Weird, weird monsters and their traditions.

There is still a gap between them that Cato doesn't seem happy to cross, but it's clear he misses his brother.

I'll bridge it for him. I step away from Cato's embrace and move towards the only family the man I care for has left.

"Right, well, we are going to need some help here, so want to join us?" I hold out my hand, and his brother looks at me.

"You would forgive me that easily?"

"We have to start somewhere," I tell him, and I offer a small smile.

He shoots an uncertain, crooked one back before taking my hand.

Obviously, I can't actually help him up, but it's symbolic, and when he wanders away to get started, Cato moves behind me.

"Tally, my perfect little Tally." The growl and possessiveness in his words sends a shiver through me, so I clear my throat.

"We are going to need more monsters for this."

THIRTY-TWO

TALIA

We work tirelessly side by side, with new monsters coming to help us wade through all the research. Some refused to come, which I understand. I told Cato's brother to only invite those who are okay being back in the lab. Some are still hesitant and confused, so I help by giving orders.

It seems to get them moving, and I smile at Cato as we fall into a routine.

Something from the notebook bugs me, though, so I take blood samples from those who are willing, including Cato and myself and even his brother, and start to work through the notes as we wait.

When I see the blood results and look back at the notebook, I know the truth.

I know what I was missing.

It shocks me, which I didn't think was possible anymore. "Cato," I murmur. He moves closer and peers at his blood and then at the notes I'm pointing out. "Do you know what this means?"

"My blood is changing," he murmurs as I nod.

"Adapting," I whisper. "But it's more than that, so is mine. It's as if being around you is…changing me too." I look up and meet his gaze. "They didn't just create monsters, they are trying to make us compatible to breed."

Honestly, what is there to say after that? Cato double-checks my findings, and I start to work through the other notes. It's always hard to come into an experiment near the end or when it has already been conducted, because you have to work backwards, but I'm trying my best to protect these innocent people.

I don't know how many hours pass, but it's not until I hear a noise and my head jerks up that I realise we are all absorbed in our work.

Standing on the stairs is Aria and her monster, Akuji.

Blinking to clear the to-do list in my mind, I hurry to her, wrapping my arms around her in a hug before blushing. She probably didn't actually want the hug, but there's something about Aria that just makes me feel safe, whole, and protected, plus she's my friend. Pulling back, I note her smile and relax. I nod at the monster at her side, not wanting to be rude since he could kill us. "Hey." I grin back at Aria. "You'll never guess what we found."

"What?" she asks me curiously, her eyes lighting up. I grab her hand and drag her after me, hearing a husky chuckle from her monster. I don't stop until she's near where I had been working. I shove her towards the microscope, to use it as an example. There's so much to tell her, but I know Aria likes to see stuff for herself, so I wait patiently as she stares through it, sharing a smile with Cato.

She lifts her head and gives me a squinty-eyed look, a familiar one that means she has no idea what I'm talking about. "Erm, babe? English? I don't do science. I do guns and knives."

I feel a blush stain my cheeks, embarrassment filling me. Of course she didn't understand it. God, sometimes I can be so dumb. "Right, right, sorry! I was analysing Cato's blood, you know, for fun—"

"Of course, what else do you do for fun?" She grins, leaning back against the table as she watches me, urging me to continue. There are no signs of reproach or boredom. She genuinely wants to hear what I have to say, and it gives me confidence. Aria would never make fun of me, and she would never tell me to be quiet or to talk less. She respects my mind, and that only makes me care for her more.

I need to start with the good news, or at least the fun stuff. "Exactly. Anyway, their blood is naturally mutating. How cool is that?"

Her eyebrows rise. "Very," she replies, so I launch into the explanation of how we found it out and what it could mean, especially for their healing properties and lifespan. She watches me, but I see her eyes flick to Cato for a moment before meeting mine again, so I suck in a breath and sag, cutting off my ramble as I remember that she probably doesn't care. I know I'm stalling. I have other things I need to tell her—things we've found that shock even me.

"We found something else. I-I swear I didn't know, Aria. You have to believe me." I take her hands, imploring her to believe me. I wouldn't blame her if she didn't. After all, I work for the people who did this. "I swear."

"Hey, it's okay. I believe you, whatever it is," she promises, squeezing my hands to urge me on and offer comfort. "Tell me."

I hesitate, glancing at Cato to make sure this is the right thing to do. He already knows, and he pulls me into his side, giving me his strength as well. I don't know what Akuji sees in my gaze, but he clears the lab until it's just us.

My eyes go to the floor, unable to look at them in case they blame me. "I've been putting together the research from this lab and the…and Cato's stash. It was hard at first, I don't understand most of it—Never mind, but…" I blow out a breath and lift my head. "The important thing is what I found. They created the monsters, Aria, by splicing genes and manipulating DNA. There were other failed experiments before…before them. They were just creating them in an attempt to make perfect soldiers, but…they were trying to bond it with human DNA."

"What are you saying?" she asks with a frown, and Akuji draws closer. Cato squeezes me, urging me to continue, to trust them and him.

"I think, from the research I can see, that they were trying to make humans and monsters compatible to create a new race, a superior race, that they could control. They were trying to extend our lives and make us stronger, faster." I raise my eyes then to meet her shocked ones. "I have a terrible feeling about why they sent me here. I think they want to continue what they started. They could not only make more monsters, Aria, but more races. They could end the world with this research."

Aria gasps, her eyes going to Akuji, and I see the information rolling between them like a seamless, silent communication before she turns back to me, her face hard and shoulders back.

"We can't ever let them get this research."

She's right—we can't.

What started as a mission to a deserted city has now become a life-threatening fight to stop humanity from destroying itself and these innocent creatures in the same breath. Monsters never asked to be created, tortured, and used. All they want is to be left alone, and I'll be damned if I won't make that happen.

I might not have known what I was sent here for, but now that I do, I won't stand idly by. Fuck my future, fuck my job, and fuck the humans.

I'm siding with the monsters, and I'll protect them all.

THIRTY-THREE

CATO

I watch Talia as her friend comforts her and they duck their heads together to whisper. I only drag my gaze away when I notice Akuji is watching me. Something in his eyes makes me lower my head with a blush, but he nods, and I follow him. We move far enough away so my mate and her friend can't overhear us, but not too far so they are still within our sight.

My eyes still flick to Talia, my hands curling in with the itch to reach out and pull her close.

"I never knew that. Did you?"

Akuji's words bring me back to our conversation, and I force myself to concentrate. He's trying to protect his people and figure out what's next, and I need to help him. We need to work together, but my sole focus is Talia. Every twitch of her hand has me glancing over to check if she's okay.

She's my entire existence.

Akuji is still waiting for an answer, and I am still a leader, so I need to answer as much as I can and help him understand. "No. For a long time, I have been trying to make sense of their research, hoping for an understanding of our race—"

"Which you did," he interrupts.

"Enough to treat our wounds and help our women during childbirth, but not to this extent. It took her human brain to figure out the rest. She truly is magnificent. Her brain—" I shake my head, knowing I'm still blushing. "I didn't know this, but are we really surprised? The humans did terrible things to our people when we were captives, so of course they would be exploring every opportunity of what our creation meant. They are correct though—we cannot let this fall into human hands. They will send others to retrieve it once they realise Talia and Aria aren't coming back."

"You're right. I'll double patrols and have eyes on the walls and tunnels at all times. We won't let them get to the lab. We will protect our city and race, and nobody will be hurt by them again," he promises, clapping me on the back in a friendly gesture I never really understood. The sound of footsteps has us turning to see Aria walking towards us. The fiery little human scares me. There's something almost unhinged in her eyes, and she's not soft like my Talia, but she suits Akuji perfectly, and it's clear he loves her madness.

"You are right about the humans being magnificent," Akuji rumbles at me, his eyes flashing as he watches the human walking towards him.

As soon as she is within reach, he grabs her and hauls her against him, touching every inch of her. I blush and look away, but my eyes land on Talia, and I notice she's watching them too.

With…longing?

I force myself to avert my eyes before I do something stupid, like bend her over right here to prove I am as much hers as Aria is Akuji's. Instead, I chuckle as Akuji purrs for his mate. "I never thought I'd see the great Akuji weak." My worries resurface. Akuji is the strongest of us all, and she holds his heart in her tiny hands. "Remember that, remember you are his weakness just as he is our strength. Do not ruin something so pure and true, human."

Without waiting for a response, I move to Talia, unable to be away from her any longer. She smiles warmly at me, all sadness gone from her gaze, and all is right in the world again. I hear Aria and Akuji talking, but I tune them out as I pull Talia into my arms and hug her tight. She sighs and buries her head into my chest, letting me hold her until Akuji's voice interrupts us, making me want to growl.

"Cato, do you want to date?" he asks me, and Aria laughs so hard, she falls against him. Talia giggles against my side as I raise my eyebrows, sliding my tail around her waist and holding her tighter against me. "What? I like Cato. We could date sometime, no?"

I frown at them.

"You could if you want." Aria wipes at her eyes and shares a look with Talia. "It's usually reserved for partners—mates."

"Oh." Akuji shrugs, not the least bit embarrassed as he waves at me to dismiss his words. "Sorry, we cannot date."

"Understood." I shrug, knowing I need to learn what this date is so I can take Talia on one. I might not be as strong and wild as Akuji, but I would make a good mate, and I need to show Talia why she has to stay with me forever.

I watch Akuji and Aria go, lost in their own little world, and Talia grins at me. "They are so sweet together. She needed someone who could match her crazy."

"Him as well." I smile. "But thank fuck they are gone."

"What? Why?" she asks, sounding concerned.

"So I can finally do this." I grab her face, haul her up as I bend down, and slam my lips to hers. She groans against my mouth, curling her hands on my chest as I sweep my tongue into her mouth, showing her without words how amazing I find her. When I pull back, her eyes are closed and her lips are slack. She blinks her glazed eyes open, and satisfaction roars through me.

No, I may not be as strong as Akuji, but when Talia looks at me like that, she makes me think I can save the entire world.

Just for her.

"Cato." The way she says my name, like a sigh filled with hope, has my heart swelling so much, it feels like it will burst. My entire body vibrates with purpose—to make her happy.

"Later, after we have finished researching, we will date as well."

She giggles, her cheeks blushing. "Is that right?"

"Yes. I will romance you with science and then date you." I grin down at her, and her smile fades as her gaze becomes distant. "Tally?"

"What? It's nothing."

"No, tell me," I demand, frowning. I hate the worry I see in her eyes, and I want to share it with her so she never has to worry again.

"I'm just worried about what they will do now." She pats my chest and tries to turn away, so I grab her hand and haul her back until she slams into my chest.

Leaning down, I kiss up her throat to her tiny ear. "We deal with this together, always together. They won't get their hands on it. Now let me send my people back, they need to rest. You and I can stay and work through everything else until you feel more confident, and then we can go through every single one of your worries one by one until you feel better." I nip her ear, loving when she melts into me. "Sound good, Tally?"

"Good." She leans back into me. "You tricky little monster."

"There's nothing little about me, Tally. I'll show you that later too," I promise before releasing her.

She shoots me a glare, but there's a smile tugging at her lips, and I feel like I could take on all the humans just to see that smile again.

THIRTY-FOUR

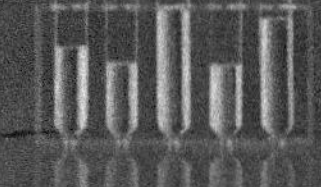

TALIA

Just like Cato promised, he dismissed everyone and then we got back to work, trying to sort through the rest of the research. As we do, he works through my worries with me one by one.

"What if they come?"

"They would have to get over the wall and through our people first. They will never get to you or the research," he promises as he labels some samples.

"What if the research isn't the only—"

"It has to be, or they wouldn't need it so desperately." He winks. I huff, and five minutes later, I fire more at him. He shoots them all down logically, and it shouldn't, but it reassures me. Now, I feel confident once more, as well as safe and sure.

Just like he knew I would.

Despite the fact I cannot allow myself to love Cato, he makes it so hard not to. He's always there for me, he holds me when I get weak, and he makes me laugh and values my intelligence. He challenges me and pushes me, all while holding my hand.

Cato is far too easy to love.

I know when this thing between us is over and he leaves for his mate, it will destroy me, because no matter how hard I try to protect my heart and soul, they already belong to him. He stole them with every soft touch, with every teasing kiss and innocent look. He made me his, and he doesn't even know it.

"What? No more?" He grins cheekily at me. His tail slides up my leg in that maddening way, as if he can't bear not to touch me, and I find myself leaning into his side. His grin slowly fades as he looks down at me, his throat bobbing as he swallows.

"Tally," he whispers, reaching down to cup my face and raise it farther as he searches my eyes. "I—"

He freezes, and I blink, ready to leap for him. I want to tell him how I feel so maybe he can love me back. "Cat—"

"Run!" he roars, starting to turn when I hear something flying through the air. I scream as he jerks and falls. Horror courses through me as I reach for him, blood spilling from a wound on his side. My head jerks around as humans pour into the lab dressed in all black, their guns turned to us. Behind them is an open hatch in the floor I didn't even know was there.

"Don't move!" they yell, but Cato roars.

His eyes are completely red as he climbs to his feet and steps before me, his arms spread wide and claws on display. "Kill him and take the girl!" That makes Cato roar even louder, and then he leaps at them.

Looking around for a weapon, I grab a microscope and slam it into the nearest guard when he reaches for me. More hands are there, however, and then I freeze when three more shots are fired. My head swivels around in horror, and a scream lodges in my throat as Cato stumbles back. Another guard steps forward and fires right into his chest, and Cato drops to his knees. His hands come up and cover his chest before he falls to his back. I sag in the man's arms as I stare at Cato and the hole in his chest.

"No!" The scream erupts from me so loudly, the man holding me lets go. "Cato!" He doesn't move.

Bodies of the men he killed are scattered around, but it's not enough, they converge on me. I refuse to leave him here, refuse to let him die. I kick and fight to get to his side, barely seeing the men attacking me. They don't want to hurt me, though, which is an advantage. I slide under someone's arm, grabbing a gun and slamming it into his head before dropping to Cato's side and pressing my hands to the wound in his chest. His blood covers my hands and arms.

"Don't you dare fucking die," I snarl. "You promised you would always be there."

He doesn't move, and then arms wrap around me again.

"Fuck you, let me go!" I yell and thrash.

"Someone shut her up," a guard snaps, and then something hard hits the back of my head, making me tumble forward as blackness claws at me. I try to fight it, to stay awake, because if I don't, it's all over…but it's so hard.

The last thing I hear before I fade into the waiting darkness are their voices. "Grab the research and leave the monster, it's already dead."

I whimper, my eyes catching on Cato as I'm hauled over someone's shoulder.

THIRTY-FIVE

CATO

I wake up with a groan. More than just the wounds are ripping my body in half, but my soul and heart as well.

"Talia!" I know I roar it.

I can't see, can't breathe, and when I feel hands, I attack. I give into the haze, needing to stay alive to save her. I promised her.

I fight, even as I'm slammed down onto something hard and straps are wrapped around my body. I twist and roar, biting and slashing while only one word leaves my lips in a desperate, anguished howl.

Her name.

Nothing else exists in the haze, only her. Her screams fill my head, I feel her hands on me, and I hear her begging me to stay. I fight until something else pierces the haze beyond the agony of my broken heart and wounded body.

A voice.

It's familiar and soft.

It doesn't belong to Tally, but it's human.

What is her name?

"I'm going to get her back."

I stare at the familiar face, trying to push back the haze and remember why I can't attack her, why Tally wouldn't like that. Tally… my mate. The agony is so deep, it rips me apart from the inside. My mate must be so scared.

The haze starts to come back.

"Mate," someone snaps.

Mate. My mate. I almost roar again. Where is she?

"I know you're in there, Cato, and that you can hear me. I'm going to get Talia back. I'm going to get your mate back, no matter what it takes. But you need to fight the haze, I know you can. Use your logic. You need to heal and be strong so you can protect her when I save her. Listen to me now, Cato. Your mate needs you."

Aria, I remember her now. Talia's friend. Her words pierce the haze as I slump. I see determination and fear in her eyes—fear for my mate. Talia needs me. It's the only thing that makes me swallow my whimper of agony when the haze starts to pull back. Instead, I ignore that agony. All that matters is Talia.

I need to get her back, and then I will never let her go again.

"You will bring her back to me?" My voice is more of a snarl, and I realise my people are standing around me, covered in wounds from my attacks. I should feel guilty, but I don't. Instead, all I feel is pain for the missing half of my soul.

My mate.

"I vow it," she states. "But I need your help." She looks at Akuji. "All of your help."

"You have it," Akuji replies instantly. "You have all of us, all of me, little human. You won't do this alone." Stepping forward, he takes Aria's hand as she looks down at me. "Let us get your Talia back."

I can feel the many wounds, some less serious, on my body, but none of it matters.

All that matters is her, my Talia, and they took her from me.

They want a war, and now they will have one.

I let them bandage my wounds. They tell me to eat, but I refuse, wanting to focus on coming up with a plan to save my mate.

Leaning against the rooftop railing, I let the pain wash through me. I deserve it. I let them sneak up on us. I let them take my mate. I deserve much worse, and I will spend the rest of my life on my knees before my mate, begging for her forgiveness. First, though, we must work together to get her back.

Fuck logic, and fuck playing it smart.

The humans want a war, and I'll give them one, even if Akuji doesn't want to. They took Talia. They took the only person in this entire world I would kill for. I feel the haze sneaking up on me every now and again, drawn by my fury, and I try to breathe through it. I need to stay present, knowing Aria is right—Talia needs me.

I ignore everything and everyone, even the worried eyes of my people and my brother. He tries to help me, but I push him away. I hate the weakness in my body, because it stops me from being as quick as I need to be. Maybe if I had been faster and stronger, they wouldn't have wounded me and taken her.

Akuji's voice calls out, interrupting my spiralling thoughts and bringing me back from the brink once more.

"Tribes, we are gathered here today for an emergency. Humans entered our city. They came over the wall and took one of us."

There's a chorus of growls and shouts.

"They have taken Talia, mate to Cato."

"A human?" someone asks in confusion.

A feral snarl rips from my throat, and those closest to me shoot me a worried look and move away. How dare they? I breathe through my anger when Akuji surges ahead with his own anger.

"A human, one of us," Akuji snarls, shutting that down. "She was happy here. She was staying here to protect our people in her own way. She is one of us, and she has been taken. We cannot let that stand. My mate has a plan to get her bac—"

"One human, and there is all this fuss?" someone snaps. "When it's our people who are missing, there is nothing!"

"Nothing?" Roroak, Akuji's general, retorts. "How many of our warriors have died going over the wall to try to retrieve children, lovers, and family? We are not giving the human special treatment, we are treating her like she is one of us because she is. Just like our Aria, our reigner's mate, our queen. She fights for us, she stands with us, and now she is asking for our help, as is Cato, another reigner. They have given so much for us—their lives, battles, and stations—yet they ask for one thing now. Are we going to turn our backs on them? The human is mated to one of us, who has given his entire existence for our happiness. I say let's give him back his happiness. Let us sacrifice for him for once."

"That's the most I've ever heard him speak," someone murmurs, making chuckles spread across the crowd.

All the talking pisses me off, and I start to pace, tuning them out. Let them squabble and hide behind their wall if they want to, but I am getting my mate back with or without them, even if I have to rip every single human to pieces to find her.

The haze is so strong, I can't hear or see anymore. I'm struggling to not attack my own people. I am weak, so fucking weak. I have to let Aria and Akuji fight my case for me, and I hate it.

When Aria looks at me, her words reach that deep place inside of me, one that still has some humanity left.

"Let's get our Talia back."

It's about time.

THIRTY-SIX

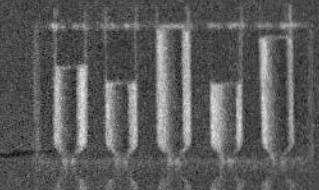

TALIA

A groan erupts from my throat, and I lift my heavy hand to prod the back of my head, where there's a sizable lump. I drop my hand with a wince and breathe through the sickness rolling through me. I try to open my eyes, but the bright light has me crying out, so I burrow into myself and just let the pain pass.

I can't remember where I am or what happened.

All I know is pain, and when it finally recedes enough for my brain to come back online, all thoughts slide to a halt.

Cato!

I scramble to my knees, nearly screaming at the agony it sends through my pained head. Hissing through it, I look around, trying to figure out where I am. They hurt Cato, and they took me and the research.

Which means…I'm back over the wall.

From the looks of the room I'm in, I'm also back at work.

Great.

The walls are that annoying, boring white colour. There are no windows, only one door, and I'm betting it's locked. They carelessly tossed me into an empty room, not even bothering to chain me, the idiots. I check the corners and notice a camera, so I flip it off before stumbling to my feet. I have to catch myself on the wall because my head spins. Breathing through the bile crawling up my throat and the weakness in my limbs, I force myself to harden my jelly legs and make my way to the door. I test the handle and find it locked like I thought, then I start to pace, not wanting to fall back into unconsciousness.

My thoughts are slow and sluggish but still pained.

Cato… God, Cato. I remember him going down, his chest ripped open… I turn my head and vomit everywhere. Wiping at my mouth and shooting a glare at the camera, I begin to pace again.

Logic, Tally. That's what he would tell me. Think logically.

He was hurt, but he can heal anything. He's practically indestructible, and if I'm right, he's safe. Someone will undoubtedly find him and get him help. That thought allows me to focus on my situation, because I'm all alone and surrounded by enemies in the one place I used to get excited to come to.

Did they get the research?

If so, then why am I alive?

I have so many questions and not enough answers. Lifting my hand, I go to scrub at my face, and that's when I see it—Cato's cracked, flaking blood on my hands and arms, and I'm sick all over again. I make sure to spray it across their perfect white walls, because fuck them.

Fuck the humans.

It's up to me to save the monsters and stop the humans from starting another war.

From playing god.

They might have been underestimating me my entire career, but it will work well for me now, because I'm going to play dumb and rip them apart from the inside.

First, I need to get out of this room.

CATO

I hurry through the streets with Aria and Akuji, trusting her plan. After all, she knows more about humans and their world than us. If it means working with them to get my Tally back, then I will do it. I will do anything.

Akuji isn't happy though. It's in every line of his body as he stares at his mate, his ferocious need to protect her evident in his gaze. When we stop to wait, Akuji turns to Aria. "Are you sure about this? Going through the wall—"

"We have no choice."

My impatience for getting Tally back makes me antsy, but I move away to give them privacy to talk, knowing I would be the same with my mate. I never should have let them get close enough to take her, and now I'll live with that fear and regret for the rest of my life.

When I get her back, I'm never letting her go again. I will lock her in my room and keep her pinned in our furs as I make her mine like I should have from the start.

I drift closer again when Aria starts to pace, trying to dismiss Akuji's worry. What they don't know is that no matter what, I am going with her over the wall to get my mate back. I listen to them bicker, not saying a word.

Let them argue, it won't stop me.

Her plan is simple—cause chaos over the wall, draw the humans who are patrolling beyond to those points, and sneak through. Next, we will make our way through the city, find Tally, and drag her home.

She isn't doing that without me. Tally would kick my ass if Aria got hurt, but I also plan on ripping apart every bastard who touched my mate.

"But how the hell do we hide you? My whole plan relies on being unseen," Aria snaps.

"We will figure it out, little mate." Akuji pulls her into his arms, but I don't miss his triumphant grin, even as jealousy fills me. He has his mate, while my arms feel empty without Talia. "As long as we are together."

"Yeah, being cute isn't going to help you," Aria mutters, smacking his chest and pulling away, propping her hands on her hips as she eyes him.

"Yeah, this will be fun." Akuji grins.

Just then, the first signal goes up, and my heart leaps.

I'm coming, Tally.

Just hold on, mate.

THIRTY-SEVEN

TALIA

"Hello? Is anybody watching, or are we all on break like normal and stroking each other's cocks?" I yell, pacing around the room as I glare at the camera. "Why kidnap me and just lock me in here? Or are you so unoriginal this is all you could come up with? Oh, I'm so scared?" I let all my fears and worries flow from my mouth until I'm just ranting at the camera. I'm so deep into a rant, I barely hear the door open, but I do, and I cut my words off and spin, glaring at the smiling face of Doctor Hayes.

"Hello, Talia. How wonderful of you to join us."

"Oh yeah, like it was a voluntary invitation," I snap, crossing my arms.

He frowns then, watching me carefully. "You work for us. We sent you on a field experiment, where you were kidnaped and held by monsters. We rescued you, and this is the thanks we get?"

"Who said I was kidnapped?" I ask, my eyes narrowed.

"You did not return with your research, despite knowing how

important it was to the company, and when we found you, you were still in the lab with a monster… Or am I wrong?" The look he gives me tells me he knows he is, but he wants me to say it. "Did you make friends, Talia? Did you make friends with some monsters and feel sorry for them?"

I grind my teeth as he smirks.

"Or maybe you looked at the research." My eye twitches, and he grins smugly. "Poor little Talia, are you fucking the monsters?"

I slap him as hard as I can, and his head snaps around, but when it comes back, he's furious. "You are going to regret that," he informs me, his eyes slitted, showing the evil underneath.

"Nah, it felt too good, and to see that perfect, anal-retentive hairstyle move out of place? It was worth it. So, Doctor Hayes, you seem obsessed with the monsters and fucking. Do you want to fuck them?" I run my eyes down his body. "It would make sense. You seem like you are strung awfully tight, so a good monster fuck might loosen that."

I blame my fear, my anger, and my head wound for my words, but in all honesty, I don't regret them. Maybe Aria is rubbing off on me, or maybe I hate the bastards who did this.

"Have you finished?" he sneers, clearly annoyed. I nod, and he sniffs, looking me over. "Good, let's get you cleaned up and back to work."

"Back to…work?" I hedge, staring at him like he's lost his mind.

"Yes. After all, we have the research now and the person who can read it."

Fuck.

CATO

The human world is terrible. No wonder my brilliant Talia didn't shine brightly here.

I follow Aria reluctantly, scanning our surroundings silently as I search for any traces of my Tally.

I don't have it in me to speak or be polite. Talia is my sole focus, and the only thing I can concentrate on is getting to her side. When Akuji talks to his mate, I block him out, not wanting the distraction.

The human world is not suitable for my sunshine Talia. It's too dark, too dull, and too full of pain. She needs pretty lights, flowers, books, and art. She needs beauty and happiness. She needs support…

She needs me, and when I get her back, I'm going to show her that.

For a moment, a dark thought spirals through my head. What if she doesn't want to come back? What if she wants to stay here with the humans? But then I remember her fighting to get to me, fighting her own people.

No, she belongs with us over the wall.

She's just as much of a monster as we are. Fuck the humans. They had her, and they mistreated her. She's ours now.

When we reach a run-down shack that seems to be on stilts and constructed of mismatched metals, Aria shoves Akuji and me into the shadows on the side of the structure. We hunch there as she glares at us, the sound of heavy breathing and muttering coming from inside the building. The stench of this place makes my nose itch. The scent of unwashed bodies, sweat, decay, and death are all too much for my oversensitive senses.

"Don't move, I won't be long." She glares at us before turning and walking away.

"Your mate is kind of scary," I murmur to Akuji, and he chuckles as he watches her retreating form.

"Isn't she just?" His voice sounds soft and loving, and I wonder if that's what I sound like when I talk about my Tally. "Yours is very smart, it must be intimidating."

"Nope, I love that she can put me on my ass, scientifically speaking." I grin at him, and he chuckles, clapping my shoulder.

"I'm happy for you, brother. I truly am. You deserve someone who sees your brilliance and your love for all things brainy."

I roll my eyes and grin back at him. "And you deserve someone who can handle your crazy."

He laughs harder than before, and we both freeze when we hear what's happening inside.

Akuji straightens and begins to growl. Sighing, I reach for him, knowing what this means, but I could no more hold him back than they could me if it were Tally. Instead, I watch him storm into the shack.

We are going to end up killing every human here.

"Monster! Monster!" I hear someone scream.

Yep, these two are as sneaky as, well, monsters.

A moment later, I hear a tell-tale death gurgle and almost smack my head. Akuji just killed someone…or maybe Aria. I wouldn't put it past her. Fuck, I better go see if they are okay. Tally would be so pissed if I let her friend get hurt.

Sliding around the corner, I'm just about to go inside when I hear a soft thunk.

Turning, I crouch automatically, but it's no use. An object flies at me, expanding and pinning me to the ground, and then electricity shocks my body. The agony rips through my still healing nerve endings as I jerk and snarl under the assault.

Through my pain, I see humans storming towards us.

Not again!

The electricity is too strong, and I start to black out, only coming to when Aria screams. That noise cuts through me. It's the same sound Tally made. I manage to turn my head to see her screaming on a human's back while Akuji lies on the ground, unmoving. With dawning horror, I watch them knock Aria out.

Not again.

Not ever again.

I release the haze, and with an anguished roar, I rip from the net. I hear them yell at each other, but I don't care. I cut through their masses, gutting them and ripping off heads. Blood splatters me while objects hit me, trying to take me down.

My only thought is of Tally.

If I die now, no one will save her.

I push through the pain, tearing into throats, but more and more soldiers converge on me until a bigger shock hits my neck, right between the connection to my brain and spine, and I cannot fight the waiting darkness anymore.

I plunge into it, her name on my lips once more.

THIRTY-EIGHT

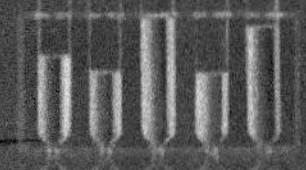

TALIA

I'm led to the emergency showers near one of the labs, and a guard stands at the door as I strip and wash, getting all the blood and vomit from me. I almost cry again as I scrub at Cato's blood before I force myself to keep moving. I can't help him if I'm an emotional wreck and break down. They are all counting on me to protect them, so I need to be strong.

I would do anything to have him here and feel him pull me into his arms and promise me everything will be okay. That's when I realise just how much I've grown to depend on Cato. I always promised myself I'd never trust another man again, but I do.

I trust him completely, and I need him.

It's not because I can't survive without him, I could, but it would hurt. Without him, I don't feel like me. Before him, I was drifting, just surviving and overworking, but then when I was with him, I learned how to smile again, laugh, trust, explore, and see beauty. I also learned how to find love, but there can't be a future with him.

There just can't.

"Hurry it up, or I'll come in there and help you," the guard yells, banging on the wall near the door, making me jump. I quickly dunk my head and step out, drying off and putting on the scrubs they left for me. I don't want to give them an excuse to come in here with me. I know better than that. This guard has *those* eyes—the ones every girl recognises. He's mentally fucking me, and all he would need is an excuse to attack. It's in the cruel, vicious tilt of his lips and the gleam in his eyes when he turns to me, blocking the doorway and my exit. I swallow my fear and tilt my head back, staring straight into his eyes.

"Move please," I tell him with a strong voice that surprises even me. "Your boss won't like being kept waiting."

The reminder of his job seems to do the trick. He moves aside and grabs my arm. "Fine, let's take you to the boss." The smirk he gives me makes me shiver, but I fake my confidence as I'm dragged down the corridor. This is a floor I haven't been on before. It has to be at the top, which requires high security clearance.

I'm dragged past offices and closed rooms before being shoved through the doors of a lab. We have to wait as it decontaminates us and then put on coats before we are allowed in. When I step through, my jaw almost drops. This lab is state of the art, top of the line, and massive, with huge, bright windows. It's better than any of the labs they gave me to work in, and it's clear where their main research happens. The fact that they probably still work on monsters here taints that beauty, though, and all I see when I look around is the horror of the lab and bunker beyond the wall.

I let the handsy guard drag me over to a workstation, where the research I found beyond the wall is waiting, and fear fills me as I'm shoved down into a comfortable chair. The guard crosses his arms and glares down at me as we wait. A few moments later, Hayes comes trotting in, sees me sitting there, and smiles.

"Good, you're ready to start work again." He smirks.

"No," I retort, narrowing my eyes. "I'm not."

"Now, Talia—"

"That's Doctor Ledger to you." I sniff, eyeing him.

His eyes narrow slightly, and the door opens again, but we continue our staring contest. "Oh, sorry, I was just hoping to steal you for a moment, sir."

The voice is familiar, achingly so, and I groan as I look over at my dickweed ex. Of course he's here, and of course he's working with the dickhead who's been experimenting on monsters. He stops when he sees me, his mouth opening and closing before he smirks and moves closer. "I heard you found her, sir. Good work."

"I wasn't a lost dog," I snap.

"No?" He arches his eyebrow. "Then maybe stop acting like a fucking stray."

All my anger and fear explode through me, and before they can stop me, I launch myself at him, punching him square in his smug, stealing face. He staggers back as I shake out my hand. "Fuck, that hurt!" I exclaim, even as he covers his nose.

"You bitch!" He goes to grab me, but the guard steps in.

"Sir?"

"Take him away for now and let him lick his wounds." Hayes chuckles, and we both watch as my ex is dragged off, shouting. I simply blow him a kiss and try to ignore my aching knuckles as I sit back down. I eye my boss, and he eyes me right back, sighing as he also sits.

"I thought you were better than this, Tal—Doctor Ledger. You have such great potential. You got the research, and I know you understand it. We need that. Work with us" —he holds his hands up in a pleading gesture— "and you can have everything you've ever wanted."

Before, I would have jumped at the chance, but not now. Now, I know what they do. "I will not be the person who helps you kill thousands."

"Of creatures!" he yells and then grabs my face, his true colours showing. The vile bastard inside him bleeds into his eyes. "You have one more chance to comply, Talia, before I force you. Do not be a fool."

"Then I guess I'm a fool." I spit right in his face.

He jerks back, wiping at his face as his expression closes down. All emotion is gone, but I refuse to be afraid. They clearly want me alive for something, they clearly need me, and I've had enough of being pushed around and used.

Fuck them.

Fuck him.

The guard comes back and glares at me, but I ignore him too. "Chain her to the desk," Hayes orders. I go to get up, but the guard pushes me down before he quickly shackles my left ankle to the table leg. He stands back as I struggle, trying to free myself, but all I do is cut into my leg. Biting back a curse, I glare at them.

"It seems you've gone feral since spending time with the monsters." Hayes sniffs.

"And don't you forget it." I grin, even as I grind my teeth. "I will never help you."

"Don't be a fool and make the same mistake your parents made," he snaps.

I stare at him, blinking in confusion. "My parents?" I ask slowly, not understanding how they have anything to do with this.

He just laughs. "Yes. You didn't know they worked for me? Poor little Talia, always left in the dark."

I feel my nostrils flare in anger. "You leave them out of this. They never would have worked for you!"

"Oh, but they did," he purrs as he leans in. "In fact, they were the best at what they did…until they grew a conscience and we had to get rid of them. We can't have any of this getting out, now can we?"

My heart slams as I stare at him. "Get rid of them?" My voice is small, panicked.

"You didn't really think the great Doctor Ledge and his wife died in an accident, did you?" He looks me over. "We had them killed. They knew too much, and they were going to tell. They even stole research to take it to the press. We couldn't have that, and then imagine our surprise when their daughter applied for a job here. Well, we couldn't let that go to waste, could we? Keep your enemies close and all that jazz."

My ears ring, and the pain in my head triples as I struggle to breathe.

No, no.

"They died in an accident."

"That's how I made it look." He grins. "Now get to work before you end up the same way." He leaves me alone, and I crumple onto the desk.

Horror wars with disbelief.

He killed them.

He killed my parents.

And now he's going to kill me unless he gets what he wants.

THIRTY-NINE

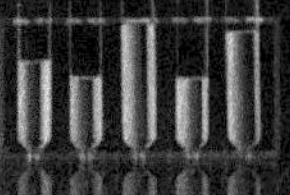

TALIA

They leave me there, obviously expecting me to work, and in all honesty, my fingers itch to explore the research they have here to see if it fills in the missing pieces like I think, but I refuse.

If they want to kill me, then let them.

I won't break my promise to Cato and his people, not even if it means my death. The only thing I regret is not getting to say goodbye to Cato and telling him how I feel.

I wish I had held on tight and took the chance when I had it. I wish I hadn't spent my last few days so terrified and working. I should have savoured every moment with him, and now my memories are all I have to get me through this. I'm alone, so completely alone. They can't come over the wall, and Aria can't risk it.

If I don't work, I'll die. I've accepted that now.

It gives me a freeing sort of peace, as does knowing my parents were fighting against this so strongly, they were willing to risk it all and died for it. It only makes me more determined. I will not let them down, and I will never help the man who killed them.

Instead, I rest my head on the desk and fall asleep, escaping into my memories, where my parents are still alive and Cato is there, holding me tight.

I wake with a jerk when something slams near my head. "If you won't take this seriously, then the boss wants you to see something."

The guard's smirk is downright evil, and I don't fight as he undoes my shackles, because where would I go? I'm at the very top of their heavily guarded skyscraper, and I'm not a fighter. Instead, I just let him lead me away.

I don't even look where we are going. What's the point? I'm a dead woman walking.

When we go to a suspicious corridor, I perk up and drag my feet. "Is this where you kill me?" I ask.

"You wish," he scoffs as he keeps dragging me, and I start to fight, my instincts kicking in when I see a cell door. When he opens it, though, I stop fighting altogether.

I gape, not believing my eyes.

I wonder if they already killed me and I've gone to heaven.

There, on the floor, is an unconscious Cato.

I shout his name as I'm tossed inside, barely listening to the door slamming closed. I scramble to his side, trying to turn him over, but he's too big. Instead, I press my fingers against his neck and wait. He has a heartbeat, thank god. I lean into his side and cry. "Cato, oh god, I thought you were dead. I didn't know you were here."

There's a groan, and he twitches below me. "Tally…" His voice is garbled, broken, and weak.

I sob harder. "Cato."

"Tally." His voice is stronger. "No cry." He slowly turns and wraps his arms around me. "Sleep, everything fine."

"Cato, please, wake up," I beg. "We are in trouble."

A moment later, I am rolled onto my back, his fully awake body poised over mine. His sharp claws slash across the floor as he searches the area. I can't help but cry harder as I reach up and cup his snarling face and turn it so he meets my gaze. He blinks his bright red eyes, but I've never been so happy to see someone before.

"Cato, you're really here," I whisper. "How?"

He grunts and relaxes a little, but he shoots a glare at the door.

"Cato," I beg.

His tongue darts out, wetting his lips and fangs, and a pulse goes through me. That has his head swinging around as he sniffs the air and growls, except nothing but comfort fills me at the sound. "Tally safe."

"Yes, yes, I'm safe," I promise, leaning up and kissing every inch of his face. When I pull back, his eyes are black again.

"Tally, my Tally." He pulls me closer, holding me tightly. "I was so scared I would never see you again." My Cato is back, and I cry harder as he rubs my back. "Shh, everything is fine. I'm here now, you're safe."

"How?" I ask, pulling back and blinking my teary eyes to bring him into view.

"Aria led us over the wall. We were on our way to you when we were ambushed, but I can't be too mad since it got me what I wanted—to be by your side." He grins, softly brushing my hair back. "Are you okay? I don't smell any fresh injuries."

"Just a headache," I reply and then groan when he starts to massage my temples. "I can't believe you came for me."

"Of course I did." He frowns. "I will always come for you, Tally."

"You shouldn't have put yourself in danger like that." My hands skate over the bandage on his chest. "I was so worried you were dead."

His claw tips my chin up until I meet his eyes. "Not even death could stop me from getting to your side."

For a moment, nothing but love and relief pour through me before I smack him over and over. "You were safe. You were alive. You risked it all!" I scold. "You big red fool!"

He watches me, his eyebrow rising. "Not exactly the thanks I thought I'd get," he deadpans.

"You risked your life for me!" I yell.

"Of course." He frowns, confused. "Did you hit your head?"

"Cato," I snap, exasperated. "You shouldn't have done that."

"Why not?" he retorts angrily.

"Because… Because your people need you!"

"And?" he replies.

"Your people need you, Cato, but no one needs me!" I finish, panting as I stare into his angry eyes.

"I need you," he roars. "Don't you see? I can't live without you, you brilliant fool." He grabs me, pulls me close, and slams his lips onto mine.

I moan, and he swallows the sound, kissing me breathless, and I give as good as I get. I lick and nip his lips, sucking the sting away as he snarls and flips us again so I'm pinned beneath him. He wedges his body between my thighs as he sucks on my tongue.

Just as suddenly as it starts, it stops when an electric shock flows through him and into me. I scream, and he throws himself away, writhing on the floor and clawing at his neck, where I hadn't even noticed a slim silver collar. "Cato!" I yell, pressing my hand to my lips, where the shock still sits.

I get to my feet and rush to the door, pounding on it until my hands cut open. "Stop it, stop it!" I scream. "Please stop!" I turn back, covering my lips as he roars as more shocks go through his body. Just then, the door opens, and I almost fall through it, only to stop when a gun is pressed to my head.

Cato snarls and narrows his eyes on us, even as he claws at the collar.

"Time's up." The gun remains against my head as I'm dragged away. "If you move, she dies." When the door slams shut, I sag, aching to rush back to Cato's side. The guard slams me against the wall and meets my eyes. "Now do you see? If you don't work, we'll kill your little pet."

"I'll work," I say instantly. I would do anything to protect him.

He's here.

Cato came for me.

They have Cato, and I refuse to let them hurt him, so I'll play nice for now.

I work for a few hours, and after, they let me change into the clothes they give me, finally getting me out of those fucking scrubs.

Honestly, though, I'm not their little lackey. They watch me with bored eyes and eventually wander off, so I start to create a plan. I don't know how it will all come together yet, but I need to get Cato and the research out of here. I sit to hide it under the desk, where there's a box for rubbish, and start to add bits and bobs as I go so they don't get suspicious.

I'm just straightening from adding some samples when the door opens behind me, making me stiffen. "Get up, Doctor, there's someone we need you to see."

With that, I'm forced to my feet at gunpoint and dragged down more corridors before being shown to a door.

"Wait here," the guard orders.

"For?" I question, but he just ignores me. "Obviously deaf as well as dumb," I mutter.

He turns to me, a scowl twisting his lips as he steps closer, towering over me. "What did you say?"

"You're going to have to try better than that to scare me," I reply sweetly, patting my hand on his chest and pushing him back. "I've been surrounded by nearly eight-foot monsters for far too long for a weak, steroid using bitch like you to intimidate me." I flutter my lashes.

His hand comes up, and he's about to slap me when his radio buzzes. "Let her into the room."

"You're a lucky bitch. Next time, you won't be," he hisses, grabbing my arm roughly, opening the door, and flinging me inside.

Turning, I smash my fist into it. "Bastard," I mutter, but then I freeze when I turn around. Chained across a table is Aria. I hurry to her side, dropping to my knees as I flutter my hand over her head.

"Aria?" I whisper "Aria?" I repeat louder, but she doesn't stir.

Running my hand under her sweaty hair, I find her pulse and breathe a sigh of relief that she's alive. She's clearly knocked out but alive. There's no water that I can use to wash her head and search for an injury, so I sit back on my heels, gnawing on my lip before looking around. They brought me here for a reason… Was it to use her against me?

Maybe.

Sighing, I get to my feet and wander around the table, keeping my eyes on her the entire time. "Hurting her won't get you anything, I barely know her. She's just someone you employed, and she's as dumb as a box of rocks if you ask me," I call, hoping they will let her go or at least won't hurt her. "I would just get rid of her now and save you a whole heap of trouble. Trust me, that's all she's good for—trouble." The words spewing from my lips make me feel sick, and I pray if she's listening, she knows I don't mean them.

The door opens again, admitting Doctor Hayes. "Now that's not nice, Talia. She came all this way to save you from us." He cocks his head as he looks her over. "I'll admit she is…lacking intelligence, but she is brave." He shuts the door behind him and leans against it as he looks me over.

"Sit."

"I'm not a dog," I snap.

"No, if you were, you'd be better behaved. Now sit," he demands, "before I decide I don't need her after all and slice that pretty little throat."

Eyes narrowed, I sit stiffly in the chair, my hands folded on the table. I glance between her and him, wondering what his plan is. She came for me with Cato…and Akuji. Oh god, he wouldn't have let her go alone. I want to ask, but I dare not. It would give away my hand, and that's what he wants. He's searching for any weaknesses, and I've already shown Cato is one, and because of that, he will be hurt.

I won't let that happen to Aria and Akuji if he's here.

Instead, I stay silent, waiting, watching, and wondering what his next move will be. Suddenly, there is a groan from Aria. My eyes snap to her as she wakes, the groans filled with pain making me wince. The noises stop, and her eyes open, squinting in the light. She lifts her head, and her eyes lock on me.

I watch as emotions cross her features, almost too fast to track—shock, guilt, worry, happiness, and fear.

I know what this must look like, but I just watch her, eyeing her bloodstained, bruised face. Her clothes are filthy, and her hair is crusted with dried dirt and blood. She looks like hell, and I'm spotless. I hate it. I want to tell her everything, to beg her to trust me, but I don't because I can't give the plan away.

Not yet.

She takes in my face before dropping her gaze to her chained hands and then looking back at me.

"You're not chained."

Her comment is casual, but I hear the accusations underneath and flinch. She doesn't trust me. My heart cracks. Aria is my friend, one of my only friends, and she doesn't trust me. I shouldn't blame her, especially given what she's woken up to, but it hurts.

I look over her shoulder to Doctor Hayes, who appears smug, and I see her stiffen and try to follow my gaze, but she can't see him. "I told her if she tried anything, I would hurt you. Talia is smart enough to know her odds, unlike you. No, our scientist here is smarter than that."

Her eyes stay locked on me, trying to read my expression as a million thoughts flicker through her own. Her fists clench, and I have no doubt she's wondering if smashing heads will help. I wish it would. I wish I were half as brave as she is, but all I have is my intelligence, and right now, they need that.

They will keep Cato, Aria, and Akuji alive as long as I play nice.

I can't stand the pain in her eyes, though, nor the anger directed at me as she questions my every motive. It hurts more than I thought it would.

"I'm so sorry, Aria," I find myself saying, knowing I shouldn't. I reach for her, hoping she won't reject me. I can't lose her, she's too important to me. Her eyes close for a moment, and it makes me worry how severe her injuries are. Did they drug her or hit her? I glare accusingly at Doctor Hayes, who just smirks at me.

When Aria says nothing, Doctor Hayes circles behind me. It's my turn to have my spine stiffen, uncomfortable with him behind me. Aria watches him, and I swallow my nerves.

"We knew you would come for her. I'm surprised about the other monster, but we knew her mate would follow her. It's exactly what we wanted."

I jerk in surprise. Did he lie to her or to me? Cato and I aren't mated, so that's a lie. What game is he playing, and why can't I figure out the rules?

"A trap," she replies, following his game and his lie better than I can. "Is Akuji okay?" she finally asks, and her voice is small and worried. Her love for her monster shines in her eyes, and I wonder if mine do that when it comes to Cato. I wonder if Doctor Hayes truly believes we are mated to monsters.

"Is that the monster we found you with?" Hayes asks, and I want to tell her not to answer, because there is interest in his voice—interest you don't want aimed at you. It means he wants something from you. I try to warn her, but she ignores me.

"Yes," she snaps. "Where is he?"

"Would you like to see?" Hayes queries softly, pretending to be nice, even though this is exactly what he wants. She's playing into his hands, and I want to scream and shout, but that will do nothing. Instead, I watch Aria nod, and then her shackles are released. Her hands are still chained together, but no longer attached to the table. She tests them while eyeing him with malice. Maybe she's not falling for his games as much as he thinks.

"I'll take you to him," Hayes offers and moves around me. I watch as he heads to the door, my eyes locked on Aria. I silently beg her to be safe and play the game, but I know she can't understand.

She struggles to her feet, keeping her eyes on me, and in her gaze is a promise to come back for me.

I wish she wouldn't. I want her to get out of here, to be safe and run away as fast as she can, because this is the true monster's nest, not over the wall.

With one last look at me, she turns and walks from the room, and I worry it will be the last time I'll see her.

FORTY

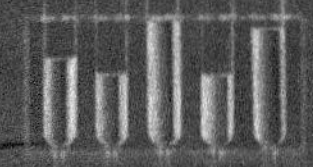

TALIA

I wait in the room, but Hayes never comes back. Instead, a guard drags me from the room and back to my lab, where he throws me down and demands I work. How can I when I'm so distracted by my worry for Cato, Aria, and Akuji?

What are they doing to them while I'm chained to a table and being forced to work on the very experiments that made them?

I'm left alone for hours without food or water. Eventually, the guard reports that I haven't been working to Hayes, and I'm dragged back to my cell and thrown inside. I scramble over to Cato. He's on his side, jerking with the force of the collar.

Oh god, tell me they didn't leave this on the entire time?

Tears fill my eyes, and when the shocks stop, he sags and his eyes roll shut. "Cato," I sob.

"Tally." He groans. "Don't cry." He cups my face, and I cradle his hand in mine. "No tears," he rasps out, forcing himself into a sitting position and pulling me into his arms, where I feel safe.

"Please, your tears kill me, Tally." He pulls my face back and wipes my cheeks. I cry harder at how kind he's being, despite the situation he's in all because of me.

"Please, mate, stop," he pleads.

I still at the word, my breath freezing in my throat as I stare at him. "Mate?" I croak out.

He frowns, his brow furrowed as his tail wraps around me. "Huh?" he asks, sounding confused, but he's happy I'm not crying anymore.

"You called me mate, as in friend or…" I trail off. He has a mate out there somewhere, a monster, so why is he calling me that? I know where I stand with him.

"Mate as in my forever, as in my destined. I mentioned mates, Tally." He scratches his head, watching me. "Did they do something to you?" Anger flares in his eyes.

"Wait, wait, I'm…I'm your mate?"

"Of course you are." He frowns, watching me carefully. "I told you that. I told you how amazing you are."

"I-I thought you were talking about someone else!" I yell, smacking his chest. "I was insanely jealous. I kept thinking I was going to have to give you up and that's why you never took things further, because you knew there would be someone you loved one day and it would never be me."

His eyes narrow with each word until I squeal when he pins me on my back, his arms on either side of my head. "As if I would ever let you give me up," he snarls. "I wouldn't let it happen. You could try to run, and I would follow you. I followed you over the fucking wall into the human city, Tally, because you are mine. I knew it the first moment I met you and every moment since. Every smile you threw my way, every time you laughed at something I said, and every small touch and kiss only solidified that. You. Are. Mine." He kisses me, but I pull away, grinning.

"I really thought you meant someone else," I whisper.

"Foolish little human. How can one person be so smart but also so dumb?" He huffs a laugh. "It's always been you, and it will always be you. Do I need to tell you every moment of every day?" I shake my head. “When I mentioned mates and what I spoke about that night, I was talking about you.”

Tears fill my eyes again, and he panics, pressing his lips to mine.

“Please, Talia, stop crying. Your tears kill me.”

“It was just what you said was so sweet, and I thought it was about someone else,” I whisper. “I was so jealous, but I couldn’t give you up, even then. I was determined to make the most of it and keep you while I could, even if it broke my heart.”

“Oh, my little Tally,” he purrs, pressing his lips to every inch of my face in small, loving kisses. “My foolish, brilliant Tally.”

“But… But you never fuck me.” My cheeks heat, but I refuse to be ashamed.

He groans and grinds his hard cock into my stomach as if to show me how much he needs me, and desire slams through me so hard, it steals my breath. My legs wrap around his waist as I grind against his length, my body catching up with our words and the fact that this huge, strong, brilliant monster is mine.

All mine.

“I wanted you to be ready. I wanted it to be your choice, Tally, to give yourself over to me, because once that happens, I could never give you up. I also wanted you to have the life you want, even if it meant going back home over the wall. But I’m selfish,” he snarls. “I realised it that night. I could never let you go, not even if that’s what you wanted. You are mine to keep, mine to mate, touch, and kiss. You are mine, and there is not a place in this world where you could ever escape from me. Even if we haven’t fully mated yet, that doesn’t matter to me, all that does is that you hold my very soul, my heart, in your tiny human hands, and I willingly put them there. If you are mine, then I am yours with every fibre of my being.”

“Prove it,” I demand as I meet his eyes, needing him so badly. I thought I had lost him. I thought he wasn’t mine, and then I did lose him. We might not make it out of here alive, and I refuse to have regrets. I want Cato. I have since that first moment he turned those soft eyes on me.

From when he danced with me.

From when he made me laugh so hard, my stomach ached.

From when he held me so tightly and promised to protect me.

"I will not mate you in this tiny little cell, Tally. When I take you for the first time, it will be in our nest, where I can spend hours making you scream."

"Fuck," I whisper, even as he continues that slow grind, digging his huge cock into my pussy. I groan at the friction. The pressure is great but not enough, and it just winds me up further until my pussy is throbbing in time with my heart.

"Tally, baby, if you don't stop, I'm going to slam into that tight little cunt and pump you full of my seed," he warns, biting my lower lip with his fangs until I'm gasping. Moaning, he rolls free of me. I get to my elbows and see him on his knees. His head hangs down, and his eyes blaze red as he watches me.

Flopping back, I cover my face, trying to breathe through my desire. He's right—they are observing, and the last thing I need is to give them more ammunition. We have waited this long, so we can wait a little while longer.

"I'm going to have such lady blue balls," I mutter, and he barks out a laugh.

"You're not the only one, Tally," he replies, even as he crawls back to me and pulls me into his arms. "But I have waited for you my entire life, so I can wait a little longer," he whispers in my ear. "Forever if I have to, because you are worth it. And this, just holding you, just having your heart, is enough."

"Maybe for you," I mutter, and he chuckles breathlessly against my ear, sending a shiver through me.

"Behave, Tally. Now tell me everything they did today." He kisses my pounding pulse, and it's hard to concentrate with every hard inch of him pressed against my back, but I recount everything that happened, and when I'm done, the desire is gone, replaced by worry and anger.

"I'm sorry, Tally," he murmurs, holding me tighter. "Now, let's work through the problem together." We do, starting to work through options for escape, just like when we work side by side, and it brings me a sense of calm I can only get from him.

We are just weighting the pros and cons of me working and not working when the cell door opens and his collar activates. He throws me away so I don't get hurt, and I watch helplessly as he writhes in agony.

"Come with us, and I will turn it off," a guard barks.

With one last look at Cato, I hurry from the cell so they will turn it off. Once outside, I glare at the two guards. "Turn it off now, or I will go nowhere," I snarl.

They chuckle but stop it, and I relax. "I wouldn't be making demands if I were you, little girl. It seems the boss has run out of patience with you."

"What do you mean?" I ask, edging away as they grin at me.

"It means if you won't work or mate the monster to give him what he needs, then he's going to give you to one that will."

FORTY-ONE

CATO

The collar cuts off, and I slump in agony. Every time they do it, it rips open my wounds, never giving them enough time to fully heal. It leaves me in pain, but not as much as having Talia taken from me again does.

I hate it. I feel helpless, useless.

She's my mate, and I can't protect her from them. I'm locked away again like a beast, kept in a cage once more, and it would usually be enough to send me into the haze, but knowing she needs me keeps it at bay for now.

They keep taking her from me, though, and that has me riding the edge as I pace the cell, wondering what is happening right now.

Think, Cato. Work through the problem.

Her voice is in my head as I slash at the walls and roar.

Think.

They need her alive. They need her brain. They need the research.

That means she's safe.

I tell myself that over and over, but it doesn't lessen my need for my mate. It just leaves me angry and my beast side champing at the bit to get to our mate and kill those who dare to touch her. She is mine.

I cannot believe she didn't know. I laugh bitterly. I am such a fool. I should have spent every moment I had with her showing her what she means to me and how much I love her.

I won't make that mistake again. She will never doubt her place in my life or the fact that I am hers and she is mine.

The collar buzzes again, dropping me to my knees. With a snarl, I fight against the current. Each time they use it, I get more used to it, and this time, I stay upright, fighting the agony as the door opens. Ten men with guns pour in.

"Behave, and we will turn it off. Misbehave, and that tiny human you're so fond of will be passed between the guards until there is nothing left of her," one barks.

I snarl but force myself to relax and not attack them.

They would hurt Talia to get to me, and I will never let that happen. I can survive whatever they wish to do to me. I have before and will again for her.

They cut the collar off, and with the guns pointed at me, they slowly lead me from the cell. I behave, despite the fact I want to rip them to pieces for simply speaking about her. The process is slow, since they won't turn the guns away, but I'm finally led to a room similar to my cell, only this one has a glass wall with an observation room, where a scientist with cruel eyes stands.

I ignore him as they order me to lie on the metal bed. I do, with my arms on the rests, and a moment later, metal bands cover my chest, arms, legs, and neck, holding me still as the guards back against the wall.

Idiots.

"I want the full workup. Let's see what the effects of its lifestyle have had," the doctor calls, his voice sort of mumbled through the glass. I resign myself to being their lab rat, bite my tongue, and hold back my snarls as they take my blood.

They scan me and check every inch of me over, even my teeth.

I take it all and let myself think of nothing but Talia. I remember her smile, her laugh, and the feel of her hands on my skin. It keeps me calm. When they wander away, leaving me here, I meet the eyes of the scientist who is watching me curiously. "Where is my mate?" I demand, needing to know she's okay.

The grin he gives me is vicious and reminds me of the men who used to torture us as kids.

"Talia?" The scientist smirks. "Right now, she's in with another beast, being rutted and fucked in every hole so I can get what I need."

The haze explodes.

With a roar, I sit upright, the metal bands snapping across my body. There's yelling, but none of it matters.

She's all that matters.

Filled with fury, anger, and resentment, the haze takes over until I'm across the lab, ripping the guns from the guards. I break them before I grab one's head and rip out his throat. I let his corpse drop to the floor as I turn to another, who's hitting me with a baton.

Everything is hazy and tinged with red, the bloodlust so extreme, I couldn't stop if I wanted to.

My movements are fast and unhinged.

Grabbing a scientist, I lift him into the air and rip him apart right down the middle, his organs and blood spraying across everything. I ignore the yells. The door is locked, so they can't get out, and I almost laugh as I tear through their masses. This is too easy.

They are so weak.

I let out an earth-shattering roar, and I hear the alarms blare. I still hear their screams, but I don't care as I drop my head, my fangs dripping blood.

They are all dead men.

I'll kill them all until I can get my mate.

TALIA

"No, let me go!" I scream as I'm dragged to a secret level I didn't even know existed. This one is equipped with so much security, I know there will never be any hope of escape. There are too many guards, cameras, sensors, locked cells, and doors, and I begin to feel hopeless.

I thought they needed my brain, so why are they doing this? Why do they want me to mate with a monster? If I were thinking clearly, I could probably figure it out, but right now, my fight-or-flight instinct is taking hold as I'm dragged screaming and kicking through the corridor.

I sag and look around as I'm led through the lab. Compared to those I worked in or even the ones downstairs, this one is a butcher's market. I cannot even begin to describe what I see. There are tubes, like those in the bunker, and inside them are half-monster children in various states of growth.

There are bigger ones spread on tables, being cut up, and there's even a pregnant monster being cut open. I turn my head and throw up on my guard, gagging and getting sick over and over.

They are monsters.

They are evil.

I knew it, but seeing this? I can't stop being sick, and the guard shouts and drops me to my knees. "Fuck. Look at my shoes, the stupid bitch!" one yells and kicks me like a dog.

I whimper, tears in my eyes as I look around.

"I'll take her, go clean up," another orders, grabbing me and dragging me quickly to avoid me being sick. At the end of the lab are rows of cells with glass walls. He picks one at random, unlocks it, and throws me in before locking it behind me.

Standing there with a grin, he stares at me and says, "Good luck, I'm going to enjoy this."

That's when I feel breath fanning across the back of my neck.

I freeze like prey, unable to move. I feel that warm breath move closer, and then I turn, unable to stop. There, towering above me, is a monster.

He's red-skinned, horned, and fanged, but this one has bright orange eyes, and instead of one tail, he has two. His legs are slightly bowed, and his back and sides are covered in long, sharp spikes. He looks absolutely terrifying, but I'm learning some of the scariest-looking things are actually the nicest and that a pretty face can hide vile souls.

"Hi," I squeak out.

There's a bang on the glass, but I don't look away from the monster. "Don't worry, bitch, we won't let it kill you. The boss just wants it to fuck you." The guard laughs.

"Human," the monster hisses, lifting his nose and sniffing. "You smell like monster."

I swallow, refusing to be afraid. I am sure he can smell my fear, but I still fake it. "Because I am the mate of a monster."

"No, not mated." He sniffs, pacing around me. "Not yet at least."

"We haven't actually had time." I huff, and he chuckles as he stops before me again.

"They want me to breed you," he snarls, hissing in my face.

"They can fuck off, and if you touch me, I'll kill you, monster or not, and then my mate will come and rip your corpse to pieces for even looking at me." I sniff.

He laughs. "I like you. You are strong, not like the other humans, who all stink of lies and fear."

"I am not like them. I'm on your side," I promise. I look back at the guard. "Hear that, fucker? I am on their side. Fuck you and your sick-ass experiments, you piece of shit!" I rage, slamming my fists into the glass. "I will never fucking help you!" Huffing, I look back at the monster. "Are you going to try to breed me?"

"No." He cocks his head. "I will never do what they want. They will have to kill me first."

I relax a little, wandering around his tiny cell with no privacy as the guard watches us, unsure what to do. "What are you? You are not like the monsters I know."

"I am a splice. I was made here. I know nothing else but this lab," he answers, watching me curiously.

I eye him, nodding. "They modified your genetics. I wonder why."

"You are a scientist," he sneers.

"Yes, and I'm using that to protect the monsters by figuring out what they want with us, and then I plan to burn all their fucking research as a giant fuck you," I tell him unashamedly.

He nods like he likes that answer. "I do not mate the unwilling. I will not be their puppet, despite how much they torture me, and they know that. For them to throw you in here, they must not like you."

"No, they want to break me." I shrug. "But they won't succeed. Men have been trying my whole life." I meet his eyes. "When I get out of here, I'll let you all free. You can go over the wall with us, meet others of your kind, and find a home, happiness, and a future."

He blinks and then offers me a slow smile. "I would like that…to be happy."

As he's facing me, the door opens and a guard storms in, lifts his gun, and blows out the monster's brains as I scream. I scream and scream, even as they drag me out before a frowning Hayes. "That was his last chance, he knew that. His death is on your hands, Talia. Not to worry, there are plenty more monsters to force into your cunt, some who will enjoy it. Take her back for now and let her calm the beast down. Hell, maybe in the madness, it will fuck her and we'll get what we want."

Shocked silent, I look back at the headless body of the kind monster I just met.

I need to get us out of here fast.

FORTY-TWO

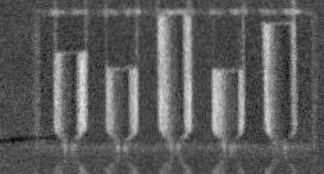

TALIA

I didn't listen to most of what they said, but by the time I'm back at my cell, it clicks and I understand, because there, covered in blood and ripping the cell apart, despite the shocks running through his system, is a red-eyed Cato.

"Cato?" I ask, unsure.

He stills, and his head snaps to me with a growl. My heart hammers from worry. His head falls back slightly as he inhales, and the howl he lets out chills me to my bones. I don't fight as he snatches me and slams me against the wall, keeping his back to the door, protecting me as he sticks his head in the crook of my neck.

This isn't my mate, this is his beast side.

"Shh, everything is okay," I promise, stroking his back and shoulders as he sniffs my chest and farther down. He sticks his head between my legs and inhales, making me squeak, but he settles a little as he comes back up.

His red eyes lock on me. "You smell of another," he snarls, his voice guttural.

"They threw me in with a male and ordered him to breed me, and when we both refused, they killed him," I whisper as I cup his face, uncaring about the blood on us. "What happened to you? Are you okay?" I query, searching his red eyes.

"You were gone," he bites out. "Told me." His words are rough, hard to get out. "Mine," he snarls, holding me tightly.

"Yours," I promise, groaning when he licks my neck and rubs himself across me as if to leave his scent there. His leg presses between my thighs, against my pussy, making my head fall back with a groan.

"Cato," I murmur, but he ignores me, licking my skin and rubbing against me. His nose goes back to my neck, and he growls, clearly not happy.

Before I can react, his hand is around my neck like a necklace, tilting it to the side before his fangs pierce my neck. I scream as he purrs, rocking his thigh into my pussy as the pain fades to pleasure. My eyes slide shut as he continues to purr before pulling his fangs out of my neck, making me whimper. He licks the wound before pressing his forehead to mine, hitting my clit with each rock of his knee until I come hard.

His lips cover mine, swallowing my sounds of pleasure as he lets me rub myself against his hard thigh, riding out the orgasm until I slump back. "What the fuck?" I demand, but my voice is breathy.

"You didn't smell like me." His words are more coherent and the red is fading from his eyes. "I needed to claim you, or I never would have calmed down. It was either the mating bite or I would fuck you right here, covered in our enemies' blood."

My eyes widen. That should make me feel disgusted, right? Instead, I moan, the idea way too hot.

He inhales and closes his eyes before they snap open and lock on me, still swirling with flickers of red. "I can smell your arousal, mate," he warns.

"Yup, sorry, but in my defence, you just made me ride your thigh until I came and then threatened to fuck me. That's like threatening me with a good time." I shrug, and a loving smile curls up his lips as he watches me.

"Tally, my Tally, how did I get so lucky?" he purrs, licking my lips as if he can't help himself. His hand tightens on my throat, and it should feel threatening, but it feels reassuring and strong—strong enough that I can let go and trust him to catch me.

"Don't forget it." I grin, and he laughs again, pressing his head to mine.

"Fuck, Tally, I thought I had lost you again." He shivers, and I wrap my arms around him, holding him as he holds me. "We are getting out of here, and when we do, I'm never letting you go again."

"Promise?" I smile, but it fades when he lifts his head, his eyes blazing red again.

"Promise," he snarls, eyeing me hungrily. "Now, if I don't move away from you, we are going to have a problem." I wrap my legs tighter.

"I don't want you to walk away. I want you right here. Fuck them, fuck what they think. I could have lost you today. I don't need our nest, I just need you." I roll my body against his, making him groan. With my mouth hovering over his, I grin. "So fuck me and claim me as your mate."

"Talia," he warns, my full name making me shiver. His tail lashes behind him, and his fangs are bared. He looks so strong and beautiful, I ache for him. I know he can smell it, as his eyes flare as his inhales.

"Stop overthinking this." Leaning in, I nip his lip. "Fuck me, Cato. Claim me, mate me."

I'm slammed back into the wall, my trousers and shirt ripped from my body as he tosses them behind him. His eyes roam over every inch of my flesh like he's never seen it before, even though he has licked it, tasted it, and impaled it, but never fucked it, and damn if I'm not dripping wet for him.

"I cannot be soft, Talia, not when I'm claiming you," he warns.

"Who the fuck said I need soft?" Gripping his horns, I yank him to me, kissing him hard and urging him on before pulling back. "Fuck me."

I gasp when he lets me down, spins me, and kicks my legs open. His chest presses to my back as he pins me there, his tail sliding up my leg to my pussy. He flicks my clit until I whine, and then it stops at my pussy as he nips my neck. "They do not get to see you," he snarls, more beast than man, and before I can reply, he thrusts his tail inside me.

Even wet, even after I just came, I groan, clenching around that length. I rock my hips as he fucks me with it before pulling out just as suddenly as he slammed it into me.

Claws on my hips, he yanks my ass out so my hands are pressed to the wall, his own sliding up my back, over my arms, and down, where his fingers twine with mine despite his warning. That touch of sweetness almost makes tears fill my eyes, because I know what he's doing.

He's reminding me he's with me and keeping me in this moment with him, even when he's brutal with my body. His huge cock presses against my pussy, dragging along my wet folds and bumping my clit as he covers himself in my cream.

"You're going to scream for me, mate," he bites out. "You're going to take every inch of me and let them know you are mine as I pump you full of my scent and cum."

Oh fuck. The dirty words go right to my clit, and I actually scream when he lines up with my entrance and slams into me, forcing me to stretch around his massive cock. It's so deep, hard, and wide, I nearly choke, unable to breathe, but he doesn't let me retreat. Instead, he pulls out and thrusts back inside me.

The dirty words that tumble from his lips have me whining and pushing back to take him deeper. "Such a good girl, Tally." His voice is a biting growl that vibrates through my body. "Look how pretty you are as you take me. Better than I could have ever imagined, like a tight, wet heat wrapped around my cock, driving me wild. You feel so good, my mate—too good. I can't stop."

Sometimes it's easy to forget Cato is a virgin, and unlike my own first fumbling attempts, he plunges into me, taking me hard and fast, knowing what to do automatically. His fangs scrape my frail skin, his claws dig into the wall to stop himself from cutting me, and his tail wraps around my stomach, helping me push back to take him.

"Cato!" I shout, my head hanging forward. Pleasure surges through me as he tilts my hips to hit that spot inside of me that has my eyes sliding shut. My clit throbs, and his tail snakes down to flick it as he hammers into me.

As he does, I notice a smell, a delicious scent that has me groaning. "What is that smell?" I beg breathlessly.

"My mating scent," he rumbles. "Filling you, covering you, so you will always smell like me and no other will touch you. You. Are. Mine!" he roars, his fangs slamming back into my neck to hold me still as he takes me rough and hard.

The pain mixes with pleasure, and before I know it, I'm coming again, screaming like he wanted as my body clenches around his invading cock. Snarling, he pulls free, and I hear him pumping himself. A minute later, his release splashes across my back, ass, and pussy, covering me in his delicious scent, and then he's back inside me, still hard as he fights my milking cunt.

His fangs lift from my neck, and then he leaves the wounds with his tongue as he fights me. "I'm nowhere near done with you yet, little mate," he promises, growling in my ear, but I slump forward.

He pulls from my body and spins me, lifts me, and slams my back into the wall as he impales me on his cock. He places one hand on the wall and the other on my neck, tilting my head back, the pressure making me suck in deep breaths. I ride him as much as I can as he takes me. His blazing eyes remain locked on me, his fangs dripping with my blood as he snarls.

"Mine, mine, mine," he chants.

"Yours," I promise, my voice just a breath as he squeezes my throat again. His mouth drops to my chest and attacks my nipples, licking and nipping and drawing blood, leaving a sting of bite marks across my chest as he powers into me.

"Mine forever," he snarls, his fangs piercing right over my heart. The sudden blast of pain is accompanied by pleasure as his fingers pinch my clit.

I can't even scream as he fucks me through one orgasm and right into another, his scent making me as wild as him. I claw at him, which only spurs him on, and he fucks me so hard, it almost hurts, as I seem to continually come until his head drops back and he roars.

He slams into me once, twice, and stills.

His release fills me as I slump back, the pleasure still circling my body, not letting up until he stops touching my clit, and then I slump like a puppet with cut strings. He catches me and withdraws from my pussy as his fingers slide through his dripping release and thrust it back inside of me.

"Love you, Tally. Love you so much."

"I love you too," I reply, opening my eyes to meet his, and he kisses me softly, even as his fingers cup my cunt and stop his release from spilling from me.

He drugs me with his kisses, and when he pulls back, I'm limp and unable to even move. I giggle, which causes him to chuckle.

Pulling my limp body into his arms, he rains kisses along my face as he carries me to a dark corner and pulls me over his body. He blocks the door and any prying eyes as he whispers how perfect I am and how much he loves me.

As I lie in his arms, everything feels right.

As if whatever will happen, I know I'm safe with him. More than safe, I'm happy. I'm loved. He might not have said the words much yet, but I'm beginning to see monsters don't need to, they show you with every little action.

The way he comforts me.

The way he holds me tighter, as if he'll never let me go.

The way he watches me.

The way he touches and kisses me.

The way he shares his world with me.

That's his way of saying I love you, now I just need to show him back, because I love him, and I choose him every time.

I always will.

FORTY-THREE

CATO

I hold my mate close as she sleeps. I managed to get her dressed before she nodded off in my arms, keeping my back to the cell door to protect her as much as I can. My heart is so full, it feels like it might burst, and for the first time in forever, I feel at peace.

It's as if that missing part of me has clicked into place with my soul and everything makes sense. My mind isn't working on a million problems at once. I'm not thinking of the next day or year or threat. I'm just here in this moment as a man holding the woman he loves more than life itself, wondering how he ever got so lucky.

I want to go back to that scared little young one clinging to his brother's hand when they set out into a city destroyed by war and tell him it gets better. I want to tell him it's worth it. Everything is worth it because we get her.

Pulling her tighter against me, I bury my head in her neck and drink in her scent. It's mixed with mine, the mating scent making me grin as I kiss the bite mark on her neck. A surge of possessiveness goes through me. I never thought I'd be the type, but with her, I'm anything but calm and collected.

I thought it would get better when we mated, but I was wrong—if anything, I'm more possessive, obsessed, and protective now than I ever was before. I need to trust my mate to do her part so we can get out of here with our friends.

I hate that she has to face them alone, but she's not afraid, my brave little human, so I will be fearless as well.

She murmurs in her sleep, turning and pressing her face to my chest. My heart skips a beat at her trust in me, so I press my lips to her forehead. "I promise you, mate, I will never let another hurt you again. I will do everything to make you happy for the rest of our long lives, because a few years with you will never be enough. Even a hundred wouldn't be. We will get out of this, and we will start our life together. I promise you. Just hold on a bit longer, and I'll hold on with you. Where you go, I go. When you hurt, I hurt." Brushing my lips over her forehead, I give my vows to her. "I will love you forever."

I relax, not daring to sleep with such a precious being in my arms. Instead, I just let myself be happy with her in my embrace and protect her while she rests.

When morning comes and they shove food through the door, waking her, it comes too soon.

I want to pull her back into my arms and hold onto her forever, but she's like a bird—she has wings and she needs to fly.

I let her go with a soft smile, pushing her hair back from her sleepy face as she yawns. She grins at me and surprises me by leaning in and kissing me. Climbing to her feet, she stretches and then wanders away to take care of business while I grab the food. We sit with our knees pressed together, and I hand feed her as she blushes but grins at me.

It's almost domestic, but it all crashes down when I hear them coming.

I sober, and she must feel my shift in mood, because her hand comes out and covers mine. "I will be fine. Don't worry about me, just hold on a bit longer." She stands, and they buzz the door. My collar starts up and I grit my teeth, fighting the surge as it lights up every nerve in my body.

Her eyes narrow as she steps before me, her legs parted to protect me.

My beautiful, strong mate.

When they beckon her out of the open door, she throws me a look that tells me she promises she will return, and I know she will.

If not, I will come for her.

TALIA

I ignore the knowing looks and dirty comments from the guards who clearly watched me mate Cato last night. I refuse to let them ruin something as special and beautiful as our love. Instead, I keep my chin tilted up, and they soon grow bored of their barbs not landing and just drag me to the desk I'm working at.

Today, they don't chain me, probably realising I won't try anything. At least they didn't shove me into another cell with a monster to mate. It seems they must be happy about the mating, and now I need to figure out why.

The monster said breeding, but they must know I can't have kids.

So why?

I wait until they get bored and wander away, and then I start the process of hiding some research before pretending to work. I take my blood and run some tests, curious why they took it when I first arrived.

An hour later, I'm staring at the results in shock.

My blood is changing. I am changing.

But how? Why? I run through multiple factors, and the only thing I can think of is Cato. I don't think they have drugged us, and all I've done is mate Cato. Is this why they want that? I need to know, so I demand to see Doctor Hayes to find out the truth.

This is so much more than them creating monsters and experimenting on them.

This is… This is my human biology changing, and I want to know how and why they have done this.

I have to wait, and then he finally arrives, watching me with an arched eyebrow. He seems happy today, probably because I mated a monster just like he wanted. "My blood is changing. Why?"

"Is it?" he asks, but he doesn't sound shocked, only happy. "And how are you feeling?"

"Cut the shit," I snap, "and tell me what is going on. How can I help with this research if I don't know?" The words are bitter in my mouth.

"I knew you couldn't resist the challenge." He chuckles and sits, observing me curiously for a moment before nodding as if coming to a decision. "I suppose it won't hurt. It's not like you are ever getting out of here, and you are brilliant, so you might spot something we did not. Plus, you have a unique perspective." He smirks. "No others have survived the change yet."

"Others?" I prompt.

He hums. "Maybe I should start at the beginning."

"That would be good," I retort.

"Well, you know we made them." He doesn't hide it nor seem embarrassed. "It was very inconvenient when they got their own minds and started a war. We tried to conduct the same research here, but some of the original scientists died in the labs and we didn't have time to get their research, so we have been guessing. You met the splice. That was an attempt to create a stronger, more obedient version. There have been others, nothing too impressive, until a team suggested a baby would be the best way to move forward. It seems human genes and monster genes are compatible, and there's a theory that their offspring would be the best of both species, so of course we wanted to explore that. It seemed, however, that forcing matings didn't work, and the offspring didn't survive long, if at all. There was a theory that it had to be from a bonded, mated pair—strange, I know—and the person's blood had to be compatible. You had your blood taken when we first employed you—a surprise, let me tell you, when we realised you were compatible. We hired you because your parents were some of the most amazing minds of our time."

The mention of my parents makes me snarl, but I bite it back since I'm getting what I want.

"So imagine our surprise when their child is also a brilliant scientist and her blood is compatible. We tried to find ways to induce you into a mating, but many suggested it needed to be natural, so we sent you over the wall. We do need the research, but we thought that was the best way to get it and the results we needed. Only you had not mated. Bonded, sure, we saw the changes in your blood, but not enough."

"So you tried to force me."

"And then you did it all by yourself. Good girl." He smirks. "So now you will start to change and adapt, sharing their qualities to prepare for offspring…or that is the theory at least."

"Change how?" I demand.

"We don't know for sure. Some are guessing the basics, such as healing, strength, and speed—all the better to protect the baby. But we will find out with you." He smiles. "We are going to do amazing things together, you and me. Just think of it."

"I'd rather not," I sneer, and he narrows his eyes.

"We have tried other ways. Trust me, if we didn't need you, you'd be gone already. Remember that," he hisses.

"Other ways?" I ask as a bad feeling starts to coil within my stomach.

"We tried other ways of adapting humans to accept monster matings." He shrugs. "Such as starting them young before their bodies are fully developed."

"Kids," I whisper.

"Kids, but not ones anyone cared about."

I gasp. "The kids…they aren't getting sick from the food."

"Oh, they are. There are drugs in them." He shrugs. "Who better to experiment on than those who do not matter?"

"You fucking bastard!" I fling myself at him, but guards grab me and hold me back as he tuts.

"Really, Talia, can't you see all the good we are doing?"

I snarl at him, vindictiveness entering my tone. "No, but you are wrong."

"About?" he asks curiously.

"I can't be what you need because I can't have kids."

The slow smile he gives me makes me shiver. "Yes you can, Talia. Between the changes in your blood from the bonding and the drugs we had been giving you every day you worked here, you can have kids and you will."

I gape in shock before I launch myself at him again.

He made me into a lab rat.

"Now, now, that's no way to act. I think you need some time alone, so get back to work, and if you're a good girl, we will put you back in with our monster. If not, we will kill him. After all, he's done his job now."

I freeze as terror fills me.

They will kill Cato.

I have to keep him alive.

"Good girl. Get back to work."

FORTY-FOUR

TALIA

What Hayes told me has me filling in missing pieces. Upstairs is a breeding farm—that's why they have captured and experimented on monsters. It's clear it's not just to create more of the same, but to create different ones.

A new species.

It's also more than that. They want to change us, change humans, so no one is safe anymore. I stash as much research away as I can, knowing we'll need to get out of here soon. It won't be long before they will hurt Cato to get me to do something, and I can only imagine what Aria and Akuji are going through. We need to get back over the wall, where they have no power.

We need to destroy their research once and for all, but that won't stop them. No, now we need to destroy them. To do that, however, I still need to understand the origins. Some of the research makes no sense to me, and I start to get frustrated, knowing I need to unlock its secrets so I can protect my people.

My people…

Is that what they are now?

Yes, I decide they are.

"Come on, scientist. Time for your check-up," a guard barks sometime later.

"Check-up?" I question, but he ignores me, and an idea sparks in my head. "Fine, one moment." I grab as much as I can, stuff it into a bag, and hoist it over my shoulder.

"What's in the bag?" one asks.

"It's to run some tests on Cato, the monster I share a cell with. Hayes wants me to understand this process, so I need these," I explain.

He seems torn, so I sweeten the pot.

"Do you really want to bother the boss to confirm what I'm saying? What else am I going to do with it?" I gesture around us. "It's not like there's anywhere to go."

"Fine," he mutters, and he, along with another guard, lead me back through the labs to a completely different one. This one more looks like a doctor's office, with a table and cupboards along the back wall, and a bad feeling starts inside of me as I look around. "What's going on?" I query, placing the bag under the metal bed so they will forget about it.

"Get on," the guard demands.

Swallowing my protests in case they take it out on Cato, I do as I'm told, and once there, I have to wait and wonder what they are going to do to me. They need me alive, but it's clear they only want me for my brain and womb. Everything else? Well, it doesn't matter.

I wait and wait, and finally, a man in a lab coat scurries in. He doesn't even look at me as he moves to a tray and pulls it closer. I frown as he draws blood and then checks me over. When he forces my thighs open and checks my vagina without gloves, I almost kick him in the face.

Instead, tears fill my eyes.

I want to scrub them away as they flow down my cheeks like hot trails of embarrassment. He doesn't care. He treats me like an animal as he scans me and conducts test after test, all while the guard watches on, only heightening my embarrassment and fear.

"Undress her," the man orders, and the guard grins wider.

"With pleasure."

"Wait, no!" I protest, leaping up.

The doctor frowns at me. "I must check every inch of you, so either he undresses you or you will undress yourself. Otherwise, we will knock you out and undress you."

I almost vomit at the idea, knowing they could do anything. Fear pounds through me so hard, my hands shake and legs turn to jelly as they tremble. The guard advances on me, ripping at my clothes as I yell and push him back, scrambling away.

"Now!" the doctor orders. "We don't have all day."

"Please." I hate the scared whisper that leaves my lips as the guard blocks the doctor's view and grins down at me, licking his lips.

"I like hearing you beg. Maybe I'll take you to my own cell on the way back," he whispers. "But first, let's see why that monster was all insane to get into your pussy."

I'm almost sick, the fear so intense, I shake like a leaf. I was so strong, so sure, but humans are vile creatures. A monster would never rape another. Women are treasured, loved, and considered equals, while here, I'm reminded that I'm nothing in this world.

My degrees, intelligence, and importance mean nothing here.

I'm still just a cunt, and that's all they see.

"No." My voice is weak, and I hate that. I hate that I have to fight to keep my body as my own. I hate that men feel like they can take that choice away from me just because I'm a woman. They act as if it's their right to use my body and that my consent means nothing. They don't care if they destroy lives, all they care about is the momentary pleasure and the feeling of being in control.

Even if she hates it.

Even if she screams.

Even if she says no.

I'm about to beg the doctor to help when the guard's radio crackles to life. "All guards, get to your stations!" the radio barks.

He snarls and turns away from me. "Copy," he answers.

The scientist frowns. "Get her back to the cell." Before I have time to grab my bag, I'm hauled out of there, sweating at having to leave it behind. They are hyper-focused on something else, however, so they don't care.

I start to panic, wondering if he's going to do exactly what he threatened, but when he tosses me back in with Cato and slams the door, I know they have something else to deal with. I thank my lucky stars and whomever has caused such a disturbance.

When I turn to Cato, who's stumbling to his feet from his collar, I burst into sobs. He yanks me to him, hurrying us to the corner. He runs his hands across me, fear and worry warring in his eyes. "Tally, Tally, tell me what's wrong. Did they hurt you?" His eyes fade to a blazing red, but I can't speak. All I can do is cry.

I've never come so close as I did right then to being touched by another without consent, and for a moment, that fear just takes over, stripping away everything that makes me me as I realise just how easy it is for them to do that.

"Tally, please, talk to me," he begs. "Tell me what happened. Let me fix this, baby. Please." The desperation and pain in his voice makes me bite back my sobs and meet his terrified gaze.

"I—" I croak before swallowing. "I'm okay, they didn't hurt me. It came close though," I admit, my lip trembling. "Closer than ever before. He was going to—" I shake my head, unable to say it out loud, and for a moment, he stares at me, not comprehending what I am trying to tell him, before realisation dawns. I feel his fury coursing through him, but he keeps it together as he gathers me close, stroking my back and face.

"Never again," he promises. "I'm sorry I wasn't there, Tally. I'm glad you're okay." His voice is a growl, but it only comforts me. "I will kill them all for even looking at you. When we get out, you point out which one, okay?"

I nod and move closer. "Can you… Can you just hold me for a bit?" I ask softly.

"Always. I'll hold you always," he murmurs, rocking me in his arms as he lets me cry it out and rebuild myself, but I can't seem to shake my fear because I know there will be a next time and I might not be so lucky.

Just then, alarms blare, and I scream. I don't mean to, but it sets Cato off even more, and he moves me behind him, where I huddle, unable to stop the tears as he crouches before me.

The alarms are followed by loud voices, gunshots, and screaming.

I want to ask what is happening, I want to be brave and tell him this is our chance to get out, but I do none of these things, only feeling safe here with him standing before me.

There is silence, and then the door swings open. Cato is up and moving before I can react, flinging himself at our attackers with a snarl, only to be flung right back.

"It's us," a snarling voice responds, and for a moment, all I see is the guard coming to finish what he started before a sweet, confused voice reaches me.

"It's a rescue." Aria? No, it can't be. "Hey, it's me, Talia."

I blink, eyeing her. It is. It's Aria. But how?

Why?

How?

"Aria?" I ask dumbly, as if my mind's playing tricks on me.

"Yes, come on, it's time to get out of here. We are going home." I feel Cato's relief as he hurries over to me and picks me up softly, like I'm a child. I feel like one, all scared and hiding while they fight to free us.

Weak, so weak.

I bury my face into him, not wanting to see the shame in Aria's eyes at how weak and useless I am. Cato stiffens against me, but he's all that feels safe to me at the moment. I hold him tight, even as he carries me. I feel us moving, and after a while, I lift my head and see we are near the labs where…where it nearly happened.

Where I left the research.

That perks me up.

I ignore the screaming scientist, the alarms, everything… We are going to get out of here, and we need to take that with us, but just then, the lights go out, plunging us into darkness, bar the red flashing alarm. I shake with fear as Cato holds me closer.

Akuji moves with ease, destroying those who come after us, and I slip from Cato's arms, feeling stronger. He follows me as I walk into the lab and stare down at the table where I was nearly raped, and an anger like I've never felt before fills me, exploding out of me like the monster's haze. With a scream that shocks me, I grab the closest thing and throw it. It happens to be a chair, and it hits a computer, smashing it to bits. For a moment, I stand there, my chest heaving as I glare at the broken computer, and something akin to satisfaction fills me.

I do it again, and before I know it, I'm tearing through the room, smashing and breaking everything I can to rid this room of the control it has over me.

I know they are all watching me, and when I'm done, I meet Aria's eyes confidently. "So they can never do this again," I state, and she just nods knowingly before turning back to Akuji. I manage to grab my bag that contains all the main research I could take. Cato slings it over his shoulder without question, eyeing me to make sure I'm okay. I just nod in response, but then Aria's voice has me looking over.

"His mum is in the cells."

I follow her gaze to a small monster child at her side, and my heart stops, but then I remember what they are doing upstairs at the breeding facility.

"Hey," Aria murmurs as she crouches near him. "These are my friends. This is Talia, another good human, that's Cato, and this is Akuji. We are going to get you home, okay?"

"Okay." His tiny whisper is filled with trust and love. We need to get him and the others out of here before they lock us back up. I watch Aria grab a gun and straighten. I should help, but I just lean against Cato's side, suddenly exhausted.

"Can you carry them both?" Aria asks Cato. "I need to be able to fight, and I can't carry him—"

He looks down at me and then the kid and nods. I know he wants to fight with them, but the thought that I could lose him makes me hold on tighter to him.

"Hey, trust my friend, okay?" She leads him to Cato and looks into his eyes. "We are going to get your mummy, but I need you to be still and quiet, all right?" I look at the little boy in awe. He's so precious and innocent. We need to save him. We need to save them all.

Dying here won't stop these bastards, so even though it hurts my heart to think of anyone we've left behind, I know we have to keep moving.

"Of course," the little boy says as Cato scoops both him and me up. I hold on tight, trusting his judgement as I smile softly at the boy to reassure him. Aria looks at us before joining Akuji in the corridor as we hear approaching boots.

I have to trust in them to protect us, and I do.

No one fights like Aria and Akuji, and he will kill anyone who comes for his mate.

I watch as they surge into the corridors to clear a path. The sounds of fighting reach us as Cato surveys the corridor protectively, shielding us both. I can't get the idea of the breeding floor out of my mind though. What if there are more children alive up there?

All I saw was death and that one monster in the cell, but that doesn't mean there aren't more. After all, they hinted at it. We don't have time to go back and search the entire building for them. It would get us all killed, and despite my guilt, I'm not selfish enough for that.

But I can do something.

Anything.

While they are killing the guards coming for us, I hurry to a terminal, ignoring Cato. I can't go back and help them, security was too tight, but I can do as much as I can for anyone left alive up there.

Using the already logged in computer, I access security and open the cells, freeing the monsters. The idiots keep it all on one software.

When I move back to Cato's side, I'm at peace with what I did—I turned them loose on the bastards who did this.

I don't know if the other cells were filled or not, but now I can leave here without feeling guilty. They are now free for the first time and able to get their vengeance.

"Come on." Cato grabs us and moves us outside to see what is happening. The corridor beyond is a mass of moving and dead bodies. Akuji rips through them as Aria fires into their masses. Both move like dancers, their actions confident and strong. Akuji roars in triumph, while Aria looks back at us, grinning, before she's thrown out of sight.

I bite back my scream, waiting with bated breath, but I soon see her back on her feet and flying at the guard who hurt her.

"I was going to offer to help," Cato deadpans, looking at me. "But I don't think she needs it."

Despite the situation, I can't help but giggle, knowing he's right—Aria fights like a monster and is just as good as one. She doesn't need our help, we would only get in the way. Instead, we protect the child and the research.

We watch as they kick ass, taking down an army of guards before they hit a red button and cells I don't remember seeing swing open, releasing more monsters.

"It's time to go home," Aria calls, her voice reaching us. "You might have to fight. Are you with us?"

"Until the end!" a female shouts, and at the voice, the kid in Cato's arms starts to wiggle before he slips free and starts to run.

"Mummy!"

"Kid!" Cato shouts, but it's too late. I just stare with everyone else as he flings himself at the woman. My heart melts when she cries, swinging him around happily as they both chatter and giggle.

How could we ever feel guilty now? We might not have been able to save everyone, but this makes it worth it.

"Mummy, Mummy, the human saved me," he tells her as he pulls back.

"Thank you. Thank you," she repeats, her eyes filled with tears as she falls to her knees before Aria. "I owe you my life, thank you."

"You owe me nothing," Aria offers and holds out her hand to the lady, looking every bit the badass monster saver she is. "Now, let's get you both home, shall we?"

The woman watches Aria for a moment before accepting her hand, and Aria looks at her mate. "Ready?"

"Let's go home, mate," he replies.

"What he said, Tally," Cato murmurs to me, holding me closer. "Home, so I can remind you I will never let you go again."

"Sounds perfect," I whisper, cupping his cheek as I lean in and kiss him.

Home.

Home is where he is.

FORTY-FIVE

CATO

After we make it through the lobby, with Akuji and Aria leading and taking down any threats, we hurry out into the fresh air of the human city.

Tally seems surer now, stronger, and each step she takes away from the building makes her stand taller. I've never been so proud. My woman is one hell of a fighter. Nothing keeps her down. She's not uncertain at all as she leads us through her lands with a tight-jawed determination that makes me ridiculously hard. Once we reach the mouth of an alley, she sighs and looks back at us. Her bright, stormy eyes flick to me for a moment.

"We have to walk down the street from here." She sounds about as happy as Aria as she curses. I look around to see why. It's open and there are too many people, strange human homes, and perfect-looking streets.

It's crude and very cold.

"Okay, we'll move fast then. Where are we going?" Aria asks.

"Straight down this road. It leads right into the slums, but there is a small bridge we have to cross and it might be guarded." She swallows nervously, but Aria nods before pursing her lips and looking at Akuji.

It's strange and funny to watch the giant monster I have looked up to all my life peer down at the tiny human as he waits for her commands. "Carry me. You're faster. We'll run as fast as we can. Do not stop for anything." She looks at the rest of us then, taking charge, and we listen because she knows best. "If we get split up, head to the wall, and we will find you."

I grab Talia while Akuji scoops up Aria, and when we are all ready, we burst out from the alley and into the streets. Aria leads the way in Akuji's arms, with me right on his heels, holding both Talia and her bag.

We race as fast as we can, the wall towering in the distance like a gleaming beacon of hope. That's where we need to be. We can do this. We are going to make it. It's chaos around us, but we stay focused until we skid to a stop before a bridge. Humans protect the crossing. I hold Talia tighter as Aria slides down Akuji and rushes across the bridge. We watch in awe as she tricks them and then begins to kick their asses.

"She's amazing." Talia giggles.

"No, you are," I murmur, kissing her quickly.

A whistle cuts through the air, and I focus on moving forward, not on how perfect my mate is in my arms. Akuji scoops Aria back up, and then we are moving through the decayed, run-down section of the human world.

It blows my mind to contemplate the differences between the two areas. Surely sharing food, wealth, and resources would mean they could all live happy lives, not this…division.

Here, the differences are obvious. People stare at us, but they almost seem resigned. There are no screams or running. They just watch and wait for their fate. It's sad really.

Aria leads us through shadows as much as she can, taking us through run-down buildings, over unsteady walkways, and down littered streets. The fact that this area is worse off than our city doesn't escape my notice either, and when I glance down at Talia, she seems sad as she looks around.

"Almost there!"

I put on a burst of speed as we take to the walkways in the sky, the wall looming closer now. I'm so close to getting my mate home.

Rumbling fills the air, like the sound of the humans' machines they call cars, and when I look back, I see soldiers advancing across the bridge—many of them. Snarling, I turn back around, refusing to let them catch us.

I flinch at the sound of their weapons, and Talia whimpers, curling into my chest. I bend over her, protecting every inch of her as I grit my teeth and follow a confident Aria and Akuji. With an epic leap, we land before the door we came in through, and Akuji rips it open, his eyes hard and determined.

"Go!" Aria yells to us, looking back at the place around us sadly.

Tally slides down my body as I protect her back, hurrying to her friend's side before hesitating. Aria pushes her towards the door, and I head there as well. It's selfish to go first with my mate and leave a friend behind, but when it comes to Talia, I'm selfish. I'm selfish with her time and with her life, even if she won't be.

I push her through the door and yank her to my side, burying my face in her neck and relaxing as the familiar feel of our city welcomes us home.

We did it.

We made it.

The slamming of the door has me looking up to see everyone is back through the wall.

Everyone is alive.

Everyone is well.

And that's when I see hundreds of monsters moving from the shadows and stepping into view.

Waiting for us.

FORTY-SIX

TALIA

I watch in astonishment as the child we saved is reunited with his father. They embrace, and when the father thanks Aria, I can sense how uncomfortable she is, but I almost whoop when the monster drops to his knees before her and then more follow until they are all on their knees facing her.

Shock and wonder cross her features, and I know she deserves this. I'm happy to be invisible at the side, but my friend, the woman who grew up in the slums, fighting to survive, and protected these monsters without a second thought for herself, deserves all the recognition in the world.

She deserves a family and happiness, even if she didn't know she was seeking it.

"I owe you my life. I offer my loyalty and my weapons until I am dead. I bow to you, our queen, our versalis."

"Queen?" Aria whispers, looking at a shocked Akuji. I grin up at Cato, and he smiles knowingly down at me. I may not know exactly what is happening, but I sense their love and respect in every bowed head.

"They are crowning you. That is an honour which has not been given since the war. It's a name for someone who protects our race, who fights for them with no tribal allegiance. It is for someone who is just loyal to our species." He meets Aria's eyes, the pride he feels for his mate evident in every line of his face. "You are our versalis." He drops to his knees before her, pressing his forehead to her hand. "My mate. My saviour."

Her head jerks back before she looks out at the gathered crowd. She doesn't think she deserves it, but that's okay. Akuji will spend the rest of their lives teaching Aria that she deserves the world. That she's an incredible person, even if she doesn't know it now.

She truly is a queen in every sense of the word.

She drops to her knees before them, unwilling to stand while they kneel, and it only makes me love her more. Unlike most people, Aria will never be happy being worshipped. All she wants is loyalty and friendship.

"We are equals here," she murmurs, trying to force the words from her throat. "No humans, no monsters, just people. A community, one I'm proud to kneel to."

I couldn't have said it better myself.

I never expected to find happiness or a home when I came over the wall, but that's exactly what I found, mixed with acceptance, friendship, and equality. Monsters aren't perfect, and I know we have a long, rocky road before us.

I look up at my mate, at the monster I chose over my own people, and I have no regrets.

We will face whatever comes together.

Cato doesn't let me go straight back to work, despite my protests. He only lets me put the research away, and then he forces me to rest, saying my body needs it. He's obviously right, since I fall deeply asleep within seconds, which shouldn't be a surprise since we celebrated our safe arrival back. Everyone danced and drank, and it was honestly one of the best nights of my life.

When I wake up, I'm lying across his chest. My hand is under my cheek, my legs are between his, and his tail is curled around the top of my thigh, holding me against him. Under my head is his slow, steady heartbeat, and I know I should move, but instead, I just listen and let the sound of it relax me.

My eyes slide closed as I listen to it beat. I've heard others say that listening to the ocean brings them peace, the waves calling them home, but Cato's heart does that for me. Here, curled in furs and wrapped around an eight-foot red monster within a forgotten city, is where I feel at home.

This life over here won't be easy, but fuck, it's worth it, and being surrounded by monsters has brought me to back to life. I'm never alone now, never lonely, and I don't overwork or just sleep, eat, work, and repeat. Cato showed me what it's like to be alive again, and I'll spend the rest of my life as a happy woman if we live like that, even if the food is weird and I have to end up wearing fur.

I must smile, because he speaks, his voice rumbly and sleepy. "I hope that smile is for me."

Lifting my head, I press my chin to the muscles on his chest. "Always you. Before you, I didn't smile," I admit.

His eyes smoulder as they watch me, his hands stroking along my back before they reach my ass.

A pulse of desire shoots through me, and before he can react, I slide up his body, nipping his chin on the way before I press my lips to his. "Thank you."

"For what, Tally?" he whispers.

"For coming for me, for saving me in every way you can save someone. For loving me even when I didn't love myself."

"Always, mate," he promises, kissing me softly.

"Now let me show you what making love is, mate, not just fucking," I murmur into his lips, his hands gripping my hips as I straighten. His blazing red eyes lock on me as I pull off my clothing. His clothes were discarded last night, but I insisted on sleeping in a shirt.

His eyes drop to my breasts, his tongue darting out to wet a fang in a sexy as hell movement. "I'm your willing pupil," he purrs.

"Good answer." I grin as I reach down and stroke his length, his eyes hooded with pleasure. Kneeling, I drag him across my pussy, groaning when his tip nudges my clit. I'm wet, I always am around him, but he's massive, so I work myself on his length until I feel comfortable enough to press him to my entrance.

Wordlessly, he grabs my hips and helps lift me onto his length. I work myself down, taking all of him in a gentle roll until we both groan as I sink down.

"Perfect." He groans, flashing his fangs.

"It gets better," I promise as I lay my hand on his chest and start to slowly grind before riding his huge cock. His eyes track and note my every movement as he lets me take my pleasure.

Grabbing his hands, I slide them up my body until they cup my swaying tits.

"Tally." He groans. "My perfect mate."

His big hands cup and tweak my nipples, arching pleasure through me as I groan. I speed up as I lift and drop and wind, hitting my clit until I can't hold back. Pleasure takes over, and with a cry, I come, milking his cock as I shudder on top of him.

Doing a flashy sit-up, he covers my mouth, swallowing my pleasure as his arms wrap around me and he rolls us, leaving me blinking. Grinning down at me, he props his hands on either side of my head. "I think I got the gist of the lesson," he purrs, wrapping his tail around one ankle and tugging it to the side as he kisses me and starts to move.

I tilt my hips, and he hits that spot that has me moaning into his mouth. His drugging kisses leave me breathless as our bodies come together and we lose ourselves in one another. This isn't a quick, hard fuck racing to our release. This is a slow build of pleasure and exploring hands.

"I love you so much, Tally," he whispers against my lips as his hips flex. I slide my hands down his back to cup his ass and hold him tighter. Nipping my chin, he tongues away the sting. "My perfect, beautiful mate."

"I love you too," I rasp out, forcing my eyes to stay open and locked on his, but the steady slide of his cock mixed with his gentle, loving touches has me reaching for another release. It happens slowly, like a cresting wave washing over me before carrying me away on the pleasure as I cry out his name.

He swallows it, groaning into my mouth as he stills and finds his own release. When it subsides and we are left panting, I smile softly at him, and he grins back at me.

"You're a fast learner," I tease.

"And I'm betting you have many things to show me, Tally," he purrs as he kisses me once more, telling me without words how much he loves me.

When Cato finally lets me leave our nest, I hurry to the bathroom and step into the shower, sighing as the water runs over my dirty, tired muscles. My head falls back, and I let the water cascade down my body before hands grab me and haul me back against a huge, hard body.

"Cato!" I laugh as I slap his wandering hands.

"What? I'm just preserving water." He grins, turning me to see his sparkling eyes. "Now be good and let your mate take care of you."

I stand here as he washes every inch of me, starting at my toes and ending with my face until I'm panting from his skilled hands, especially since he spent five minutes washing my nipples with his tongue.

When he drops to his knees and grins up at me, I can't help but snort. "Preserving water?" I tease.

"Exactly, and how can you ask me not to take care of my mate when I can smell her pretty cunt demanding my attention?" Grabbing my ass with sharp nails, he tugs me closer, presses his face to my pussy, and inhales with a groan. "You always smell so delicious. I think I might need to have you walk around with my cum on every inch of you so no other smells it."

"Cato," I protest, feeling my cheeks heat, even as the idea has me licking my lips.

"Beautiful little Tally, tell me, shall we do an experiment?" The smirk he aims my way has my thighs clenching.

"Experiment?" I echo dumbly.

"To see how long it takes my mate to come on my tongue," he purrs.

Oh fuck.

FORTY-SEVEN

TALIA

When Cato finally lets me escape the shower, I'm grinning way too widely. He helps me dress in tight jeans and a top before leading me downstairs hand in hand, where we eat with everyone else.

I would have felt awkward before, but I don't any longer. If they don't like me, then that's on them. I don't blame them, nor will I hold it against them, but I'm not going anywhere, and that gives me a sense of confidence as I walk into the old lecture hall they turned into a cafeteria.

A dinosaur skeleton hangs from the ceiling, and mismatched tables are spread around the space, with food tables along the back and many monsters gathered about. Nearly all turn to me when we enter, but I just smile and wave as Cato greets people, assuaging their worries with a confident smile. He never once lets go of my hand.

When we finally make our way to a table, he sits me down with a kiss and promises he will return.

He heads to the queue and stands at the back, making me grin as I watch him. Despite the conversation he's in, he glances back at me and winks.

"He's happier than I've ever seen him."

I jump at the voice that's close to me and turn to see his brother sitting at my table, a tray before him as he nods his head at Cato.

"I'm glad you're both okay. We got the word when you crossed back over the wall, but I couldn't relax until I saw him."

"I'm sorry. I should have had him go see you last night," I reply. "You're his family, after all."

"So are you. You're his mate, and you come first. I don't blame him for that. I'm just glad he's okay…that you're both okay," he admits as he watches me. "I was a bastard to you. I'm sorry, Talia. I truly am. How could I ever hate someone who makes the only family I have left that happy?"

Swallowing, I smile softly at him. "Thank you, but he's the one who makes me happy. I was never happy over the wall. I don't think I even remember what being happy felt like."

"I know that feeling." He nods, watching me carefully. "I would like for us to be friends."

"I would like that, and I know Cato would as well." I offer my hand to shake, but he takes it and presses it to his chest and then to mine, over my heart.

"That is how we accept apologies," he explains, and I nod.

"Thank you, I will remember." I cherish their lessons. After all, this is my home now, so I need to learn their ways.

"Are you both okay?" he inquires.

I glance back at Cato to see him nodding along to something a monster is saying to him, but his eyes are on us and he wears a frown on his face. "Are you okay?" he mouths.

I smile. "Fine." I turn back to his brother. "We will be."

He nods again, and my stomach rumbles loudly, reminding me I haven't eaten recently. His eyebrows rise before he laughs. "Humans are funny." He takes what looks to be some form of bread or pastry and hands it over to me.

I dare not tell him I'll wait for Cato, not when he's being kind, so I accept it and take a bite. I chew with a cringe. It tastes like stale crisps.

He chuckles at my expression. "You get used to it. It's good for healing and health."

Despite the fact that it's like chomping on cardboard, I swallow it. My stomach does feel better, and I seem to have more energy as well, so I smile. "Thank you."

He shrugs like it's nothing, and I lean in with a wicked grin. "So now that we are friends, want to tell me all the funny stories from when Cato was a kid?"

He throws his head back with a laugh, and I join in, glancing over to see Cato smiling so wide, his face might break, and my heart fills with so much happiness, I don't know what to do with it.

"Where are we going?" I giggle, letting him tug me after him.

"You'll see," is all he will say as he leads me through the city. We arrive in front of a building that's standing, but that doesn't mean anything. We go through an open side door, and dust and dirt follow us in, but the farther we go down the corridor, the cleaner it becomes as we wind through half ruined back areas before we cross a huge black curtain. It's dark at first, but then lights suddenly flicker on, and I turn to see Cato at a switch. Turning forward, I step out onto a wooden stage and gasp.

A stage! I'm on a stage at a theatre!

There are seats and stands to the left, curling around the stage, with boxes up top. Some are crumbling, but it's still beautiful. The filigree decorations are gold and red to match the seats, and the stage is dark hardwood.

In the middle is a piano.

Not just any piano, but a gleaming black Yamaha GB1 Grand Piano, just like the one my mum had.

"Cato." I stare at the piano on the stage, swallowing as he steps before me.

"I know you miss playing, and I know you miss your parents and that it hurt to play after, but I thought if we played together, it might not hurt as much." He holds out his hand, a slight tremor in it. How could I not lay my hand in his? He leads me over the bench and sits down, trying not to break it as I grin. Lifting the lid, I run my hands nervously over the keys. "I haven't played in a long time, I'm probably terrible."

"So we can both be." His hands smash the keys, making a horrific noise, and a laugh bursts out of me. He always knows what to say to make me feel better. Turning back, I start to run through random songs, and he joins in. It sounds terrible, and it makes me giggle, but then I find my feet with it again, my fingers flying across the keys with sure movements born from years of practice.

The music consumes me, and I don't even realise he's not playing anymore. I'm alone on the bench, my eyes closing as I play the song my mum wrote. The music whisks me away, and I recall the feel of her warmth next to me as her hands dance across my own as she smiles at me.

Pure happiness swells within me, and when the last note fades, I open my eyes and glance up at Cato. "Thank you," I whisper. "Thank you for giving me my mum back."

"Always. Can you teach me?"

The words echo the ones I asked my mum as a kid, and I swallow as my past and present collide. She would love him, I think to myself, monster or not. I pat the bench, and just like my mum did, I start to teach him, carrying on her memory through him.

Through us.

He's a quick learner, and despite his huge size, he's delicate with the keys. When he does well, he looks at me proudly, and I fall completely and utterly in love with him harder than before. He sees my expression and leans in.

Cupping my cheeks, he kisses me softly. "Remembering the past is good, but so is making new memories to override the sadness." He grins, and I gasp as he lifts me, pushes down the top, and lays me across it.

"Cato," I warn, but he ignores me, tugs down my pants, and seals his mouth on my cunt, making me cry out at the sudden attack.

Lifting his head, he grins wickedly at me. "Now that's music," he purrs.

"You're evil—" It ends in a scream when he nips my clit.

"Want to try that one again, mate?" he teases as he grips my thighs and thrusts his tongue inside me. My voice echoes around the stage like music, the keys depressing under our weight, sending out random bursts of song.

Gripping his head, I tug him closer and ride his tongue before he replaces it with his fingers, lashing my clit until I'm coming on his face. Chuckling, he licks me through it before he climbs up my body, tugging me farther off the piano as he kneels on the bench to get close enough to kiss me as his cock presses to my pussy.

Crack.

Cato disappears as the bench crushes under his weight, sending us sprawling to the floor. I stare down at him, unable to help the laughter that bursts from my lips. Grinning, he starts to laugh too as he looks at the splintered wood around us.

"I guess I'll remember that for the future." He chuckles, which only makes me laugh harder. "Do not laugh at your mate, Tally." He pouts before his clawed fingers dig into my side, tickling me and sending me into hysterics on the stage.

My heart and soul feel light, lighter than they ever have, with my mate at my side.

"Please, stop!" I eventually call, and he grins down at me where he's poised above me.

"I like playing the piano again," I tell him, and he chuckles as he kisses me.

"Then we will come here every day. It will be our place, and you can teach me everything."

I grin up at him. "I would love that."

FORTY-EIGHT

CATO

"Don't overdo it if you still need to res—"

"Cato," she snaps.

"You went through a lot, answers can wait…" I try again.

"Cato!" She slaps my chest, and I wince.

"Yes, Tally?" I reach for her, but she smacks my hand away.

"Nope, you are not distracting me with sex." I smell her desire, and she quickly steps away as if knowing I'm going to grope her, so I pout.

"What about just letting me lick your pretty pussy?" I purr, advancing on her.

"No." She points in my face, licking her lips. "We need to work. I'm fine, I'm rested. I've eaten. I've had fresh air and everything else you deemed necessary, now we need to work."

"Can I eat your cunt after?" I grin.

"If you're good." She huffs and turns around to face the table, so I grab her hips and haul her back, grinding my hard cock into her perky little ass as I lean down and nip her neck.

"I'm always good, mate," I coo.

"Work."

"Fine," I mumble, but I place another kiss on her neck before stepping away, instantly feeling cold and unsatisfied. I help her nonetheless, and soon, we are lost in the work. She managed to steal a lot of the research, and the stuff we have kept here is helping her fill in the gaps. She works tirelessly, and if I weren't here, she wouldn't remember to take a break, eat, or drink. I make sure she does, and every time she kisses me gratefully, I vow to do it for the rest of my life.

The idea of working here, side by side forever, almost makes me giddy.

My people drop by with gifts for her or just to say hello, and she's nothing but polite and kind. I see them falling in love with her just like I did. Even my brother checks on us and laughs when she answers him distractedly. He says she reminds him of me.

He's not wrong, and I couldn't be happier.

It seems I'm not the only one, because the news spreads about Akuji and Aria's mating, and we have to finish work early so we can get Talia over to his territory to help Aria with the preparations.

I'm forced to leave her with some of the other women of Akuji's tribe. I watch her disappear into his rooms before Akuji claps me on the shoulder and drags me away.

All the while, I want to turn around and go to her side.

"So, brother, when is your mating?" Akuji grins at me.

I chuckle. "Tally and I are private people, so we might do a little ceremony, nothing…"

"Over the top." Akuji grins. "The bane of being leader—your people won't allow anything small."

I groan, knowing he's right, and he laughs again. "It's worth it, brother, because at the end, she's yours." The love shining in his eyes makes me smile.

"You love her a lot," I remark as we wander with his general at his side, listening happily.

"More than I knew possible, but you understand that." I nod, and he stops, watching me wistfully. "Who would have guessed this is where I would be?"

"Not me." I grin. "But I have no regrets, do you?"

"Only waiting this long to claim her," he jokes. "I cannot wait to see how this changes our people and lands. We have been stagnant for far too long, brother."

"True." I nod. "And Samael?" I hate bringing him up on such an occasion, but it's a worry I have.

"I have a feeling he's got his hands full right now." He smirks mysteriously. "Now, let's go get me ready to claim my female, and then we will plan yours. Fuck the humans, fuck their experiments. Let's focus on nothing but the future, brother, because it's so bright."

"That it is." I turn and walk with him, thinking of Talia. "That it is."

Akuji and Aria's mating ceremony is perfect, and the tribes rejoice at their union, accepting their human queen. It gives me hope for our future, our healing, and for my own mating, which I have been thinking about non-stop since Akuji mentioned it.

I know they will want a big ceremony since I'm a tribe leader, but all I really need is my mate. As I watch her dance with my people, an idea comes to mind, and without waiting around, I grab my brother and my mate and yank them from the celebrations.

"Where are we going?" my brother grouses. "There was a busty woman—"

"You can romance after." I grin, holding onto my mate until we reach the museum. I head to my favourite place and turn to her. "This is the place where I first felt you, where I first knew my life would change. It's also the place where you chose me. I can't think of a better place to cement our bonding."

"Cato?" she asks with confusion.

"They will want a big ceremony, but I don't want that. All I need are you and my brother. Just us, my family. They don't get another piece of you. You are all mine, and I have been waiting for this moment my whole life. So, Tally, my love, will you agree to be mine forever?"

Her eyes fill with tears as she wraps her arms around me. "I will."

I swing her around as I kiss her. It's not tradition, but it's us, and that's all that matters.

Putting her down, I look at my brother. "Will you do us the honour?"

"I couldn't think of anything that would make me happier." He claps us both on the shoulder. "They got a big ceremony, plus you've always been weird, so they'll accept it."

That only makes me laugh.

"Hold on, let me get the supplies." He hurries away as I look at Tally.

"Are you sure this is what you want?"

"I'm yours, and you're mine, I want that forever. I don't want to be eyed by a million monsters or perform in front of them and vow our love. I only need this to know how much you mean to me…as long as you are okay with that?" she asks worriedly.

"More than okay," I whisper as I cup her face.

"Your people will be mad," she whispers as I lower my head.

"Let them," I murmur before I kiss her. I don't care, so long as she agrees to be mine forever.

"Kissing later," my brother scolds as he skids to a stop before me with a knife in his hand and paste in the other. "Let's get this done, lovers."

TALIA

Cato kisses me once more before holding my hand as we stand side by side and face his brother. His brother hands over the knife, and Cato turns to me. "Talia, I here tonight vow to be yours forever. I offer you my heart." He bangs his chest. "I offer you my soul and my blade." He kneels.

I try to remember everything Aria did earlier. I swallow nervously but take my strength from him. "Cato, I here tonight vow to be yours forever. I offer you my heart." I bang my own chest, copying what he did and wincing at the pain. "I offer you my soul and my blade." After I finish speaking, I kneel as well.

"Cato, my brother, leader of Acumen, do you here tonight take Talia as your mate?" He grins at us both.

"Forever," Cato replies immediately.

"Usually we repeat it, but since there's no one here, and I think if I make Cato wait any longer, he might hit me, we'll skip that part. Cato, bleed for her and show your dedication. Make your body hers. Give her every inch of you," he orders.

I get queasy at the idea, but I know it's tradition. I spent enough time listening to the women tell Aria about what to expect.

I won't dishonour him by stopping him.

He leans forward, nuzzling into my chest as he presents his back to his brother. His brother seems far too happy to carve my name into his back—overjoyed, actually—which only highlights our differences. When it's done, Cato kisses my chest and leans back, tracing the knife as I blink.

"Brother—"

Cato ignores him as he takes the bloodied blade and winks at me. "Your name is over my back as a symbol that you will always protect it." He presses the tip to his heart. "However this has belonged to you since the day I was born, so it should be emblazoned across it as well." I gasp as he carves my name over his heart, grinning at me the entire time.

The crazy, crazy man.

"Cato…" I shake my head, tears in my eyes. "You crazy bastard."

They both chuckle. "Well then, let's carry on." His brother claps. "Tally, my new sister, do you take Cato, leader of Acumen, as your mate?"

"Yes," I reply without hesitation.

"Thank fuck," his brother whispers, making us laugh, and then I make a split-second decision. The same as Aria. I won't dishonour this tradition.

I will show them exactly how strong humans are. "And I offer my skin willingly."

Cato's head snaps around to me. "Tally, no—"

"You wear my name, and I want to wear yours." I reach out and kiss him. "It will be okay."

"Don't you dare, brother," Cato snaps at his brother as he steps towards me, taking my face as he searches my gaze. "You do not have to do this. I know you love me, I know I am your mate."

"It's not just for us, but for them. I am yours, and you are mine. I am doing this with or without your blessing."

He grinds his teeth, but he must see the determination in my eyes. "Fine." He keeps the blade in his grip and circles me. "Then I will do it." I hear the horror in his voice as I pull up the back of my shirt and kneel. When I feel the blade pressing to my skin, I brace for the pain.

Before he begins, he tries again. "Tally, you do not need—"

"Fucking do it," I order, and his brother chuckles.

The next few minutes are agony, and I can tell Cato hates every minute of it. When it's done, he kisses me all over, telling me how brave I am and how much he loves me. "You can show me later with your tongue," I murmur, shaking from the shock and pain, but I have no regrets.

"I did not need to know that," his brother mutters before carrying on. "Cato and Talia, you have bled and vowed to be mates before our people. Rise as one." Cato lifts me into his arms and kisses me soundly.

"We are officially mated, Tally," he murmurs.

"And that is my cue to leave so you can bone." His brother gently touches both of our arms. "Thank you for letting me be part of it. I'm going to find someone myself. Night, mates," he calls, and I can't help but giggle as we watch him go.

"What do you want to do now, mate?" Cato wiggles his eyebrows.

"Well, you did mention that thing with your tongue…"

He's moving before I finish, and I can't stop laughing. He sprints back to our rooms and barricades the door before laying me on the bed. "Let me paste your back."

Who am I to refuse?

He rolls me softly onto my front, and a moment later, all my clothes are ripped away and a wet, cold paste is tenderly massaged into his name. I wince, the pain making me bite my lip, but as the paste starts to work, it fades into a pleasurable hum.

"There," he purrs, his voice filled with hunger. He turns over, his eyes dragging down the length of my body as he reaches for me. Batting his hands away, I take the cream and get to my knees.

"Before you fuck me, let me do yours." I grin, and he grunts as if he's feeling put out. While I'm covering the words on his chest, he leans in and sucks my nipples and massages my ass, making me groan. I have to drag myself away and move around to his back as I carefully cover that too.

I'm wet and shivering in anticipation, knowing as soon as I'm done, I'm his.

Just as soon as I've covered the last letter, he hauls me forward and pins me to his nest. His mating instincts are undoubtedly kicking in as he tangles his fingers in my hair, and I rub my ass against him as his lips cover mine in a brutal, claiming kiss.

I try to roll, to kiss him deeper, but he pulls away, leaving me confused and horny.

"On your knees, mate. Let me look at my name while I claim you."

He doesn't have to tell me twice. I hurry to my knees, groaning when his hand covers my pussy and he grinds the heel of his palm into my core, making me cry out. "Hold on, mate. Seeing my name on you is driving me crazy, and I need to be inside of you. I need to fill you with my cum and see you covered in it." His voice is a growl, one that makes me shiver in need.

I love sweet sex with Cato, but rough, claiming sex?

It could make a girl an addict.

Gripping the fur beneath me, I push back into his hand, grinding my wet cunt into it. Snarling, he digs his teeth into my shoulder to pin me as he thrusts his fingers into me. He works me quickly on them before adding another, stretching me for his cock while his thumb rubs my clit. When I'm on the verge of coming, he pulls away, leaving me whining and pushing back, seeking the pleasure I know he can give me.

One hand lifts from the bed and wraps around my throat to hold me in place as his cock lines up with my entrance and, with a hard thrust, slams inside me. Both of us groan, his length forcing me to stretch around him. The bite of pain turns into a burning lust for my mate.

"Cato," I beg, needing to move. I feel way too full with him just sitting inside me.

"Behave, mate," he snaps, his other hand tracing over his name as he starts to move, the burn making me gasp. "Fuck, I love seeing my name on you. I never thought I'd be a possessive man, but it seems I am when it comes to you, Tally. I want everyone to see it and know you are mine." His words tumble out with a growl, leaving me breathless and pushing back, taking him deeper as he fucks me.

Snarling, he drags his hand down my back and grips my hips, lifting me until I'm off the nest. The deeper angle makes each thrust slide across those nerves that have me fighting his hand, unable to do anything but cry out.

"Please," I implore, tears squeezing from my eyes. The pleasure is too much, and the burn on my back only adds to the sensations as he growls. The vibrations move through his body to mine until I feel myself clenching around him.

I'm already reaching for the release he denied me earlier.

He feels it and stills. "Not yet, mate. You come when I say so. Your body and your pleasure are mine."

"Bastard," I hiss, trying to fight his hold, but he just holds still, chuckling until I relax, and then he hammers into me. He fucks me hard and fast, building me up once more with each stroke of his cock and each drag of his teeth as he leans down to bite me. It drives me crazy.

Finally, he pinches my clit. "Come for me, Tally. Coat my cock in my mate's cum."

I do, screaming my release as I clench around his cock. The pleasure is so great, I see stars, but he doesn't relent. He fights my milking cunt, fucking me through it, and starts to bring me to another release. "Good girl," he praises. "Again, let me feel it again. Let everyone hear you."

"I can't—" I gasp as he rubs my clit, and then a scream erupts from my mouth as he makes me a liar and I come again.

He holds me to him as he continues to pummel into me, brutally taking my cunt. His voice is just a growl now as he lets go and mates me like a beast. His hand keeps me still for him, not that I could move anyway.

"Mine," he snarls, his teeth catching on my throat before he sits back, the slap of our hips loud as he fucks me.

The paste burns on my back now, the smell of his mating scent wrapping around me.

"Mine!" he roars as his hips jerk and he thrusts into me wildly, and when his release fills me, he pulls out and sprays it across my pussy, ass, and back. I cry out as I come again, unable to stop myself.

Falling forward, I hit the nest, unable to do anything but pant.

His hands cover my body, massaging his cum and his scent into my skin before they slip over my dripping cunt. Scooping up his release, he thrusts it back inside me. I whine but don't protest, and when he's happy, he blankets my body, curling around me and purring contently.

"My Tally, my mate," he murmurs in my ear. My eyes don't even open as I snuggle back into him, my body limp and still shivering from aftershocks.

"We are so doing that again…maybe when I can move." I grin, making him chuckle in my ear.

"We have our whole lives, Tally, and I plan on making the most of every day I have with you, knowing how lucky I am."

Well, fuck.

Tears roll down my cheek as I find the effort to roll and kiss him. "I feel the same way, Cato. Together, we can do anything, and I can't wait to find out what that is."

"Me too, mate," he murmurs against my lips before I feel his tip up in a grin. "But for now…" He rolls me onto my back as I groan and try to smack him away.

"Insatiable. I created a monster!" I complain as he crawls down my body.

"Yes you did, Tally, and now it's time you pay the price."

FORTY-NINE

TALIA

We spent three days straight in our nest. Cato wouldn't let me leave it, not even for food, and I couldn't be happier. Every muscle in my body is sore and well used, but I'm grinning widely.

Cato announces we have mated, and the news is met with stunned silence. For a moment, I start to panic, but then roars of joy go up and we are surrounded by monsters celebrating and congratulating us. Cato drinks it up, proud of me as he presents me to them with nothing but joy, and I've never felt such acceptance and warmth.

I'm finally a part of a family.

I find myself sitting amongst them all, our table overflowing with gifts and food as they clamber to be close, welcoming me with open arms. It's so different from when I first came and I hid upstairs in hopes of not dying. Now, I can't imagine my life without such happiness and chatter. They see my differences, and some are still wary, but others celebrate it, and after a day spent revelling, I am forced to read bedtime stories to the kids and tuck them in before heading to my nest with my mate, where we spend the rest of the day exploring each other, lost in pleasure.

How could life get any more perfect?

The next morning, I leave Cato asleep in the nest and sneak out before the sun sets, focusing on the problems before me.

I know the humans wanted to breed humans and monsters and were altering us with drugs to do that. I know only some humans are compatible. I know they created monsters, including splicing new ones. They experimented on them and tried to make more…but this is something else.

I can almost taste it.

Before I know it, hours have passed and Cato forces me to stop and eat, and then we dive back in. He must feel my determination, as if my fingertips are reaching for the solution.

It takes two days, two days of hardly any sleep or breaks, until I figure it out. It just clicks, and I instantly sit back, horrified by what this means.

What they have done.

I look at Cato, barely able to say the words as shock and revulsion lodge in my throat.

"Tally, whatever it is, we'll deal with it together," he urges.

Nodding, I turn and explain what I've found, and when I'm done, he shudders out a shocked breath.

"If this is right…"

"Everything will change." I nod. "Everything."

"We need to call a meeting.

FIFTY

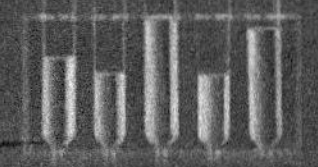

TALIA

A meeting is called, the urgency and importance stressed. It cannot be held until tomorrow, due to it being close to sunrise, and I find myself struggling to sleep, so I get up and work through the rest of the notes, double- and triple-checking what I've found.

Cato silently sits with me, supporting me, and a few hours later, I shower and let him make it all better before sitting on our nest. I need to get dressed, but I just stare at my hands, wondering what this means for me.

"It changes nothing, mate," he states, cupping my cheeks and searching my eyes. "Nothing."

"Promise?" I ask like a child.

"Promise," he rumbles before pressing his forehead to mine. "They need to know. We will face this problem head-on, and we will do this together."

"Together," I whisper and let him help me stand.

Cato thinks I look fine, but something about this meeting and attending as Cato's mate makes it important to both him and the tribes. Aria has embraced all that comes with being a monster's mate, and so do I. It's time to cast off my human clothes and find something in between. So while Cato does that, I quickly smoke out my eyes and add lipstick from some makeup they found, and when he announces that he's left some options, I hurry out and grab them before he can see me.

I want it to be a surprise.

Some of it are furs I wouldn't be caught dead in, but I manage to find some black, skin-tight ripped jeans, boots, and a fur band top I create. It ties at the back like it would if it were a skirt and is surprisingly comfortable. For my hair, I manage to slick the normally crazy blonde waves, and with much cursing and aching arms, I achieve an elaborate updo that has me bouncing in excitement.

"Are you ready?" I call.

"Yes, Tally, let me see," he replies, amusement lacing his voice. Grinning widely, I open the door and step out.

"Ta-da!" I spin "What do you think?"

His jaw actually drops as he gapes, sitting as still as a statue, and I start to panic, touching the outfit self-consciously.

"Does it look silly?"

"No." His voice is almost soundless, and when he stands and prowls towards me, I gulp at the intensity in his eyes. "I should pin you to my nest and never let you out. You look like one of us, my perfect mate." When he stops before me, he strokes the fur with a purr before his hands trace my makeup and then hesitate over my hair as his lips quirk.

"You made your hair into horns," he whispers.

"So we match." I giggle as I turn and check them out in the mirror once more. The blonde waves have been twisted into two, if not small, bending horns, and the rest of my hair flows down in waves. I look good, if I do say so myself, and every bit a monster's mate.

"You look good enough to eat," he rumbles, and I start to back away with a laugh.

"Bad monster!" I scold as I start to run.

"Don't you know not to run from a predator, Tally?" he teases as he prowls after me. "We always catch our prey."

By the time we get to the meeting spot, I'm having to bat Cato away, his hands continually wandering, but he soon sobers when we head into the lab. I thought this was the best place to meet, since it's where this all started and hopefully where it will end. My happiness dissolves in the face of my nerves as I wait for them to arrive.

What I'm going to tell them will change everything, and I almost feel bad for being the bearer of the news. I hoped I was wrong, but I know I'm not. What they did… I shake my head in disgust, still trying to wrap my mind around it all.

There's no more time to second-guess or worry, though, because Aria appears at the top of the stairs, grinning at me. Mated life suits her. She wears a short fur skirt and top, and her fiery hair is braided, showing off her marked back.

Akuji is on her heels, barely letting his mate out of his sight, even as he greets us. "Tally." Aria wraps me in her arms, making me wince, and she pulls back instantly. "What happened?" She tries to turn me, so I go willingly. "Talia!" she yells.

Laughing, I take Cato's hand. "We mated too."

She squeals and goes to hug me again before slapping my arm. "And we didn't get invited!"

"It was just us, small and intimate." I shrug sheepishly.

"Congratulations, brother." Akuji slaps Cato's back with a grin. "Knew you would be next."

"How could I not be?" Cato winks at me.

"Is that the news?" Aria asks excitedly, and I sober, swallowing hard.

"No, I-I found something in the research, something…something I can barely believe, but I think it's best I just explain without questions, okay? I don't know what it means yet or where to go, but this affects everyone… This affects us, Aria."

She watches me carefully and crosses her arms. "Whatever you have to say, we can handle it. We trust you, Talia. Tell us."

Akuji places his palm on his mate's shoulder, and she leans into him. Cato comes to my side, offering his strength to me as well, basically mirroring the others' poses.

Licking my lips, I glance at him, and he nods. "Okay, so we know humans made monsters. They experimented on them to push their limits. Whilst at the HQ, I found out not only that, but since the wall was erected, they have been trying to create more by splicing different DNA together. I think they did that here as well, which means some monsters might have different traits or strengths, but they also…they also created a breeding programme."

Aria's eyes narrow, and I nod.

"They want humans and monsters to mate. They need their offspring for the next generation, and they realised mated pairs were the way to go. That's why they sent us over the wall, in hopes we would. That's why…that's why…" Cato pulls me closer, and I carry on. "They tried to have me raped before the monster refused." Aria snarls, so I push forward. "It turns out our bodies change when we mate." Her eyes flash, and I realise she knows that. "Our blood, our entire beings rearrange. It's magnificent actually and scientifically impossible, but it's happening, and that's what they wanted. They have been trying to recreate that by pumping the slums with drugs. That's why there is so much sickness and death. They are weeding out the weak, but when I looked into it further…"

"What?" Aria prompts.

"They are changing our DNA, and it's not natural, but it made me realise some of our DNA wasn't natural to begin with. I think they are experimenting on us. I think this is one big experiment." Swallowing hard, I meet their eyes. "And I don't think we are human at all."

This news goes off like a bomb, and Aria just stares.

I stare back, unsure what else to say.

The sound of booted feet hitting the stairs causes us to turn. Standing at the top with a grin is a dark-haired, curvy female. She looks familiar, and then I realise she's the same woman from my job when I first got it—a journalist, they called her. She grins knowingly at us, her eyes hard with a strength that scares me. Behind her, standing like a scarred shadow, looms Samael, who snarls and glares at us all.

"She's right, and I have proof," the woman calls.

EPILOGUE

A MONTH LATER...

TALIA

I wait nervously for Cato to arrive, biting my lip. Drinks are flowing at The Hideout, and everyone is celebrating, making the most of the time they have. They need to with everything going on, but me? I'm not. I'm waiting for my mate, who walks through the door, clapping Akuji on the shoulder as he grins. His eyes instantly find me, and his grin widens as he heads straight for me.

Aria snickers at my side. "Good luck," she whispers as she slides from the booth and throws herself at her mate, who catches her mid-air with a chuckle. Their tiger winds through their legs, but I stay clear of him—bad memories and all. I can agree, however, that he looks after Aria.

"Tally." Cato sighs, as if he's finally happy now that he's with me as he slides in to sit by my side, kissing me soundly before smiling at me. "How was your girls' day?"

"It was good. I found something out," I hedge.

His eyebrows rise. "You told me you weren't working."

"I wasn't." I've been working non-stop since the bombshell I dropped in the lab all those weeks ago, collecting proof and trying to find out just what exactly we are. Aria tries to help but mostly annoys me, and Cato assists when he can, but with the humans prepping for war at our walls, they are busy upgrading the city every night.

This war has brought all the monsters back together again, even Samuel's Darklings, although just thinking of him makes me shiver in fear. He hates humans more than any monster, and I feel sorry for the woman, the human, who is with their tribe. He wouldn't let her go. No one knows why, but I have my theories it's to torture her. She didn't seem afraid, however, so we let her walk away with a promise to show us the proof she spoke of.

We are still waiting, and I'm starting to believe she might not have it.

Hell, maybe she's just as crazy as Samael. After all, only a madwoman would walk back into hell, which is what their tribe land is. I saw it once with Cato, and it haunts me to this day.

It's filled with scarred, criminal monsters, the worst of the worst, and it's a total wasteland.

They make Akuji's warriors look non-threatening.

"No, not working." I fidget nervously, and he frowns.

"Tally," he warns.

"I'm pregnant," I blurt out. His eyes widen, and I start to ramble. "I wasn't sure, but I missed my period a lot, and I was sick, and then the cravings—"

His lips cover mine before he pulls back with a grin. "You're sure?"

"I'm sure," I whisper. "We are going to have a baby. I didn't think I ever would, Cato. I don't care who made this happen, but we are going to be parents. We are going to have a family."

He leaps to his feet, whooping, and I fall back with a giggle.

"I'm guessing you're happy?"

"Happy?" He grabs me and tugs me to my feet, kissing me hard. "You gave me the best gift in the world when you agreed to be my mate, and now you're telling me we are starting our own family?" His eyes shine bright as his hand covers my stomach. "I couldn't even put into words how happy I am."

"But the war, the experiments—"

"Doesn't matter. There's never a good time to have a baby, but it will be so loved, so protected. It will wish for nothing…unless you don't want this?" he asks suddenly.

"I want this," I reply automatically, covering his hand with mine. I never thought I would have kids, so all I wanted was to work, but with Cato? The idea of a family is almost a need I can't control, and when I saw the tenth test saying positive, I knew I was happy—worried but so happy.

I cried, and Aria panicked and slapped me.

"I'm going to be a dad!" he yells, and everyone looks at us. "We are having a baby!"

Cheers and roars go up, and Aria toasts me from the other side of the room with a smirk on her lips. Akuji grins at us as drinks get passed around and everyone congratulates us. Laughing and grinning widely, I can't help but wonder what kind of world my child will be born into or what they will be. My perfect rainbow baby, the one I never thought I could have.

But it doesn't matter. Cato is right—it will be so loved, unlike most of us over that wall.

Here, in the forgotten city, I found my happiness, my future, my destiny, and my family.

One I always needed.

No matter what is to come, the truth is out now, and one thing's for certain—we won't do this alone.

For a moment, I swear I hear a roar of fury shaking under our feet, but I soon forget about it as my mate kisses me.

BONUS SCENE

TALIA

"I hate being pregnant," I whine.

Cato grins, sliding his hands around my waist, but I slap them away.

"No touchy. This is your magic penis' fault anyway."

"Tally." He pouts. "I know how to make it better."

"You know how to stop me from almost pissing myself and eating everything in sight?" I narrow my eyes, knowing I'm being unreasonable. I would take all the downsides in a heartbeat to have this child—a child I've always wanted and never thought I could have. It doesn't mean I'm not allowed to complain though.

"You are perfect." He grins, uncaring about my irritable mood. I soften when he cups my face and kisses me, and when he crouches, I sigh, softening further for my amazing mate. His hand covers my round stomach as he presses his lips there. "Your mother is having a bad day. Be a good boy for me and take it easy on her, okay, bud?"

"It could be a girl," I retort for the hundredth time—an argument we never get sick of.

He grins up at me, his fangs turning me on instantly. He knows it, and his grin stretches, the bastard. We've been inseparable, and our appetites for each other even scare the monsters here. One look from him, and I'm wet, which he loves. "Then it would be an incredible little girl, taking after her amazing mother."

"Sweet talker." I huff. "You're still not getting your dick anywhere near me today."

"How about my tongue then?" He wiggles his eyebrows, and I laugh just like he knew I would, but it ends in a gasp when our baby kicks. Cato feels it, and I press my hands over his as tears fill my eyes.

"You are going to be the best mother," he whispers, looking at me.

"You'll be the best father," I respond, and he leans up and kisses me. When he pulls away, I laugh at the mischievous look on his face.

"So, about my tongue—"

"Ew, Cato!" Noya calls as he rushes into our nest. "Auntie Tally, will you read to us now?"

"Of course, my favourite boy," I promise as I clamber to my swollen feet with Cato's help.

"I thought I was your favourite." Cato huffs, mock glaring at Noya. "Do I need to fight this little beast for the title?" He holds up his hands and starts to fake swipe, and Noya squeaks and runs away. With a wink at me, Cato hurries after him.

Boys.

Looking down, I smile at my round stomach. "Please be a girl. I need the backup." I giggle, and there's a kick, and my smile widens. "You will be so loved, so very loved. I can teach you about science, and Aria can teach you to shoot. Akuji can teach you how to punch, and Cato can chase all the boys away. The world is waiting for you, and whatever is to come, you will always be protected and happy, no matter how this war ends."

I waddle downstairs to my people, to my family and friends, the future of our races held in my belly.

ARE YOU READY FOR THE END?

The last installment of The Forgotten City series is coming soon...

ABOUT K.A KNIGHT

K.A Knight is an international bestselling indie author trying to get all of the stories and characters out of her head, writing the monsters that you love to hate. She loves reading and devours every book she can get her hands on, and she also has a worrying caffeine addiction.

She leads her double life in a sleepy English town, where she spends her days writing like a crazy person.

Read more at K.A Knight's website or join her Facebook Reader Group.
Sign up for exclusive content and my newsletter here
http://eepurl.com/drLLoj

ALSO BY K.A KNIGHT

THEIR CHAMPION SERIES *Dystopian RH*

The Wasteland

The Summit

The Cities

The Nations

Their Champion Coloring Book

Their Champion Boxed Set

The Forgotten

The Lost

The Damned

Their Champion Companion Boxed Set

DAWNBREAKER SERIES *SCI FI RH*

Voyage to Ayama

Dreaming of Ayama

THE LOST COVEN SERIES *PNR RH*

Aurora's Coven

Aurora's Betrayal

HER MONSTERS SERIES *PNR RH*

Rage

Hate

THE FALLEN GODS SERIES *PNR*

PrettyPainful

Pretty Bloody

PrettyStormy

Pretty Wild

Pretty Hot

Pretty Faces

Pretty Spelled

Fallen Gods Boxed Set 1

Fallen Gods Boxed Set 1

FORBIDDEN READS *(STANDALONES)* *CONTEMPORARY*

Daddy's Angel

Stepbrothers' Darling

FORGOTTEN CITY

Monstrous Lies

STANDALONES

IN DEN OF VIPERS' UNIVERSE - CONTEMPORARY

Scarlett Limerence

Nadia's Salvation

Den of Vipers

Gangsters and Guns (Co-Write with Loxley Savage)

CONTEMPORARY

The Standby

Divers Heart

SCI FI RH

Crown of Stars

AUDIOBOOKS

The Wasteland

The Summit

Rage

Hate

Den of Vipers *(From Podium Audio)*

Gangsters and Guns *(From Podium Audio)*

Daddy's Angel *(From Podium Audio)*

Stepbrother's Darling *(From Podium Audio)*

Blade of Iris *(From Podium Audio)*

Deadly Affair *(From Podium Audio)*

Stolen Trophy *(From Podium Audio)*

SHARED WORLD PROJECTS

Blade of Iris - Mafia Wars *CONTEMPORARY*

CO-AUTHOR PROJECTS - *Erin O'Kane*

HER FREAKS SERIES *PNR RH*

Circus Save Me

Taming The Ringmaster

Walking the Tightrope

Boxed Set

STANDALONES

PNR RH

The Hero Complex

Collection of Short Stories

Dark Temptations (contains One Night Only and Circus Saves Christmas)

THE WILD BOYS SERIES *CONTEMPORARY*

The Wild Interview

The Wild Tour

The Wild Finale

The Wild Boys Boxed Set

CO-AUTHOR PROJECTS - *Ivy Fox*

Deadly Love Series *CONTEMPORARY*

Deadly Affair

Deadly Match

Deadly Encounter

CO-AUTHOR PROJECTS - *Kendra Moreno*

STANDALONES

CONTEMPORARY

Stolen Trophy

CO-AUTHOR PROJECTS - *Loxley Savage*

THE FORSAKEN SERIES *SCI FI RH*

Capturing Carmen

Stealing Shiloh

Harboring Harlow

STANDALONES

Gangsters and Guns - IN DEN OF VIPERS' UNIVERSE

OTHER CO-WRITES

Shipwreck Souls *(with Kendra Moreno & Poppy Woods)*

The Horror Emporium *(with Kendra Moreno & Poppy Woods)*

CPSIA information can be obtained
at www.ICGtesting.com
Printed in the USA
BVHW081031180123
656503BV00019B/136